The Cords of Vanity

The Cords of Vanity

A Comedy of Shirking

James Branch Cabell

MINT EDITIONS

The Cords of Vanity: A Comedy of Shirking was first published in 1909.

This edition published by Mint Editions 2021.

ISBN 9781513295800 | E-ISBN 9781513297309

Published by Mint Editions®

 MINT
EDITIONS

minteditionbooks.com

Publishing Director: Jennifer Newens
Design & Production: Rachel Lopez Metzger
Project Manager: Micaela Clark
Typesetting: Westchester Publishing Services

Contents

An Introduction   7

The Prologue

The Prologue: Which Deals with the Essentials   13

The Cords of Vanity

1. He Sits Out a Dance   21

2. He Loves Extensively   26

3. He Earns a Stick-pin   33

4. He Talks with Charteris   40

5. He Revisits Fairhaven and the Play   46

6. He Chats Over a Hedge   53

7. He Goes Mad in a Garden   57

8. He Duels with a Stupid Woman   64

9. He Puts His Tongue in His Cheek   70

10. He Samples New Emotions   79

11. He Postures Among Chimney-Pots   88

12. He Faces Himself and Remembers   98

13. He Baits Upon the Journey   105

14. HE PARTICIPATES IN A BRAVE JEST   112

15. HE DECIDES TO AMUSE HIMSELF   117

16. HE SEEKS FOR COPY   123

17. HE PROVIDES COPY   129

18. HE SPENDS AN AFTERNOON IN ARDEN   139

19. HE PLAYS THE IMPROVIDENT FOOL   148

20. HE DINES OUT, IMPEDED BY SUPERSTITIONS   159

21. HE IS URGED TO DESERT HIS GALLEY   167

22. HE CLEANS THE SLATE   176

23. HE REVILES DESTINY AND CLIMBS A WALL   182

24. HE RECONCILES SENTIMENT AND REASON   188

25. HE ADVANCES IN THE ATTACK ON SELWOODE   195

26. HE ASSISTS IN THE DIVERSION OF BIRDS   200

27. HE CALLS, AND COUNSELS, AND CONSIDERS   205

28. HE PARTICIPATES IN SUNDRY CONFIDENCES   217

29. HE ALLOWS THE MERITS OF IMPERFECTION   226

30. HE GILDS THE WEATHER-VANE   233

THE EPILOGUE: WHICH SUGGESTS THAT
SECOND THOUGHTS—   238

An Introduction

by Wilson Follett

M r. Cabell, in making ready this second or intended edition of The Cords Of Vanity, performs an act of reclamation which is at the same time an act of fresh creation.

For the purely reclamatory aspect of what he has done, his reward (so far as that can consist in anything save the doing) must come from insignificantly few directions; so few indeed that he, with a wrily humorous exaggeration, affects to believe them singular. The author of this novel has been pleased to describe the author of this introduction as "the only known purchaser of the book" and, further, as "the other person to own a Cords Of Vanity." I could readily enough acquit myself, with good sound legal proofs, of any such singularity as stands charged in this soft impeachment—and that without appeal to *The Cleveland Plain Dealer* of eleven years ago ("slushy and disgusting"), or to *The New York Post* ("sterile and malodorous. . . worse than immoral—dull"), or to *Ainslee's Magazine* ("inconsequent and rambling. . . rather nauseating at times"). These devotees of the adjective that hunts in pairs are hardly to be discussed, I suppose, in connection with any rewards except such as accrue to the possessors of a certain obtuseness, who always and infallibly reap at least the reward of not being hurt by what they do not know—or, for that matter, by what they do know. He who writes such a book as The Cords Of Vanity is committing himself to the supremely irrational faith that this dullness is somehow not the ultimate arbiter; and for him the pronouncements of this dullness simply do not figure among either his rewards or his penalties. So, it is not exactly to these tributes of the press that one reverts in noting that The Cords Of Vanity, on its publication eleven years ago, promptly became a book which there were—almost—none to praise and very few to love. After all, its author's computation of that former audience of his—his actual individual voluntary readers of a decade ago—appears to be but slightly and pardonably exaggerated on the more modest side of the fact. If there were a Cabell Club of membership determined solely by the number of those who, already possessing The Cords Of Vanity in its first edition, recognize it as the work of a serious artist of high achievement and higher capacity, I suspect that the smallness of that club would be in inordinate disproportion to everything but its selectness and its members' pride in "belonging."

Be that as it may, the economist-author, on the eve of his book's emergence from the limbo of "out of print," prefers that it come into its redemption carrying a foreword by someone who knew it without dislike in its former incarnation. No contingent liability, it seems, can dissuade Mr. Cabell from this preference. An author who once elected to precede a group of his best tales with an introduction eloquently setting forth reasons why the collection ought not to be published at all, is hardly to be deterred now by the mere inexpediency of hitching his star to a farm-wagon. His own graciously unreasonable insistence must be the excuse, such as it is, for the present introduction, such as it is. If there may be said to exist a sort of charter membership in Mr. Cabell's audience, this document is to be construed as representing its very enthusiastic welcome to the later and vastly larger elective membership.

And if, weighed as such a welcome, it proves hopelessly inadequate, at least it provides a number of possible compensations by the way. For instance, that *New York World* critic who damned the book but praised its frontispiece of 1909, has now a uniquely pat opportunity to balance his ledger by praising the book and damning this foreword, which, more or less, replaces the frontispiece. Similarly, the more renowned critic and anthologist who so well knows the "originals" of the verses in *From the Hidden Way*, can now render poetically perfect justice to all who will care by perceiving that both the earlier edition of this book and the author of this foreword are but figments of Mr. Cabell's slightly puckish invention.

But these pages must not be, like those which follow, a comedy of shirking. They will have flouted a plain duty unless they speak of the sense and the degree in which this novel, during the process of reclaiming it, has been actually recreated. Perhaps the matter can be packed most succinctly into the statement that Mr. Cabell's hero has been subjected to such a process of growth as has made him commensurate in stature with the other two modern writers of Mr. Cabell's invention. As *The Cream of the Jest* is essentially the book of Felix Kennaston and *Beyond Life* that of John Charteris, so THE CORDS OF VANITY is essentially the book of Robert Etheridge Townsend. Now, this Townsend has accomplished a deal of growing since 1909. By this I do not mean that he is taken at a later period of his own imagined life, or that he fails to act consonantly with the extreme youth imputed to him: I mean that he is the creation of a more mature mind, a deeper philosophy, a more probing insight into the implications of things. A given youth of twenty-five will be very differently interpreted by an observer of thirty and by the same observer at forty, very much as a given era of the past will be understood differently by a single historian before and after certain cycles of his own social and political experience. The past never remains to us the same past; it grows up along with us; the physical facts may remain admittedly the same, but our understanding accents them differently, finds more in them at some points and less at others. So Robert Etheridge Townsend remains an example of that special temperament which, being unable to endure the contact of unhappiness, consistently shirks every responsibility that entails or threatens discomfort; and the truth about him, taking him as an example of just that temperament, is still inexorably told. But his weakness as a man becomes much more tolerable in this second version, because it is much more intimately and poignantly correlated with his strength as an artist. One is made to feel that he, like Charteris, may the better consummate in his art the auctorial virtues of distinction and clarity, beauty and symmetry, tenderness and truth and urbanity, precisely because his personal life is bereft of those virtues. Less than before, the accent is on the wastrel in Townsend; more than before, it is on the potential creator of beauty in him. The earlier readers will hardly count it as a fault that Mr. Cabell has contrived to make his novel, without detriment to any truth whatsoever, a far less unpleasant book. Sardonic it still is, by a necessary implication, but not wantonly, and with a mellowness. The irony, which at its harshest was capable of rasping the nerves, has become capable of wringing the heart.

Other reasons there are, too, for holding that THE CORDS OF VANITY is certain to make its second appeal to a many times multiplied audience. Since divers momentous transactions of the years just gone, the whole world stands in a moral position extraordinarily well adapted to the comprehension of just such a comedy of shirking; and especially the world of thought has received a powerful impulsion toward the area long occupied by Mr. Cabell's romantic pessimism. There is perhaps somewhat more demand for satire, or at least a growing toleration of it. Moreover, by sheer patience and reiteration Mr. Cabell has procured no little currency for some of his most characteristic ideas. Chivalry and gallantry, as he analyzes them, are concepts which play their part in the inevitable present re-editing of social and literary history. *The Rivet in Grandfather's Neck*, *The Cream of the Jest*, and *The Certain Hour* have somewhat to say to the discriminating, even on other than purely aesthetic grounds; *Beyond Life* is on the threshold of its day as the *Sartor Resartus* of one side, the aesthetic side, of modernism; "*Of* Jurgen *eke they maken mencion*"; and THE CORDS OF VANITY is but the first of the earlier books to be reissued in the format of the uniform and accessible Intended Edition.

While THE CORDS OF VANITY was out of print, a fresh copy is known to have been acquired for twenty-five cents. Copies of a more recent work by the same hand—a tale which has been rendered equally unavailable to the public, though by slightly different considerations—have fetched as much as one hundred times that sum. This arithmetic may be, in part, the gauge of an unsought and distasteful notoriety; but that very notoriety, by the most natural of transitions, will lead the curious on from what cannot be obtained to what can, and some who have begun by seeking one particular work of a great artist will end by discovering the artist. In short, it is rational to expect that the fortunes hereafter of this rewritten novel will very excellently illustrate the uses of adversity.

Not, I repeat, that any great part of the reward for such writing can come from without. According to Robert Etheridge Townsend, "a man writes admirable prose not at all for the sake of having it read, but for the more sensible reason that he enjoys playing solitaire"—a not un-Cabellian saying. And, even of the reward from without, it may be questioned whether the really indispensable part ever comes from the multitude. A lady with whose more candid opinions the writer of this is more frequently favored nowadays than of old has said: "Every time I hear of somebody who has wanted one of these books without being able to get it, or who, having got it, has conceded it nothing better than the disdain of an ignoramus, I feel as if I must forthwith get out the copy and read it through again and again, until I have read it once for every person who has rejected it or been denied it." One may feel reasonably sure that it is this kind of solicitude, rather than any possible sanction from the crowd, which would be thought of by the author of this book as "the exact high prize through desire of which we write."

WILSON FOLLETT
CHESHIRE, CONNECTICUT
May, 1920

THE PROLOGUE

"In the house and garden of his dream he saw a child moving, and could divide the main streams at least of the winds that had played on him, and study so the first stage in that mental journey."

The Prologue: Which Deals with the Essentials

1—Writing

It appeared to me that my circumstances clamored for betterment, because never in my life have I been able to endure the contact of unhappiness. And my mother was always crying now, over (though I did not know it) the luckiest chance which had ever befallen her; and that made me cry too, without understanding exactly why.

So the child, that then was I, procured a pencil and a bit of wrapping-paper, and began to write laboriously:

> Dear Lord
> You know that Papa died and please comfort Mama and give Father a crown of Glory Ammen
> > Your lamb and very sincerely yours
> > Robert Etheridge Townsend

This appeared to the point as I re-read it, and of course God would understand that children were not expected to write quite as straight across the paper as grown people. The one problem was how to deliver this, my first letter, most expeditiously, because when your mother cried you always cried too, and couldn't stop, not even when you wanted to, not even when she promised you five cents, and it all made you horribly uncomfortable.

I knew that the big Bible on the parlor table was God's book. Probably God read it very often, since anybody would be proud of having written a book as big as that and would want to look at it every day. So I tiptoed into the darkened parlor. I use the word advisedly, for there was not at this period any drawing-room in Lichfield, and besides, a drawing-room is an entirely different matter.

Everywhere the room was cool, and, since the shades were down, the outlines of the room's contents were uncomfortably dubious; for just where the table stood had been, five days ago, a big and oddly-shaped black box with beautiful silver handles; and Uncle George had lifted me so that I could see through the pane of glass, which was a part of this funny box, while an infinity of decorous people rustled and whispered. . .

I remember knowing they were "company" and thinking they coughed and sniffed because they were sorry that my father was dead. In the light of knowledge latterly acquired, I attribute these actions to the then prevalent weather, for even now I recall how stiflingly the room smelt of flowers—particularly of magnolia blossoms—and of rubber and of wet umbrellas. For my own part, I was not at all sorry, though of course I pretended to be, since I had always known that as a rule my father whipped me because he had just quarreled with my mother, and that he then enjoyed whipping me.

I desired, in fine, that he should stay dead and possess his crown of glory in Heaven, which was reassuringly remote, and that my mother should stop crying. So I slipped my note into the Apocrypha. . .

I felt that somewhere in the room was God and that God was watching me, but I was not afraid. Yet I entertained, in common with most children, a nebulous distrust of this mysterious Person, a distrust of which I was particularly conscious on winter nights when the gas had been turned down to a blue fleck, and the shadow of the mantelpiece flickered and plunged on the ceiling, and the clock ticked louder and louder, in prediction (I suspected) of some terrible event very close at hand.

Then you remembered such unpleasant matters as Elisha and his bears, and those poor Egyptian children who had never even spoken to Moses, and that uncomfortably abstemious lady, in the fat blue-covered *Arabian Nights*, who ate nothing but rice, grain by grain—in the daytime. . . And you called Mammy, and said you were very thirsty and wanted a glass of water, please.

Today, though, while acutely conscious of that awful inspection, and painstakingly careful not to look behind me, I was not, after all, precisely afraid. If God were a bit like other people I knew He would say, "What an odd child!" and I liked to have people say that. Still, there was sunlight in the hall, and lots of sunlight, not just long and dusty shreds of sunlight, and I felt more comfortable when I was back in the hall.

2—Reading

I LAY FLAT UPON MY stomach, having found that posture most conformable to the practice of reading, and I considered the cover of this slim, green book; the name of John Charteris, stamped thereon in fat-bellied letters of gold, meant less to me than it was destined to signify thereafter.

A deal of puzzling matter I found in this book, but in my memory, always, one fantastic passage clung as a burr to sheep's wool. That fable, too, meant less to me than it was destined to signify thereafter, when the author of it was used to declare that he had, unwittingly, written it about me. Then I read again this

Fable of the Foolish Prince

"As to all earlier happenings I choose in this place to be silent. Anterior adventures he had known of the right princely sort. But concerning his traffic with Schamir, the chief talisman, and how through its aid he won to the Sun's Sister for a little while; and concerning his dealings with the handsome Troll-wife (in which affair the cat he bribed with butter and the elm-tree he had decked with ribbons helped him); and with that beautiful and dire Thuringian woman whose soul was a red mouse: we have in this place naught to do. Besides, the Foolish Prince had put aside such commerce when the Fairy came to guide him; so he, at least, could not in equity have grudged the same privilege to his historian.

"Thus, the Fairy leading, the Foolish Prince went skipping along his father's highway. But the road was bordered by so many wonders—as here a bright pebble and there an anemone, say, and, just beyond, a brook which babbled an entreaty to be tasted,—that many folk had presently overtaken and had passed the loitering Foolish Prince. First came a grandee, supine in his gilded coach, with half-shut eyes, uneagerly meditant upon yesterday's statecraft or tomorrow's gallantry; and now three yokels, with ruddy cheeks and much dust upon their shoulders; now a haggard man in black, who constantly glanced backward; and now a corporal with an empty sleeve, who whistled as he went.

"A butterfly guided every man of them along the highway. 'For the Lord of the Fields is a whimsical person,' said the Fairy, 'and such is his very old enactment concerning the passage even of his cowpath; but princes each in his day and in his way may trample this domain as prompt their will and skill.'

"'That now is excellent hearing,' said the Foolish Prince; and he strutted.

"'Look you,' said the Fairy, 'a man does not often stumble and break his shins in the highway, but rather in the byway.' . . .

"Thus, the Fairy leading, the Foolish Prince went skipping on his allotted journey, though he paused once in a while to shake his bauble at the staring sun.

"'The stars,' he considered, 'are more sympathetic. . .

"And thus, the Fairy leading, they came at last to a tall hedge wherein were a hundred wickets, all being closed; and those who had passed the Foolish Prince disputed before the hedge and measured the hundred wickets with thirty-nine articles and with a variety of instruments, and each man entered at his chosen wicket, and a butterfly went before him; but no man returned into the open country.

"'Now beyond each wicket,' said the Fairy, 'lies a great crucible, and by ninety and nine of these crucibles is a man consumed, or else transmuted into this animal or that animal. For such is the law in these parts and in human hearts.'

"The Prince demanded how if one found by chance the hundredth wicket? But she shook her head and said that none of the Tylwydd Teg was permitted to enter the Disenchanted Garden. Rumor had it that within the Garden, beyond the crucibles, was a Tree, but whether the fruit of this Tree were sweet or bitter no person in the Fields could tell, nor did the Fairy pretend to know what happened in the Garden.

"'Then why, in heaven's name, need a man test any of these wickets?' cried the Foolish Prince; 'with so much to lose and, it may be, nothing to gain? For one, I shall enter none of them.'

"But once more she shook her glittering head. 'In your House and in your Sign it was decreed. Time will be, my Prince; today the kid gambols and the ox chews his cud. Presently the butcher cries, *Time is!* Comes the hour and the power, and the cook bestirs herself and says, *Time was!* The master has his dinner, either way, all say, and every day.'

"And the Fairy vanished as she talked with him, her radiances thinning into the neutral colors of smoke, and thence dwindling a little by a little into the vaulting spiral of a windless and a burnt-out fire, until nothing remained of her save her voice; and that was like the moving of dead leaves before they fall.

"'Truly,' said the Foolish Prince, 'I am compelled to consider this a vexatious business. For, look you, the butterfly I just now admire flits over this wicket, and then her twin flutters over that wicket, and between them there is absolutely no disparity in attraction. Hoo! here is a more sensible insect.'

"And he leaped and cracked his heels together and ran after a golden butterfly that drifted to the rearward Fields. There was such a host of butterflies about that presently he had lost track of his first choice, and was in boisterous pursuit of a second, and then of a third, and then of yet others; but none of them did he ever capture, the while that one by one he followed divers butterflies of varying colors, and never a golden butterfly did he find any more.

"When it was evening, the sky drew up the twilight from the east as a blotter draws up ink, and stars were kindling everywhere like tiny signal-fires, and a light wind came out of the murky east and rustled very plaintively in places where the more ambiguous shadows were; and the Foolish Prince shivered, for the air was growing chill, and the tips of his fingers were aware of it.

"'A crucible,' he reflected, 'possesses the minor virtue of continuous warmth.'

"And before the hedge he found a Rational Person, led hither by a Clothes' Moth, working out the problem of the hundred wickets in consonance with the most approved methods. 'I have very nearly solved it,' the Rational Person said, in genteel triumph, 'but this evening grows too dark for any further ciphering, and again I must wait until tomorrow. I regret, sir, that you have elected to waste the day, in pursuit of various meretricious Lepidoptera.'

"A happy day, my brother, is never wasted."

"'That appears to me to be nonsense,' said the Rational Person; and he put up his portfolio, preparatory to spending another night under his umbrella in the Fields.

"'Indeed, my brother?' laughed the Foolish Prince. 'Then, farewell, for I am assured that yonder, as here, our father makes the laws, and that to dispute his appreciation of the enticing qualities of butterflies were an impertinence.'

"Thereafter, pushing open the wicket nearest to his hand, the Foolish Prince tucked his bauble under his left arm and skipped into the Disenchanted Garden; and as he went he sang, not noting that, from somewhere in the thickening shadows, had arisen a golden butterfly which went before him through the wicket.

"Sang the Foolish Prince:

"Farewell to Fields and Butterflies
And levities of Yester-year!
For we espy, and hold more dear,
The Wicket of our Destinies.

"Whereby we enter, once for all,
A Garden which such fruit doth yield
As, tasted once, no more Afield
We fare where Youth holds carnival.

"Farewell, fair Fields, none found amiss
When laughter was a frequent noise
And golden-hearted girls and boys
Appraised the mouth they meant to kiss.

"Farewell, farewell! but for a space
We, being young, Afield might stray,
That in our Garden nod and say,
Afield is no unpleasant place.'"

3—Arithmetic

IN SUCH DISCONNECTED FASHION, AS hereafter, I record the moments of my life which I most vividly remember. For it is possible only in the last paragraphs of a book, and for a book's people only, to look back upon an ordered and proportionate progression to what one has become; in life the thing arrives with scantier dignity; and one appears, in retrospection, less to have marched toward any goal than always to have jumped and scrambled from one stepping-stone to another because, however momentarily, "just this or that poor impulse seemed the sole work of a lifetime."

Well! at least I have known these moments and the rapture of their dominance; and I am not lightly to be stripped of recollection of them, nor of the attendant thrill either, by any cheerless hour wherein, as sometimes happens, my personal achievements confront me like a pile of flimsy jack-straws.

What does it all amount to?—I do not know. There may be some sort of supernal bookkeeping, somewhere, but very certainly it is not conformable to any human mathematics.

THE CORDS OF VANITY

"His has been the summer air, and the sunshine, and the flowers; and gentle ears have listened to him, and gentle eyes have been upon him. Let others eat his honey that please, so that he has had his morsel and his song."

Chapter 1

He Sits Out a Dance

When I first knew Stella she was within a month of being fifteen, which is for womankind an unattractive age. There were a startling number of corners to her then, and she had but vague notions as to the management of her hands and feet. In consequence they were perpetually turning up in unexpected places and surprising her by their size and number. Yes, she was very hopelessly fifteen; and she was used to laugh, unnecessarily, in a nervous fashion, approximating to a whinny, and when engaged in conversation she patted down her skirts six times to the minute.

It seems oddly unbelievable when I reflect that Rosalind—"daughter to the banished Duke"—and Stella and Helen of Troy, and all the other famous fair ones of history, were each like that at one period or another.

As for myself, I was nine days younger than Stella, and so I was at this time very old—much older than it is ever permitted anyone to be afterward. I cherished the most optimistic ideas as to my impendent moustache, and was wont in privacy to encourage it with the manicure-scissors. I still entertained the belief that girls were upon the whole superfluous nuisances, but was beginning to perceive the expediency of concealing this opinion, even in private converse with my dearest chum, where, in our joyous interchange of various heresies, we touched upon this especial sub-division of fauna very lightly, and, I now suspect, with some self-consciousness.

2

All this was at a summer resort, which was called the Green Chalybeate. Stella and I and others of our age attended the hotel hops in the evening with religious punctuality, for well-meaning elders insisted these dances amused us, and it was easier to go than to argue the point. At least, that was the feeling of the boys.

Stella has since sworn the girls liked it. I suspect in this statement a certain parsimony as to the truth. They giggled too much and were never entirely free from that haunting anxiety concerning their skirts.

We danced together, Stella and I, to the strains of the last Sousa two-step (it was the *Washington Post*), and we conversed, meanwhile, with careful disregard of the amenities of life, since each feared lest the other might suspect in some common courtesy an attempt at—there is really no other word—spooning. And spooning was absurd.

Well, as I once read in the pages of a rare and little known author, one lives and learns.

I asked Stella to sit out a dance. I did this because I had heard Mr. Lethbury—a handsome man with waxed mustachios and an absolutely piratical amount of whiskers,—make the same request of Miss Van Orden, my just relinquished partner, and it was evident that such whiskers could do no wrong.

Stella was not uninfluenced, it may be, by Miss Van Orden's example, for even in girlhood the latter was a person of extraordinary beauty, whereas, as has been said, Stella's corners were then multitudinous; and it is probable that those two queer little knobs at the base of Stella's throat would be apt to render their owner uncomfortable and a bit abject before—let us say—more ample charms. In any event, Stella giggled and said she thought it would be just fine, and I presently conducted her to the third piazza of the hotel.

There we found a world that was new.

3

IT WAS A WORLD OF sweet odors and strange lights, flooded with a kindly silence which was, somehow, composed of many lispings and trepidations and thin echoes. The night was warm, the sky all transparency. If the comparison was not manifestly absurd, I would liken that remembered sky's pale color to the look of blue plush rubbed the wrong way. And in its radiance the stars bathed, large and bright and intimate, yet blurred somewhat, like shop-lights seen through frosted panes; and the moon floated on it, crisp and clear as a new-minted coin. This was the full midsummer moon, grave and glorious, that compelled the eye; and its shield was obscurely marked, as though a Titan had breathed on its chill surface. Its light suffused the heavens and lay upon the earth beneath us in broad splashes; and the foliage about us was dappled with its splendor, save in the open east, where the undulant, low hills wore radiancy as a mantle.

For the trees, mostly maples of slight stature, clustered thickly about the hotel, and their branches mingled in a restless pattern of blacks and silvers and dim greens that mimicked the laughter of the sea under an April wind. Looking down from the piazza, over the expanse of tree-tops, all this was strangely like the sea; and it gave one, somehow, much the same sense of remote, unbounded spaces and of a beauty that was a little sinister. At times whippoorwills called to one another, eerie and shrill; and the distant dance-music was a vibration in the air, which was heavy with the scent of bruised growing things and was filled with the cool, healing magic of the moonlight.

Taking it all in all, we had blundered upon a very beautiful place. And there we sat for a while and talked in an aimless fashion. We did not know quite how one ought to "sit out" a dance, you conceive. . .

4

THEN, MOVED BY SOME QUEER impulse, I stared over the railing for a little at this great, wonderful, ambiguous world, and said solemnly:

"It is good."

"Yes," Stella agreed, in a curious, quiet and tiny voice, "it—it's very large, isn't it?" She looked out for a moment over the tree-tops. "It makes me feel like a little old nothing," she said, at last. "The stars are so big, and—so uninterested." Stella paused for an interval, and then spoke again, with an uncertain laugh. "I think I am rather afraid."

"Afraid?" I echoed.

"Yes," she said, vaguely; "of—of everything."

I understood. Even then I knew something of the occasional insufficiency of words.

"It is a big world," I assented, "and lots of people are having a right hard time in it right now. I reckon there is somebody dying this very minute not far off."

"It's all—waiting for us!" Stella had forgotten my existence. "It's bringing us so many things—and we don't know what any of them are. But we've got to take them, whether we want to or not. It isn't fair. We've got to—well, got to grow up, and—marry, and—die, whether we want to or not. We've no choice. And it may not matter, after all. Everything will keep right on like it did before; and the stars won't care; and what we've done and had done to us won't really matter!"

"Well, but, Stella, you can have a right good time first, anyway, if you keep away from ugly things and fussy people. And I reckon you really go to Heaven afterwards if you haven't been really bad,—don't you?"

"Rob,—are you ever afraid of dying?" Stella asked, "very much afraid—Oh, you know what I mean."

I did. I was about ten once more. It was dark, and I was passing a drug-store, with huge red and green and purple bottles glistening in the gas-lit windows; and it had just occurred to me that I, too, must die, and be locked up in a box, and let down with trunk-straps into a hole, like Father was. . . So I said, "Yes."

"And yet we've got to! Oh, I don't see how people can go on living like everything was all right when that's always getting nearer,—when they know they've got to die before very long. Because they dance and go on picnics and buy hats as if they were going to live forever. I—oh, I can't understand."

"They get used to the idea, I reckon. We're sort of like the rats in the trap at home, in our stable," I suggested, poetically. "We can bite the wires and go crazy, like lots of them do, if we want to, or we can eat the cheese and kind of try not to think about it. Either way, there's no getting out till they come to kill us in the morning."

"Yes," sighed Stella; "I suppose we must make the best of it."

"It's the only sensible thing to do, far as I can see."

"But it is all so big—and so careless about us!" she said, after a little. "And we don't know—we can't know!—what is going to happen to you and me. And we can't stop its happening!"

"We'll just have to make the best of that, too," I protested, dolefully.

Stella sighed again, "I hope so," she assented; "still, I'm scared of it."

"I think I am, too—sort of," I conceded, after reflection. "Anyhow, I am going to have as good a time as I can."

There was now an even longer pause. Pitiable, ridiculous infants were pondering, somewhat vaguely but very solemnly, over certain mysteries of existence, which most of us have learned to accept with stolidity. We were young, and to us the miraculous insecurity and inconsequence of human life was still a little impressive, and we had not yet come to regard the universe as a more or less comfortable place, well-meaningly constructed anyhow—by Somebody—for us to reside in.

Therefore we moved a trifle closer together, Stella and I, and were commonly miserable over the *Weltschmerz*. After a little a distant whippoorwill woke me from a chaos of reverie, and I turned to Stella, with a vague sense that we two were the only people left in the whole world, and that I was very, very fond of her.

Stella's head was leaned backward. Her lips were parted, and the moonlight glinted in her eyes. Her eyes were blue.

"Don't!" said Stella, faintly.

I did. . .

It was a matter out of my volition, out of my planning. And, oh, the wonder, and sweetness, and sacredness of it! I thought, even in the instant; and, oh, the pity that, after all, it is slightly disappointing. . .

Stella was not angry, as I had half expected. "That was dear of you," she said, impulsively, "but don't try to do it again." There was the wisdom of centuries in this mandate of Stella's as she rose from the bench. The spell was broken, utterly. "I think," said Stella, in the voice of a girl of fifteen, "I think we'd better go and dance some more."

5

IN THE CRUDE MORNING I approached Stella, with a fatuous smile. She apparently both perceived and resented my bearing, although she never once looked at me. There was something of great interest to her in the distance, apparently down by the springhouse; she was flushed and indignant; and her eyes wouldn't, couldn't, and didn't turn for an instant in my direction.

I fidgeted.

"If," said she, impersonally, "if you believe it was because of *you*, you are very much mistaken. It would have been the same with anybody. You don't understand, and I don't either. Anyhow, I think you are a mess, and I hate you. Go away from me!"

And she stamped her foot in a fine rage.

For the moment I entertained an un-Christian desire that Stella had been born a boy. In that case, I felt, I would, just then, have really enjoyed sitting upon the back of her head, and grinding her nose into the lawn, and otherwise persuading her to cry "'Nough." These virile pleasures being denied me, I sought for comfort in discourteous speech.

"Umph-huh!" said I, "and you think you're mighty smart, don't you? Well, I don't want you pawing around me any more, either. I won't have it, do you understand! That was what I was going to tell you anyhow, you kissing-bug, even if you hadn't acted so smart. And you can just stick that right in your pipe and smoke it, you old Miss Smart Alec."

Thereupon I—wisely—departed without delay. A rock struck me rather forcibly between the shoulder blades, but I did not deign to notice this phenomenon.

"You can't fight girls with fists," I reflected. "You've just got to talk to them in the right way."

Chapter 2

He Loves Extensively

I saw no more of Stella for a lengthy while, since within two days of the events recorded it pleased my mother to seek out another summer resort.

"For in September," she said, "I really must have perfect quiet and unimpeachable butter, and falling leaves, and only a very few congenial people to be melancholy with,—and that sort of thing, you know. I find it freshens one up so against the winter."

It was a signal feature of my mother's conversation that you never understood, precisely, what she was talking about.

Thus in her train the silly, pretty woman drew otherwhither her hobbledehoy son, as indeed Claire Bulmer Townsend had aforetime drawn an armament of more mature and stolid members of my sex. I was always proud of my handsome mother, but without any aspirations, however theoretical, toward intimacy; and her periods of conscientious if vague affection, when she recollected its propriety, I endured with consolatory foreknowledge of an impendent, more agreeable era of neglect.

I fancy that at bottom I was without suspecting it lonely. I was an only child; my father had died, as has been hinted, when I was in kilts. . . No, I must have graduated from kilts into "knee-pants" when the Democracy of Lichfield celebrated Grover Cleveland's first election as President, for I was seven years old then, and was allowed to stay up ever so late after supper to watch the torchlight parade. I recollect being rather pleasantly scared by the yells of all those marching people and by the glistening of their faces as the irregular flaring torches heaved by; and I recollect how delightfully the cold night air was flavored with kerosene. In any event, it was on this generally festive November night that my father again took too much to drink, and, coming home toward morning, lay down and went to sleep in the vestibule between our front-door and the storm-doors; and five days later died of pneumonia. . . In that era I was accounted an odd boy; given to reading and secretive ways, and, they record, to long silences throughout which my lips would move noiselessly. "Just talking to one of my friends," they tell me I was used to explain; though it was not until my career at King's College that I may be said to have pretended to intimacy with anybody.

2

FOR IN OLD FAIRHAVEN I spent, of course, a period of ostensible study, as four generations of my fathers had done aforetime. But in that leisured, slatternly and ancient city I garnered a far larger harvest of (comparatively) innocuous cakes and ale than of authentic learning, and at my graduation carried little of moment from the place save many memories of Bettie Hamlyn. . . Her father taught me Latin at King's College, while Bettie taught me human intimacy—almost. Looking back, I have not ever been intimate with anybody. . .

Not but that I had my friends. In particular I remember those four of us who always called ourselves—in flat defiance, just as Dumas did, of mere arithmetic—"The Three Musketeers." I think that we loved one another very greatly during the four years we spent together in our youth. I like to believe we did, and to remember the boys who were once unreasonably happy, even now. It does not seem to count, somehow, that Aramis has taken to drink and every other inexpedient course, I hear, and that I would not recognize him today, were we two to encounter casually—or Athos, either, I suppose, now that he has been so long in the Philippines.

And as for D'Artagnan—or Billy Woods, if you prefer the appellation which his sponsors gave him,—why we are still good friends and always will be, I suppose. But we are not particularly intimate; and very certainly we will never again read *Chastelard* together and declaim the more impassioned parts of it,—and in fine, I cannot help seeing, nowadays, that, especially since his marriage, Billy has developed into a rather obvious and stupid person, and that he considers me to be a bit of a bad egg. And in a phrase, when we are together, just we two, we smoke a great deal and do not talk any more than is necessary.

And once I would have quite sincerely enjoyed any death, however excruciating, which promoted the well-being of Billy Woods; and he viewed me not dissimilarly, I believe. . . However, after all, this was a long, long while ago, and in a period almost antediluvian.

And during this period they of Fairhaven assumed I was in love with Bettie Hamlyn; and for a very little while, at the beginning, had I assumed as much. More lately was my error flagrantly apparent when I fell in love with someone else, and sincerely in love, and found to my amazement that, upon the whole, I preferred Bettie's companionship to that of the woman I adored. By and by, though, I learned to accept this odd, continuing phenomenon much as I had learned to accept the sunrise.

3

ONCE BETTIE DEMANDED OF ME, "I often wonder what you really think of me? Honest injun, I mean."

I meditated, and presently began, with leisure:

"Miss Hamlyn is a young woman of considerable personal attractions, and with one exception is unhandicapped by accomplishments. She plays the piano, it is true, but she does it divinely and she neither crochets nor embroiders presents for people, nor sketches, nor recites, nor sings, or in fine annoys the public in any way whatsoever. Her enemies deny that she is good-looking, but even her friends concede her curious picturesqueness and her knowledge of it. Her penetration, indeed, is not to be despised; she has even grasped the fact that all men are not necessarily fools in spite of the fashion in which they talk to women. It must be admitted, however, that her emotions are prone to take precedence of her reasoning powers: thus she is not easily misled from getting what she desires, save by those whom she loves, because in argument, while always illogical, she is invariably convincing—"

Miss Hamlyn sniffed. "This is, perhaps, the inevitable effect of twenty cigarettes a day," was her cryptic comment. "Nevertheless, it does affect me with ennui."

"—For, the mere facts of the case she plainly demonstrates, with the abettance of her dimples, to be an affair of unimportance; the real point is what she wishes done about it. Yet the proffering of any particular piece of advice does not necessarily signify that she either expects or wishes it to be followed, since had she been present at the Creation she would have cheerfully pointed out to the Deity His various mistakes, and have offered her co-operation toward bettering matters, and have thought a deal less of Him had He accepted it; but this is merely a habit—" "Yes?" said Bettie, yawning; and she added: "Do you know, Robin, the saddest and most desolate thing in the world is to practise an *etude* of Schumann's in nine flats, and the next is to realize that a man who has been in love with you has recovered for keeps?"

"—It must not be imagined, however, that Miss Hamlyn is untruthful, for when driven by impertinences into a corner she conceals her real opinion by voicing it quite honestly as if she were joking. Thereupon you credit her with the employment of irony and the possession of every imaginable and super-angelical characteristic—"

"Unless we come to a better understanding," Miss Hamlyn crisply began, "we had better stop right here before we come to a worse—"

"—Miss Hamlyn, in a word, is possessed of no insufferable virtues and of many endearing faults; and in common with the rest of humanity, she regards her disapproval of any proceeding as clear proof of its impropriety." This was largely apropos of a fire-new debate concerning the deleterious effects of cigarette-smoking; and when I had made an end, and doggedly lighted another one of them, Bettie said nothing. . . She minded chiefly that one of us should have thought of the other without bias. She said it was not fair. And I know now that she was right.

But of Bettie Hamlyn, for reasons you may learn hereafter if you so elect, I honestly prefer to write not at all. Four years, in fine, we spent to every purpose together, and they were very happy years. To record them would be desecration.

4

MEANTIME, DURING THESE YEARS, I had fallen in and out of love assiduously. Since the Anabasis of lad's love traverses a monotonous country, where one hill is largely like another, and one meadow a duplicate of the next to the last daffodil, I may with profit dwell upon the green-sickness lightly. It suffices that in the course of these four years I challenged superstition by adoring thirteen girls, and, worse than that, wrote verses of them.

I give you their names herewith—though not their workaday names, lest the wives of divers people be offended (and in many cases, surprised), but the appellatives which figured in my rhymes. They were Heart's Desire, Florimel, Dolores, Yolande, Adelais, Sylvia, Heart o' My Heart, Chloris, Felise, Ettarre, Phyllis, Phyllida, and Dorothy. Here was a rosary of exquisite names, I even now concede; and the owner of each *nom de plume* I, for however brief a period, adored for this or that peculiar excellence; and by ordinary without presuming to mention the fact to any of these divinities save Heart o' My Heart, who was, after all, only a Penate.

Outside the elevated orbits of rhyme she was called Elizabeth Hamlyn; and it afterward became apparent to me that I, in reality, wrote all the verses of this period solely for the pleasure of reading them aloud to Bettie, for certainly I disclosed their existence to no one else—except just one or two to Phyllida, who was "literary."

And the upshot of all this heart-burning is most succinctly given in my own far from impeccable verse, as Bettie Hamlyn heard the summing-up one evening in May. It was the year I graduated from King's College, and the exact relation of the date to the Annos Domini is trivial. But the battle of Manila had just been fought, and off Santiago Captain Sampson and Commander Schley were still hunting for Cervera's "phantom fleet." And in Fairhaven, as I remember it, although there was a highly-colored picture of Commodore Dewey in the barber-shop window, nobody was bothering in the least about the war except when Colonel Snawley and Dr. Jeal foregathered at Clarriker's Emporium to denounce the colossal errors of "imperialism" . . .

> "Thus, then, I end my calendar
> Of ancient loves more light than air;—
> And now Lad's Love, that led afar
> In April fields that were so fair,
> Is fled, and I no longer share
> Sedate unutterable days
> With Heart's Desire, nor ever praise
> Felise, or mirror forth the lures
> Of Stella's eyes nor Sylvia's,
> Yet love for each loved lass endures.
>
> "Chloris is wedded, and Ettarre
> Forgets; Yolande loves otherwhere,
> And worms long since made bold to mar
> The lips of Dorothy and fare
> Mid Florimel's bright ruined hair;
> And Time obscures that roseate haze
> Which glorified hushed woodland ways
> When Phyllis came, as Time obscures
> That faith which once was Phyllida's,—
> Yet love for each loved lass endures.
>
> "That boy is dead as Schariar,
> Tiglath-pileser, or Clotaire,

Who once of love got many a scar.
And his loved lasses past compare?—
None is alive now anywhere.
Each is transmuted nowadays
Into a stranger, and displays
No whit of love's investitures.
I let these women go their ways,
Yet love for each loved lass endures.

"Heart o' My Heart, thine be the praise
If aught of good in me betrays
Thy tutelage—whose love matures
Unmarred in these more wistful days,—
Yet love for each loved lass endures."

For this was the year that I graduated, and Chloris—I violate no confidence in stating that her actual name was Aurelia Minns, and that she had been, for a greater number of years than it would be courteous to remember, the undisputed belle of Fairhaven,—had that very afternoon married a promising young doctor; and I was draining the cup of my misery to the last delicious drop, and was of course inspired thereby to the perpetration of such melancholy bathos as only a care-free youth of twenty is capable of evolving.

5

"DEAR BOY," SAID BETTIE, WHEN I had made an end of reading, "and are you very miserable?"

Her fingers were interlocked behind her small black head; and the sympathy with which she regarded me was tenderly flavored with amusement.

This much I noticed as I glanced upward from my manuscript, and mustered a Spartan smile. "If misery loves company, then am I the least unhappy soul alive. For I don't want anybody but just you, and I believe I never will."

"Oh—? But I don't count." The girl continued, with composure: "Or rather, I have always counted your affairs, so that I know precisely what it all amounts to."

"Sum total?"

"A lot of imitation emotions." She added hastily: "Oh, quite a good imitation, dear; you are smooth enough to see to that. Why, I remember once—when you read me that first sonnet, sitting all hunched up on the little stool, and pretending you didn't know I knew who you meant me to know it was for, and ending with a really very effective, breathless sob—and caught my hand and pressed it to your forehead for a moment—Why, that time I was thoroughly rattled and almost believed—even I—that—" She shrugged. "And if I had been younger—!" she said, half regretfully, for at this time Bettie was very nearly twenty-two.

"Yes." The effective breathless sob responded to what had virtually been an encore. "I have not forgotten."

"Only for a moment, though." Miss Hamlyn reflected, and then added, brightly: "Now, most girls would have liked it, for it sounded all wool. And they would have gone into it, as you wanted, and have been very, very happy for a while. Then, after a time—after you had got a sonnet or two out of it, and had made a sufficiency of pretty speeches,—you would have gone for an admiring walk about yourself, and would have inspected your sensations and have applauded them, quite enthusiastically, and would have said, in effect: 'Madam, I thank you for your attention. Pray regard the incident as closed.'"

"You are doing me," I observed, "an injustice. And however tiny they may be, I hate 'em."

"But, Robin, can't you see," she said, with an odd earnestness, "that to be fond of you is quite disgracefully easy, even though—" Bettie Hamlyn said, presently: "Why, your one object in life appears to be to find a girl who will allow you to moon around her and make verses about her. Oh, very well! I met today just the sort of pretty idiot who will let you do it. She is visiting Kathleen Eppes for the Finals. She has a great deal of money, too, I hear." And Bettie mentioned a name.

"That's rather queer," said I. "I used to know that girl. She will be at the K. A. dance tomorrow night, I suppose,"—and I put up my manuscript with a large air of tolerance. "I dare say that I have been exaggerating matters a bit, after all. Any woman who treated me in the way that Miss Aurelia did is not, really, worthy of regret. And in any event, I got a ballade out of her and six—no, seven—other poems."

For the name which Bettie had mentioned was that of Stella Musgrave, and I was, somehow, curiously desirous to come again to Stella, and nervous about it, too, even then. . .

JAMES BRANCH CABELL

Chapter 3

He Earns a Stick-pin

D ear me!" said Stella, wonderingly; "I would never have known you in the world! You've grown so fa—I mean, you are so well built. I've grown? Nonsense!—and besides, what did you expect me to do in six years?—and moreover, it is abominably rude of you to presume to speak of me in that abstracted and figurative manner—quite as if I were a debt or a taste for drink. It is really only French heels and a pompadour, and, of course, you can't have this dance. It's promised, and I hop, you know, frightfully. . . Why, naturally, I haven't forgotten—How could I, when you were the most disagreeable boy I ever knew?"

I ventured a suggestion that caused Stella to turn an attractive pink, and laugh. "No," said she, demurely, "I shall never never sit out another dance with you."

So she did remember!

Subsequently: "Our steps suit perfectly—Heavens! you are the fifth man who has said that tonight, and I am sure it would be very silly and very tiresome to dance through life with anybody. Men are so absurd, don't you think? Oh, yes, I tell them all—every one of them—that our steps suit, even when they have just ripped off a yard or so of flounce in an attempt to walk up the front of my dress. It makes them happy, poor things, and injures nobody. You liked it, you know; you grinned like a pleased cat. I like cats, don't you?"

Later: "That is absolute nonsense, you know," said Stella, critically. "Do you always get red in the face when you make love? I wouldn't if I were you. You really have no idea how queer it makes you look."

Still later: "No, I don't think I am going anywhere tomorrow afternoon," said Stella.

2

So that during the fleet moments of these Finals, while our army was effecting a landing in Cuba, I saw as much of Stella as was possible; and veracity compels the admission that she made no marked effort to prevent my doing so. Indeed, she was quite cross, and scornful, about the crowning glory being denied her, of going with me to the Baccalaureate Address the morning I received my degree. To that of course I took Bettie.

3

I SAID GOOD-BYE TO BETTIE Hamlyn rather late one evening. It was in her garden. The Finals were over, and Stella had left Fairhaven that afternoon. I was to follow in the morning, by an early train.

It was a hot, still night in June, with never a breath of air stirring. In the sky was a low-hung moon, full and very red. It was an evil moon, and it lighted a night that was unreasonably ominous. And Bettie and I had talked of trifles resolutely for two hours.

"Well—good-bye Bettie," I said at last. "I'm glad it isn't for long." For of course we meant never to let a month elapse without our seeing each other.

"Good-bye," she said, and casually shook hands.

Then Bettie Hamlyn said, in a different voice: "Robin, you come of such a bad lot, and already you are by way of being a rather frightful liar. And I'm letting you go. I'm turning you over to Stellas and mothers and things like that just because I have to. It isn't fair. They will make another Townsend of my boy, and after all I've tried to do. Oh, Robin, don't let anybody or anything do that to you! Do try to do the unpleasant thing sometimes, my dear!—But what's the good of promising?"

"And have I ever failed you, Bettie?"

"No,—not me," she answered, almost as though she grudged the fact. Then Bettie laughed a little. "Indeed, I'm trying to believe you never will. Oh, indeed, I am. But just be honest with me, Robin, and nothing else will ever matter very much. I don't care what you do, if only you are always honest with me. You can murder people, if you like, and burn down as many houses as you choose. You probably will. But you'll be honest with me—won't you?—and particularly when you don't want to be?"

So I promised her that. And sometimes I believe it is the only promise which I ever tried to keep quite faithfully. . .

4

AND ALL THE ENSUING SUMMER I followed Stella Musgrave from one watering place to another, with an engaging and entire candor as to my desires. I was upon the verge of my majority, when, under the terms of my father's will, I would come into possession of such fragments of his patrimony as he had omitted to squander. And afterward I intended to become excessively distinguished in this or that profession, not as yet irrevocably fixed upon, but for choice as a writer of immortal verse; and I was used to dwell at this time very feelingly, and very frequently, upon the wholesome restraint which matrimony imposes upon the possessor of an artistic temperament.

Stella promised to place my name upon her waiting list, and to take up the matter in due season; and she lamented, with a tiny and pre-meditated yawn, that as a servitor of system she was compelled to list her "little lovers and suitors in alphabetical order, Mr. Townsend. Besides, you would probably strangle me before the year was out."

"I would thoroughly enjoy doing it," I said, grimly, "right now." She regarded me for a while. "You would, too," she said at last, with an alien gravity; "and that is why—Oh, Rob dear, you are out of my dimension. I am rather afraid of you. I am a poor bewildered triangle who is being wooed by a cube!" the girl wailed, and but half humorously.

And I began to plead. It does not matter what I said. It never mattered.

And persons more sensible than I found then far more important things to talk about, such as General Alger's inefficiency, and General Shafter's hammock, and "embalmed beef," and the folly of taking over the Philippines, and Admiral von Diedrich's behavior, and the yellow fever in our camps and the comparative claims of Messrs. Sampson and Schley to be made rear-admiral; and everybody more or less was demanding "an investigation," as the natural aftermath of a war.

5

STELLA'S MOTHER HAD CLOSED BELLEMEADE for the year, however, and they were to spend the winter in Lichfield; and Stella, to reduplicate her phrase, promised to "think it over very seriously."

But I suppose I had never any real chance against Peter Blagden. To begin with,—though Stella herself, of course, would inherit plenty of money when her mother died,—Peter was the only nephew of a childless uncle who was popularly reported to "roll in wealth"; and in addition, Peter was seven years older than I and notoriously dissipated. No other girl of twenty would have hesitated between us half so long as Stella did. She hesitated through a whole winter; and even now there is odd, if scanty, comfort in the fact that Stella hesitated. . .

Besides Peter was eminently likeable. At times I almost liked him myself, for all my fervent envy of his recognized depravity and of the hateful ease with which he thought of something to say in those uncomfortable moments when he and I and Stella were together. At most other times I could talk glibly enough, but before this seasoned scapegrace I was dumb, and felt my reputation to be hopelessly immaculate. . . If only Stella would believe me to be just the tiniest bit depraved! I blush to think of the dark hints I dropped as to entirely fictitious women who "had been too kind to me. But then"—as I would feelingly lament,—"we could never let women alone, we Townsends, you know—"

6

ONE WOMAN AT LEAST I was beginning to "let alone," in that I was writing Bettie Hamlyn letters which grew shorter and shorter. . . Her mother had fallen ill, not long after I left college; and she and Bettie were now a great way off, in Colorado, where the old lady was dying, with the most selfish sort of laziness about it, and so was involving me in endless correspondence. . . At least, I wrote to Bettie punctually, if briefly, though I had not seen her since that night when the moon was red, and big, and very evil. I had to do it, because she had insisted that I write.

"But letters don't mean anything, Bettie. And besides, I hate writing letters."

"That is just why you must write to me regularly. You never do the things you don't want to do. I know it. But for me you always will, and that makes all the difference."

"Shylock!" I retorted.

"If you like. In any event, I mean to have my pound of flesh, and regularly."

So I wrote to Bettie Hamlyn on the seventh of every month— because that was her birthday,—and again on the twenty-third, because that was mine. The rest of my time I gave whole-heartedly to Stella. . .

7

THEY NAMED HER STELLA, I fancy, because her eyes were so like stars. It is manifestly an irrelevant detail that there do not happen to be any azure stars. Indeed, I am inclined to think that Nature belatedly observed this omission, and created Stella's eyes to make up for it; at any rate, if you can imagine Aldebaran or Benetnasch polished up a bit and set in a speedwell-cup, you will have a very fair idea of one of them. You cannot, however, picture to yourself the effect of the pair of them, because the human mind is limited.

Really, though, their effect was curious. You noticed them casually, let us say; then, without warning, you ceased to notice anything. You simply grew foolish and gasped like a newly-hooked trout, and went mad and babbled as meaninglessly as a silly little rustic brook trotting under a bridge.

I have seen the thing happen any number of times. And, strangely enough, you liked it. Numbers of young men would venture into the same room with those disconcerting eyes the very next evening, even appearing to seek them out and to court peril, as it were,—young men who must have known perfectly well, either by report or experience, the unavoidable result of such fool-hardy conduct. For eventually it always culminated in Stella's being deeply surprised and grieved,—at a dance, for choice, with music and color and the unthinking laughter of others to heighten the sadness and the romance of it all,—she never having dreamed of such a thing, of course, and having always regarded you only as a dear, dear friend. Yes, and she used certainly to hope that nothing she had said or done could have led you to believe she had even for a moment considered such a thing. Oh, she did it well, did Stella, and endured these frequent griefs and surprises with, I must protest, quite exemplary patience. In a phrase, she was the most adorable combination of the prevaricator, the jilt and the coquette I have ever encountered.

8

So, FOR THE SEVENTH TIME, I asked Stella to marry me. Nearly every fellow I knew had done as much, particularly Peter Blagden; and it is always a mistake to appear unnecessarily reserved or exclusive. And this time in declining—with a fluency that bespoke considerable practice,—she informed me that, as the story books have it, she was shortly to be wedded to another.

And Peter Blagden clapped the pinnacle upon my anguish by asking me to be the best man. I knew even then whose vanity and whose sense of the appropriate had put him up to it. . .

"For I haven't a living male relative of the suitable age except two second cousins that I don't see much of—praise God!" said Peter, fervently; "and Hugh Van Orden looks about half-past ten, whereas I class John Charteris among the lower orders of vermin."

I consented to accept the proffered office and the incidental stick-pin; and was thus enabled to observe from the inside this episode of Stella's life, and to find it quite like other weddings.

Something like this:

"Look here," a perspiring and fidgety Peter protested, at the last moment, as we lurked in the gloomy vestry with not a drop left in either flask; "look here, Henderson hasn't blacked the soles of these blessed shoes. I'll look like an ass when it comes to the kneeling part—like an ass, I tell you! Good heavens, they'll look like tombstones!"

"If you funk now," said I, severely, "I'll never help you get married again. Oh, sainted Ebenezer in bliss, and whatever have I done with that ring? No, it's here all right, but you are on the wrong side of me again. And there goes the organ—Good God, Peter, look at her! simply look at her, man! Oh, you lucky devil! you lucky jackass!"

I spoke enviously, you understand, simply to encourage him.

Followed a glaring of lights, a swishing of fans, a sense that Peter was not keeping step with me, and the hum of densely packed, expectant humanity; a blare of music; then Stella, an incredible vision with glad, frightened eyes. My shoulders straightened, and I was not out of temper any longer. The organist was playing softly, *Oh, Promise Me*, and I was thinking of the time, last January, that Stella and I heard The Bostonians, and how funny Henry Clay Barnabee was. . . "—so long as ye both may live?" ended the bishop.

"I will," poor Peter quavered, with obvious uncertainty about it.

And still one saw in Stella's eyes unutterable happiness and fear, but her voice was tranquil. I found time to wonder at its steadiness, even though, just about this time, I resonantly burst a button off one of my new gloves. I fancy they must have been rather tight.

"And thereto," said Stella, calmly, "I give thee my troth."

And subsequently they were Mendelssohned out of church to the satisfaction of a large and critical audience. I came down the aisle with Stella's only sister—who afterward married the Marquis d'Arlanges,—and found Lizzie very entertaining later in the evening. . .

YES, IT WAS QUITE LIKE other weddings. I only wonder for what conceivable reason I remember its least detail, and so vividly. For it all happened a great while ago, when—of such flimsy stuff is glory woven,—Emilio Aguinaldo and Captain Coghlan were the persons most talked of in America; and when the Mazet committee was "investigating" I forget what, but with column after column about it in the papers every day; and when *Me und Gott* was a famous poem, and "to hobsonize" was the most popular verb; and when I was twenty-one. *Sic transit gloria mundi*, as it says in the back of the dictionary.

Chapter 4

He Talks with Charteris

It was upon the evening of this day, after Mr. and Mrs. Blagden had been duly rice-pelted and entrained, that I first talked against John Charteris. The novelist was, as has been said, a cousin of Peter Blagden, and as such, was one of the wedding guests at Bellemeade; and that evening, well toward midnight, the little man, midway in the consumption of one of his interminable cigarettes, happened to come upon me seated upon the terrace and gazing, rather vacantly, in the direction of the moon.

I was not thinking of anything in particular; only there was a by-end of verse which sang itself over and over again, somewhere in the back of my brain—"Her eyes were the eyes of a bride whom delight makes afraid, her eyes were the eyes of a bride"—and so on, all over again, as at night a traveller may hear his train jogging through a monotonous and stiff-jointed song; and in my heart there was just hunger.

2

Charteris had heard, one may presume, of my disastrous love-business; and with all an author's relish of emotion, in others, chose his gambit swiftly. "Mr. Townsend, is it not? Then may a murrain light upon thee, Mr. Townsend,—whatever a murrain may happen to be,—since you have disturbed me in the concoction of an ever-living and entrancing fable."

"I may safely go as far," said I, "as to offer the proverbial penny."

"Done!" cried Mr. Charteris. He meditated for a moment, and then began, in a low and curiously melodious voice, to narrate

The Apologue of the First Conjugation

"When the gods of Hellas were discrowned, there was a famous scurrying from Olympos to the world of mortals, where each deity must henceforward make shift to do without godhead:—Aphrodite in her hollow hill, where the good knight Tannhauser revels yet, it may be; Hephaestos, in some smithy; whilst Athene, for aught I know, established a girls' boarding school, and Helios, as is notorious, died under priestly torture, and Dionysos cannily took holy orders, and Hermes set up as a merchant in Friesland. But Eros went to the Grammarians. He would be a schoolmaster.

"The Grammarians, grim, snuffy and wrinkled though they might be, were no more impervious to his allures than are the rest of us, and in consequence appointed him to an office. This office was, I glean of mediaeval legend, that of teaching dunderheaded mortals the First Conjugation. So Eros donned cap and gown, took lodgings with a quiet musical family, and set *amo* as the first model verb; and ever since this period has the verb 'to love' been the first to be mastered in all well-constituted grammars, as it is in life.

"Heigho! it is not an easy verb to conjugate. One gets into trouble enough, in floundering through its manifold nuances, which range inevitably through the bold-faced 'I love', the confident 'I will love', the hopeful 'I may be loved', and so on to the wistful, pitiful Pluperfect Subjunctive Passive, 'I might have been loved if'—Then each of us may supply the Protasis as best befits his personal opinion and particular scars, and may tear his hair, or scribble verses, or adopt the cynical, or, in fine, assume any pose which strikes his fancy. For he has graduated into the Second Conjugation, which is *moneo*; and may now admonish to his heart's content, whilst looking back complacently into the First Classroom, where others—and so many others!—are still struggling with that mischancy verb, and are involved in the very conditions—verbal or otherwise—which aforetime saddened him, or showed him a possible byway toward recreation, or played the deuce with his liver, according to the nature of the man.

"Eros is a hard, implacable pedagogue, and for the fact his scholars suffer. He wields a rod rather than a filigree bow, as old romancers fabled,—no plaything, but a most business-like article, well-poised in the handle, and thence tapering into graceful, stinging nothingness; and not a scholar escapes at least a flick of it.

"I can fancy the class called up as Eros administers, with zest, his penalties. Master Paris! for loving his neighbor a little less than himself, and his neighbor's wife a little more. Master Lancelot! ditto. Masters Petrarch, Tristram, Antony, Juan Tenorio, Dante Alighieri, and others! ditto. There are a great many called up for this particular form of peccancy, you observe; even Master David has to lay aside his Psalm Book, and go forward with the others for chastisement. Master Romeo!

for trespassing in other people's gardens and mausoleums. Master Leander! for swimming in the Hellespont after dark; and Master Tarquin! for mistaking his bedroom at the Collatini's house-party.

"Thus, one by one, each scholar goes into the darkened private office. The master handles his rod—eia! 'tis borrowed from the Erinnyes,— lovingly, caressingly, like a very conscientious person about the performance of his duty. Then comes the dreadful order, 'Take down your breeches, sir!' . . . But the scene is too horrible to contemplate. He punishes all, this schoolmaster, for he is unbelievably old, and with the years' advance has grown querulous.

"Well, now I approach my moral, Mr. Townsend. One must have one's birching with the others, and of necessity there remains but to make the best of it. Birching is not a dignified process, and the endurer comes therefrom both sore and shamefaced. Yet always in such contretemps it is expedient to brazen out the matter, and to present as stately an appearance, we will say, as one's welts permit.

"First, to the world—"

3

BUT AT THIS POINT I raised my hand. "That is easily done, Mr. Charteris, inasmuch as the world cares nothing whatever about it. The world is composed of men and women who have their own affairs to mind. How in heaven's name does it concern them that a boy has dreamed dreams and has gone mad like a star-struck moth? It was foolish of him. Such is the verdict, given in a voice that is neither kindly nor severe; and the world, mildly wondering, passes on to deal with more weighty matters. For vegetables are higher than ever this year, and, upon my word, Mrs. Grundy, ma'am, a housekeeper simply doesn't know where to turn, with the outrageous prices they are asking for everything these days. No, believe me, the world does not take love-affairs very seriously—not even the great ones," I added, in noble toleration.

And with an appreciative chuckle, Charteris sank beside me upon the bench.

"My adorable boy! so you have a tongue in your head."

"But can't you imagine the knights talking over Lancelot's affair with Guenevere, at whatever was the Arthurian substitute for a club? and sniggering over it? and Lamoracke sagaciously observing that there was always a crooked streak in the Leodograunce family? Or one Roman matron punching a chicken in the ribs, and remarking to her neighbor at the poultry man's stall: 'Well, Mrs. Gracchus, they do say Antony is absolutely daft over that notorious Queen of Egypt. A brazen-faced thing, with a very muddy complexion, I'm told, and practically no reputation, of course, after the way she carried on with Caesar. And that reminds me, I hear your little Caius suffers from the croup. Now *my* remedy'—and so they waddle on, to price asparagus."

Charteris said: "Well! we need not go out of our way to meddle with the affairs of others; the entanglement is most disastrously apt to come about of itself quite soon enough. Yet a little while and Lancelot will be running Lamoracke through the body, while the King storms Joyeuse Garde; a few months and your Roman matron will weep quietly on her unshared pillow—not aloud, though, for fear of disturbing the children,—while Gracchus is dreadfully seasick at Actium."

"But that doesn't prove anything," I stammered. "Why, it doesn't follow logically—"

"Nor does anything else. This fact is the chief charm of life. You will presently find, I think, that living means a daily squandering of interest upon the first half of a number of two-part stories which have not ever any sequel. Oh, my adorable boy, I envy you tonight's misery so profoundly I am half unwilling to assure you that in the ultimate one finds a broken heart rather fattening than otherwise; and that a blighted life has never yet been known to prevent queer happenings in conservatories and such-like secluded places or to rob a solitude *a deux* of possibilities. I grant you that love is a wonderful thing; but there are a many emotions which stand toward love much as the makers of certain marmalades assert their wares to stand toward butter—'serving as an excellent occasional substitute.' At least, so you will find it. And unheroic as it is, within the month you will forget."

"No,—I shall not quite forget," said I.

"Then were you the more unwise. To forget, both speedily and frequently, is the sole method of rendering life livable. One is here; the importance of the fact in the eternal scheme of things is perhaps a shade more trivial than one is disposed to concede, but in any event, one is here; and here, for a very little while in youth, one is capable of happiness. For it is a colorful world, Mr. Townsend, containing much, upon the whole, to captivate both eye and taste; a world manured and fertilized by the no longer lovely bodies of persons who died in youth. Oh, their coffins lie everywhere beneath our feet, thick as raisins in a pudding, whithersoever we tread. Yet every one of these poor relics was once a boy or a girl, and wore a body that was capable of so much pleasure! Today, unused to gain the fullness of that pleasure, and now not ever to be used, they lie beneath us, in their coffins, these white, straight bodies, like swords untried that rust in the scabbard. Meanwhile, on every side is apparent the not yet out-wasted instrument, and one is naturally inquisitive,—so that one's fingers and one's nostrils twitch at times, even in the hour when one is most miserable, very much as yours do now."

For a long while I meditated. Then I said: "I am not really miserable, because, all in all, one is content to pay the price of happiness. I have been very happy sometimes during the past year; and whatever the blind Fate that mismanages the world may elect to demand in payment, I shall not haggle. No, by heavens! I would have nothing changed, and least of all would I forget; having drunk nectar neat, one would not qualify it with the water of Lethe."

I rose, not unhandsome, I trusted, in the moonlight. I was hoping Mr. Charteris would notice my new dress-suit, procured in honor of Stella's wedding. And I said: "The play is over, the little comedy is played out. She must go; at least she has tarried for a little. She does not love you; ah! but she did. God speed her, then, the woman we have all loved and lost, and still dream of on sleepy Sundays; and all possible happiness to her! One must be grateful that through her one has known the glory of loving. Even though she never cared—'and never could understand',—one may not but be glad that one has known and loved in youth the Only Woman."

"The Only Woman has a way of leaving many heirs, Mr. Townsend, that play the deuce with the estate."

"—So tomorrow, like the person in *Lycidas*, I am for fresh fields, Mr. Charteris. And indeed it is high time that I were journeying, since she and I have rested, and have laughed and eaten and drunk our fill at this particular tavern; and now it is closing time. A plague on these foolish and impertinent laws, say I quite heartily; for it is cold and cheerless outside, whereas here within I was perfectly comfortable. None the less I must go, or else be evicted by the constable; so good-night, my sweet; and as for you, Madam Clotho, pray what unconscionable score have you chalked up against me?"

I grimaced. "Heavens! what an infinity of sighs, sonnets, lamentations, and heart-burnings is this that I owe to Fate and Decency!"

Charteris applauded as though it were a comedy. "In effect, Marian's married and you stand here, alive and merry at—pray what precise period of life, Mr. Townsend?"

"I confess to twenty-one at present, sir, though I trust to live it down in time."

"I would hardly have thought you that venerable. Well, I predict for you a life without achievements but of gusto. Yes, you will bring a seasoned palate to your grave,—and I envy you. We open Willoughby Hall next week, and of course you will make one of the party. For you write, I know; and you will want to talk to me about editors and read me all your damnable verses. Nothing could please me more. Good-night, you glorious boy."

And the little man wheeled and departed, leaving me to reflect, with appropriate emotions, that I had been formally invited to visit the founder of the Economist school of writers.

4

"HE SAID IT," I MORE lately observed—"yes, he undoubtedly said it. And he wrote *Ashtaroth's Lackey* and *In Old Lichfield* and *The Foolish Prince*, and he knows all the magazine editors personally, and they are probably only too glad to oblige him about anything, and—Oh, may be, it is only a dream, after all." My heart was pounding, but not with sorrow or despair or any other maudlin passion; and Stella was now as remote from my thoughts as was Joan of Arc or Pharaoh's daughter.

Chapter 5

He Revisits Fairhaven and the Play

So I went to Willoughby Hall, which stands, as you may be aware, upon the eastern outskirt of Fairhaven. My reappearance created some stir among the older students and the town-folk, though, one and all, they presently declared me to be "too stuck-up for any use," inasmuch as I ignored them in favour of the Charteris house-party,— after, of course, one visit to Chapel, which I paid a little obviously *en prince*, and affably shook hands with all the Faculty, and was completely conscious of how such happenings impressed us when I, too, was a student.

So much had happened since then, and I felt so much older,— with my existence so delightfully blighted, too,—that it seemed droll to find Colonel Snawley and Dr. Jeal still sitting in arm chairs before Clarriker's Emporium, very much as I had left them there ten months ago.

2

By a disastrous chance did Bettie Hamlyn spend that spring, as well as the preceding year, in Colorado with her mother, who died there that summer; and to me Fairhaven proper without Bettie Hamlyn seemed a tawdry and desolate place; and I know that but for Mrs. Hamlyn's illness—a querulous woman for whom I never cared a jot,—my future life had been quite otherwise. For, as I told Bettie once, and it was true, I have found in the world but three sorts of humanity— "Myself, and Bettie Hamlyn, and the other people."

So I still wrote to Bettie Hamlyn on the seventh of every month— because that was her birthday,—and again on the twenty-third, because that was mine.

And I thought of many things as I walked by the deserted garden, where there was nothing which concerned me now, not even a ghost. I did not go in to leave a card upon Professor Hamlyn. The empty house confronted me too blankly, with its tight-shuttered windows, like blind eyes, and I hurried by.

MEANWHILE, THIS WAS THE FIRST time for many years that Willoughby Hall had been occupied by any other than caretakers; and Fairhaven, to confess the truth, was a trifle ill-at-ease before the modish persons who now tenanted the old mansion; and consoled itself after an immemorial usage by backbiting.

And meanwhile I enjoyed myself tremendously. It was the first time I was ever thrown with people who were unanimously agreed that, after all, nothing is very serious. Mrs. Charteris, of course, was different; but she, like the others, found me divertingly naive and, in consequence, petted and cosseted me. I like petting; and since everyone seemed agreed to regard me as "the Child in the House"—that was Alicia Wade's nickname, and it clung,—and to like having a child in the house, I began a little to heighten my very real boyishness. There was no harm in it; and if people were fonder of me because I sat upon the floor by preference, and drolly exaggerated what I really thought, it became a sort of public duty to do these things. So I did, and found it astonishingly pleasant.

4

AND MEANWHILE TOO, JOHN CHARTERIS could never see enough of me, whom, as I today suspect, Charteris was studying conscientiously, to the end that I should be converted into "copy." For me, I was waiting cannily until he should actually ask to see those manuscripts I had brought to Willoughby Hall, and should help me to get them published. So there were two of us. . . In any event, it was just three weeks after Stella's marriage that Charteris coaxed me into Fairhaven's Opera House to witness a performance of *Romeo and Juliet*, by the Imperial Dramatic Company.

I went under protest; I had witnessed the butchery of so many dramas within these walls during my college days, that I knew what I must anticipate, I said. I had, as a matter of fact, always enjoyed the Opera House "shows," but I did not wish to acknowledge the harboring of such crude tastes to Charteris. In any event, at the conclusion of the second act,—

"By Jove!" said I, in a voice that shook a little. "She's a stunner!" I jolted out, as I proceeded to applaud, vigorously, with both hands and feet. "And who would have thought it! Good Lord, who would have thought it!"

Charteris smiled, in that infernally patronizing way he had sometimes. "A beautiful woman, my dear boy,—an inordinately beautiful woman, in fact, but entirely lacking in temperament."

"Temperament!" I scoffed; "what's temperament to two eyes like those? Why, they're as big as golf-balls! And her voice—why, a violin—a very superior violin—if it could talk, would have just such a voice as that woman has! Temperament! Oh, you make me ill! Why, man, just look at her!" I said, conclusively.

Charteris looked, I presume. In any event, the Juliet of the evening stood before the curtain, smiling, bowing to right and left. The citizens of Fairhaven were applauding her with a certain conscientious industry, for they really found Romeo and Juliet a rather dull couple. The general opinion, however, was that Miss Montmorenci seemed an elegant actress, and in some interesting play, like *The Two Orphans* or *Lady Audley's Secret*, would be well worth seeing. Upon those who had witnessed her initial performance, she had made a most favorable impression in *The Lady of Lyons*; while at the Tuesday matinee, as Lady Isabel in *East Lynne*, she had wrung the souls of her hearers, and had brought forth every handkerchief in the house. Moreover, she was very good-looking,—quite the lady, some said; and, after all, one cannot expect everything for twenty-five cents; considering which circumstances, Fairhaven applauded with temperate ardor, and made due allowance for Shakespeare as being a classic, and, therefore, of course, commendable, but not necessarily interesting.

5

"Well?" I queried, when she had vanished. I was speaking under cover of the orchestra,—a courtesy title accorded a very ancient and very feeble piano. "Well, and what do you think of her—of her looks, I means? Who cares for temperament in a woman!"

Charteris assumed a virtuous expression. "I don't dare tell you," said he; "you forget I am a married man."

Then I frowned a little. I often resented Charteris's flippant allusion to a wife whom I considered, with some reason, to be vastly too good for her husband. And I considered how near I had come to remaining with the others at Willoughby Hall—for that new game they called bridge-whist! And I decided I would never care for bridge. How on earth could presumably sensible people be content to coop themselves in a drawing-room on a warm May evening, when hardly a mile away was a woman with perfectly unfathomable eyes and a voice which was a love-song? Of course, she couldn't act, but, then, who wanted her to act? I indignantly demanded of my soul.

One simply wanted to look at her, and hear her speak. Charteris, with his prattle about temperament, was an ass; when a woman is born with such eyes and with a voice like that, she has done her full duty by the world, and has prodigally accomplished all one has the tiniest right to expect of her.

It was impossible she was in reality as beautiful as she seemed, because no woman was quite so beautiful as that; most of it was undoubtedly due to rouge and rice-powder and the footlights; but one could not be mistaken about the voice. And if her speech was that, what must her singing be! I thought; and in the outcome I remembered this reflection best of all.

I consulted my programme. It informed me, in large type at the end, that Juliet was "old Capulet's daughter," and that the part was played by Miss Annabelle Alys Montmorenci.

And I sighed. I admitted to myself that from a woman who wilfully assumed such a name little could be hoped. Still, I would like to see her off the stage. . . without all those gaudy fripperies and gewgaws. . . merely from curiosity. . . Then too, they said those actresses were pretty gay. . .

6

"A MOST ENJOYABLE PERFORMANCE," SAID Mr. Charteris, as we came out of the Opera House. "I have always had a sneaking liking for burlesque."

Thereupon he paused to shake hands with Mrs. Adrian Rabbet, wife to the rector of Fairhaven.

"Such a sad play," she chirped, "and, do you know, I am afraid it is rather demoralizing in its effects on young people. No, of course, I didn't think of bringing the children, Mr. Charteris—Shakespeare's language is not always sufficiently obscure, you know, to make that safe. And besides, as I so often say to Mr. Rabbet, it is sad to think of our greatest dramatist having been a drinking man. It quite depressed me all through the play to think of him hobnobbing with Dr. Johnson at the Tabard Inn, and making such irregular marriages, and stealing sheep—or was it sheep, now?"

I said that, as I remembered, it was a fox, which he hid under his cloak until the beast bit him.

"Well, at any rate, it was something extremely deplorable and characteristic of genius, and I quite feel for his wife." Mrs. Rabbet sighed, and endeavored, I think, to recollect whether it was *Ingomar* or *Spartacus* that Shakespeare wrote. "However," she concluded, "they play *Ten Nights in a Barroom* on Thursday, and I shall certainly bring the children then, for I am always glad for them to see a really moral and instructive drama. That reminds me! I absolutely must tell you what Tom said about actors the other day—"

And she did. This led naturally to Matilda's recent and blasphemous comments on George Washington, and her observations as to the rector's dog, and little Adey's personal opinion of Elisha. And so on, in a manner not unfamiliar to fond parents. Mrs. Rabbet said toward the end that it was a most enjoyable chat, although to me it appeared to partake rather of the nature of a monologue. It consumed perhaps a half-hour; and when we two at last relinquished Mrs. Rabbet to her husband's charge, it was with a feeling not altogether unakin to relief.

7

WE WALKED SLOWLY DOWN FAIRHAVEN'S one real street, which extends due east from the College for as much as a mile, to end inconsequently in those carefully preserved foundations, which are now the only remnant of a building wherein a number of important matters were settled in Colonial days. There Cambridge Street divides like a Y, one branch of which leads to Willoughby Hall.

Our route from the Opera House thus led through the major part of Fairhaven, which, after an evening of unwonted dissipation, was now largely employed in discussing the play, and turning the cat out for the night. The houses were mostly dark, and the moon, nearing its full, silvered row after row of blank windows. There was an odour of growing things about, for in Fairhaven the gardens are many.

Then it befell that I made a sudden exclamation.

"Eh?" said Charteris.

"Why, nothing," I explained, lucidly.

It may be mentioned, however, that we were, at this moment, passing

JAMES BRANCH CABELL

a tall hedge of box, set about a large garden. The hedge was perhaps five feet six in height; Charteris was also five feet six, whereas I was an unusually tall young man, and topped my host by a good half-foot.

"I say," I observed, after a little, "I'm all out of cigarettes. I'll go back to the drug-store," I suggested, as seized with a happy thought, "and get some. I noticed it was still open. Don't think of waiting for me," I urged, considerately.

"Why, great heavens!" Charteris exclaimed; "take one of mine. I can recommend them, I assure you—and, in any event, there are all sorts, I fancy, at the house. They keep only the rankest kind of domestic tobacco yonder."

"I prefer it," I insisted, "oh, yes, I really prefer it. So much milder and more wholesome, you know. I never smoke any other sort. My doctor insists on my smoking the very rankest tobacco I can get. It is much better for the heart, he says, because you don't smoke so much of it, you know. Besides," I concluded, virtuously, "it is infinitely cheaper; you can get twenty cigarettes all for five cents at some places. I really must economize, I think."

Charteris turned, and with great care stared in every direction. He discovered nothing unusual. "Very well!" assented Mr. Charteris; "I, too, have an eye for bargains. I will go with you."

"If you do alive," quoth I, quite honestly, "I devoutly desire that all sorts of unpleasant things may happen to me for not having wrung your neck first."

Charteris grinned. "Immoral young rip!" said he; "I warn you, before entering the ministry, Mr. Rabbet was accounted an excellent shot."

"Get out!" said I.

And the fervour of my utterance was such that Charteris proceeded to obey. "Don't be late for breakfast, if you can help it," he urged, kindly. "Of course, though, you are up to some new form of insanity, and I shall probably be sent for in the morning, to bail you out of the lock-up."

Thereupon he turned on his heel, and went down the deserted street, singing sweetly.

Sang Mr. Charteris:

> *"Curly gold locks cover foolish brains,*
> *Billing and cooing is all your cheer,*
> *Sighing and singing of midnight strains*
> *Under bonnybells" window-panes.*
> *Wait till you've come to forty year!*

"Forty times over let Michaelmas pass,
Grizzling hair the brain doth clear;
Then you know a boy is an ass,
Then you know the worth of a lass,
Once you have come to forty-year."

Chapter 6

He Chats Over a Hedge

L eft to myself, I began to retrace my steps. Solitude had mitigated my craving for tobacco in a surprising manner; indeed, a casual observer might have thought it completely forgotten, for I walked with curious leisure. When I had come again to the box-hedge my pace had degenerated, a little by a little, into an aimless lounge. Mr. Robert Etheridge Townsend was rapt with admiration of the perfect beauty of the night.

Followed a strange chance. There was only the mildest breeze about; it was barely audible among the leaves above; and yet—so unreliable are the breezes of still summer nights,—with a sudden, tiny and almost imperceptible outburst, did this treacherous breeze lift Mr. Townsend's brand-new straw hat from his head, and waft it over the hedge of trim box-bushes. This was unfortunate, for, as has been said, the hedge was a tall and sturdy hedge. So I peeped over it, with disconsolate countenance.

2

"Beastly awkward," said I, as meditatively; "I'd give a great deal to know how I'm going to get my hat back without breaking through the blessed hedge, and rousing the house, and being taken for a burglar, may be—"

"It is terrible," assented a quite tranquil voice; "but if gentlemen *will* venture abroad on such terrible nights—"

"Eh?" said I. I looked up quickly at the moon; then back toward the possessor of the voice. It was peculiar I had not noticed her before, for she sat on a rustic bench not more than forty feet away, and in full view of the street. It was, perhaps, the strangeness of the affair that was accountable for the great wonder in my soul; and the little tremor which woke in my speech.

"—so windy," she complained.

"Er—ah—yes, quite so!" I agreed, hastily.

"I am really afraid that it must be a tornado. Ah," she continued, emotion catching at her voice, "heaven help all poor souls at sea! How the wind must whistle through the cordage! how the marlin-spikes must quiver, and the good ship reel on such a night!" She looked up at a cloudless sky, and sighed.

"Er h'm!" I observed.

For she had come forward and had held out my hat toward me, and I could see her very plainly now; and my mouth was making foolish sounds, and my heart was performing certain curious and varied gymnastics which could not, by any stretch of the imagination, be included among its proper duties, and which interfered with my breathing.

3

"Didn't I know it—didn't I know it?" I demanded of my soul, and my pulses sang a paean; "I knew, with that voice, she couldn't be a common actress—a vulgar, raddled creature out of a barn! You not a gentlewoman! Nonsense! Why—why, you're positively incredible! Oh, you great, wonderful, lazy woman, you are probably very stupid, and you certainly can't act, but your eyes are black velvet, and your voice is evidently stolen from a Cremona, and as for your hair, there must be pounds of it, and, altogether, you ought to be set up on a pedestal for men to worship! There is just one other woman in the whole wide world as beautiful as you are; and she is two thousand years old, and is securely locked up in the Louvre, and belongs to the French Government, and, besides, she hasn't any arms, so that even there you have the advantage!"

Indeed, Miss Annabelle Alys Montmorenci was of much the same large, placid type as the Venus of Milo, nor were the upper portions of the two faces dissimilar. Miss Montmorenci's lips, however, were far more curved, more buxom, and were, at the present moment, bordered by an absolutely bewildering assemblage of dimples which the statue may not boast.

4

"I really think," said Miss Montmorenci, judicially, "that it would be best for you to seek some shelter from this devastating wind. It really is not safe, you know, in the open. You might be swept away, just as your hat was."

"The shelter of a tree—" I began, looking doubtfully into the garden, which had any number of trees.

"The very thing," she assented. "There is a splendid oak yonder, just half a block up the street." And she graciously pointed it out.

I regarded it with disapproval. "Such a rickety old tree," I objected, sulkily.

Followed a silence. She bent her head to one side, and looked up at me. She was now grave with a difference. "A strolling actress isn't supposed to be very particular, is she?" asked Miss Montmorenci. "She wouldn't object to a man's coming by night and trying to scrape acquaintance with her,—a man who wouldn't think of being seen with her by day? She would like it, probably. She—she'd probably be accustomed to it, wouldn't she?" And Miss Montmorenci smiled.

And I, on a sudden, was abjectly ashamed of myself. "Why, you can't think that of me!" I babbled. "I—oh, don't think me that sort, I beg of you! I'm not—really, I'm not, Miss Montmorenci! But I admired you so much tonight—I—oh, of course, I was very silly and very presumptuous, but, really, you know—"

I paused for a little. This was miles apart from the glib talk I had designed.

"My name is Robert Townsend," I then continued; "I am staying at Mr. Charteris's place, just outside of Fairhaven. And I am delighted to meet you, Miss Montmorenci. So now, you see, we have been quite properly introduced, haven't we? And, by the way," I suggested, after a moment's meditation, "there is a very interesting old college here—old pictures, records, historical association and such like. I would like to inspect it, vastly. Can't I call for you in the morning. We can do it together, if you don't mind, and if you haven't already seen it. Won't you, Miss Montmorenci? You really ought to see King's College, you know; it is quite famous, because I was educated there, and no end of other interesting things have happened within its venerable confines."

She had drawn close to the hedge. "You really mean it?" she asked. "You would walk through the streets of this Fairhaven with me—with a barn-stormer, with a strolling actress? You'd be afraid!" she cried, suddenly; "oh, yes, you talk bravely enough, but you'd be afraid, of course, when the time came! You'd be afraid!"

I had taken the hat, but my head was still uncovered. "I don't think," said I, reflectively, "that I am afraid of many things, somehow. But of one thing I am certainly not afraid, and that is of mistaking a good woman for—for anything else. Their eyes are different somehow," I haltingly explained, as to myself; then I smiled. "Shall we say eleven o'clock?"

Miss Montmorenci laid one hand upon the hedgetop and slowly twisted off four box-leaves what while I waited. "I—I believe you," she said, in meditation; "oh, yes, I believe you, somehow, Mr. Townsend. But we rehearse in the morning, and there is a matinee every day, you know, and—and there are other reasons—" She paused, irresolutely. "No," said Miss Montmorenci, "I thank you, but—good night."

"Oh, I say! am I never to see any more of you?"

A century or so of silence now. Her deliberation seemed endless.

At last: "Matinees and rehearsal keep us busy by day. But I am boarding here for the week, and—and I rest here in the garden after the evening performance. It is cool, it—it is like a glass of water after taking rather bitter medicine. And you aren't a bad sort, are you? No; you look too big and strong and clean, Mr. Townsend. And, besides, you're just a boy—"

"In that case," cried Mr. Townsend, "I shall say goodnight with a light heart." And I turned to go.

"A moment—" said she.

"An eternity," I proffered.

"Promise me," she said, "that you will not come again this week to the Opera House."

My brows were raised a trifle. "I adore the drama," I pleaded.

"And I loathe it. And I act very badly—hopelessly so," said Miss Montmorenci, with an indolent shrug; "and, somehow, I don't want you to see me do it. Why did you mind my calling you a boy? You *are*, you know."

So I protested I had not minded it at all; and I promised. "But at least," I said, triumphantly, "you can't prevent my remembering Juliet!"

She said of course not, only I was not to be silly.

"And therefore," quoth I, "Juliet shall be remembered always." I smiled and waved my hand. "*Au revoir*, Signorina Capulet," said I.

And I took my departure. My blood rejoiced, with a strange fervor, in the summer moonlight. It was good to be alive.

Chapter 7

He Goes Mad in a Garden

And, oh, but it is good to be with you again, Signorina!" cried I, as I came with quick strides into the moonlit garden. I caught both her hands in mine, and laughed like an ineffably contented person. There was nothing very subtle about the boy that then was I; at worst, he overacted what he really felt; and just at present he was pleased with the universe, and he saw no possible reason for concealing the fact.

It was characteristic, also, that she made no pretence at being surprised by my coming. She was expecting me and she smiled very frankly at seeing me. Also, in place of the street dress of Tuesday, she wore something that was white and soft and clinging, and left her throat but half concealed. This, for two reasons, was sensible and praiseworthy; one being that the night was warm, and the other that it really broadened my ideas as to the state of perfection which it is possible for the human throat to attain.

2

"So you don't like my stage-name?" she asked, as I sat down beside her. "Well, for that matter, no more do I." "It doesn't suit you," I protested—"not in the least. Whereas, you might be a Signorina Somebody-or-other, you know. You are dark and stately and—well, I can't tell you all the things you are," I complained, "because the English language is so abominably limited. But, upon the whole, I am willing to take the word of the playbill,—yes, I am quite willing to accept you as Signorina Capulet. She had a habit of sitting in gardens at night, I remember. Yes," I decided, after reflection, "I really think it highly probable that you are old Capulet's daughter. I shall make a point of it to pick a quarrel as soon as possible, with that impertinent, trespassing young Montague. He really doesn't deserve you, you know."

Unaccountably, her face saddened. Then, "Signorina? Signorina?" she appraised the title. "It *is* rather a pretty name. And the other is horrible. Yes, you may call me Signorina, if you like."

SHE WOULD NOT TELL ME her real name. She was unmarried,—this much she told me, but of her past life, her profession, or of her future she never spoke. "I don't want to talk about it," she said, candidly. "We play for a week in Fairhaven, and here, once off the stage, I intend to forget I am an actress. When I am on the stage," she added, in meditative wise, "of course everyone knows I am not."

I laughed. I found her very satisfying; she was not particularly intelligent, perhaps, but then I was beginning to consider clever women rather objectionable creatures. There was a sufficiency of them among the Charteris house-party—Alicia Wade, for instance, and Pauline Ashmeade and Cynthia Chaytor,—and I thought of them almost resentfully. The world had accorded them not exactly what they most wanted, perhaps, but, at least, they had its luxuries; and they said sharp, cynical things about the world in return. In a woman's mouth epigrams were as much out-of-place as a meerschaum pipe.

Here, on the contrary, was a woman whom the world had accorded nothing save hard knocks, and she regarded it, upon the whole, as an eminently pleasant place to live in. She accepted its rebuffs with a certain large calm, as being all in the day's work. There was, no doubt, some good and sufficient reason for these inconveniences; not for a moment, however, did she puzzle her handsome head in speculating over this reason. She was probably too lazy. And the few favours the world accorded her she took thankfully.

"You see," she explained to me—this was on Thursday night, when I found her contentedly eating cheap candy out of a paper bag,—"the world is really very like a large chocolate drop; it's rather bitter on the outside, but when you have bitten through, you find the heart of it sweet. Oh, how greedy!—you've taken the last candied cherry, and I am specially fond of candied cherries!" And indeed, she looked frankly regretful as I munched it.

I thought her adorable; and in exchange for that last candied cherry I promised her some of the new books,—*David Harum* certainly, and, *When Knighthood Was in Flower*, because everybody was reading it, and Mr. Dooley, because they said this young fellow Dunne was nearly as funny as Bill Nye. . .

IN FACT, THE MOON SEEMED to shine down each night upon that particular garden in a more and more delightful and dangerous manner. And I being a fairly normal and healthy young man, the said moonshine affected me in a fashion which has been peculiar to moonshine since Noah was a likely stripling; my blood appeared to me, at times, to leap and bubble in my veins as if it had been some notably invigorating and heady tipple; and my heart was unreasonably contented, and I gave due thanks for this woman who had come to me unsullied through the world's gutter. For she came unsullied; there was no questioning that.

I pictured her in certain execrable rhymes as the Lady in *Comus*, moving serene and unafraid among a rabble of threatening, bestial shapes. And I rejoiced that there were women like this in the world,— brave, wholesome, unutterably honest women, whose very lack of cleverness—oh, subtle appeal to my vanity!—demanded a gentleman's protection.

As has been said, I was a well-grown lad, but when I thought in this fashion I seemed to myself, at a moderate computation, ten feet in height,—and just the person, in short, who would be an ideal protector.

Thus far my callow meditations. My course of reasoning was perhaps faulty, but then there are, at twenty-one, many processes more interesting and desirable than the perfecting of a mathematical demonstration. And so, for a little, my blood rejoiced with a strange fervour in the summer moonlight, and it was good to be alive.

5

THURSDAY WAS THE TWENTY-THIRD OF the month, so upon that afternoon I wrote to Bettie Hamlyn, in far-off Colorado.

It was a lengthy letter. It told her of how desolate her garden was and of how odd Fairhaven seemed without her. It told how I had half changed my mind, and would probably not go to Europe with Mr. Charteris, after all. Bettie had been at pains, in the letter I was answering, to expatiate upon her hatred of Charteris, whom she had never seen. My letter told her, in fine, of a variety of matters. And it ended:

"I went to the Opera House on Monday. But that, like everything else, isn't the same without you, dear. The woman who played Juliet was, I believe, rather good-looking, but I scarcely noticed her in worrying over the pitiful circumstance that the Apothecary and the Populace of Verona had only one pair of shoes between them. Besides, Mercutio kept putting on a bathrobe and insisting he was Friar Laurence. . . I would write more about it, if I had not almost used up all my paper. There is just room to say—"

6

THIS WAS, AS I HAVE stated, on Thursday afternoon. Upon the following evening—

"And why not?" I demanded, for the ninth time.

But she was resolute. "Oh, it is dear of you!" she cried; "and I—I do care for you,—how could I help it? But it can't be,—it can't ever be," she repeated wearily; and then she looked at me, and smiled a little. "Oh, boy, boy! dear, dear boy!" she murmured, half in wonder, "how foolish of you and—how dear of you!"

"And why not?" said I—for the tenth time.

She gave a sobbing laugh. "Oh, the great, brave, stupid boy!" she said, and, for a moment, her hand rested on my hair; "he doesn't know what he is doing,—ah, no, he doesn't know! Why, I might hold you to your word! I might sue you for breach of promise! I might marry you out of hand! Think of that! Why I am only a strolling actress, and fair game for any man,—any man who isn't particular," she added, with the first trace of bitterness I had ever observed in her odd, throaty voice. "And you would marry me,—you! you would give me your name, you would make me your wife! You have actually begged me to be your wife, haven't you? Ah, my brave, strong, stupid Bobbie, how many women must love you,—women who have a right to love you! And you would give them all up for me,—for me, you foolish Bobbie, whom you haven't known a week! Ah, how dear of you!" And she caught her breath swiftly, and her voice broke.

"Yes," I brazenly confessed; "I really believe I would give them all up—every blessed one of them—for you." I inspected her, critically, and then smiled. "And I don't think that I would be deserving any very great credit for self sacrifice, either, Signorina."

"My dear," she answered, "it pleases you to call me old Capulet's daughter,—but if I were only a Capulet, and you a Montague, don't you see how much easier it would be? But we don't belong to rival families, we belong to rival worlds, to two worlds that have nothing in common, and never can have anything in common. They are too strong for us, Bobbie,—my big, dark, squalid world, that you could never sink to, and your gay little world which I can never climb to,—your world that would have none of me, even if—even *if*—" But the condition was not forthcoming.

"The world," said I, in an equable tone—"My dear, I may as well warn you I am shockingly given to short and expressive terms, and as we are likely to see a deal of each other for the future, you will have to be lenient with them,—accordingly, I repeat, the world may be damned."

And I laughed, in unutterable content. "Have none of you!" I cried. "My faith, I would like to see a world which would have none of you! Ah, Signorina, it is very plain to me that you don't realize what a beauty, what a—a—good Lord, what an unimaginative person it was that invented the English language! Why, you have only to be seen, heart's dearest,—only to be seen, and the world is at your feet,—my world, to which you belong of rights; my world, that you are going to honour by living in; my world, that in a little will go mad for sheer envy of blundering, stupid, lucky me!" And I laughed her to scorn.

There was a long silence. Then, "I belonged to your world once, you know."

"Why, of course, I knew as much as that."

"And yet—you never asked—" "Ah, Signorina, Signorina!" I cried; "what matter? Don't I know you for the bravest, tenderest, purest, most beautiful woman God ever made? I doubt you—I! My word!" said I, and stoutly, "that *would* be a pretty go! You are to tell me just what you please," I went on, almost belligerently, "and when and where you please, my lady. And I would thank you," I added, with appropriate sternness, "to discontinue your pitiful and transparent efforts to arouse unworthy suspicions as to my future wife. They are wasted, madam,—utterly wasted, I assure you."

"Oh, Bobbie, Bobbie!" she sighed; "you are such a beautiful baby! Give me time," she pleaded weakly.

And, when I scowled my disapproval, "Only till tomorrow—only a little, little twenty-four hours. And promise me, you won't speak of this—this crazy nonsense again tonight. I must think."

"Never!" said I, promptly; "because I couldn't be expected to keep such an absurd promise," I complained, in indignation.

"And you look so strong," she murmured, with evident disappointment,— "so strong and firm and—and—admirable!"

So I promised at once. And I kept the promise—that is, I did subsequently refer to the preferable and proper course to pursue in divers given circumstances "when we are married;" but it was on six occasions only, and then quite casually,—and six times, as I myself observed, was, all things considered, an extremely moderate allowance and one that did great credit to my self-control.

7

"AND BESIDES, WHY *NOT*?" I said,—for the eleventh time.

"There are a thousand reasons. I am not your equal, I am just an ostensible actress—Why, it would be your ruin!"

"My dear Mrs. Grundy, I confess that, for the moment, your disguise had deceived me. But now: I recognize your voice."

She laughed a little. "And after all," the grave voice said, which was, to me at least, the masterwork of God, "after all, hasn't one always to answer Mrs. Grundy—in the end?"

"Why, then, you disgusting old harridan," said I, "I grant you it is utterly impossible to defend my behaviour in this matter, and, believe me, I don't for an instant undertake the task. To the contrary, I agree with you perfectly,—my conduct is most thoughtless and reprehensible, and merits your very severest condemnation. For look you, here is a young man, well born, well-bred, sufficiently well endowed with this world's goods, in short, an eminently eligible match, preparing to marry an 'ostensible actress' a year or two his senior,—why, of course, you are,—and of whose past he knows nothing,—absolutely nothing. Don't you shudder at the effrontery of the minx? Is it not heart-breaking to contemplate the folly, the utter infatuation of the misguided youth who now stands ready to foist such a creature upon the circles of which your ladyship is a distinguished ornament? I protest it is really incredible. I don't believe a word of it."

"I cannot quite believe it, either, Bobbie—"

"But you see, he loves her. You, my dear madam, blessed with a wiser estimation of our duties to society, of the responsibilities of our position, of the cost of even the most modest establishment, and, above all, of the sacredness of matrimony and the main chance, may well shrug your shoulders at such a plea. For, as you justly observe, what, after all, is this love? only a passing madness, an exploded superstition, an irresponsible *ignis fatuus* flickering over the quagmires and shallows of the divorce court. People's lives are no longer swayed by such absurdities; it is quite out of date."

"Yes; you are joking, Bobbie, I know; yet it is really out of date—"

"But I protest, loudly, my hand upon my heart, that it is true; people no longer do mad things for love, or ever did, in spite of lying poets; any more than the birds mate in the spring, or the sun rises in the morning; popular fallacies, my dear madam, every one of them. You and I know better, and are not to be deceived by appearances, however specious they may be. Ah, but come now! Having attained this highly satisfactory condition, we can well afford to laugh at all our past mistakes,—yes, even at our own! For let us be quite candid. Wasn't there a time, dear lady, before Mr. Grundy came a-wooing, when, somehow, one was constantly meeting unexpected people in the garden, and, somehow, one sat out a formidable number of dances during the evening, and, somehow, the poets seemed a bit more plausible than they do today? It was very foolish, of course,—but, ah, madam, there *was* a time,—a time when even our staid blood rejoiced with a strange fervour in the summer moonlight, and it was good to be alive! Come now, have you the face to deny it,— Mrs. Methuselah?"

"It has not been quite bad to be alive, these last few hours—"

"And, oh, my dear, how each of us will look back some day to this very moment! And we are wasting it! And I have not any words to tell you how I love you! I am just a poor, dumb brute!" I groaned.

Then very tenderly she began to talk with me in a voice I cannot tell you of, and concerning matters not to be recorded.

And still she would not promise anything; and I would give an arm, I think, could it replevin all the idiotic and exquisite misery I knew that night.

Chapter 8

He Duels with a Stupid Woman

Yet I approached the garden on Saturday night with an elated heart. This was the last evening of the engagement of the Imperial Dramatic Company. Tomorrow the troupe was to leave Fairhaven; but I was very confident that the leading lady would not accompany them, and by reason of this confidence, I smiled as I strode through the city of Fairhaven, and hummed under my breath an inane ditty of an extremely sentimental nature.

As I bent over the little wooden gate, and searched for its elusive latch, a man came out of the garden, wheeling sharply about the hedge that, until this, had hidden him; and simultaneously, I was aware of the mingled odour of bad tobacco and of worse whiskey. Well, she would have done with such people soon! I threw open the gate, and stood aside to let him pass; then, as the moon fell full upon the face of the man, I gave an inarticulate, startled sound.

"Fine evening, sir," suggested the stranger.

"Eh?" said I; "eh? Oh, yes, yes! quite so!" Afterward I shrugged my shoulders, and went into the garden, a trifle puzzled.

2

I found her beneath a great maple in the heart of the enclosure. It was a place of peace; the night was warm and windless, and the moon, now come to its full glory, rode lazily in the west through a froth of clouds. Everywhere the heavens were faintly powdered with stardust, but even the planets seemed pale and ineffectual beside the splendour of the moon.

The garden was drenched in moonshine—moonshine that silvered the unmown grass-plots, and converted the white rose-bushes into squat-figured wraiths, and tinged the red ones with dim purple hues. On every side the foliage blurred into ambiguous vistas, where fireflies loitered; and the long shadows of the nearer trees, straining across the grass, were wried patterns scissored out of blue velvet. It was a place of peace and light and languid odours, and I came into it, laughing, the possessor of an over-industrious heart and of a perfectly unreasoning joy over the fact that I was alive.

"I say," I observed, as I stretched luxuriously upon the grass beside her, "you put up at a shockingly disreputable place, Signorina." "Yes?" said she.

"That fellow who just went out," I explained—"do you know the police want his address, I think? No," I continued, after consideration, "I am sure I'm not mistaken,—that is either Ned Lethbury, the embezzler, or his twin-brother. It's been five years since I saw him, but that is he. And that," said I, with proper severity, "is a sample of the sort of associate you prefer to your humble servant! Ah, Signorina, Signorina, I am a tolerably worthless chap, I admit, but at least I never forged and embezzled and then skipped my bail! So you had much better marry me, my dear, and say good-bye to your peculating friends. But, deuce take it! I forgot—I ought to notify the police or something, I suppose."

She caught my arm. Her mouth opened and shut again before she spoke. "He—he is my husband," she said, in a toneless voice. Then, on a sudden, she wailed: "Oh, forgive me! Oh, my great, strong, beautiful boy, forgive me, for I am very unhappy, and I cannot meet your eyes— your honest eyes! Ah, my dear, my dear, do not look at me like that,— you don't know how it hurts!"

The garden noises lisped about us in the long silence that fell. Then the far-off whistling of some home going citizen of Fairhaven tinkled shrilly through the night, and I shuddered a bit.

"I don't understand," I commenced, strangely quiet. "You told me—"

"Ah, I lied to you! I lied to you!" she cried. "I didn't, mean to—hurt you. I did not know—I couldn't know—I was so lonely, Bobbie," she pleaded, with wide eyes; "oh, you don't know how lonely I am. And when you came to me that first night, you—why, you spoke to me as the men I once knew used to speak. There was respect in your voice, and I wanted that so; I hadn't had a man speak to me like that for years, you know, Bobbie. And, boy dear, I was so lonely in my squalid world,— and it seemed as if the world I used to know was calling me—your world, Bobbie—the world I am shut out from."

"Yes," I said; "I think I understand."

"And I thought for a week—just to peep into it, to be a lady again for an hour or two—why, it didn't seem wicked, then, and I wanted it so much! I—I knew I could trust you, because you were only a boy. And I was hungry—*so* hungry for a little respect, a little courtesy, such as men don't accord strolling actresses. So I didn't tell you till the very last I was married. I lied to you. Oh, but you don't understand, this stupid, honest boy doesn't understand anything except that I have lied to him!"

"Signorina," I said, again, and I smiled, resolutely, "I think I understand." I took both her hands in mine, and laughed a little. "But, oh, my dear, my dear," I said, "you should have told me that you loved another man; for you have let me love you for a week, and now I think that I must love you till I die."

"Love him!" she echoed. "Oh, boy dear, boy dear, what a Galahad it is! I don't think Ned ever cared for anything but Father's money; and I—why, you have seen him. How *could* I love him?" she asked, as simply as a child.

I bowed my head. "And yet—" said I. Then I laughed again, somewhat bitterly. "Don't let's tell stories, Mrs. Lethbury," I said; "it is kindly meant, I know, but I remember you now. I even danced with you once, some seven years ago,—yes, at the Green Chalybeate. I remember the night, for a variety of reasons. You are Alfred Van Orden's daughter; your father is a wealthy man, a very wealthy man; and yet, when your—your husband disappeared you followed him—to become a strolling actress. Ah, no, a woman doesn't sacrifice everything for a man in the way you have done, unless she loves him."

I caught my breath. Some unknown force kept tugging down the corners of my mouth, in a manner that hampered speech; moreover, nothing seemed worth talking about. I had lost her. That was the one thing which mattered.

"Why, of course, I went with him," she assented, a shade surprised; "he was my husband, you know. But as for loving,—no, I don't think Ned ever really loved me," she reflected, with puckering brows. "He took that money for—for another woman, if you remember. But he is fond of me, and—and he *needs* me."

I did not say anything; and after a little she went on, with a quick lift of speech.

"Oh, what a queer life we have led since then! You can't imagine it, my dear. He has been a tavern-keeper, a drummer,—everything! Why, last summer we sold rugs and Turkish things in Atlantic City! But he is always afraid of meeting someone who knows him, and—and he drinks too much. So we have not got on in the world, Ned and I; and now, after three years, I'm the leading lady of the Imperial Dramatic Company, and he is the manager. I forgot, though,—he is advance-agent this week, for he didn't dare stay in Fairhaven, lest some of the men at Mr. Charteris's should recognize him, you know. He came back only this evening—"

She paused for a moment; a wistful quaver crept into her speech. "Oh, it's queer, it's queer, Bobbie! Sometimes—sometimes when I have time to think, say on long Sunday afternoons, I remember my old life, every bit of it,—oh, I do remember such strange little details! I remember the designs on the bread and butter plates, and all the silver things on my desk, and the plank by my door that always creaked and somehow never got fixed, and the big, shiny buttons on the coachman's coat,—just trifles like that. And—and they hurt, they hurt, Bobbie, those little, unimportant things! They—grip my throat."

She laughed, not very mirthfully. "Then I am like the old lady in the nursery rhyme, and say, Surely, this can't be I. But it is I, boy dear,—a strolling actress, a barn-stormer! Isn't it queer, Bobbie? But, oh, you don't know half—"

I was remembering many things. I remembered Lethbury, a gross man, superfluously genial, whom I had never liked, although I recalled my admiration of his whiskers. I recollected young Amelia Van Orden, not come to her full beauty then, the bud of girlhood scarce slipped; and I remembered very vividly the final crash, the nine days' talk over Lethbury's flight in the face of certain conviction,—by his father-in-law's advice (as some said) who had furnished and forfeited heavy bail for the absconder. Oh, the brave woman who had followed! Oh, the brave, foolish woman! And, for the action's recompense, he was content to exhibit her to yokels, to make of her beauty an article of traffic. Heine was right; there is an Aristophanes in heaven. And then hope blazed.

"Your husband," I said, quickly, "he does not love you? He—he is not faithful to you?"

"No," she answered; "there is a Miss Fortescue—she plays second parts—"

"Ah, my dear, my dear!" I cried, with a shaking voice; "come away, Signorina,—come away with me! He *doesn't* need you,—and, oh, my dear, I need you so! You can get your divorce and marry me. Ah, Signorina, come away,—come away from this squalid life that is killing you, to the world you are meant for, to the life you hunger for! Come back to the clean, lighthearted world you love, the world that is waiting to pet and caress you just as it used to do,—our world, Signorina! You don't belong here with—with the Fortescues. You belong to us."

I sprang to my feet. "Come now!" said I. "There's Anne Charteris; she is a good woman, if ever lived one. She used to know you, too, didn't she? Well, then, come with me to her, dearest—and tonight! You shall see your father tomorrow. Your father—why, think how that old man loves you, how he has longed for you, his only daughter, all these years. And I?" I spread out my hands, in the tiniest, impotent gesture. "I love you," I said, simply. "I cannot do without you, heart's dearest."

Impulsively, she rested both hands upon my breast; then bowed her head a little. The nearness of her seemed to shake in my blood, to catch at my throat, and my hands, lifted for a moment, trembled with desire of her.

"You don't understand," she said. "I am a Catholic—my mother was one, you know. There is no divorce for us. And—and besides, I'm not modern. I am very old-fashioned, I suppose, in my ideas. Do you know," she asked, with a smile upon the face which lifted confidingly toward me, "I—I *really* believe the world was made in six days; and that the whale swallowed Jonah, and that there is a real purgatory and a hell of fire and brimstone. You don't, do you, Bobbie? But I do,—and I promised to stay with him till death parted us, you know, and I must do it. I am all he has. He would get even worse without me. I—oh, boy dear, boy dear, I love you so!" And her voice broke, in a great, choking sob.

"A promise—a promise made by an ungrown girl to a brute—a thief—!"

"No, dear," she answered, quietly; "a promise made to God."

And looking into her face, I saw love there, and anguish, and determination. It seemed monstrous, but of a sudden I knew with a dull surety; she loved me, but she thought she had no right to love me; she would not go with me. She would go with that drunken, brutish thief.

And I suddenly recalled certain clever women—Alicia Wade, Pauline Ashmeade, Cynthia Chaytor—the women of that world wherein I was novitiate; beyond question, they would raise delicately penciled eyebrows to proclaim this woman a fool—and to wonder.

They would be right, I thought. She was only a splendid, tender-hearted, bright-eyed fool, the woman that I loved. My heart sickened as her folly rose between us, an impassable barrier. I hated it; and I revered it.

Thus we two stood silent for a time. The wind murmured above in the maples, lazily, ominously. Then the gate clicked, with a vicious snap that pierced the silence like the report of a distant rifle. "That is probably Ned," she said wearily. "I had forgotten they close the barrooms earlier on Saturday nights. So good-bye, Bobbie. You—you may kiss me, if you like."

So for a moment our lips met. Afterward I caught her hands in mine, and gripped them close to my breast, looking down into her eyes. They glinted in the moonlight, deep pools of sorrow, and tender—oh, unutterably tender and compassionate.

But I found no hope there. I lifted her hand to my lips, and left her alone in the garden.

3

LETHBURY WAS FUMBLING AT THE gate.

"Such nuishance," he complained, "havin' gate won't unlock. Latch mus' got los'—po' li'l latch," murmured Mr. Lethbury, plaintively—"all 'lone in cruel worl'!"

I opened the gate for him, and stood aside to let him pass toward his wife.

Chapter 9

He Puts His Tongue in His Cheek

It was not long before John Charteris knew of the entire affair, for in those days I had few concealments from him: and the little wizened man brooded awhile over my misery, with an odd wistfulness.

"I remember Amelia Van Orden perfectly," he said—"now. I ought to have recognized her. Only, she was never, in her best days, the paragon you depict. She sang, I recollect; people made quite a to-do over her voice. But she was very, very stupid, and used to make loud shrieking noises when she was amused, and was generally reputed to be 'fast.' I never investigated. Even so, there was not any real doubt as to her affair, in any event, with Anton von Anspach, after that night the sleigh broke down—"

"Oh, spare me all those ancient Lichfield scandals! She is an angel, John, if there was ever one."

"In your eyes, doubtless! So your heart is broken. Yet do you not realize that not a month ago you were heartbroken over Stella Musgrave? Child, I repeat, I envy you this perpetual unhappiness, for I have lost, as you will presently lose, the capacity of being quite miserable."

"But, John, it seems as if there were nothing left to live for, now—"

"At twenty-one! Well, certainly, at that age one loves to think of life as being implacable. But you will soon discover that she is merely inconsequential, and that none of her antics are of lasting importance; and you will learn to smile a deal more often than you weep or laugh."

Then we talked of other matters. It was presently settled that Charteris was to take me abroad with him that summer; and with the thorough approval of my mother.

"Mr. Charteris will be of incalculable benefit to you," she told me, "in introducing you to the very best people, all of whom he knows, of course, and besides you are getting to look older than I, and it is unpleasant to have to be always explaining you are only my stepson, particularly as your father never married anybody but me, though, heaven knows, I wish he had. Of course you will be just as wild as your father and your Uncle George. I suppose that is to be expected, and I daresay it will break my heart, but all I ask of you is please to keep out of the newspapers, except of course the social items. And if you *must* associate with abandoned women, please for my sake, Robert, don't have anything to do with those who can prove that they are only misunderstood, because they are the most dangerous kind."

I kissed her. "Dear little mother, I honestly believe that when you get to heaven you will refuse to speak to Mary Magdalen."

"Robert, let us remember the Bible says, 'in my Father's house are many mansions,' and of course nobody would think of putting me in the same mansion with her."

It was well-nigh the last conversation I was to hold with my mother; and I was to remember it with an odd tenderness. . .

2

UPON THE DOINGS OF MYSELF in Europe during the ensuing two years I prefer to dwell as lightly as possible. I had long anticipated a sojourn in divers old-world cities; but the London I had looked to find was the London of Dickens, say, and my Paris the Paris of Dumas, or at the very least of Balzac. It is needless to mention that in the circles to which the, quite real, friendship of John Charteris afforded an entry I found little that smacked of such antiquity. I had entered a world inhabited by people who amused themselves and apparently did nothing else; and I was at first troubled by their levity, and afterward envious of it, and in the end embarked upon sedulous attempt to imitate it. I continued to be very boyish; indeed, I found myself by this in much the position of an actor who has made such a success in one particular role that the public declines to patronize him in any other.

3

IT WAS DURING THIS FIRST year abroad that I wrote *The Apostates*, largely through the urging of John Charteris.

"You have the ability, though, that dances most gracefully in fetters. You will never write convincingly about the life you know, because life is, to you, my adorable boy, a series of continuous miracles, to which the eyes of other men are case-hardened. Write me, then, a book about the past."

"I have thought of it," said I, "for being over here makes the past seem pretty real, somehow. Last month when I was at Ingilby I was on fire with the notion of writing something about old Ormskirk— my mother's ancestor, you know. And since I've seen what's left of

Bellegarde I have wanted to write about his wife's people too,—the dukes and vicomtes of Puysange, or even about the great Jurgen. You see, I am just beginning to comprehend that these are not merely characters in Lowe's and La Vrilliere's books, but my flesh and blood kin, like Uncle George Bulmer—"

"And for that reason you want to write about them! You would, though; it is eminently characteristic. Well, then, why should you not immortalize the persons who had the honor of begetting you—oh, most handsome and most naive of children!—by writing your very best about them?" "Because to succeed—not only among the general but with the 'cultured few,' God save the mark!—it is now necessary to write not badly but abominably."

"What would you demand, then, of a book?"

I meditated. "What one most desiderates in the writings of today is clarity, and beauty, and tenderness and urbanity, and truth."

"Not a bad recipe, upon the whole, though I would stipulate for symmetry and distinction also—Write the book!"

"Ah," said I, "but this is the kind of book I wish to read when, of course, the mood seizes me. It is not at all the sort of book, though, I would elect to write. The main purpose of writing any book, I take it, is to be read; and people simply will not read a book when they suspect it of being carefully written. That sort of thing gets on a reader's nerves; it's too much like watching a man walk a tight-rope and wondering if he won't slip presently."

"Oh, 'people!'" Charteris flung out, in an extremity of scorn. "Since time was young, a generally incompetent humanity has been willing to pardon anything rather than the maddening spectacle of labour competently done. And they are perfectly right; it is abominable how such weak-minded persons occasionally thrust themselves into a world quite obviously designed for persons who have not any minds at all. But I was not asking you to write a 'best-seller.'"

"No, you were asking me to become an Economist, and be one of 'the few rare spirits which every age providentially affords,' and so on. That is absolute and immoral nonsense. When you publish a novel you are at least pretending to supply a certain demand; and if you don't endeavour honestly to supply it, you are a swindler, no more and no less. No, it is all very well to write for posterity, if it amuses you, John; personally, I cannot imagine what possible benefit you will derive from it, even though posterity *does* read your books. And for myself, I want to be read and to be a power while I can appreciate the fact that I *am* a sort of power, however insignificant. Besides, I want to make some money out of the blamed thing. Mother is a dear, of course, but, like all the Bulmers, with age she is becoming tight-fisted."

"And Esau—" Charteris began.

"Yes,—but that's Biblical, and publishing a book is business. People say to authors, just as they do to tailors: 'I want such and such an article. Make it and I'll pay you for it.' Now, your tailor may consider the Imperial Roman costume more artistic than that of today, and so may you in the abstract, but if he sent home a toga in place of a pair of trousers, you would discontinue dealing with him. So if it amuses you to make togas, well and good; I don't quarrel with it; but, personally, I mean to go into the gents' furnishing line and to do my work efficiently."

"Yes,—but with your tongue in your cheek."

"It is the one and only attitude," I sweetly answered, "in which to write if you indeed desire to be read with enjoyment." And presently I rose and launched upon

A Defence of That Attitude

"The main trouble with you, John Charteris, is that you will never recover from being *fin de siecle*. Yes, you belong to that queer dying nineteenth century. And even so, you have quite overlooked what is, perhaps, the signal achievement of the nineteenth century,—the relegation of its literature to the pharmacopoeia. The comparison of the tailor, I willingly admit, is a bad one. Those who write successfully nowadays must appeal to men and women who seek in fiction not only a means of relaxation, but spiritual comfort as well, and an uplifting rather than a mere diversion of the mind; so that they are really druggists who trade exclusively in intoxicants and hypnotics.

"Half of the customers patronize the reading-matter shops because they want to induce delusions about a world they know, and do not find particularly roseate and the other half skim through a book because they haven't anything else to do and aren't sleepy, as yet.

"Oh, in filling either prescription the trick is much the same; you have simply to avoid bothering the reader's intellect in any way whatever. You have merely to drug it, you have merely to caress it with interminable platitudes, or else with the most uplifting avoidances of anything which happens to be unprintably rational. And you must remember always that the crass emotions of half-educated persons are, in reality, your chosen keyboard; so play upon it with an axe if you haven't any handier implement, but hit it somehow, and for months your name will be almost as famous as that of my mother's father remains the year round because he invented a celebrated baking-powder.

"It is all very well for you to sneer, and talk about art. But there are already in this world a deal more Standard Works than any man can hope to digest in the average lifetime. I don't quarrel with them, for, personally, I find even Ruskin, like the python in the circus, entirely endurable so long as there is a pane of glass between us. But why, in heaven's name, should you endeavour to harass humanity with one more battalion of morocco-bound reproaches for sins of omission, whenever humanity goes into the library to take a nap? For what other purpose do you suppose a gentleman goes into his library, pray? When he is driven to reading he does it decently in bed.

"Besides, if I like a book, why, then, in so far as I am concerned, it *is* a good book. No, please don't talk to me about 'the dignity of literature'; modern fiction has precisely as much to do with dignity as has vaudeville or billiards or that ridiculous Prohibitionist Party, since the object of all four, I take it, is to afford diversion to people who haven't anything better to do. Thus, a novel which has diverted a thousand semi-illiterate persons is exactly ten times as good as a novel that has pleased a hundred superior persons. It is simply a matter of arithmetic.

"You prefer to look upon writing as an art, rather than a business? Oh, you silly little man, the touchstone of any artist is the skill with which he adapts his craftsmanship to his art's limitations. He will not attempt to paint a sound or to sculpture a colour, because he knows that painting and sculpture have their limitations, and he, quite consciously, recognizes this fact whenever he sets to work.

"Well, the most important limitation of writing fiction nowadays is that you have to appeal to people who would never think of reading you or anybody else, if they could possibly imagine any other employment for that particular vacant half-hour. And you cannot hope for an audience of even moderately intelligent persons, because intelligent persons do not attempt to keep abreast with modern fiction. It is probably ascribable to the fact that they enjoy being intelligent, and wish to remain so.

"You sneer at the 'best-sellers.' I tell you, in sober earnest, that the writing of a frankly trashy novel which will 'sell,' is the highest imaginable form of art. For true art, in its last terms, is the adroit circumvention of an unsurmountable obstacle. I suppose that form and harmony and colour are very difficult to tame; and the sculptor, the musician and the painter quite probably earn their hire. But people don't go to concerts unless they want to hear music; whereas the people who buy the 'best-sellers' are the people who would prefer to do *anything* rather than be reduced to reading. I protest that the man who makes these people read on until they see how 'it all came out' is a deal more than an artist; he is a sorcerer."

And I paused, a little out of breath.

"What a boy it is!" said Charteris. "Do you know, you are uncommonly handsome when you are talking nonsense? Write the trashy book, then. I never argue with children; and besides, I do not have to read it."

4

IT THUS FELL ABOUT THAT in the second European year, not very long after my mother's death, *The Apostates* was given to the world, with what result the world has had a plenty of time wherein to forget. . . It was first published in *The Quaker Post*, with pictures by Roderick King Hill, and in the autumn was brought out as a book by Stuyvesant and Brothers. I made rather a good thing cut of it financially; but the numerous letters I received from the people who had liked it I found extremely objectionable. They were not the right sort of people, I felt forlornly. . . So I endured my plaudits without undue elation, for I always held *The Apostates* to be, at best, a medley of conventional tricks and extravagant rhetoric, inanimate by any least particle of myself,— and its success, say, as though the splendiferous trappings of an emperor were hung upon a clothier's dummy, and the result accepted as an adequate presentation of Charlemagne.

In other words, the book was the most unbridled kind of balderdash, founded on my callow recollections of the Green Chalybeate,—not the least bit accurate, as I was afterward to discover,—with all the good people exceedingly oratorical and the bad ones singularly epigrammatic and abandoned and obtuse. I introduced a depraved nobleman, of course, to give the requisite touch of high society, seasoned the mixture with French and botany and with a trifle of Dolly Dialoguishness, and inserted, at judicious intervals, the most poetical of descriptions, so that the skipping of them might afford an agreeable rest to the reader's eye. There was also a sufficiency of piddling with unsavoury matters to insure the suffrage of schoolgirls.

And a number of persons, in fine, were so misguided as to enthuse over the result. The verb is carefully selected, for they one and all were just the sort of people who "enthuse."

5

I WAS VEXED, HOWEVER, AT the time to find I could not achieve an appropriate emotion over my mother's death. The news came, to be sure, at a season when I was preoccupied with getting rid of Agnes Faroy. . . I have not ever heard of any rational excuse for the quite common assumption that children ought to be particularly fond of their parents. Still, my mother was the prettiest woman I had ever known, though without any claim to beauty, and I had always gloried in our kinship; for I believed her nature to be generous and amiable when she thought of it; and the cablegram which announced the event aroused in me sincere regret that a comely ornament to my progress had been smashed irrevocably.

For a little I reflected as to whither she had vanished, and decided she had been too futile and well-meaning ever to be punished by any reasonable Being. Yet how she would have enjoyed the publication of my book!—without any attempt to read it, however, since she had never, to my knowledge, read anything, with the exception of the daily papers. . . And besides, I disliked being unable to have the appropriate emotion.

But I simply could not manage it. For here, in the midst of the Faroy mess,—with Agnes weeping all over the place, and her brothers flourishing pistols and declaiming idiocies,—came the news from Uncle George that my mother had left me virtually nothing. She must have used up, of course, a good share of her Bulmer Baking Powder money in supporting my father comfortably; but she had always lived in such estate as to make me assume she had retained, anyhow, enough of the Bulmer money to last my time. So it was naturally a shock to discover that this monetary attitude was inherited from my mother, who had been cheerfully "living on her principle" all these years, without considering my future. I had no choice but to regard it as abominably selfish.

"I think Claire was afraid to tell you," wrote Uncle George, "how little there was left. In any event, she always shirked doing it, so as to stave off unpleasantness. And when we cabled you how ill she was, it now seems most unfortunate you could not see your way clear to giving up your trip through the chateau country, as your not coming appeared to be on her mind a great deal at the last. I do not wish to seem to criticize you in any way, Robert, but I must say. . ."

Well, but you know what sort of nonsense that smug gambit heralds in letters from your kindred. Even so, I now owned the Townsend house and an income sufficient for daily bread; and it looked just then as though the magazine editors were willing to furnish the butter, and occasional cakes. So the future promised to be pleasant enough.

6

CHARTERIS HAD RETURNED TO ALGIERS in the autumn my book was published, but I elected to pass the winter in England. "Of course," was Mr. Charteris's annotation—"because it is precisely the most dangerous spot in the world for you. And you are to spend October at Negley? I warn you that Jasper Hardress is in love with his wife, and that the woman has an incurable habit of making experiments and an utter inability to acquire experience. Take my advice, and follow Mrs. Monteagle to the Riviera, instead. Cissie will strip you of every penny you have, of course, but in the end you will find her a deal less expensive than Gillian Hardress."

"You possess a low and evil mind," I observed, "since I am fond, in all sincerity, of Hardress, whereas his wife is not even civil to me. Why, she goes out of her way to be rude to me."

"Yes," said Mr. Charteris; "but that is because she is getting worried about her interest in you. And what is the meaning of this, by the way? I found it on your table this morning." He read the doggerel aloud with an unkindly and uncalled-for exaggeration of the rhyming words.

> *"We did not share the same inheritance,—*
> *I and this woman, five years older than I,*
> *Yet daughter of a later century,—*
> *Who is therefore only wearied by that dance*
> *Which has set my blood a-leaping.*
>
> *"It is queer*
> *To note how kind her face grows, listening*
> *To my wild talk, and plainly pitying*
> *My callow youth, and seeing in me a dear*
> *Amusing boy,—yet somewhat old to be*

Still reading Alice Through the Looking-Glass
And Water-Babies. . . *With light talk we pass,*

> *"And I that have lived long in Arcady—*
> *I that have kept so many a foolish tryst,*
> *And written drivelling rhymes—feel stirring in me*
> *Droll pity for this woman who pities me,*
> *And whose weak mouth so many men have kissed."*

"That," I airily said, "is, in the first place, something you had no business to read; and, in the second, simply the blocking out of an entrancingly beautiful poem. It represents a mood."

"It is the sort of mood that is not good for people, particularly for children. It very often gets them shot too full of large and untidy holes."

"Nonsense!" said I, but not in displeasure, because it made me feel like such a devil of a fellow. So I finished my letter to Bettie Hamlyn,—for this was on the seventh,—and I went to Negley precisely as I had planned.

7

"WE WERE JUST SPEAKING OF you," Mrs. Hardress told me, the afternoon of my arrival,—"Blanche and I were talking of you, Mr. Townsend, the very moment we heard your wheels."

I shook hands. "I trust you had not entirely stripped me of my reputation?"

"Surely, that is the very last of your possessions any reasonable person would covet?"

"A palpable hit," said I. "Nevertheless, you know that all I possess in the world is yours for the asking."

"Yes, you mentioned as much, I think, at Nice. Or was it Colonel Tatkin who offered me a heart's devotion and an elopement? No, I believe it was you. But, dear me, Jasper is so disgustingly healthy that I shall probably never have any chance of recreation."

I glanced toward Jasper Hardress. "I have heard," said I, hopefully, "that there is consumption in the family?"

"Heavens, no! he told me that before marriage to encourage me, but I find there is not a word of truth in it."

Then Jasper Hardress came to welcome his guest, and save from a distance I saw no more that evening of Gillian Hardress.

Chapter 10

He Samples New Emotions

It was the following day, about noon, as I sat intent upon my Paris *Herald* that a tiny finger thrust a hole in it. I gave an inaudible observation, and observed a very plump young person in white with disfavour.

"And who may you happen to be?" I demanded.

"I'm Gladys," the young lady responded; "and I've runned away."

"But not without an escort, I trust, Miss Gladys? Really—upon my word, you know, you surprise me, Gladys! An elopement without even a tincture of masculinity is positively not respectable." I took the little girl into my lap, for I loved children, and all helpless things. "Gladys," I said, "why don't you elope with me? And we will spend our honeymoon in the Hesperides."

"All right," said Gladys, cheerfully. She leaned upon my chest, and the plump, tiny hand clasped mine, in entire confidence; and the contact moved me to an irrational transport and to a yearning whose aim I could not comprehend. "Now tell me a story," said Gladys.

So that I presently narrated to Gladys the ensuing

Story of the Flowery Kingdom

"Fair Sou-Chong-Tee, by a shimmering brook
Where ghost-like lilies loomed tall and straight,
Met young Too-Hi, in a moonlit nook,
Where they cooed and kissed till the hour was late:
Then, with lanterns, a mandarin passed in state,
Named Hoo-Hung-Hoo of the Golden Band,
Who had wooed the maiden to be his mate—
For these things occur in the Flowery Land.

"Now, Hoo-Hung-Hoo had written a book,
In seven volumes, to celebrate
The death of the Emperor's thirteenth cook:
So, being a person whose power was great,

He ordered a herald to indicate
He would blind Too-Hi with a red-hot brand
And marry Sou-Chong at a quarter-past-eight,—
For these things occur in the Flowery Land.

"And the brand was hot, and the lovers shook
In their several shoes, when by lucky fate
A Dragon came, with his tail in a crook,—
A Dragon out of a Nankeen Plate,—
And gobbled the hard-hearted potentate
And all of his servants, and snorted, and
Passed on at a super-cyclonic rate,—
For these things occur in the Flowery Land.

"The lovers were wed at an early date,
And lived for the future, I understand,
In one continuous tete-a-tete,—
For these things occur. . . in the Flowery Land."

Gladys wanted to know: "But what sort of house is a tete-a-tete? Is it like a palace?"

"It is very often much nicer than a palace," I declared,—"provided of course you are only stopping over for a week-end."

"And wasn't it odd the Dragon should have come just when he did?"

"Oh, Gladys, Gladys! don't tell me you are a realist."

"No, I'm a precious angel," she composedly responded, with a flavour of quotation.

"Well! it is precisely the intervention of the Dragon, Gladys, which proves the story is literature," I announced. "Don't you pity the poor Dragon, Gladys, who never gets a chance in life and has to live always between two book-covers?"

She said that couldn't be so, because it would squash him.

"And yet, dear, it is perfectly true," said Mrs. Hardress. The lean and handsome woman was regarding the pair of us curiously. "I didn't know you cared for children, Mr. Townsend. Yes, she is my daughter." She carried Gladys away, without much further speech.

Yet one Parthian comment in leaving me was flung over her shoulder, snappishly. "I wish you wouldn't imitate John Charteris so. You are

JAMES BRANCH CABELL

getting to be just a silly copy of him. You are just Jack where he is John. I think I shall call you Jack."

"I wish you would," I said, "if only because your sponsors happened to christen you Gillian. So it's a bargain. And now when are we going for that pail of water?"

Mrs. Hardress wheeled, the child in her arms, so that she was looking at me, rather queerly, over the little round, yellow head. "And it was only Jill, as I remember, who got the spanking," she said. "Oh, well! it always is just Jill who gets the spanking—Jack."

"But it was Jack who broke his crown," said I; "Wasn't it—Jill?" It seemed a jest at the time. But before long we had made these nicknames a habit, when just we two were together. And the outcome of it all was not precisely a jest. . .

2

SHE TOLD ME NOT LONG after this, "When I saw Gladys loved you, of course I loved you too." And I hereby soberly record the statement that to have a woman fall thoroughly in love with him is the most uncomfortable experience which can ever befall any man.

I am tolerably sure I never made any amorous declaration. Rather, it simply bewildered me to observe the shameless and irrational infatuation this woman presently bore for me, and before it I was powerless. When I told her frankly I did not love her, had never loved her, had no intention of ever loving her, she merely bleated, "You are cruel!" and wept. When I attempted to restrain her paroxysms of anguish, she took it as a retraction of what I had told her.

I would then have given anything in the world to be rid of Gillian Hardress. This led to scenes, and many scenes, and played the very devil with the progress of my second novel. You cannot write when anyone insists on sitting in the same room with you, on the irrelevant plea that she is being perfectly quiet, and therefore is not disturbing you. Besides, she had no business in my room, and was apt to get caught there.

3

I REMEMBER ONE OF THESE contentions. She is abominably rouged, and before me she is grovelling, as she must have seen some actress do upon the stage.

"Oh, I lied to you," she wailed; "but you are so cruel! Ah, don't be cruel, Jack!"

Then I lifted the scented woman to her feet, and she stayed motionless, regarding me. She had really wonderful eyes.

"You are evil," I said, "through and through you are evil, I think, and I can't help thinking you are a little crazy. But I wish you would teach me to be as you are, for tonight the hands of my dead father strain from his grave and clutch about my ankles. He has the right because it is his flesh I occupy. And I must occupy the body of a Townsend always. It is not quite the residence I would have chosen—Eh, well, for all that, I am I! And at bottom I loathe you!"

"You love me!" she breathed.

I thrust her aside and paced the floor. "This is an affair of moment. I may not condescend to sell, as Faustus did, but of my own volition must I will to squander or preserve that which is really Robert Townsend."

I wheeled upon Gillian Hardress, and spoke henceforward with deliberation. You must remember I was very young as yet.

"I have often regretted that the colour element of vice is so oddly lacking in our life of today. We appear, one and all, to have been born at an advanced age and with ladylike manners, and we reach our years of indiscretion very slowly; and meanwhile we learn, too late, that prolonged adherence to morality trivialises the mind as hopelessly as a prolonged vice trivialises the countenance. I fear this has been said by someone else, my too impetuous Jill, and I hope not, for in that event I might possibly be speaking sensibly, and to be sensible is a terrible thing and almost as bad as being intelligible."

"You are not being very intelligible now, sweetheart. But I love to hear you talk."

"Meanwhile, I am young, and in youth—*il faut des emotions*, as Blanche Amory is reported to have said, by a novelist named Thackeray, whose productions are now read in public libraries. Still, for a respectable and brougham-supporting person, Thackeray came then as near to speaking the truth as is possible for people of that class. In youth emotions are necessary. Find me, therefore, a new emotion!"

"So many of them, dear!" she promised.

"I do not love you, understand,—and your husband is my friend, and I admire him. But I am I! I have endowments, certain faculties which many men are flattering enough to envy—and I will to make of them

JAMES BRANCH CABELL

a carpet for your quite unworthy feet. I will to degrade all that in me is most estimable, and in return I demand a new emotion."

4

WELL, BUT WOMEN ARE QUEER. There is positively no way of affronting them, sometimes. She had not even the grace to note that I had taken a little too much to drink that night. . . But over all this part of my life I prefer to pass as quickly as may be expedient.

5

I REMEMBERED, ANYWAY, AFTER GILLIAN had gone from my room, to write Bettie Hamlyn a post-card. It was no longer, strictly speaking, the twenty-third, but considerably after midnight, of course. Still, it was the writing regularly when I loathed writing letters that counted with Bettie, I reflected; and virtually I was writing on the twenty-third, and besides, Bettie would never know.

6

AND THEREAFTER GILLIAN HARDRESS MADE almost no concealment of her feeling toward me, or employed at best the flimsiest of disguises. All that winter she wrote to me daily, and, when the same roof sheltered us, would slip the scribblings into my hand at odd moments, but preferably before her husband's eyes. She demanded an account of every minute I spent apart from her, and never believed a syllable of my explanations; and in a sentence, she pestered me to the verge of distraction.

And always the circumstance which chiefly puzzled me was the host of men that were infatuated by Gillian Hardress. There was no doubt about it; she made fools of the staidest, if for no better end than that the spectacle might amuse me.

"Now you watch me, Jack!" she would say. And I obediently would watch her wriggling beguilements, and the man's smirking idiocy, with bewilderment.

For in me her allurements aroused, now, absolutely no sensation save that of boredom. Often I used to wonder for what reason it seemed impossible for me, alone, to adore this woman insanely. It would have been so much more pleasant, all around.

But, I repeat, I wish to have done with this portion of my life as quickly as may be expedient. I am not particularly proud of it. I would elide it altogether, were it possible, but as you will presently see, that is not possible if I am to make myself intelligible. And I find that the more I write of myself the more I am affected by the same poor itch for self-exposure which has made Pepys and Casanova and Rousseau famous, and later feminine diarists notorious.

Were I writing fiction, now, I would make the entire affair more plausible. As it stands, I am free to concede that this chapter in my life history rings false throughout, just as any candid record of an actual occurrence does invariably. It is not at all probable that a woman so much older than I should have taken possession of me in this fashion, almost against my will. It is even less probable that her husband, who was by ordinary absurdly jealous of her, should have suspected nothing and have been sincerely fond of me.

But then I was only twenty-two, as age went physically, and he looked upon me as an infant. I was, I think, quite conscientiously childish with Jasper Hardress. I prattled with him, and he liked it. And so often, especially when we three were together—say, at luncheon,—I was teased by an insane impulse to tell him everything, just casually, and see what he would do.

I think it was the same feeling which so often prompted her to tell him, in her flighty way, of how profoundly she adored me. I would wriggle and blush; and Jasper Hardress would laugh and protest that he adored me too. Or she would expatiate upon this or that personal feature of mine, or the becomingness of a new cravat, say; and would demand of her husband if Jack—for so she always called me,—wasn't the most beautiful boy in the world? And he would laugh and answer that he thought it very likely.

7

THEY WERE AMERICANS, I SHOULD have said earlier, but to all intents they lived abroad, and had done so for years. Hardress's father had been thoughtful enough to leave him a sufficient fortune to countenance the indulgence of this or any other whim, so that the Hardresses divided the year pretty equally between their real home at Negley and a tiny chateau which they owned near Aix-les-Bains. I visited them at both places.

It was a pleasant fiction that I came to see Gladys. Regularly, I was told off to play with her, as being the only other child in the house. It was rather hideous, for the little girl adored me, and I was beginning to entertain an odd aversion toward her, as being in a way responsible for everything. Had Gillian Hardress never found me cuddling the child, whose sex was visibly a daily aggrievement to Jasper Hardress, however conscientiously he strove to conceal the fact,—so that in consequence "I have to love my precious lamb for two, Jack,"—Gillian would never, I think, have distinguished me from the many other men who, so lightly, tendered a host of gallant speeches. . . But I never fathomed Gillian Hardress, beyond learning very early in our acquaintance that she rarely told me the truth about anything.

Also I should have said that Hardress cordially detested Charteris, just as Bettie Hamlyn did, because for some reason he suspected the little novelist of being in love with Hardress's wife. I do not know; but I imagine Charteris had made advances to her, in his own ambiguous fashion, as he was apt to do, barring strenuous discouragement, to every passably handsome woman he was left alone with. I do know he made love to her a little later.

Hardress distrusted a number of other men, for precisely the same reason. Heaven only is familiar with what grounds he had. I merely know that Gillian Hardress loathed John Charteris; she was jealous of his influence over me. But me her husband never distrusted. I was only an amusing and ingenuous child of twenty-two, and not for a moment did it occur to him that I might be in love with his wife.

Indeed, I believe upon reflection that he was in the right. I think I never was.

8

"Yes," I said, "I am to meet the Charterises in Genoa. Yes, it is rather sudden. I am off tomorrow. I shall not see you dear good people for some time, I fancy. . ."

When Hardress had gone the woman said in a stifled voice: "No, I will not dance. Take me somewhere—there is a winter-garden, I know—"

"No, Jill," said I, with decision. "It's no use. I am really going. We will not argue it."

Gillian Hardress watched the dancers for a moment, as with languid interest. "You fear that I am going to make a scene. Well! I can't. You have selected your torture chamber too carefully. Oh, after all that's been between us, to tell me here, to my husband's face, in the presence of some three hundred people, without a moment's warning, that you are 'off tomorrow!' It—it is for good, isn't it?"

"Yes," I said. "It had to be—some time, you know."

"No, don't look at me. Watch the dancing, I will fan myself and seem bored. No, I shall not do anything rash."

I was uncomfortable. Yet at bottom it was the theatric value of this scene which impressed me,—the gaiety and the brilliance on every side of her misery. And I did not look at her. I did just as she ordered me.

"I was proud once. I haven't any pride now. You say you must leave me. Oh, dearest boy, if you only knew how unhappy I will be without you, you could not leave me. Sweetheart, you must know how I love you. I long every minute to be with you, and to see you even at a distance is a pleasure. I know it is not right for me to ask or expect you to love me always, but it seems so hard."

"It's no use, Jill—"

"Is it another woman? I won't mind. I won't be jealous. I won't make scenes, for I know you hate scenes, and I have made so many. It was because I cared so much. I never cared before, Jack. You have tired of me, I know. I have seen it coming. Well, you shall have your way in everything. But don't leave me, dear! oh, my dear, my dear, don't leave me! Oh, I have given you everything, and I ask so little in return—just to see you sometimes, just to touch your hand sometimes, as the merest stranger might do. . ."

So her voice went on and on while I did not look at her. There was no passion in this voice of any kind. It was just the long monotonous wail of some hurt animal. . . They were playing the *Valse Bleu*, I remember. It lasted a great many centuries, and always that low voice was pleading with me. Yes, it was uncommonly unpleasant; but always at the back of my mind some being that was not I was taking notes as to precisely how I felt, because some day they might be useful, for the book I had already outlined. "It is no use, Jill," I kept repeating, doggedly.

Then Armitage came smirking for his dance. Gillian Hardress rose, and her fan shut like a pistol-shot. She was all in black, and throughout that moment she was more beautiful than any other woman I have ever seen.

"Yes, this is our dance," she said, brightly. "I thought you had forgotten me, Mr. Armitage. Well! good-bye, Mr. Townsend. Our little talk has been very interesting—hasn't it? Oh, this dress *always* gets in my way—"

She was gone. I felt that I had managed affairs rather crudely, but it was the least unpleasant way out, and I simply had not dared to trust myself alone with her. So I made the best of an ill bargain, and remodeled the episode more artistically when I used it later, in *Afield*.

Chapter 11

He Postures Among Chimney-Pots

I met the Charterises in Genoa, just as I had planned. Anne's first exclamation was, "Heavens, child, how dissipated you look! I would scarcely have known you."

Charteris said nothing. But he and I lunched at the Isotta the following day, and at the conclusion of the meal the little man leaned back and lighted a cigarette.

"You must overlook my wife's unfortunate tendency toward the most unamiable of virtues. But, after all, you are clamantly not quite the boy I left at Liverpool last October. Where are your Hardresses now?"

"In London for the season. And why is your wife rushing on to Paris, John?"

"Shopping, as usual. Yes, I believe I did suggest it was as well to have it over and done with. Anne is very partial to truisms. Besides, she has an aunt there, you know. Take my advice, and always marry a woman who is abundantly furnished with attractive and visitable relations, for this precaution is the true secret of every happy marriage. We may, then, regard the Hardress incident as closed?"

"Oh, Lord, yes!" said I, emphatically.

"Well, after all, you have been sponging off them for a full year. The adjective is not ill-chosen, from what I hear. I fancy Mrs. Hardress has found you better company after she had mixed a few drinks for you, and so—But a truce to moral reflections! for I am desirous once more to hear the chimes at midnight. I hear Francine is in Milan?"

"There is at any rate in Milan," said I, "a magnificent Gothic Cathedral of international reputation; and upon the upper gallery of its tower, as my guidebook informs me, there is a watchman with an efficient telescope. Should I fail to meet that watchman, John, I would feel that I had lived futilely. For I want both to view with him the Lombard plain, and to ask him his opinion of Cino da Pistoia, and as to what was in reality the middle name of Cain's wife."

Francine proved cordial; but John Charteris was ever fickle, and not long afterward an Italian countess, classic in feature, but in coloring smacking of an artistic renaissance, had drawn us both to Switzerland, and thence to Liege. It was great fun, knocking about the Continent with John, for he knew exactly how to order a dinner, and spoke I don't know how many languages, and seemed familiar with every side-street and back-alley in Europe. For myself, my French as acquired in Fairhaven appeared to be understood by everybody, but in replying very few of the natives could speak their own foolish language comprehensibly. I could rarely make head or tail out of what they were jabbering about.

I was alone that evening, because Annette's husband had turned up unexpectedly; and Charteris had gone again to hear Nadine Neroni, the new prima donna, concerning whom he and his enameled Italian friend raved tediously. But I never greatly cared for music; besides, the opera that night was *Faust*; the last act of which in particular, when three persons align before the footlights and scream at the top of their voices, for a good half hour, about how important it is not to disturb anybody, I have never been able to regard quite seriously.

So I was spending this evening sedately in my own apartments at the Continental; and meanwhile I lisped in numbers that (or I flattered myself) had a Homeric tang; and at times chewed the end of my pencil meditatively. "From present indications," I was considering, "that Russian woman is cooking something on her chafing-dish again. It usually affects them that way about dawn."

I began on the next verse viciously, and came a cropper over the clash of two sibilants, as the distant clamour increased. "Brutes!" said I, disapprovingly. "Sere, clear, dear—Now they have finished, '*Jamais, monsieur*', and begun crying, 'Fire!' Oh, this would draw more than three souls out of a weaver, you know! Mere, near, hemisphere—no, but the Greeks thought it was flat. By Jove! I do smell smoke!"

Wrapping my dressing-gown about me—I had afterward reason to thank the kindly fates that it was the green one with the white fleurs-de-lis, and not my customary, unspeakably disreputable bath-robe, scorched by the cigarette ashes of years,—I approached the door and peeped out into the empty hotel corridor. The incandescent lights glimmered mildly through a gray haze which was acrid and choking to breathe; little puffs of smoke crept lazily out of the lift-shaft just opposite; and down-stairs all Liége was shouting incoherently, and dragging about the heavier pieces of hotel furniture.

"By Jove!" said I, and whistled a little disconsolately as I looked downward through the bars about the lift-shaft.

"Do you reckon," spoke a voice—a most agreeable voice,—"we are in any danger?"

The owner of the voice was tall; not even the agitation of the moment prevented my observing that, big as I am, her eyes were almost on a level with my shoulder. They were not unpleasant eyes, and a stray dream or two yet lingered under their heavy lids. The owner of the voice wore a strange garment that was fluffy and pink,—pale pink like the lining of a sea-shell—and billows of white and the ends of various blue ribbons peeped out about her neck. I made mental note of the fact that disordered hair is not necessarily unbecoming; it sometimes has the effect of an unusually heavy halo set about the face of a half-awakened angel.

"It would appear," said I, meditatively, "that, in consideration of our being on the fifth floor, with the lift-shaft drawing splendidly, and the stairs winding about it,—except the two lower flights, which have just fallen in,—and in consideration of the fire department's probable incompetence to extinguish anything more formidable than a tar-barrel,—yes, it would appear, I think, that we might go further than 'dangerous' and find a less appropriate adjective to describe the situation."

"You mean we cannot get down?" The beautiful voice was tremulous.

And my silence made reply.

"Well, then," she suggested, cheerfully, after due reflection, "since we can't go down, why not go up?"

As a matter of fact, nothing could be more simple. We were on the top floor of the hotel, and beside us, in the niche corresponding to the stairs below, was an iron ladder that led to a neatly-whitewashed trapdoor in the roof. Adopting her suggestion, I pushed against this trap-door and found that it yielded readily; then, standing at the top of the ladder, I looked about me on a dim expanse of tiles and chimneys; yet farther off were the huddled roofs and gables of Liége, and just a stray glimpse of the Meuse; and above me brooded a clear sky and the naked glory of the moon.

I LOWERED MY HEAD WITH a distinct sigh of relief.

"I say," I called, "it is infinitely nicer up here—superb view of the city, and within a minute's drop of the square! Better come up."

"Go first," said she; and subsequently I held for a moment a very slender hand—a ridiculously small hand for a woman whose eyes were almost on a level with my shoulder,—and we two stood together on the roof of the Hôtel Continental. We enjoyed, as I had predicted, an unobstructed view of Liége and of the square, wherein two toy-like engines puffed viciously and threw impotent threads of water against the burning hotel beneath us, and, at times, on the heads of an excited throng erratically clad.

But I looked down moodily, "That," said I, as a series of small explosions popped like pistol shots, "is the café; and, oh, Lord! there goes the only decent Scotch in all Liége!"

"There is Mamma!" she cried, excitedly; "there!" She pointed to a stout woman, who, with a purple? shawl wrapped about her head, was wringing her hands as heartily as a bird-cage, held in one of them, would permit. "And she has saved Bill Bryan!"

"In that case," said I, "I suppose it is clearly my duty to rescue the remaining member of the family. You see," I continued, in bending over the trap-door and tugging at the ladder, "this thing is only about twenty feet long; but the kitchen wing of the hotel is a little less than that distance from the rear of the house behind it; and with this as a bridge I think we might make it. In any event, the roof will be done for in a half-hour, and it is eminently worth trying." I drew the ladder upward.

Then I dragged this ladder down the gentle slant of the roof, through a maze of ghostly chimneys and dim skylights, to the kitchen wing, which was a few feet lower than the main body of the building. I skirted the chimney and stepped lightly over the eaves, calling, "Now then!" when a muffled cry, followed by a crash in the courtyard beneath, shook my heart into my mouth. I turned, gasping; and found the girl lying safe, but terrified, on the verge of the roof.

"It was a bucket," she laughed, "and I stumbled over it,—and it fell—and—and I nearly did,—and I am frightened!"

And somehow I was holding her hand in mine, and my mouth was making irrelevant noises, and I was trembling. "It was close, but—look here, you must pull yourself together!" I pleaded; "because we haven't, as it were, the time for airy badinage and repartee—just now."

"I can't," she cried, hysterically. "Oh, I am so frightened! I can't!"

"You see," I said, with careful patience, "we must go on. I hate to seem too urgent, but we *must*, do you understand?" I waved my hand toward the east. "Why, look!" said I, as a thin tongue of flame leaped through the open trap-door and flickered wickedly for a moment against the paling gray of the sky.

She saw and shuddered. "I'll come," she murmured, listlessly, and rose to her feet.

4

I HEAVED ANOTHER SIGH OF relief, and waving her aside from the ladder, dragged it after me to the eaves of the rear wing. As I had foreseen, this ladder reached easily to the eaves of the house behind the rear wing, and formed a passable though unsubstantial-looking bridge. I regarded it disapprovingly.

"It will only bear one," said I; "and we will have to crawl over separately after all. Are you up to it?"

"Please go first," said she, very quiet. And, after gazing into her face for a moment, I crept over gingerly, not caring to look down into the abyss beneath.

Then I spent a century in impotence, watching a fluffy, pink figure that swayed over a bottomless space and moved forward a hair's breadth each year. I made no sound during this interval. In fact, I do not remember drawing a really satisfactory breath from the time I left the hotel-roof, until I lifted a soft, faint-scented, panting bundle to the roof of the Councillor von Hollwig.

5

"YOU ARE," I CRIED, WITH conviction, "the bravest, the most—er—the bravest woman I ever knew!" I heaved a little sigh, but this time of content. "For I wonder," said I, in my soul, "if you have any idea what a beauty you are! what a wonderful, unspeakable beauty you are! Oh, you are everything that men ever imagined in dreams that left them weeping for sheer happiness—and more! You are—you, and I have held you in my arms for a moment; and, before high heaven, to repurchase that privilege I would consent to the burning of three or four more hotels and an odd city or so to boot!" But, aloud, I only said, "We are quite safe now, you know."

She laughed, bewilderingly. "I suppose," said she, "the next thing is to find a trap-door."

But there were, so far as we could discover, no trapdoors in the roof of the Councillor von Hollwig, or in the neighbouring roofs; and, after searching three of them carefully, I suggested the propriety of waiting till dawn to be melodramatically rescued.

"You see," I pointed out, "everybody is at the fire over yonder. But we are quite safe here, I would say, with an entire block of houses to promenade on; moreover, we have cheerful company, eligible central location in the very heart of the city, and the superb spectacle of a big fire at exactly the proper distance. Therefore," I continued, and with severity, "you will please have the kindness to explain your motives for wandering about the corridors of a burning hotel at four o'clock in the morning."

She sat down against a chimney and wrapped her gown about her. "I sleep very soundly," said she, "and we did both museums and six churches and the Palais de Justice and a deaf and dumb place and the cannon-foundry today,—and the cries awakened me,—and I reckon Mamma lost her head."

"And left you," thought I, "left you—to save a canary-bird! Good Lord! And so, you are an American and a Southerner as well."

"And you?" she asked.

"Ah—oh, yes, me!" I awoke sharply from admiration of her trailing lashes. The burning hotel was developing a splendid light wherein to see them. "I was writing—and I thought that Russian woman had a few friends to supper,—and I was looking for a rhyme when I found you," I concluded, with a fine coherence.

She looked up. It was incredible, but those heavy lashes disentangled quite easily. I was seized with a desire to see them again perform this interesting feat. "Verses?" said she, considering my slippers in a new light.

"Yes," I admitted, guiltily—"of Helen."

She echoed the name. It is an unusually beautiful name when properly spoken. "Why, that is my name, only we call it Elena."

"Late of Troy Town," said I, in explanation.

"Oh!" The lashes fell into their former state. It was hopeless this time; and manual aid would be required, inevitably. "I should think," said my compatriot, "that live women would be more—inspiring"

"Surely," I assented. I drew my gown about me and sat down. "But, you see, she is alive—to me." And I dwelt a trifle upon the last word.

"One would gather," said she, meditatively, "that you have an unrequited attachment for Helen of Troy."

I sighed a melancholy assent. The great eyes opened to their utmost. The effect was as disconcerting as that of a ship firing a broadside at you, but pleasanter. "Tell me all about it," said she, coaxingly.

"I have always loved her," I said, with gravity. "Long ago, when I was a little chap, I had a book—*Stories of the Trojan War*, or something of the sort. And there I first read of Helen—and remembered. There were pictures—outline pictures,—of quite abnormally straight-nosed warriors, with flat draperies which amply demonstrated that the laws of gravity were not yet discovered; and the pictures of slender goddesses, who had done their hair up carefully and gone no further in their dressing. Oh, the book was full of pictures,—and Helen's was the most manifestly impossible of them all. But I knew—I knew, even then, of her beauty, of that flawless beauty which made men's hearts as water and drew the bearded kings to Ilium to die for the woman at sight of whom they had put away all memories of distant homes and wives; that flawless beauty which buoyed the Trojans through the ten years of fighting and starvation, just with delight in gazing upon Queen Helen day by day, and with the joy of seeing her going about their streets. For I remembered!" And as I ended, I sighed effectively.

"I know," said she.

> *"'Or ever the knightly years had gone*
> *With the old world to the grave,*
> *I was a king in Babylon*
> *And you were a Christian slave.'"*

"Yes, only I was the slave, I think, and you—er—I mean, there goes the roof, and it is an uncommonly good thing for posterity you thought of the trap-door. Good thing the wind is veering, too. By Jove! look at those flames!" I cried, as the main body of the Continental toppled inward like a house of cards; "they are splashing, actually splashing, like waves over a breakwater!"

I drew a deep breath and turned from the conflagration, only to encounter its reflection in her widened eyes. "Yes, I was a Trojan warrior," I resumed; "one of the many unknown men who sought and found death beside Scamander, trodden down by Achilles or Diomedes. So they died knowing they fought in a bad cause, but rapt with that joy they had in remembering the desire of the world and her perfect loveliness. She scarcely knew that I existed; but I had loved her; I had overheard some laughing words of hers in passing, and I treasured them as men treasure gold. Or she had spoken, perhaps—oh, day of days!— to me, in a low, courteous voice that came straight from the back of the throat and blundered very deliciously over the perplexities of our alien speech. I remembered—even as a boy, I remembered."

She cast back her head and laughed merrily. "I reckon," said she, "you are still a boy, or else you are the most amusing lunatic I ever met."

"No," I murmured, and I was not altogether playacting now, "that tale about Polyxo was a pure invention. Helen—and the gods be praised for it!—can never die. For it is hers to perpetuate that sense of unattainable beauty which never dies, which sways us just as potently as it did Homer, and Dr. Faustus, and the Merovingians too, I suppose, with memories of that unknown woman who, when we were boys, was very certainly some day, to be our mate. And so, whatever happens, she

"Abides the symbol of all loveliness,
Of beauty ever stainless in the stress
Of warring lusts and fears.

"For she is to each man the one woman that he might have loved perfectly. She is as old as youth, she is more old than April even, and she is as ageless. And, again like youth and April, this Helen goes about the world in varied garments, and to no two men is her face the same. Oh, very often she transmutes her fleshly covering. But through countless ages I, like every man alive, have followed her, and fought for her, and won her, and have lost her in the end,—but always loving her as every man must do. And I prefer to think that some day—" But my voice here died into a whisper, which was in part due to emotion and partly to an inability to finish the sentence satisfactorily. The logic of my verses when thus paraphrased from memory, seemed rather vague.

"Yes—like Pythagoras" she said, a bit at random. "Oh, I know. There really must be something in it, I have often thought, because you actually do remember having done things before sometimes."

"And why not? as the March Hare very sensibly demanded." But now my voice was earnest. "Yes, I believe that Helen always comes. Is it simply a proof that I, too, am qualified to sit next to the Hatter?" I spread out my hands in a helpless little gesture. "I do not know. But I believe that she will come,—and by and by pass on, of course, as Helen always does."

"You will know her?" she queried, softly.

Now I at last had reached firm ground. "She will be very tall," I said, "very tall and exquisite,—like a young birch-tree, you know, when its new leaves are whispering over to one another the secrets of spring. Yes, that is a ridiculous sounding simile, but it expresses the general effect of her— the *coup d'oeil*, so to speak,—quite perfectly. Moreover, her hair will be a miser's dream of gold; and it will hang heavily about a face that will be— quite indescribable, just as the dawn yonder is past the utmost preciosity of speech. But her face will flush and will be like the first of all anemones to peep through black, good-smelling, and as yet unattainable earth; and her eyes will be deep, shaded wells where, just as in the proverb, truth lurks."

But now I could not see her eyes.

"No," I conceded, "I was wrong. For when men talk to her as—as they cannot but talk to her, her face will flush dull red, almost like smouldering wood; and she will smile a little, and look out over a great fire, such as that she saw on the night when Ilium was sacked and the slain bodies were soft under her stumbling feet, as she fled through flaming Troy Town. And then I shall know her."

My companion sighed; and the woes of centuries weighed down her eyelids obstinately. "It is bad enough," she lamented, "to have lost all one's clothes—that new organdie was a dream, and I had never worn it; but to find yourself in a dressing-gown—at daybreak, on a strange roof—and with an unintroduced lunatic—is positively terrible!"

The unintroduced lunatic rose to his feet and waved his hand toward the east. The dawn was breaking in angry scarlet and gold that spread like fire over half the visible horizon; the burning hotel shut out the remaining half with tall flames, which shouldered one another monotonously, and seemed lustreless against the pure radiance of the sky. Chill daylight showed in melting patches through the clouds of black smoke overhead.

It was a world of fire, transfigured by the austere magnificence of dawn and the grim splendour of the shifting, roaring conflagration; and at our feet lay the orchard of the Councillor von Hollwig, and there the awakened birds piped querulously, and sparks fell crackling among apple-blossoms.

"Ilium is ablaze," I quoted; "and the homes of Pergamos and its towering walls are now one sheet of flame."

JAMES BRANCH CABELL

She inspected the scene, critically. "It does look like Ilium," she admitted. "And that," peering over the eaves into the deserted by-street, "looks like a milkman."

I was unable to deny this, though an angry concept crossed my mind that any milkman, with commendable tastes and feelings, would at this moment be gaping at the fire at the other end of the block, rather than prosaically measuring quarts at the Councillor's side-entrance. But there was no help for it, when chance thus unblushingly favoured the proprieties; in consequence I clung to a water-pipe, and explained the situation to the milkman, with a fretted mind and King's College French.

I turned to my companion. She was regarding the burning hotel with an impersonal expression.

"Now I would give a deal," I thought, "to know just how long you would prefer that milkman to take in coming back."

Chapter 12

HE FACES HIMSELF AND REMEMBERS

Into the lobby of the Hôtel d'Angleterre strolled, an hour later, a tall young man, in a green dressing-gown, and inquired for Charteris. The latter, in evening dress, was mournfully breakfasting in his new quarters.

Charteris sprang to his feet. I saw, with real emotion, that he had been weeping; but now he was all flippancy. "My dear boy! I have just torn my hair and the rough drafts of several cablegrams on your account! Sit down at once, and try the bacon, since, for a wonder, it is not burnt—and, in passing, I had thought of course that you were."

Instead, I took a drink, and went to sleep upon the nearest sofa.

2

I WAS VERY TIRED, BUT I awakened about noon and managed to procure enough clothes to make myself not altogether unpresentable to the public eye. Charteris had gone already about his own affairs, and I did not regret it, for I meant, without delay, to follow up my adventure of the night before.

But when I had come out of the Rue de la Casquette, and was approaching the statue of Gretry, I came upon a very ornately-dressed woman, who was about to enter en open carriage. I stared; and preposterous as it was, I knew that I was not mistaken. And I said aloud, "Signorina!"

It was a long while before she said, "Don't—don't ever call me that again!" And since the world in general appeared just then to be largely flavoured with the irresponsibility of dreams, it did not surprise me that we were presently alone in somebody's sitting-room.

"I have seen you twice in Liége," she said. "I suppose this had to come about. I would have preferred to avoid it, though. Well! *che sara!* You don't care for music, do you? No,—otherwise you would have known earlier that I am Nadine Neroni now."

"Ah!" I said, very quietly. I had heard, as everybody had, a deal concerning the Neroni. "I think, if you will pardon me, I will not intrude upon Baron von Anspach's hospitality any longer," I said.

"That is unworthy of you,—no, I mean it would have been unworthy of a boy we knew of." There was a long pier-glass in these luxurious rooms. She led me to it now. "Look, Bobbie. We have altered a little, haven't we? I at least, am unmistakable. 'Their eyes are different, somehow', you remember. You haven't changed as much,—not outwardly. I think you are like Dorian Gray. Yes, as soon—as soon as I could afford it, I read every book you ever talked about, I think. It was damnably foolish of me. For I've heard things. And there was a girl I tried to help in London—an Agnès Faroy—"

"Ah!" I said.

"She had your picture even then, poor creature. She kissed it just before she died. She didn't know that I had ever heard of you. She never knew. Oh, how *could* you!" the Neroni said, with something very like a sob, "Or were you always—just that, at bottom?"

"And have you ever noticed, Mademoiselle Neroni, that every one of us is several people? In consequence I must confess to have been wondering—?"

"Well! I wasn't. You won't believe it now, perhaps. And it doesn't matter, anyhow." Her grave voice lifted and upon a sudden was changed. "Bobbie, when you had gone I couldn't stand it! I couldn't let you ruin your life for me, but I could not go on as I had done before—Oh, well, you'll never understand," she added, wearily. "But Von Anspach had always wanted me to go with him. So I wrote to him, at the Embassy. And after all, what is the good of talking—now!"

We two were curiously quiet. "No, I suppose there is no good in talking now." We stood there, as yet, hand in hand. The mirror was candid. "Oh, Signorina, I want to laugh as God laughs, and I cannot!"

3

BUT I LACK THE HEART to set down all that brief and dreary talk of ours. How does it matter what we said? We two at least knew, even as we talked, that all we said meant in the outcome, nothing. Yet we talked awhile and spoke, I think, quite honestly.

She was not unhappy; and there were inbred Lichfeldian traditions which prompted me to virtuous indignation over her defects in remorse and misery. There were my memories, too.

"I don't sing very well, of course, but then I'm not dependent on my singing, you know. Oh, why not be truthful? And Von Anspach always sees to it I get the tendered of criticism—in print. And, moreover, I've a deal put by. I'm a miser, *he* says, and I suppose I am, because I know what it is to be poor. So when the rainy day comes—as of course it will,—I'll have quite enough to purchase a serviceable umbrella. Meanwhile, I have pretty much everything I want. People talk of course, but it is only on the stage they ever drive you out into a snow-storm. Besides, they don't talk to *me*."

In fine, I found that the Neroni was a very different being from Miss Montmorenci. . .

4

THEN I LEFT HER. I had not any inclination just now to pursue my fair Elena. Rather I sat alone in my new bedroom, thinking, confusedly, first of Amelia Van Orden, and how I danced with her a good eight years ago; of that woman who had come to me in remote Fairhaven, coming through the world's gutter, unsullied,—because that much I yet believe, although I do not know. . . She may have been always the same, even in the old days when Lichfield thought her "fast," and she was more or less "compromised,"—and years before I met her, a blind, inexperienced boy. Only she may then have been a better actress than I suspected. . . I thought, in any event, of those execrable rhymes that likened her to the Lady in *Comus*, moving serene and unafraid among a rabble of threatening bestial shapes; and I thought of the woman who would, by this time, be with Von Anspach.

For here again were inbred Lichfieldian traditions of the sort I rarely dare confess to, even to myself, because they are so patently hidebound and ridiculous. These traditions told me that this woman, whom I had loved, was Von Anspach's harlot. I might—and I did—endeavor to be ironical and to be broadminded and to be up-to-date about the whole affair, and generally to view the matter through the sophisticated eyes of the author of The Apostates, that Robert Etheridge Townsend who was a connoisseur of ironies and human foibles; but these futilities did no good at all. Lichfield had got at and into me when I was too young to defend myself; and I could no more alter the inbred traditions of Lichfield, that were a part of me, than a carpet could change its texture. My traditions merely told me that the dear woman whom I remembered had come—in fleeing from discomforts which were unbearable, if that mattered—to be Von Anspach's harlot: and finding her this, my traditions declined to be the least bit broadminded. In Lichfield such women were simply not respectable; nor could you get around that fact by going to Liége.

There was in the room a *Matin,* which contained a brief account of the burning of the Continental, and a very lengthy one of the Neroni's appearance the night before. Drearily, to keep from thinking, I read a deal concerning *la gracieuse cantatrice américaine.* Whether or not she had made a fool of me with histrionics in Fairhaven, there was no doubt that she had chosen wisely in forsaking Lethbury, and the round of village "Opera Houses." She had chosen, after all, and precisely as I had done, to make the most of youth while it lasted; and she appeared, just now, to harvest prodigally.

"On jouait Faust," I read, "et jamais le célèbre personnage de Goethe n'adore plus exquise Gretchen. Miss Nadine Neroni est, en effet, une idéale Marguerite à la taille bien prise, au visage joli éclairé des deux yeux grands et doux. Et lorsqu'elle commença à chanter, ce fut un véritable ravissement: sa voix se fit l'interprète rêvée de la divine musique de Gounod, tandis que sa personne et son coeur incarnaient physiquement et moralement l'héroïne de Goethe" . . .

And so on, for Von Anspach had "seen to it," prodigally. And "Oh, well!" I thought; "if everybody else is so extravagantly pleased, what in heaven's name is the use of my being squeamish? Besides, she is only doing what I am doing, and getting all the pleasure out of life that is possible. She and I are very sensible people. At least, I suppose we are. I wonder, though? Meanwhile, I had better go and look for that preposterously beautiful Elena. And a fig for the provincial notions of Lichfield, that are poisoning me with their nonsense! and for the notions of Fairhaven, too, I suppose—"

5

THEN CHARTERIS CAME INTO THE room. "John," said I, "this is a truly remarkable world, and only hypercriticism would venture to suggest that it is probably conducted by an inveterate humourist. So lend me that pocket-piece of yours, and we will permit chance to settle the entire matter. That is the one intelligent way of treating anything which is really serious. You probably believe I am Robert Etheridge Townsend, but as a matter of fact, I am Hercules in the allegory. So! the beautiful lady or America? Why, the eagle flutters uppermost, and from every mountain side let praises ring. Accordingly I am off."

"And you will cross half the world," said Charteris, "in the green dressing-gown, or in the coat which Byam borrowed for you this morning? I do not wish to seem inquisitive, you understand—"

"No, I believe I am through with borrowed coats—as with yours, for instance. But I am quite ready to go in my own dressing-gown if necessary—"

I wheeled at the door.

"By the way, I am done with you, John. I am fond of you, and all that, and I sincerely admire my chimney-pot coquette—of whom you haven't heard,—but, after all, there are real people yonder. And by God, even after two years of being pickled in alcohol and chasing after women that are quite used to being chased—well, even now I am one of those real people. So I am done with you and this perpetual making light of things—!"

"The Declaration of Independence," Charteris observed, "is undoubtedly the best thing in imaginative literature that we Americans have as yet accomplished; but I am sufficiently familiar with it, thank you, and I find, with age, that only the more untruthful platitudes are endurable. Oh, I predicted for you, at our first meeting, a life without achievements but of gusto! Now, it would appear, you plan to prance among an interminable saturnalia of the domestic virtues. So be it! but I warn you that the house of righteousness is but a wayside inn upon the road to being a representative citizen."

"You are talking nonsense," I rapped out—"and immoral nonsense."

"It is very strange," John Charteris complained, "how so many of us manage to reduce everything to a question of morality,—that is, to the alternative of being right or wrong. Now a man's personality, as somebody or other very properly observes, has many parts besides the moral area; and the intelligent, the artistic, even the religious part, need not necessarily have anything to do with ethics—"

"Ah, yes," said I, "so there is a train at noon—"

"And a virtuous man," continued Charteris, amicably, "is no more the perfect type of humanity than an intellectual man. In fact, the lowest and certainly the most disagreeable type of all troublesome people is that which combines an immaculate past with a limited understanding. The religious tenets of this class consist of an unshakable belief that the Bible was originally written in English, and contains nothing applicable to any of the week-days. And in consequence—"

I left him mid-course in speech. "Words, words!" said I; and it appeared to me for the moment that words were of astonishingly trivial import,

JAMES BRANCH CABELL

however carefully selected, which was in me a wholesome, although fleet, apostacy of yesterday's creed. And I sent a cablegram to Bettie Hamlyn.

6

IT WAS ON THE TRIP homeward I first met with Celia Reindan. I then considered her a silly little nuisance. . .

For I crossed the Atlantic in a contained fury of repentance for the wasted months. I had achieved nothing that was worthy of me, and presently I would be dead. Why, I might die within the five minutes! I might never see the lagging minute-hand of my little traveling clock pass that next numeral, say! The thought obsessed me, especially at night. Once, in a panic, I rose from my berth, and pushed the minute-hand forward a half-hour. "Now, I have tricked You!" I said, aloud; for nervously I was footing a pretty large bill. At twenty-three one has the funds wherewith to balance these accounts. . .

I wanted to live normally—to live as these persons thick about me, who seemed to grow up, and mate, and beget, and die, in the incurious fashion of oxen. I wanted to think only from hand to mouth, to think if possible not at all, and to be guided always in the conduct of my life by gross and obvious truisms, so that I must be judged at last but as one of the herd. "And what is accustomed—what holds of familiar usage—had come to seem the whole essence of wisdom, on all subjects"; for I wanted just the sense of companionship, irrevocable and eternal and commonly shared with every one of my kind. And yonder was Bettie Hamlyn. . . "Oh, make a man of me, Bettie! just a common man!"

And Bettie might have done it, one considers, even then, for I was astir with a new impetus. Now, with a grin, the Supernal Aristophanes slipped the tiniest temptation in my way; to reach Fairhaven I was compelled to spend some three hours of an April afternoon in Lichfield, where upon Regis Avenue was to be met, in the afternoon, everyone worth meeting in Lichfield; and Stella drove there on fine afternoons, under the protection of a trim and preternaturally grave tiger; and the afternoon was irreproachable.

7

BY THE WAY SHE LOOKED back over her shoulder, I knew that Stella had not recognized me. I stood with a yet lifted hat, irresolute.

"By Jove!" said I, in my soul, "then the Blagdens are in Lichfield! Why, of course! they always come here after Lent. And Bettie would not mind; to call on them would be only courteous; and besides, Bettie need not ever know. And moreover, I was always very fond of Peter."

So the next afternoon but four, Stella was making tea for me. . .

Chapter 13

He Baits Upon the Journey

Y ou are quite by way of being a gentleman," had been Stella's greeting, that afternoon. Then, on a sudden, she rested both hands upon my breast. When she did that you tingled all over, in an agreeable fashion. "It was uncommonly decent of you to remember," said this impulsive young woman. "It was dear of you! And the flowers were lovely."

"They ought to have been immortelles, of course," I apologised, "but the florist was out of them. Yes, and of daffodils, too." I sat down, and sighed, pensively. "Dear, dear!" said I, "to think it was only two years ago I buried my dearest hopes and aspirations and—er—all that sort of thing."

"Nonsense!" said Stella, and selected a blue cup with dragons on it. "At any rate," she continued, "it is very disagreeable of you to come here and prate like a death's-head on my wedding anniversary."

"Gracious gravy!" said I, with a fine surprise, "so it is an anniversary with you, too?" She was absorbed in the sugar-bowl. "What a coincidence!" I suggested, pleasantly.

I paused. The fire crackled. I sighed.

"You are such poor company, nowadays, even after the advantages of foreign travel," Stella reflected. "You really ought to do something to enliven yourself." After a little, she brightened as to the eyes, and concentrated them upon the tea-making, and ventured a suggestion. "Why not fall in love?" said Stella.

"I am," I confided, "already in that deplorable condition." And I ventured on sigh number two.

"I don't mean—anything silly," said she, untruthfully. "Why," she continued, with a certain lack of relevance, "why not fall in love with somebody else?" Thereupon, I regret to say, her glance strayed toward the mirror. Oh, she was vain,—I grant you that. But I must protest she had a perfect right to be.

"Yes," said I, quite gravely, "that is the reason."

"Nonsense!" said Stella, and tossed her head. She now assumed her most matronly air, and did mysterious things with a perforated silver ball. I was given to understand I had offended, by a severe compression of her lips, which, however, was not as effective as it might have been. They twitched too mutinously.

2

Stella was all in pink, with golden fripperies sparkling in unanticipated localities. Presumably the gown was tucked and ruched and appliquéd, and had been subjected to other processes past the comprehension of trousered humanity; it was certainly becoming.

I think there was an eighteenth-century flavour about it,—for it smacked, somehow, of a patched, mendacious, dainty womanhood, and its artfulness was of a gallant sort that scorned to deceive. It defied you, it allured you, it conquered you at a glance. It might have been the last cry from the court of an innocent Louis Quinze. It was, in fine, inimitable; and if only I were a milliner, I would describe for you that gown in some not unbefitting fashion. As it is, you may draft the world's modistes to dredge the dictionary, and they will fail, as ignominiously as I would do, in the attempt.

For, after all, its greatest charm was that it contained Stella, and converted Stella into a marquise—not such an one as was her sister, the Marquise d'Arlanges, but a marquise out of Watteau or of Fragonard, say. Stella in this gown seemed out of place save upon a high-backed stone bench, set in an *allée* of lime-trees, of course, and under a violet sky,—with a sleek abbé or two for company, and with beribboned gentlemen tinkling on their mandolins about her.

I had really no choice but to regard her as an agreeable anachronism the while she chatted with me, and mixed hot water and sugar and lemon into ostensible tea. She seemed so out of place,—and yet, somehow, I entertained no especial desire upon this sleety day to have her different, nor, certainly, otherwhere than in this pleasant, half-lit room, that consisted mostly of ambiguous vistas where a variety of brass bric-à-brac blinked in the firelight.

We had voted it cosier without lamps or candles, for this odorous twilight was far more companionable. Odorous, for there were a great number of pink roses about. I imagine that someone must have sent them—because there were not any daffodils obtainable, by reason of the late and nipping frost—in honour of Stella's second wedding anniversary.

"PETER SAYS YOU TALK TO everybody that way," quoth she,—almost resentfully, and after a pause.

"Oh!" said I. For it was really no affair of Peter's. And so—

"Peter, everybody tells me, is getting fat," I announced, presently.

Stella witheringly glanced toward the region where my waist used to be. "He isn't!" said she, indignant.

"Quite like a pig, they assure me," I continued, with relish. She objected to people being well-built. "His obscene bloatedness appears to be an object of general comment."

Silence. I stirred my tea.

"Dear Peter!" said she. And then—but unless a woman of Stella's sort is able to exercise a proper control over her countenance, she has absolutely no right to discuss her husband with his bachelor friends. It is unkind; for it causes them to feel like social outcasts and lumbering brutes and Peeping Toms. If they know the husband well, it positively awes them; for, after all, it is a bit overwhelming, this sudden glimpse of the simplicity, and the credulity, and the merciful blindness of women in certain matters. Besides, a bachelor has no business to know such things; it merely makes him envious and uncomfortable.

Accordingly, "Stella," said I, with firmness, "if you flaunt your connubial felicity in my face like that, I shall go home."

She was deaf to my righteous rebuke. "Peter is in Washington this week," she went on, looking fondly into the fire. "I had planned a party to celebrate today, but he was compelled to go—business, you know. He is doing so well nowadays," she said, after a little, "that I am quite insufferably proud of him. And I intend for him to be a great lawyer—oh, much the greatest in America. And I won't ever be content till then."

"H'm!" said I. "H'm" seemed fairly non-committal.

"Sometimes," Stella declared, irrelevantly, "I almost wish I had been born a man."

"I wish you had been," quoth I, in gallant wise. "There are so few really attractive men!"

Stella looked up with a smile that was half sad.

"I'm just a little butterfly-woman, aren't I?" she asked.

"You are," I assented, with conviction, "a butterfly out of a queen's garden—a marvellous pink-and-gold butterfly, such as one sees only in dreams and—er—in a London pantomime. You are a decided ornament to the garden," I continued, handsomely, "and the roses bow down in admiration as you pass, and—ah—at least, the masculine ones do."

"Yes,—we butterflies don't love one another overmuch, do we? Ah, well, it scarcely matters! We were not meant to be taken seriously, you know,—only to play in the sunlight, and lend an air to the garden and—amuse the roses, of course. After all," Stella summed it up, "our duties are very simple; first, we are expected to pass through a certain number of cotillions and a certain number of various happenings in various tête-à-têtes; then to make a suitable match,—so as to enable the agreeable detrimentals to make love to us, with perfect safety—as you were doing just now, for instance. And after that, we develop into bulbous chaperones, and may aspire eventually to a kindly quarter of a column in the papers, and, quite possibly, the honour of having as many as two dinners put off on account of our death. Yes, it is very simple. But, in heaven's name," Stella demanded, with a sudden lift of speech, "how can any woman—for, after all, a woman is presumably a reasoning animal—be satisfied with such a life! Yet that is everything—everything!—this big world offers to us shallow-minded butterfly-women!"

Personally, I disapprove of such morbid and hysterical talk outside of a problem novel; there I heartily approve of it, on account of the considerable and harmless pleasure that is always to be derived from throwing the book into the fireplace. And, coming from Stella, this farrago doubly astounded me. She was talking grave nonsense now, whereas Nature had, beyond doubt, planned her to discuss only the lighter sort. So I decided it was quadruply absurd, little Stella talking in this fashion,—Stella, who, as all knew, was only meant to be petted and flattered and flirted with.

And therefore, "Stella," I admonished, "you have been reading something indigestible." I set down my teacup, and I clasped my hands. "Don't tell me," I pleaded, "that you want to vote!"

She remained grave. "The trouble is," said she, "that I am not really a butterfly, for all my tinsel wings. I am an ant."

"Oh," said I, shamelessly, "I hadn't heard that Lizzie had an item for the census man. I don't care for brand-new babies, though; they always look so disgracefully sun-burned."

The pun was atrocious and, quite properly, failed to win a smile or even a reproof from the morbid young person opposite. "My grandfather," said she in meditation, "began as a clerk in a country store. Oh, of course, we have discovered, since he made his money and since Mother married a Musgrave, that his ancestors came over with William the Conqueror, and that he was descended from any number of potentates. But he lived. He was a rip at first—ah, yes, I'm glad of that as well,—and he became a religious fanatic because his oldest son died very horribly of lockjaw. And he browbeat people and founded banks, and made a spectacle of himself at every Methodist conference, and everybody was afraid of him and honoured him. And I fancy I am prouder of Old Tim Ingersoll than I am of any of the emperors and things that make such a fine show in the Musgrave family tree. For I am like him. And I want to leave something in the world that wasn't there before I came. I want my life to count, I want—why, a hundred years from now I *do* want to be something more than a name on a tombstone. I—oh, I daresay it *is* only my ridiculous egotism," she ended, with a shrug and Stella's usual quick smile,—a smile not always free from insolence, but always satisfactory, somehow.

"It's late hours," I warned her, with uplifted forefinger, "late hours and too much bridge and too many sweetmeats and too much bothering over silly New Women ideas. What is the sense of a woman's being useful," I demanded, conclusively, "when it is so much easier and so much more agreeable all around for her to be adorable?"

She pouted. "Yes," she assented, "that is my career—to be adorable. It is my one accomplishment," she declared, unblushingly,—yet not without substantiating evidence.

After a little, though, her gravity returned. "When I was a girl— oh, I dreamed of accomplishing all sorts of beautiful and impossible things! But, you see, there was really nothing I could do. Music, painting, writing—I tried them all, and the results were hopeless. Besides, Rob, the women who succeed in anything like that are always so queer looking. I couldn't be expected to give up my complexion for a career, you know, or to wear my hair like a golf-caddy's. At any rate, I couldn't make a success by myself. But there was one thing I could do,—I could make a success of Peter. And so," said Stella, calmly, "I did it."

I said nothing. It seemed expedient.

"You know, he was a little—"

"Yes," I assented, hastily. Peter had gone the pace, of course, but there was no need of raking that up. That was done with, long ago.

"Well, he isn't the least bit dissipated now. You know he isn't. That is the first big thing I have done." Stella checked it off with a small, spear-pointed, glinting finger-nail. "Then—oh, I have helped him in lots of ways. He is doing splendidly in consequence; and it is my part to see that the proper people are treated properly."

Stella reflected a moment. "There was the last appointment, for instance. I found that the awarding of it lay with that funny old Judge Willoughby, with the wart on his nose, and I asked him for it—not the wart, you understand,—and got it. We simply had him to dinner, and I was specially butterfly; I fluttered airily about, was as silly as I knew how to be, looked helpless and wore my best gown. He thought me a pretty little fool, and gave Peter the appointment. That is only an instance, but it shows how I help." Stella regarded me, uncertainly. "Why, but an authorman ought to understand!"

Of a sudden I understood a number of things—things that had puzzled. This was the meaning of Stella's queer dinner the night before, and the ensuing theatre-party, for instance; this was the explanation of those impossible men, vaguely heralded as "very influential in politics," and of the unaccountable women, painfully condensed in every lurid shade of satin, and so liberally adorned with gems as to make them almost valuable. Stella, incapable by nature of two consecutive ideas, was determined to manipulate the unseen wires, and to be, as she probably phrased it, the power behind the throne. . .

"Eh, it would be laughable," I thought, "were not her earnestness so pathetic! For here is Columbine mimicking Semiramis."

Yet it was true that Peter Blagden had made tremendous strides in his profession, of late. For a moment, I wondered—? Then I looked at this butterfly young person opposite, and I frowned. "I don't like it," I said, decisively. "It is a bit cold-blooded. It isn't worthy of you, Stella."

"It is my career," she flouted me, with shrugging shoulders. "It is the one career the world—our Lichfield world—has left me. And I am doing it for Peter."

The absurd look that I objected to—on principle, you understand— returned at this point in the conversation. I arose, resolutely, for I was really unable to put up with her nonsense.

"You are in love with your husband," I grumbled, "and I cannot countenance such eccentricities. These things are simply not done—"

She touched my hand. "Old crosspatch, and to think how near I came to marrying you."

"I do think of it—sometimes. So you had better stop pawing at me. It isn't safe."

I wish I could describe her smile. I wish I knew just what it was that Stella wanted me to say or do as we stood for a moment silent, in this pleasant, half-lit room where brass things blinked in the firelight.

"Old crosspatch!" she repeated. . .

"Stella," said I, with dignity, "I wish it distinctly understood that I am not a funny old judge with a wart on his nose."

Whereupon I went away.

Chapter 14

He Participates in a Brave Jest

S tella drove on fine afternoons, under the protection of a trim and preternaturally grave tiger. The next afternoon, by a Lichfieldian transition, was irreproachable. I was to remember, afterward, wondering in a vague fashion, as the equipage passed, if the boy's lot was not rather enviable. There might well be less attractive methods of earning the daily bread and butter than to whirl through life behind Stella. One would rarely see her face, of course, but there would be such compensations as an unfailing sense of her presence, and the faint odour of her hair at times and, always, blown scraps of her laughter or shreds of her talk, and, almost always, the piping of the sweet voice that was stilled so rarely.

Perhaps the conscienceless tiger listened when she was "seeing the proper people were treated properly"? Yes, one would. Perhaps he ground his teeth? Well, one would, I suspected. And perhaps—?

There was a nod of recognition from Stella; and I lifted my hat as they bowled by toward the Reservoir. I went down Regis Avenue, mildly resentful that she had not offered me a lift.

2

A VAGRANT PUFF OF WIND was abroad in the Boulevard that afternoon. It paused for a while to amuse itself with a stray bit of paper. Presently the wind grew tired of this plaything and tossed between the eyes of a sorrel horse. Prince lurched and bolted; and Rex, always a vicious brute, followed his mate. One fancies the vagabond wind must have laughed over that which ensued.

After a moment it returned and lifted a bit of paper from the roadway, with a new respect, perhaps, and the two of them frolicked away over close-shaven turf. It was a merry game they played there in the spring sunlight. The paper fluttered a little, whirled over and over, and scuttled off through the grass; with a gust of mirth, the wind was after it, now gained upon it, now lost ground in eddying about a tree, and now made up the disadvantage in the open, and at last chuckled over its playmate pinned to the earth and flapping in sharp, indignant remonstrances. Then *da capo*.

It was a merry game that lasted till the angry sunset had flashed its final palpitant lance through the treetrunks farther down the roadway. There were gaping people in this place, and broken wheels and shafts, and a policeman with a smoking pistol, and two dead horses, and a horrible looking dead boy in yellow-topped boots. Somebody had charitably covered his face with a handkerchief; and men were lifting a limp, white heap from among the splintered rubbish.

Then wind and paper played half-heartedly in the twilight until the night had grown too chilly for further sport. There was no more murder to be done; and so the vagabond wind was puffed out into nothingness, and the bit of paper was left alone, and at about this season the big stars—the incurious stars—peeped out of heaven, one by one.

3

IT WAS STELLA'S SISTER, THE Marquise d'Arlanges, who sent for me that night. Across the street a hand-organ ground out its jingling tune as Lizzie's note told me what the playful wind had brought about. It was a despairing, hopeless and insistent air that shrilled and piped across the way. It seemed very appropriate.

The doctors feared—Ah, well, telegrams had failed to reach Peter in Washington. Peter Blagden was not in Washington, he had not been in Washington. He could not be found. And did I think—?

No, I thought none of the things that Stella's sister suggested. Of a sudden I knew. I stood silent for a little and heard that damned, clutching tune cough and choke and end; I heard the renewed babblement of children; and I heard the organ clatter down the street, and set up its faint jingling in the distance. And I knew with an unreasoning surety. I pitied Stella now ineffably, not for the maiming and crippling of her body, for the spoiling of that tender miracle, that white flower of flesh, but for the falling of her air-castle, the brave air-castle which to her meant everything. I guessed what had happened.

Later I found Peter Blagden, no matter where. It is not particularly to my credit that I knew where to look for him. Yet the French have a saying of infinite wisdom in their *qui a bu boira*. The old vice had gripped the man, irresistibly, and he had stolen off to gratify it in secret; and he had not been sober for a week. He was on the verge of collapse even when I told him—oh, with a deliberate cruelty, I grant you,—what had happened that afternoon.

Then, swiftly, his demolishment came; and I could not—could not for very shame—bring this shivering, weeping imbecile to the bedside of Stella, who was perhaps to die that night. Such was the news I brought to Stella's sister; through desolate streets already blanching in the dawn.

Stella was calling for Peter. We manufactured explanations.

4

NICE CUSTOMS CURTSEY TO DEATH. I am standing at Stella's bedside, and the white-capped nurse has gone. There are dim lights about the room, and heavy carts lumber by in the dawn without. A petulant sparrow is cheeping somewhere.

"Tell me the truth," says Stella, pleadingly. Her face, showing over billows of bedclothes, is as pale as they. But beautiful, and exceedingly beautiful, is Stella's face, now that she is come to die.

It heartened me to lie to her. Peter had been retained in the great Western Railway case. He had been called to Denver, San Francisco and—I forget today just why or even whither. He had kept it as a surprise for her. He was hurrying back. He would arrive in two days. I showed her telegrams from Peter Blagden,—clumsy forgeries I had concocted in the last half-hour.

Oh, the story ran lamely, I grant you. But, vanity apart, I told it with conviction. Stella must and should die in content; that much at least I could purchase for her; and my thoughts were strangely nimble, there was a devilish fluency in my speech, and lie after lie was fitted somehow into an entity that surprised even me as it took plausible form. And I got my reward. Little by little, the doubt died from her eyes as I lied stubbornly in a drug-scented silence; a little by a little, her cheeks flushed brighter, and ever brighter, as I dilated on this wonderful success that had come to Peter Blagden, till at last her face was all aflame with happiness.

She had dreamed of this, half conscious of her folly; she had worked toward this consummation for months. But she had hardly dared to hope for absolute success; it almost worried her; and she could not be certain, even now, whether it was the soup or her blue silk that had influenced Allardyce most potently. Both had been planned to wheedle him, to gain this glorious chance for Peter Blagden. . .

"You—you are sure you are not lying?" said Stella, and smiled in speaking, for she believed me infinitely.

"Stella, before God, it is true!" I said, with fervour. "On my word of honour, it is as I tell you!" And my heart was sick within me as I thought of the stuttering brute, the painted female thing with tumbled hair, and the stench of liquor in the room—Ah, well, the God I called to witness strengthened me to smile back at Stella.

"I believe you," she said, simply. "I—I am glad. It is a big thing for Peter." Her eyes widened in wonder and pride, and she dreamed for just a moment of his future. But, upon a sudden, her face fell. "Dear, dear!" said Stella, petulantly; "I'd forgotten. I'll be dead by then."

"Stella! Stella!" I cried, and very hoarsely; "why—why, nonsense, child! The doctor thinks—he is quite sure, I mean—" I had a horrible desire to laugh. Heine was right; there is an Aristophanes in heaven.

"Ah, I know," she interrupted. "I am a little afraid to die," she went on, reflectively. "If one only knew—" Stella paused for a moment; then she smiled. "After all," she said, "it isn't as if I hadn't accomplished anything. I have made Peter. The ball is at his feet now; he has only to kick it. And I helped."

"Yes," said I. My voice was shaken, broken out of all control. "You have helped. Why, you have done everything, Stella! There is not a young man in America with his prospects. In five years, he will be one of our greatest lawyers,—everybody says so—everybody! And you have done it all, Stella—every bit of it! You have made a man of him, I tell you! Look at what he was!—and then look at what he is! And—and you talk of leaving him now! Why, it's preposterous! Peter needs you, I tell you—he needs you to cajole the proper people and keep him steady and—and—Why, you artful young woman, how could he possibly get on without you, do you think? Oh, how can any of us get on without you? You *must* get well, I tell you. In a month, you will be right as a trivet. You die! Why, nonsense!" I laughed. I feared I would never have done with laughter over the idea of Stella's dying.

"But I have done all I could. And so he doesn't need me now." Stella meditated for yet another moment. "I believe I shall always know when he does anything especially big. God would be sure to tell me, you see, because He understands how much it means to me. And I shall be proud—ah, yes, wherever I am, I shall be proud of Peter. You see, he didn't really care about being a success, for of course he knows that Uncle Larry will leave him a great deal of money one of these days. But I am such a vain little cat—so bent on making a noise in the world,—that, I think, he did it more to please my vanity than anything else. I nagged him, frightfully, you know," Stella confessed, "but he was always—oh, *so* dear about it, Rob! And he has never failed me—not even once, although I know at times it has been very hard for him." Stella sighed; and then laughed. "Yes," said she, "I think I am satisfied with my life altogether. Somehow, I am sure I shall be told about it when he is a power in the world—a power for good, as he will be,—and then I shall be very perky—somewhere. I ought to sing *Nunc Dimittis*, oughtn't I?" I was not unmoved; nor did it ever lie within my power to be unmoved when I thought of Stella and how gaily she went to meet her death. . .

5

"Good-bye," said she, in a tired voice.

"Good-bye, Stella," said I; and I kissed her.

"And I don't think you are a mess. And I *don't* hate you." She was smiling very strangely. "Yes, I remember that first time. And no matter what they said, I always cared heaps more about you, Rob, than I dared let you know. And if only you had been as dependable as Peter—But, you see, you weren't—"

"No, dear, you did the right thing—what was best for all of us—"

"Then don't mind so much. Oh, Bob, it hurts me to see you mind so much! You aren't—being dependable, like Peter, even now," she said, reproachfully. . .

Heine was right; there is an Aristophanes in heaven.

Chapter 15

HE DECIDES TO AMUSE HIMSELF

I came to Fairhaven half-bedrugged with memories of Stella's funeral,—say, of how lightly she had lain, all white and gold, in the grotesque and horrid box, and of Peter's vacant red-rimmed eyes that seemed to wonder why this decorous company should have assembled about the deep and white-lined cavity at his feet and find no answer. Nor, for that matter, could I.

"But it was flagrant, flagrant!" my heart screeched in a grill of impotent wrath. "Eh, You gave me power to reason, so they say! and will You slay me, too, if I presume to use that power? I say, then, it was flagrant and tyrannical and absurd! 'Let twenty pass, and stone the twenty-first, Loving not, hating not, just choosing so!' O Setebos, it wasn't worthy of omnipotence. You know it wasn't!" In such a frame of mind I came again to Bettie Hamlyn.

2

IT WAS VERY ODD TO see Bettie again. I had been sublimely confident, though, that we would pick up our intercourse precisely where we had left off; and this, as I now know, is something which can never happen to anybody. So I was vaguely irritated before we had finished shaking hands, and became so resolutely boyish and effusive in my delight at seeing her that anyone in the world but Bettie Hamlyn would have been quite touched. And my conversational gambit, I protest, was masterly, and would have made anybody else think, "Oh how candid is the egotism of this child!" and would have moved that person, metaphorically anyhow, to pat me upon the head.

But Bettie only smiled, a little sadly, and answered:

"Your book?—Why, dear me, did I forget to write you a nice little letter about how wonderful it was?"

"You wrote the letter all right. I think you copied it out of *The Complete Letter Writer*. There was not a bit of you in it."

"Well, that is why I dislike your book—because there was not a bit of *you* in it. Of course I am glad it was the big noise of the month, and also a little jealous of it, if you can understand that phase of the feminine mind. I doubt it, because you write about women as though they were pterodactyls or some other extinct animal, which you had never seen, but had read a lot about."

"Which attests, in any event, my morals to be above reproach. You should be pleased."

"To roll it into a pill, your book seems pretty much like any other book; and it has made me hold my own particular boy's picture more than once against my cheek and say, 'You didn't write books, did you, dear?—You did nicer things than write books'—and he did. . . I hear many things of you. . ."

"Oh, well!" I brilliantly retorted, "you mustn't believe all you hear." And I felt that matters were going very badly indeed.

"Robin, do you not know that your mess of pottage must be eaten with you by the people who care for you?—and one of them dislikes pottage. Indeed, I *would* have liked the book, had anybody else written it. I almost like it as it is, in spots, and sometimes I even go to the great length of liking you,—because 'if only for old sake's sake, dear, you're the loveliest doll in the world.' There might be a better reason, if you could only make up your mind to dispense with pottage. . ."

The odd part of it, even today, is that Bettie was saying precisely what I had been thinking, and that to hear her say it made me just twice as petulant as I was already.

"Now, please don't preach," I said. "I've heard so much preaching lately—dear," I added, though I am afraid the word was rather obviously an afterthought.

"Oh, I forgot you stayed over for Stella Blagden's funeral. You were quite right. Stella was a dear child, and I was really sorry to hear of her death."

"Really!" It was the lightest possible additional flick upon the raw, but it served.

"Yes,—I, too, was rather sorry, Bettie, because I have loved Stella all my life. She was the first, you see, and, somehow, the others have been different. And—she disliked dying. I tell you, it is unfair, Bettie,—it is hideously unfair!"

"Robin—" she began.

"And why should you be living," I said, in half-conscious absurdity, "when she is dead? Why, look, Bettie! even that fly yonder is alive. Setebos accords an insect what He grudges Stella! Her dying is not even particularly important. The big news of the day is that the President has started his Pacific tour, and that the Harvard graduates object to his being given an honorary degree, and are sending out seven thousand protests to be signed. And you're alive, and I'm alive, and Peter Blagden is alive, and only Stella is dead. I suppose she is an angel by this. But I don't care for angels. I want just the silly little Stella that I loved,—the Stella that was the first and will always be the first with me. For I want her—just Stella—! Oh, it is an excellent jest; and I will cap it with another now. For the true joke is, I came to Fairhaven, across half the world, with an insane notion of asking you to marry me,—you who are 'really' sorry that Stella is dead!" And I laughed as pleasantly as one may do in anger.

But the girl, too, was angry. "Marry you!" she said. "Why, Robin, you were wonderful once; and now you are simply not a bad sort of fellow, who imagines himself to be the hit of the entire piece. And whether she's dead or not, she never had two grains of sense, but just enough to make a spectacle of you, even now."

"I regret that I should have sailed so far into the north of your opinion," said I. "Though, as I dare assert, you are quite probably in the right. So I'll be off to my husks again, Bettie." And I kissed her hand. "And that too is only for old sake's sake, dear," I said.

Then I returned to the railway station in time for the afternoon train. And I spoke with no one else in Fairhaven, except to grunt "Good evening, gentlemen," as I passed Clarriker's Emporium, where Colonel Snawley and Dr. Jeal were sitting in arm chairs, very much as I had left them there two years ago.

3

IT WAS A LONG WHILE afterward I discovered that "some damned good-natured friend," as Sir Fretful has immortally phrased it, had told Bettie Hamlyn of seeing me at the theatre in Lichfield, with Stella and her marvellous dinner-company. It was by an odd quirk the once Aurelia Minns, in Lichfield for the "summer's shopping," who had told Bettie. And the fact is that I had written Bettie upon the day of Stella's death and, without explicitly saying so, had certainly conveyed the impression I had reached Lichfield that very morning, and was simply stopping over for Stella's funeral. And, in addition, I cannot say that Bettie and Stella were particularly fond of each other.

As it was, I left Fairhaven the same day I reached it, and in some dissatisfaction with the universe. And I returned to Lichfield and presently reopened part of the old Townsend house. . . "Robert and I," my mother had said, to Lichfield's delectation, "just live downstairs in the two lower stories, and ostracise the third floor. . ." And I was received by Lichfield society, if not with open arms at least with acquiescence. And Byam, an invaluable mulatto, the son of my cousin Dick Townsend and his housekeeper, made me quite comfortable.

Depend upon it, Lichfield knew a deal more concerning my escapades than I did. That I was "deplorably wild" was generally agreed, and a reasonable number of seductions, murders and arsons was, no doubt, accredited to me "on quite unimpeachable authority, my dear."

But I was a Townsend, and Lichfield had been case-hardened to Townsendian vagaries since Colonial days; and, besides, I had written a book which had been talked about; and, as an afterthought, I was reputed not to be an absolute pauper, if only because my father had taken the precaution, customary with the Townsends, to marry a woman with enough money to gild the bonds of matrimony. For Lichfield, luckily, was not aware how near my pleasure-loving parents had come, between them, to spending the last cent of this once ample fortune.

And, in fine, "Well, really now—?" said Lichfield. Then there was a tentative invitation or two, and I cut the knot by accepting all of them, and talking to every woman as though she were the solitary specimen of feminity extant. It was presently agreed that gossip often embroidered the actual occurrence and that wild oats were, after all, a not unheard-of phenomenon, and that though genius very often, in a phrase, forgot to comb its hair, these tonsorial deficiencies were by the broadminded not appraised too strictly.

I did not greatly care what Lichfield said one way or the other. I was too deeply engrossed: first, in correcting the final proofs of *Afield*, my second book, which appeared that spring and was built around—there is no harm in saying now,—my relations with Gillian Hardress; secondly, in the remunerative and uninteresting task of writing for *Woman's Weekly* five "wholesome love-stories with a dash of humor," in which She either fell into His arms "with a contented sigh" or else "their lips met" somewhere toward the ending of the seventh page; and, thirdly, in diverting myself with Celia Reindan. . .

4

THAT, THOUGH, IS A BUSINESS I shall not detail, because it was one of the very vulgarest sort. It was the logical outgrowth of my admiration for her yellow hair,—she did have extraordinary hair, confound her!— and of a few moonlit nights. It was simply the result of our common vanity and of her book-fed sentimentality and, eventually, of her unbridled temper; and in nature the compound was an unsavoury mess which thoroughly delighted Lichfield. Lichfield will be only too glad, even nowadays, to discourse to you of how I got wedged in that infernal transom, and of how Celia alarmed everybody within two blocks of her bedroom by her wild yells.

5

I HAD MEANWHILE DECIDED, FIRST, to write another and a better book than *The Apostates* or *Afield* had ever pretended to be; and afterward to marry Rosalind Jemmett, whom I found, in my too-hackneyed but habitual phrase, "adorable." For this Rosalind was an eminently "sensible match," and as such, I considered, quite appropriate for a Townsend.

The main thing though, to me, was to write the book of which I had already the central idea,—very vague, as yet, but of an unquestionable magnificence. Development of it, on an at all commensurate scale, necessitated many inconveniences, and among them, the finding of someone who would assist me in imbuing the love-scenes—of which there must unfortunately be a great many—with reality; and for the tale's *milieu* I again pitched upon the Green Chalybeate,—where, as you may remember, I first met with Stella.

So I said a not unpromising farewell to Rosalind Jemmett, who was going into Canada for the summer. She was quite frankly grieved by the absolute necessity of my taking a rigorous course of the Chalybeate waters, but agreed with me that one's health is not to be trifled with. And of course she would write if I really wanted her to, though she couldn't imagine *why*—But I explained why, with not a little detail. And she told me, truthfully, that I was talking like an idiot; and was not, I thought, irrevocably disgusted by my idiocy. So that, all in all, I was not discontented when I left her.

Then I ordered Byam to pack and, by various unveracious representations, induced my Uncle George Bulmer—as a sort of visible and outward sign that I forgave him for declining to lend me another penny—to accompany me to the Green Chalybeate. Besides, I was fond of the old scoundrel. . .

6

WHEN I BEGAN TO SCRIBBLE these haphazard memories I had designed to be very droll concerning the "provincialism" of Lichfield; for, as every inhabitant of it will tell you, it is "quite hopelessly provincial,"—and this is odd, seeing that, as investigation will assure you, the city is exclusively inhabited by self-confessed cosmopolitans. I had meant to depict Fairhaven, too, in the broad style of *Cranford*, say; and to be so absolutely side-splitting when I touched upon the Green Chalybeate as positively to endanger the existence of any apoplectic reader, who presumed to peruse the chapter which dealt with this resort.

But, upon reflection, I am too familiar with these places to attempt to treat them humorously. The persons who frequent their byways are too much like the persons who frequent the byways of any other place, I find, at bottom. For to write convincingly of the persons peculiar to any locality it is necessary either to have thoroughly misunderstood them, or else perseveringly to have been absent from daily intercourse with them until age has hardened the brain-cells, and you have forgotten what they are really like. Then, alone, you may write the necessary character studies which will be sufficiently abundant in human interest.

For, at bottom, any one of us is tediously like any other. Comprehension is the grave of sympathy; scratch deeply enough and you will find not any livelily-coloured Tartarism, but just a mediocre and thoroughly uninteresting human being. So I may not ever be so droll as I had meant to be; and if you wish to chuckle over the grotesque places I have lived in, you must apply to persons who have spent two weeks there, and no more.

For the rest, Lichfield, and Fairhaven also, got at and into me when I was too young to defend myself. Therefore Lichfield and Fairhaven cannot ever, really, seem to me grotesque. To the contrary, it is the other places which must always appear to me a little queer when judged by the standards of Fairhaven and Lichfield.

JAMES BRANCH CABELL

Chapter 16

HE SEEKS FOR COPY

I had aforetime ordered Mr. George Bulmer to read *The Apostates*, and, as the author of this volume explained, from motives that were purely well-meaning. Tonight I was superintending the process.

"For the scene of the book is the Green Chalybeate," said I; "and it may be my masterly rhetoric will so far awaken your benighted soul, Uncle George, as to enable you to perceive what the more immediate scenery is really like. Why, think of it! what if you should presently fall so deeply in love with the adjacent mountains as to consent to overlook the deficiencies of the more adjacent café! Try now, nunky! try hard to think that the right verb is really more important than the right vermouth! and you have no idea what good it may do you."

Mr. Bulmer read on, with a bewildered face, while I gently stirred the contents of my tall and delectably odored glass. It was "frosted" to a nicety. We were drinking "Mamie Taylors" that summer, you may remember; and I had just brought up a pitcherful from the bar.

"Oh, I say, you know!" observed Uncle George, as he finished the sixth chapter, and flung down the book.

"Rot, utter rot," I assented pleasantly; "puerile and futile trifling with fragments of the seventh commandment, as your sturdy common-sense instantly detected. In fact," I added, hopefully, "I think that chapter is trivial enough to send the book into a tenth edition. In *Afield*, you know, I tried a different tack. Actuated by the noblest sentiments, the heroine mixes prussic acid with her father's whiskey and water; and 'Old-Fashioned' and 'Fair Play' have been obliging enough to write to the newspapers about this harrowing instance of the deplorably low moral standards of today. Uncle George, do you think that a real lady is ever justified in obliterating a paternal relative? You ought to meditate upon that problem, for it is really a public question nowadays. Oh, and there was a quite lovely clipping last week I forgot to show you—all about Electra, as contrasted with Jonas Chuzzlewit, and my fine impersonal attitude, and the survival of the fittest, and so on."

But Uncle George refused to be comforted. "Look here, Bob!" said he, pathetically, "why don't you brace up and write something—well! we'll put it, something of the sort you *can* do. For you can, you know."

"Ah, but is not a judicious nastiness the market-price of a second edition before publication?" I softly queried. "I had no money. I was ashamed to beg, and I was too well brought up to steal anything adroitly enough not to be caught. And so, in view of my own uncle's deafness to the prayers of an impecunious orphan, I have descended to this that I might furnish butter for my daily bread." I refilled my glass and held the sparkling drink for a moment against the light. "This time next year," said I, as dreamily, "I shall be able to afford cake; for I shall have written *As the Coming of Dawn*."

Mr. Bulmer sniffed, and likewise refilled his glass. "You catch me lending you any money for your—brief Biblical words!" he said.

"For the reign of subtle immorality," I sighed, "is well-nigh over. Already the augurs of the pen begin to wink as they fable of a race of men who are evilly scintillant in talk and gracefully erotic. We know that this, alas, cannot be, and that in real life our peccadilloes dwindle into dreary vistas of divorce cases and the police-court, and that crime has lost its splendour. We sin very carelessly—sordidly, at times,—and artistic wickedness is rare. It is a pity; life was once a scarlet volume scattered with misty-coated demons; it is now a yellow journal, wherein our vices are the hackneyed formulas of journalists, and our virtues are the not infrequent misprints. Yes, it is a pity!"

"Dearest Robert!" remonstrated Mr. Bulmer, "you are sadly *passé*: that pose is of the Beardsley period and went out many magazines ago."

"The point is well taken," I admitted, "for our life of today is already reflected—faintly, I grant you,—in the best-selling books. We have passed through the period of a slavish admiration for wickedness and wide margins; our quondam decadents now snigger in a parody of primeval innocence, and many things are forgiven the latter-day poet if his botany be irreproachable. Indeed, it is quite time; for we have tossed over the contents of every closet in the *menage à trois*. And I—*moi, qui vous parle*,—I am wearied of hansom-cabs and the flaring lights of great cities, even as so alluringly depicted in *Afield*; and henceforth I shall demonstrate the beauty of pastoral innocence."

"Saul among the prophets," Uncle George suggested, helpfully.

"Quite so," I assented, "and my first prophecy will be *As the Coming of Dawn*."

Mr. Bulmer tapped his forehead significantly. "Mad, quite mad!" said he, in parenthesis.

"I shall be idyllic," I continued, sweetly; "I shall write of the ineffable glory of first love. I shall babble of green fields and the keen odours of spring and the shamefaced countenances of lovers, met after last night's kissing. It will be the story of love that stirs blindly in the hearts of maids and youths, and does not know that it is love,—the love which manhood has half forgotten and that youth has not the skill to write of. But I, at twenty-four, shall write its story as it has never been written; and I shall make a great book of it, that will go into thousands and thousands of editions. Yes, before heaven, I will!"

I brought my fist down, emphatically, on the table.

"H'm!" said Mr. Bulmer, dubiously; "going back to renew associations with your first love? I have tried it, and I generally find her grandchildren terribly in the way."

"It is imperative," said I,—"yes, imperative for the scope of my book, that I should view life through youthful and unsophisticated eyes. I discovered that, upon the whole, Miss Jemmett is too obviously an urban product to serve my purpose. And I can't find any one who will."

Uncle George whistled softly. "'Honourable young gentleman,'" he murmured, as to himself, "'desires to meet attractive and innocent young lady. Object: to learn how to be idyllic in three-hundred pages.'"

There was no commentary upon his text.

"I say," queried Mr. Bulmer, "do you think this sort of thing is fair to the girl? Isn't it a little cold-blooded?"

"Respected nunky, you are at times very terribly the man in the street! Anyhow, I leave the Green Chalybeate tomorrow in search of *As the Coming of Dawn*."

"Look here," said Mr. Bulmer, rising, "if you start on a tour of the country, looking for assorted dawns and idylls, it will end in my abducting you from some rustic institution for the insane. You take a liver-pill and go to bed! I don't promise anything, mind, but perhaps about the first I can manage a little cheque if only you will make oath on a few Bibles not to tank up on it in Lichfield. The transoms there," he added unkindlily, "are not built for those full rich figures."

Next morning, I notified the desk-clerk, and, quite casually, both the newspaper correspondents, that the Green Chalybeate was about to be bereft of the presence of a distinguished novelist. Then, as my train did not leave till night, I resolved to be bored on horseback, rather than on the golf-links, and had Guendolen summoned, from the stable, for a final investigation of the country roads thereabouts.

Guendolen this afternoon elected to follow a new route; and knowing by experience that any questioning of this decision could but result in undignified defeat, I assented. Thus it came about that we circled parallel to the boardwalk, which leads uphill to the deserted Royal Hotel, and passed its rows of broken windows; and went downhill again, always at Guendolen's election; and thus came to the creek, which babbled across the roadway and was overhung with thick foliage that lisped and whispered cheerfully in the placid light of the declining sun. It was there that the germ of *As the Coming of Dawn* was found.

For I had fallen into a reverie over the deplorable obstinacy of my new heroine, who declined, for all my labours, to be unsophisticated; and taking advantage of this, Guendolen had twitched the reins from my hand and proceeded to satisfy her thirst in a manner that was rather too noisy to be quite good form. I sat in patience, idly observing the sparkling reflection of the sunlight on the water. I was elaborating a comparison between my obstinate heroine and Guendolen. Then Guendolen snorted, as something rustled through the underbrush, and turning, I perceived a Vision.

The Vision was in white, with a profusion of open-work. There were blue ribbons connected with it. There were also black eyes, of the almond-shaped, heavy-lidded variety that I had thought existed only in Lely's pictures, and great coils of brown hair which was gold where the chequered sunlight fell upon it, and two lips that were inexpressibly red. I was filled with pity for my tired horse, and a resolve that for this once her thirst should be quenched.

Thereupon, I lifted my cap hastily; and Guendolen scrambled to the other bank, and spluttered, and had carried me well past the Iron Spring, before I announced to the evening air that I was a fool, and that Guendolen was describable by various quite picturesque and derogatory epithets. And I smiled.

"Now, Robert Etheridge Townsend, you writer of books, here is a subject made to your hand!" And then:

"Only 'twixt the light and shade Floating memories of my maid Make me pray for Guendolen."

After this we retraced our steps. I was peering anxiously about the roadway.

"Pardon me," said I, subsequently; "but *have* you seen anything of a watch—a small gold one, set with pearls?"

"Heavens!" said the Vision, sympathetically, "what a pity! Are you sure it fell here?"

"I don't seem to have it about me," I answered, with cryptic, but entire veracity. I searched about my pockets, with a puckered brow. "And as we stopped here—"

I looked inquiringly into the water.

"From this side," observed the Vision, impersonally, "there is less glare from the brook."

Having tied Guendolen to a swinging limb, I sat down contentedly in these woods. The Vision moved a little, lest I be crowded.

"It might be further up the road," she suggested.

"Oh, I must have left it at the hotel," I observed.

"You might look—" said she, peering into the water.

"Forever!" I assented.

The Vision flushed, "I didn't mean—" she began.

"But I did," quoth I,—"and every word of it."

"Why, in that case," said she, and rose to her feet, "I'd better—" A frown wrinkled her brow; then a deep, curved dimple performed a similar office for her cheek. "I wonder—" said she.

"Why, you would be a bold-faced jig," said I, composedly; "but, after all there is nobody about. And, besides,—for I suspect you of being one of the three dilapidated persons in veils who came last night,—we are going to be introduced right after supper, anyway."

The Vision sat down. "You mentioned your sanatorium?" quoth she.

"The Asylum of Love," said I; "discharged—under a false impression,—as cured, and sent to paradise.

"Oh!" said I, defiant, "but it *is*!"

She looked about her. "The woods *are* rather beautiful," she conceded, softly.

"They form a quite appropriate background," said I. "It is a veritable Eden, before the coming of the snake."

"Before?" she queried, dubiously.

"Undoubtedly," said I, and felt my ribs, in meditative wise. "Ah, but I thought I missed something! We participate in a historic moment. This is in Eden immediately after the creation of—Well, but of course you are acquainted with that famous bull about Eve's being the fairest of her daughters?"

"It is *quite* time," said she, judicially, "for me to go back to the hotel, before—since we are speaking of animals,—your presence here is noticed by one of the squirrels."

"It is not good," I pleaded, "for man to be alone."

"I have heard," said she, "that—almost any one can cite scripture to his purpose."

I thrust out a foot for inspection. "No suggestion of a hoof," said I; "and not the slightest odour of brimstone, as you will kindly note; and my inoffensive name is Robert Townsend."

"Of course," she submitted, "I could never think of making your acquaintance in this irregular fashion; and, therefore, of course, I could not think of telling you that my name is Marian Winwood."

"Of course not," I agreed; "it would be highly improper."

"—And it is more than time for me to go to supper," she concluded again, with a lacuna, as it seemed to me, in the deduction.

"Look here!" I remonstrated; "it isn't anywhere near six yet." I exhibited my watch to support this statement.

"Oh!" she observed, with wide, indignant eyes.

"I—I mean—" I stammered.

She rose to her feet.

"—I will explain how I happened to be carrying two watches—"

"I do not care to listen to any explanations. Why should I?"

"—upon," I firmly said, "the third piazza of the hotel. And this very evening."

"You will not." And this was said even more firmly. "And I hope you will have the kindness to keep away from these woods; for I shall probably always walk here in the afternoon." Then, with an indignant toss of the head, the Vision disappeared.

3

I WHISTLED. SUBSEQUENTLY I GALLOPED back to the hotel.

"See here!" said I, to the desk-clerk; "how long does this place keep open?"

"Season closes latter part of September, sir."

I told him I would need my rooms till then.

Chapter 17

He Provides Copy

So it was Uncle George Bulmer who presently left the Green Chalybeate, to pursue Mrs. Chaytor with his lawless arts. I stayed out the season.

Now I cannot conscientiously recommend the Green Chalybeate against your next vacation. Once very long ago, it was frequented equally for the sake of gaiety and of health. In the summer that was Marian's the resort was a beautiful and tumble-down place where invalids congregated for the sake of the nauseous waters,—which infallibly demolish a solid column of strange maladies I never read quite through, although it bordered every page of the writing-paper you got there from the desk-clerk,—and a scanty leaven of persons who came thither, apparently, in order to spend a week or two in lamenting "how very dull the season is this year, and how abominable the fare is."

But for one I praise the place, and I believe that Marian Winwood also bears it no ill-will. For we two were very happy there. We took part in the "subscription euchres" whenever we could not in time devise an excuse which would pass muster with the haggard "entertainer." We danced conscientiously beneath the pink and green icing of the ballroom's ceiling, with all three of the band playing *Hearts and Flowers*; and with a dozen "chaperones"—whom I always suspected of taking in washing during the winter months,—lined up as closely as was possible to the door, as if in preparation for the hotel's catching fire any moment, to give us pessimistic observal. And having thus discharged our duty to society at large, we enjoyed ourselves tremendously.

For instance, we would talk over the book I was going to write in the autumn. That was the main thing. Then one could golf, or drive, or—I blush to write it even now—croquet. Croquet, though, is a much maligned game, as you will immediately discover if you ever play it on the rambling lawn of the Chalybeate, about six in the afternoon, say, when the grass is greener than it is by ordinary, and the shadows are long, and the sun is well beneath the tree-tops of the Iron Bank, and your opponent makes a face at you occasionally, and on each side the old, one-storied cottages are builded of unusually red bricks and are quite ineffably asleep.

Or again there is always the creek to divert yourself in. Once I caught five crawfishes there, while Marian waited on the bank; and afterward we found an old tomato-can and boiled them in it, and they came out a really gorgeous crimson. This was the afternoon that we were Spanish Inquisitors. . . Oh, believe me, you can have quite a good time at the Chalybeate, if you set about it in the proper way.

2

ONLY IT IS TRUE THAT sometimes, when it rained, say, with that hopeless insistency which, I protest, is unknown anywhere else in the world; and when Marian was not immediately accessible, and cigarettes were not quite satisfactory, because the entire universe was so sodden that matches had to be judiciously coaxed before they would strike; and when if you happened to be writing a fervid letter to Rosalind Jemmett, let us say, the ink would not dry for ever so long:—why, it is true that in these circumstances you would feel a shade too like the wicked Lord So-and-So of a melodrama to be comfortable.

Yet even in these circumstances, reason told me that the Book was the main thing, that the girl would be thoroughly over the affair by November at latest, and that at the cost of a few inconsequent tears, she would have meanwhile immeasurably obliged posterity. And I knew that no man may ever write in perdurable fashion save by ruthlessly converting his own life into "copy," since of other persons' lives he can, at most, reproduce but the blurred and misinterpreted by-ends, by reason of almost any author's deplorable lack of omniscience. Yes, the Book was the main thing; and yet the girl—knowingly to dip my pen into her heart as into an inkstand was not, at best, chivalric. . .

"But the Book!" said I. "Why, I must be quite idiotically in love to think of letting that Book perish!" And I viciously added: "Confound the pretty simpleton!" . . .

3

SO THE BOOK WAS BUILDED, after all, a little by a little. Hardly an evening came when after leaving Marian I had not at least one excellent and pregnant jotting to record in my note-book. Now it would be just an odd turn of language, or a description of some gesture she had made, or of a gown she had worn that day; and now a simile or some other rather good figure of speech which had popped into my mind when I was making love to her.

Nor had I any difficulty in preserving nearly all she said to me, for Marian was never a chatterbox; yet her responses had, somehow, that long-sought tang it wasn't in me to invent for any imaginary young woman who must be, for the sake of my new novel, quite heels over head in love.

And I began to see that Bettie was right, as usual. I had portrayed Gillian Hardress pretty well in *Afield*; but by and large, I had always written about women as though they were "pterodactyls or some other extinct animal, which you had never seen, but had read a lot about."

And now, in looking over my notes, I knew, and my heart glowed to know, that I was not about to repeat the error.

So the Book was builded, after all, a little by a little. And a little by a little the summer wore on; and in the lobby of the Main Hotel was hung the beautiful Spirit of the Falls poster of the Buffalo Exposition; and we talked of Oom Paul Krüger, and Shamrock II, and the Nicaragua Canal, and lanky Bob Fitzsimmons, and the Boxer outrages; and we read *To Have and To Hold* and *The Cardinal's Snuff Box*, and thought it droll that the King of England was not going to call himself King Albert, after all.

And then came the news of how the President had been shot, "with a poisoned bullet," and a week of contradictory bulletins from the Milburn House in Buffalo. And there were panicky surmises raised everywhere as to "what these anarchists may do next," so that Maggio was mobbed in Columbus, and Emma Goldman in Chicago; and Colonel Roosevelt was found, after days of search, on Mt. Marcy in the Adirondacks, and was told in the heart of a forest that tomorrow he would be at the head of a nation. And the country's guidance was entrusted to a mere lad of forty-three, with general uneasiness as to what might come of it; and the dramatic tale of Colonel Roosevelt's taking of the oath of office was in that morning's paper; and Marian and I were about to part.

4

"It will be dreadful," sighed she; "for we have to stay a whole week longer, and I shall come here every afternoon. And there will be only ghosts in the woods, and I shall be very lonely."

"Dear," said I, "is it not something to have been happy? It has been such a wonderful summer; and come what may, nothing can rob us now of its least golden moment. And it is only for a little."

"You will come back?" said she, half-doubtingly.

"Yes," I said. "You wonderful, elfin creature, I shall undoubtedly come back—to your real home, and claim you there. Only I don't believe you do live in Aberlin,—you probably live in some great, gnarled oak hereabouts; and at night its bark uncloses to set you free, and you and your sisters dance out the satyrs' hearts in the moonlight. Oh, I know, Marian! I simply *know* you are a dryad,—a wonderful, laughing, clear-eyed dryad strayed out of the golden age."

"What a boy it is!" she said. "No, I am only a really and truly girl, dear,—a rather frightened girl, with very little disposition to laughter, just now. For you are going away—Oh, my dear, you have meant so much to me! The world is so different since you have come, and I am so happy and so miserable that—that I am afraid." An infinitesimal handkerchief went upward to two great, sparkling eyes, and dabbed at them.

"Dear!" said I. And this remark appeared to meet the requirements of the situation.

There was a silence now. We sat in the same spot where I had first encountered Marian Winwood. Only this was an autumnal forest that glowed with many gem-like hues about us; and already the damp odour of decaying leaves was heavy in the air. It was like the Tosti thing translated out of marine terms into a woodland analogue. The summer was ended; but *As the Coming of Dawn* was practically complete.

It was not the book that I had planned, but a far greater one which was scarcely mine. There was no word written as yet. But for two months I had viewed life through Marian Winwood's eyes; day by day, my half-formed, tentative ideas had been laid before her with elaborate fortuitousness, to be approved, or altered, or rejected, just as she decreed; until at last they had been welded into a perfect whole that was a Book, bit by bit, we had planned it, I and she; and, as I dreamed of it as it would be in print, my brain was fired with exultation, and I defied my doubt and I swore that the Book, for which I had pawned a certain portion of my self-respect, was worth—and triply worth—the price which had been paid. . . This was in Marian's absence.

"Dear!" said she. . .

Her eyes were filled with a tender and unutterable confidence that thrilled me like physical cold. "Marian," said I, simply, "I shall never come back."

The eyes widened a trifle, but she did not seem to comprehend.

"Have you not wondered," said I, "that I have never kissed you, except as if you were a very holy relic or a cousin or something of that sort?"

"Yes," she answered. Her voice was quite emotionless.

"And yet—yet—" I sprang to my feet. "Dear God, how I have longed! Yesterday, only yesterday, as I read to you from the verses I had made to other women, those women that are colourless shadows by the side of your vivid beauty,—and you listened wonderingly and said the proper things and then lapsed into dainty boredom,—*how* I longed to take you in my arms, and to quicken your calm blood a little with another sort of kissing. You knew—you must have known! Last night, for instance—"

"Last night," she said, very simply, "I thought—And I hoped you would."

"What a confession for a nicely brought up girl! Well! I didn't. And afterward, all night, I tossed in sick, fevered dreams of you. I am mad for love of you. And so, once in a while I kiss your hand. Dear God, your hand!" My voice quavered, effectively.

"Yes," said she; "still, I remember—"

"I have struggled; and I have conquered this madness,—for a madness it is. We can laugh together and be excellent friends; and we can never, never be anything more. Well! we have laughed, have we not, dear, a whole summer through? Now comes the ending. Ah, I have seen you puzzling over my meaning before this. You never understood me thoroughly; but it is always safe to laugh."

She smiled; and I remember now it was rather as Mona Lisa smiles.

"For we can laugh together,—that is all. We are not mates. You were born to be the wife of a strong man and the mother of his sturdy children; and you and your sort will inherit the earth and make the laws for us weaklings who dream and scribble and paint. We are not mates. But you have been very kind to me, Marian dear. So I thank you and say good-bye; and I pray that I may never see you after today."

There was a sub-tang of veracity in my deprecation of an unasked-for artistic temperament; the thing is very often a nuisance, and was just then a barrier which I perceived plainly; and with equal plainness I perceived the pettier motives that now caused me to point it out as a barrier to Marian. My lips curled half in mockery of myself, as I framed the bitter smile I felt the situation demanded; but I was fired with the part I was playing; and half-belief had crept into my mind that Marian Winwood was created, chiefly, for the purpose which she had already served.

I regarded her, in fine, as through the eyes of future readers of my biography. She would represent an episode in my life, as others do in that of Byron or of Goethe. I pitied her sincerely; and, under all, what moralists would call my lower nature, held in leash for two months past, chuckled, and grinned, and leaped, at the thought of a holiday.

She rose to her feet. "Good-bye," said she.

"You—you understand, dear?" I queried, tenderly.

"Yes," she answered; "I understand—not what you have just told me, for in that, of course, you have lied. That Jemmett girl and her money is at the bottom of it all, of course. You didn't want to lose her, and still you wanted to play with me. So you were pulled two ways, poor dear."

"Oh, well, if that is what you think of me—!"

"You see, you are not an uncommon type,—a type not strong enough to live life healthily, just strong enough to dabble in life, to trifle with emotions, to experiment with other people's lives. Indeed, I am not angry, dear; I am only—sorry; for you have played with me very nicely indeed, and very boyishly, and the summer has been very happy."

5

I RETURNED TO LICHFIELD AND wrote *As the Coming of Dawn*.

I spent six months in this. My work at first was mere copying of the book that already existed in my brain; but when it was transcribed therefrom, I wrote and rewrote, shifted and polished and adorned until it seemed I would never have done; and indeed I was not anxious to have done with any labour so delightful.

Particularly did I rejoice in the character for which Marian Winwood had posed. Last summer's note-book here came into play; and now, for once, my heroine was in no need of either shoving or prompting. She did things of her own accord, and I was merely her scribe. . .

I would vain-gloriously protest, just to myself, that the love scenes in this story were the most exquisite and, with all that, the most genuine love scenes I knew of anywhere. "By God!" I would occasionally say with Thackeray; "I *am* a genius!"

Besides, the story of the book, I knew, was novel and astutely wrought; its progress caught at once and teased your interest always, so that having begun it, most people would read to the end, if only to discover "how it all came out." I knew the book, in fine, could hardly fail to please and interest a number of people by reason of its plot alone.

I ought to have been content with this. But I had somehow contracted an insane notion that a novel is the more enjoyable when it is adroitly written. In point of fact, of course, no man who writes with care is ever read with pleasure; you may toil through a page or two perhaps, but presently you are noting how precisely every word is fitted to the thought, and later you are noting nothing else. You are insensibly beguiled into a fidgety-footed analysis of every clause, which fatigues in the outcome, and by the tenth page you are yawning.

But I did not comprehend this then. And so I fashioned my apt phrases, and weighed my synonyms, and echoed this or that vowel very skilfully, I thought, and alliterated my consonants with discretion. In fine, I did not overlook the most meticulous device of the stylist; and I enjoyed it. It was a sort of game; and they taught me at least, those six delightful months, that a man writes admirable prose not at all for the sake of having it read, but for the more sensible reason that he enjoys playing solitaire.

I led a hermit's life that winter; and I enjoyed that too. Night, after all, is the one time for writing, particularly when you are inane enough to hanker after perfected speech, and so misguided as to be the slave of the "right word." You sit alone in a bright, comfortable room; the clock ticks companionably; there is no other sound in the world except the constant scratching of your pen, and the occasional far-off puffing of a freight-train coming into Lichfield; there is snow outside, but before your eyes someone, that is not you exactly, arranges and redrills the scrawls which will bring back the sweet and languid summer and remarshal all its pleasant trivialities for anyone that chooses to read through the printed page, although he read two centuries hence, in Nova Zembla. . .

Then you dip into an Unabridged, and change every word that has been written, for a better one, and do it leisurely, rolling in the mouth, as it were, the flavour of every possible synonym, before decision. Then you reread, with a corrective pen in hand the while, and you venture upon the whole to agree with Mérimée that it is preferable to write one's own books, since those of others are not, after all, particularly worth reading in comparison.

And by this time the windows are pale blue, like the blue of a dying flame, and you peep out and see the sparrows moving like rather poorly made mechanical toys about the middle of the deserted street, where there is neither light nor shade. The colour of everything is perfectly discernible, but there is no lustre in the world as yet, though yonder the bloat sun is already visible in the blue and red east, which is like a cosmic bruise; and upon a sudden you find it just possible to stay awake long enough to get safely into bed. . .

6

THUS I DANDLED THE CHILD of my brain for a long while, and arrayed it in beautiful and curious garments, adorning each beloved notion with far-sought words that had a taste in the mouth, and would one day lend an aroma to the printed page; and I rejoiced shamelessly in that which I had done. Then it befell that I went forth and sought the luxury of a Turkish bath, and in the morning, after a rub-down and an ammonia cocktail, awoke to the fact that the world had been going on much as usual, that winter.

Young Colonel Roosevelt seemed not to have wrecked civilization, after all, according to the morning *Courier-Herald*, despite that Democratic paper's colorful prophecies last autumn in the vein of Jeremiah. To the contrary, Major-General McArthur was testifying before the Senate as to the abysmal unfitness of the Filipinos for self-government; the Women's Clubs were holding a convention in Los Angeles; there had been terrible hailstorms this year to induce the annual ruining of the peach-crop, and the submarine Fulton had exploded; the California Limited had been derailed in Iowa, and in Memphis there was some sort of celebration in honor of Admiral Schley; and the Boer War seemed over; and Mr. Havemeyer also was before the Senate, to whom he was making it clear that his companies were in no wise responsible for sugar having reached the unprecedentedly high price of four and a half cents a pound.

The world, in short, in spite of my six months' retiring therefrom, seemed to be getting on pleasantly enough, as I turned from the paper to face the six months' accumulation of mail.

7

A FEW WEEKS LATER, I sent for Mr. George Bulmer, and informed him of his avuncular connection with a genius; and waved certain typewritten pages to establish his title.

Subsequently I read aloud divers portions of *As the Coming of Dawn*, and Mr. Bulmer sipped Chianti, and listened.

"Look here!" he said, suddenly; "have you seen *The Imperial Votaress?*"

I frowned. It is always annoying to be interrupted in the middle of a particularly well-balanced sentence. "Don't know the lady," said I.

"She is advertised on half the posters in town," said Mr. Bulmer. "And it is the book of the year. And it is your book."

At this moment I laid down my manuscript. "I *beg* your pardon?" said I.

"Your book!" Uncle George repeated firmly; "and scarcely a hair's difference between them, except in the names."

"H'm!" I observed, in a careful voice. "Who wrote it?"

"Some female woman out west," said Mr. Bulmer. "She's a George Something-or-other when she publishes, of course, like all those authorines when they want to say about mankind at large what less gifted women only dare say about their sisters-in-law. I wish to heaven they would pick out some other Christian name when they want to cut up like pagans. Anyhow, I saw her real name somewhere, and I remember it began with an S—Why, to be sure! it's Marian Winwood."

"Amaimon sounds well," I observed; "Lucifer, well; Larbason, well; yet they are devils' additions, the names of fiends: but—Marian Winwood!"

"Dear me!" he remonstrated. "Why, she wrote *A Bright Particular Star*, you know, and *The Acolytes*, and lots of others."

The author of *As the Coming of Dawn* swallowed a whole glass of Chianti at a gulp.

"Of course," I said, slowly, "I cannot, in my rather peculiar position, run the risk of being charged with plagiarism—by a Chinese-eyed mental sneak-thief. . ."

Thereupon I threw the manuscript into the open fire, which my preference for the picturesque rendered necessary, even in May.

"Oh, look here!" my uncle cried, and caught up the papers. "It is infernally good, you know! Can't you—can't you fix it,—and—er—change it a bit? Typewriting is so expensive these days that it seems a pity to waste all this."

I took the manuscript and replaced it firmly among the embers. "As you justly observe," said I, "it is infernally good. It is probably a deal better than anything else I shall ever write."

"Why, then—" said Uncle George.

"Why, then," said I, "the only thing that remains to do is to read *The Imperial Votaress.*"

AND I READ IT WITH an augmenting irritation. Here was my great and comely idea transmuted by "George Glock"—which was the woman's foolish pen-name,—into a rather clever melodrama, and set forth anyhow, in a hit or miss style that fairly made me squirm. I would cheerfully have strangled Marian Winwood just then, and not upon the count of larceny, but of butchery.

"And to cap it all, she has assigned her hero every pretty speech I ever made to her! I honestly believe the rogue took shorthand jottings on her cuffs. 'There is a land where lovers may meet face to face, and heart to heart, and mouth to mouth'—why, that's the note I wrote her on the day she wasn't feeling well!"

Presently, however, I began to laugh, and presently sitting there alone, I began to applaud as if I were witnessing a play that took my fancy.

"Oh, the adorable jade!" I said; and then: "George Glock, forsooth! *George Dandin, tu l' as voulu.*"

9

NATURALLY I PUT THE ENTIRE affair into a short story. And—though even to myself it seems incredible,—Miss Winwood wrote me within three days of the tale's appearance, a very indignant letter.

For she was furious, to the last exclamation point and underlining, about my little magazine tale. . . "Why don't you stop writing, and try plumbing or butchering or traveling for scented soap? *You can't write!* If you had the light of creation you wouldn't be using my material" . . .

—Which caused me to reflect forlornly that I had wasted a great deal of correct behavior upon Marian, since any of the more intimately amorous advances which I might have made, and had scrupulously refrained from making, would very probably have been regarded as raw "material," to be developed rather than shocked by. . .

Chapter 18

He Spends an Afternoon in Arden

I had, in a general way, intended to marry Rosalind Jemmett so soon as I had completed *As the Coming of Dawn*; but in the fervour of writing that unfortunate volume, I had at first put off a little, and then a little longer, the answering of her last letter, because I was interested just then in writing well and not particularly interested in anything else; and I had finally approximated to forgetfulness of the young lady's existence.

Now, however, my thoughts harked back to her; and I found, upon inquiry, that Rosalind had spent all of May and a good half of April in Lichfield, in the same town with myself, and was now engaged to Alfred Chaytor,—an estimable person, but popularly known as "Sissy" Chaytor.

2

AND THIS GAVE AN ADDITIONAL whet to my intentions. So I called upon the girl, and she, to my chagrin, received me with an air of having danced with me some five or six times the night before; our conversation was at first trivial and, on her part, dishearteningly cordial; and, in fine, she completely baffled me by not appearing to expect any least explanation of my discourteous neglect. This, look you, when I had been at pains to prepare a perfectly convincing one.

It must be conceded I completely lost my temper; shortly afterward neither of us was speaking with excessive forethought; and each of us languidly advanced a variety of observations which were more dexterous than truthful. But I followed the intractable heiress to the Moncrieffs that spring, in spite of this rebuff, being insufferably provoked by her unshakable assumptions of my friendship and of nothing more.

3

IT WAS PERHAPS A WEEK later she told me: "This, beyond any reasonable doubt, is the Forest of Arden."

"But where Rosalind is is always Arden," I said, politely. Yet I made a mental reservation as to a glimpse of the golf-links, which this particular nook of the forest afforded, and of a red-headed caddy in search of a lost ball.

But beyond these things the sun was dying out in a riot of colour, and its level rays fell kindlily upon the gaunt pines that were thick about us two, converting them into endless aisles of vaporous gold.

There was primeval peace about; an evening wind stirred lazily above, and the leaves whispered drowsily to one another over the waters of what my companion said was a "brawling loch," though I had previously heard it reviled as a particularly treacherous and vexatious hazard. Altogether, I had little doubt that we had reached, in any event, the outskirts of Arden.

"And now," quoth she, seating herself on a fallen log, "what would you do if I were your very, very Rosalind?"

"Don't!" I cried in horror. "It wouldn't be proper! For as a decent self-respecting heroine, you would owe it to Orlando not to listen."

"H'umph!" said Rosalind. The exclamation does not look impressive, written out; but, spoken, it placed Orlando in his proper niche.

"Oh, well," said I, and stretched myself at her feet, full length,— which is supposed to be a picturesque attitude,—"why quarrel over a name? It ought to be Gamelyn, anyhow; and, moreover, by the kindness of fate, Orlando is golfing."

Rosalind frowned, dubiously.

"But golf is a very ancient game," I reassured her. Then I bit a pine-needle in two and sighed. "Foolish fellow, when he might be—"

"Admiring the beauties of nature," she suggested.

Just then an impudent breeze lifted a tendril of honey-coloured hair and toyed with it, over a low, white brow,—and I noted that Rosalind's hair had a curious coppery glow at the roots, a nameless colour that I have never observed anywhere else. . .

"Yes," said I, "of nature."

"Then," queried she, after a pause, "who are you? And what do you in this forest?"

"You see," I explained, "there were conceivably other men in Arden—"

"I suppose so," she sighed, with exemplary resignation.

"—For you were," I reminded her, "universally admired at your uncle's court,—and equally so in the forest. And while Alfred—or, strictly speaking, Gamelyn, or, if you prefer it, Orlando,—is the great love of your life, still—"

"Men are so foolish!" said Rosalind, irrelevantly.

"—it did not prevent you—"

JAMES BRANCH CABELL

"Me!" cried she, indignant.

"You had such a tender heart," I suggested, "and suffering was abhorrent to your gentle nature."

"I don't like cynicism, sir," said she; "and inasmuch as tobacco is not yet discovered—"

"It is clearly impossible that I am smoking," I finished; "quite true."

"I don't like cheap wit, either," said Rosalind. "You," she went on, with no apparent connection, "are a forester, with a good cross-bow and an unrequited attachment,—say, for me. You groan and hang verses and things about on the trees."

"But I don't write verses—any longer," I amended. "Still how would this do,—for an oak, say,—

> *I found a lovely centre-piece*
> *Upon the supper-table,*
> *But when I looked at it again*
> *I saw I wasn't able,*
> *And so I took my mother home*
> *And locked her in the stable."*

She considered that the plot of this epic was not sufficiently inevitable. It hadn't, she lamented, a quite logical ending; and the plot of it, in fine, was not, somehow, convincing.

"Well, in any event," I optimistically reflected, "I am a nickel in. If your dicta had emanated from a person in Peoria or Seattle, who hadn't bothered to read my masterpiece, they would have sounded exactly the same, and the clipping-bureau would have charged me five cents. Maybe I can't write verses, then. But I am quite sure I can groan." And I did so.

"It sounds rather like a fog-horn," said Rosalind, still in the critic's vein; "but I suppose it is the proper thing. Now," she continued, and quite visibly brightening, "you can pretend to have an unrequited attachment for me."

"But I can't—" I decisively said.

"Can't," she echoed. It has not been mentioned previously that Rosalind was pretty. She was especially so just now, in pouting. And, therefore, "—pretend," I added.

She preserved a discreet silence.

"Nor," I continued, with firmness, "am I a shambling, nameless, unshaven denizen of Arden, who hasn't anything to do except to carry a spear and fall over it occasionally. I will no longer conceal the secret of my identity. I am Jaques."

"You can't be Jaques," she dissented; "you are too stout."

"I am well-built," I admitted, modestly; "as in an elder case, sighing and grief have blown me up like a bladder; yet proper pride, if nothing else, demands that my name should appear on the programme."

"But would Jaques be the sort of person who'd—?"

"Who wouldn't be?" I asked, with appropriate ardour. "No, depend upon it, Jaques was not any more impervious to temptation than the rest of us; and, indeed, in the French version, as you will find, he eventually married Celia."

"Minx!" said she; and it seemed to me quite possible that she referred to Celia Reindan, and my heart glowed.

"And how," queried Rosalind, presently, "came you to the Forest of Arden, good Jaques?"

I groaned once more. "It was a girl," I darkly said.

"Of course," assented Rosalind, beaming as to the eyes. Then she went on, and more sympathetically: "Now, Jaques, you can tell me the whole story."

"Is it necessary?" I asked.

"Surely," said she, with sudden interest in the structure of pine-cones; "since for a long while I have wanted to know all about Jaques. You see Mr. Shakespeare is a bit hazy about him."

"*So!*" I thought, triumphantly.

And aloud, "It is an old story," I warned her, "perhaps the oldest of all old stories. It is the story of a man and a girl. It began with a chance meeting and developed into a packet of old letters, which is the usual ending of this story."

Rosalind's brows protested.

"Sometimes," I conceded, "it culminates in matrimony; but the ending is not necessarily tragic."

I dodged exactly in time; and the pine-cone splashed into the hazard.

"It happened," I continued, "that, on account of the man's health, they were separated for a whole year's time before—before things had progressed to any extent. When they did progress, it was largely by letters. That is why this story ended in such a large package.

"Letters," Rosalind confided, to one of the pines, "are so unsatisfactory. They mean so little."

"To the man," I said, firmly, "they meant a great deal. They brought him everything that he most wished for,—comprehension, sympathy, and, at last, comfort and strength when they were sore needed. So the man, who was at first but half in earnest, announced to himself that he had made a discovery. 'I have found,' said he, 'the great white love which poets have dreamed of. I love this woman greatly, and she, I think, loves me. God has made us for each other, and by the aid of her love I will be pure and clean and worthy even of her.' You have doubtless discovered by this stage in my narrative," I added, as in parenthesis, "that the man was a fool."

"Don't!" said Rosalind.

"Oh, he discovered it himself in due time—but not until after he had written a book about her. *As the Coming of Dawn* the title was to have been. It was—oh, just about her. It tried to tell how greatly he loved her. It tried—well, it failed of course, because it isn't within the power of any writer to express what the man felt for that girl. Why, his love was so great—to him, poor fool!—that it made him at times forget the girl herself, apparently. He didn't want to write her trivial letters. He just wanted to write that great book in her honour, which would *make* her understand, even against her will, and then to die, if need be, as Geoffrey Rudel did. For that was the one thing which counted—to make her understand—" I paused, and anyone could see that I was greatly moved. In fact, I was believing every word of it by this time.

"Oh, but who wants a man to *die* for her?" wailed Rosalind.

"It is quite true that one infinitely prefers to see him make a fool of himself. So the man discovered when he came again to bring his foolish book to her,—the book that was to make her understand. And so he burned it—in a certain June. For the girl had merely liked him, and had been amused by him. So she had added him to her collection of men,— quite a large one, by the way,—and was, I believe, a little proud of him. It was, she said, rather a rare variety, and much prized by collectors."

"And how was *she* to know?" said Rosalind; and then, remorsefully: "Was it a very horrid girl?"

"It was not exactly repulsive," said I, as dreamily, and looking up into the sky.

There was a pause. Then someone in the distance—a forester, probably,—called "Fore!" and Rosalind awoke from her reverie.

"Then—?" said she.

"Then came the customary Orlando—oh, well! Alfred, if you like. The name isn't altogether inappropriate, for he does encounter existence with much the same abandon which I have previously noticed in a muffin. For the rest, he was a nicely washed fellow, with a sufficiency of the mediaeval equivalents for bonds and rubber-tired buggies and country places. Oh, yes! I forgot to say that the man was poor,—also that the girl had a great deal of common-sense and no less than three longheaded aunts. And so the girl talked to the man in a common-sense fashion—and after that she was never at home."

"Never?" said Rosalind.

"Only that time they talked about the weather," said I. "So the man fell out of bed just about then, and woke up and came to his sober senses."

"He did it very easily," said Rosalind, almost as if in resentment.

"The novelty of the process attracted him," I pleaded. "So he said—in a perfectly sensible way—that he had known all along it was only a game they were playing,—a game in which there were no stakes. That was a lie. He had put his whole soul into the game, playing as he knew for his life's happiness; and the verses, had they been worthy of the love which caused them to be written, would have been among the great songs of the world. But while the man knew at last that he had been a fool, he was swayed by a man-like reluctance against admitting it. So he laughed—and lied—and broke away, hurt, but still laughing."

"You hadn't mentioned any verses before," said Rosalind.

"I told you he was a fool," said I. "And, after all, that is the entire story."

Then I spent several minutes in wondering what would happen next. During this time I lost none of my interest in the sky. I believed everything I had said: my emotions would have done credit to a Romeo or an Amadis.

"The first time that the girl was not at home," Rosalind observed, impersonally, "the man had on a tan coat and a brown derby. He put on his gloves as he walked down the street. His shoulders were the most indignant—and hurt things she had ever seen. Then the girl wrote to him,—a strangely sincere letter,—and tore it up."

"Historical research," I murmured, "surely affords no warrant for such attire among the rural denizens of tranquil Arden."

"You see," continued Rosalind, oblivious to interruption, "I know all about the girl,—which is more than you do."

"That," I conceded, "is disastrously probable."

"When she realised that she was to see the man again—*Did* you ever feel as if something had lifted you suddenly hundreds of feet above rainy days and cold mutton for luncheon, and the possibility of other girls' wearing black evening dresses, when you wanted yours to be the only one in the room? Well, that is the way she felt at first, when she read his note. At first, she realised nothing beyond the fact that he was nearing her, and that she would presently see him. She didn't even plan what she would wear, or what she would say to him. In an indefinite way, she was happier than she had ever been before—or has been since—until the doubts and fears and knowledge that give children and fools a wide berth came to her,—and *then* she saw it all against her will, and thought it all out, and came to a conclusion."

I sat up. There was really nothing of interest occurring overhead.

"They had played at loving—lightly, it is true, but they had gone so far in their letter writing that they could not go backward,—only forward, or not at all. She had known all along that the man was but half in earnest—believe me, a girl always knows that, even though she may not admit it to herself,—and she had known that a love affair meant to him material for a sonnet or so, and a well-turned letter or two, and nothing more. For he was the kind of man that never quite grows up. He was coming to her, pleased, interested, and a little eager—in love with the idea of loving her,—willing to meet her half-way, and very willing to follow her the rest of the way—if she could draw him. And what was she to do? Could she accept his gracefully insulting semblance of a love she knew he did not feel? Could they see each other a dozen times, swearing not to mention the possibility of loving,—so that she might have a chance to reimpress him with her blondined hair—it *is* touched up, you know—and small talk? And—and *besides*—"

"It is the duty of every young woman to consider what she owes to her family," said I, absentmindedly. Rosalind Jemmett's family consists of three aunts, and the chief of these is Aunt Marcia, who lives in Lichfield. Aunt Marcia is a portly, acidulous and discomposing person, with eyes like shoe-buttons and a Savonarolan nose. She is also a well-advertised philanthropist, speaks neatly from the platform, and has wide experience as a patroness, and extreme views as to ineligibles.

Rosalind flushed somewhat. "And so," said she, "the girl exercised her common-sense, and was nervous, and said foolish things about new plays, and the probability of rain—to keep from saying still more foolish things about herself; and refused to talk personalities; and let him go, with the knowledge that he would not come back. Then she went to her room, and had a good cry. Now," she added, after a pause, "you understand."

"I do not," I said, very firmly, "understand a lot of things."

"Yet a woman would," she murmured.

This being a statement I was not prepared to contest, I waved it aside. "And so," said I, "they laughed; and agreed it was a boy-and-girl affair; and were friends."

"It was the best thing—" said she.

"Yes," I assented,—"for Orlando."

"—and it was the most sensible thing."

"Oh, eminently!"

This seemed to exhaust the subject, and I lay down once more among the pine-needles.

"And that," said Rosalind, "was the reason Jaques came to Arden?"

"Yes," said I.

"And found it—?"

"Shall we say—Hades?"

"Oh!" she murmured, scandalised.

"It happened," I continued, "that he was cursed with a good memory. And the zest was gone from his little successes and failures, now there was no one to share them; and nothing seemed to matter very much. Oh, he really was the sort of man that never grows up! And it was dreary to live among memories of the past, and his life was now somewhat perturbed by disapproval of his own folly and by hunger for a woman who was out of his reach."

"And Rosalind—I mean the girl—?"

"She married Orlando—or Gamelyn, or Alfred, or Athelstane, or Ethelred, or somebody,—and, whoever it was, they lived happily ever afterward," I said, morosely.

Rosalind pondered over this dénouement for a moment.

"Do you know," said she, "I think—"

"It's a rather dangerous practice," I warned her.

Rosalind sighed, wearily; but in her cheek at about this time occurred a dimple.

"—I think that Rosalind must have thought the play very badly named."

"*As You Like It*?" I queried, obtusely.

"Yes—since it wasn't, for her."

It is unwholesome to lie on the ground after sunset.

4

"I HAD RATHER A SCENE with Alfred yesterday morning. He said you drank, and gambled, and were always running after—people, and weren't in fine, a desirable person for me to know. He insinuated, in fact, that you were a villain of the very deepest and non-crocking dye. He told me of instances. His performance would have done credit to Ananias. I was *mad*! So I gave him his old ring back, and told him things I can't tell *you*,—no, not just yet, dear. He is rather like a muffin, isn't he?" she said, with the lightest possible little laugh—"particularly like one that isn't quite done."

"Oh, Rosalind," I babbled, "I mean to prove that you were right. And I *will* prove it, too!"

And indeed I meant all that I said—just then.

Rosalind said: "Oh, Jaques, Jaques! what a child you are!"

Chapter 19

He Plays the Improvident Fool

Now was I come near to the summit of my desires, and advantageously betrothed to a girl with whom I was, in any event, almost in love; but I presently ascertained, to my dismay, that sophisticated, "proper" little Rosalind was thoroughly in love with me, and always in the back of my mind this knowledge worried me.

Imprimis, she persisted in calling me Jaques, which was uncomfortably reminiscent of that time wherein I was called Jack. Yet my objection to this silly nickname was a mischancy matter to explain. There was no way of telling her that I disliked anything which reminded me of Gillian Hardress, without telling more about Gillian than would be pleasant to tell. So Rosalind went on calling me Jaques; and I was compelled to put up with a trivial and unpremeditated, but for all that a daily, annoyance; and I fretted under it.

Item, she insisted on presenting me with all sorts of expensive knick-knacks, and being childishly grieved when I remonstrated.

"But I have the money," Rosalind would say, "and you haven't. So why shouldn't I? And besides, it's really only selfishness on my part, because I like doing things for you, and *if* you liked doing things for me, Jaques, you'd understand."

So I would eventually have to swear that I did like "doing things" for her; and it followed—somehow—that in consequence she had a perfect right to give me anything she wanted to.

And this too fretted me, mildly, all the summer I spent at Birnam Beach with Rosalind and with the opulent friends of Rosalind's aunt from St. Louis. . . They were a queer lot. They all looked so unspeakably new; their clothes were spick and span, and as expensive as possible, but that was not it; even in their bathing suits these middle-aged people— they were mostly middle-aged—seemed to have been very recently finished, like animated waxworks of middle-aged people just come from the factory. And they spent money in a continuous careless way that frightened me.

But I was on my very best, most dignified behavior; and when Aunt Lora presented me as "one of the Lichfield Townsends, you know," these brewers and breweresses appeared to be properly impressed. One of them—actually—"supposed that I had a coat-of-arms"; which in Lichfield would be equivalent to "supposing" that a gentleman possessed a pair of trousers. But they were really very thoughtful about never letting me pay for anything; in this regard there seemed afoot a sort of friendly conspiracy.

So the summer passed pleasantly enough; and we bathed, and held hands in the moonlight, and danced at the Casino, and rode the merry-go-round, and played ping-pong, and read *Dorothy Vernon of Haddon Hall*,—which was much better, I told everybody, than that idiotic George Clock book, *The Imperial Votaress*. And we drank interminable suissesses, and it was all very pleasant.

Yet always in the rear of my mind was stirring restively the instinct to get back to my writing; and these sedately frolicsome benevolent people—even Rosalind—plainly thought that "writing things" was just the unimportant foible of an otherwise fine young fellow.

2

AND IN SEPTEMBER ROSALIND CAME to visit her Aunt Marcia in Lichfield, to get clothes and all other matters ready for our wedding in November; and Lichfield, as always, made much of Rosalind, and she had the honor of "leading" the first Lichfield German with Colonel Rudolph Musgrave. My partner at that dance was the Marquise d'Arlanges. . .

I was seeing a deal of the Marquise d'Arlanges. She was Stella's only sister, as you may remember, and was that autumn paying a perfunctory visit to her parents—the second since her marriage.

I shall not expatiate, however, concerning Madame la Marquise. You have doubtless heard of her. For Lizzie has not, even yet, found a time wherein to be idle; she has been busied since the hour of her birth in acquiring first, plain publicity, and then social power, and every other amenity of life in turn. I had not the least doubt even then of her ending where she is now. . .

She was at this time still well upon the preferable side o! thirty, and had no weaknesses save a liking for gossip, cigarettes, and admiration. Lizzie was never the woman to marry a Peter Blagden. Once Stella was settled, Lizzie Musgrave had sailed for Europe, and eventually had arrived at Monaco with an apologetic mother, several letters of introduction, and a Scotch terrier; and had established herself at the

Hôtel de la Paix, to look over the "available" supply of noblemen in reduced circumstances. Before the end of a month Miss Musgrave had reached a decision, had purchased her Marquis, much as she would have done any other trifle that took her fancy, and had shipped her mother back to America. Lizzie retained the terrier, however, as she was honestly attached to it.

Her marriage had been happy, and she found her husband on further acquaintance, as she told me, a mild-mannered and eminently suitable person, who was unaccountably addicted to playing dominoes, and who spent a great deal of money, and dined with her occasionally. In a sentence, the marquise was handsome, "had a tongue in her head," and, to utilise yet another ancient phrase, was as hard as nails.

And yet there was a family resemblance. Indeed, in voice and feature she was strangely like an older Stella; and always I was cheating myself into a half-belief that this woman I was talking with was Stella; and Lizzie would at least enable me to forget, for a whole half-hour sometimes, that Stella was dead. . .

"I MUST THANK YOU," I said, one afternoon, when I arose to go, "for a most pleasant dream of—what we'll call the Heart's Desire. I suppose I have been rather stupid, Lizzie; and I apologise for it; but people are never exceedingly hilarious in dreams, you know."

She said, very gently: "I understand. For I loved Stella too. And that is why the room is never really lighted when you come. Oh, you stupid man, how could I have *helped* knowing it—that all the love you have made to me was because you have been playing I was Stella? That knowledge has preserved me, more than once, my child, from succumbing to your illicit advances in this dead Lichfield."

And I was really astonished, for she was not by ordinary the sort of woman who consents to be a makeshift.

I said as much, "And it *has* been a comfort, Lizzie, because she doesn't come as often now, for some reason—"

"Why—what do you mean?"

The room was very dark, lit only by the steady, comfortable glow of a soft-coal fire. For it was a little after sunset, and outside, carriages were already rumbling down Regis Avenue, and people were returning from the afternoon drive. I could not see anything distinctly, excepting my own hands, which were like gold in the firelight; and so I told her all about *The Indulgences of Ole-Luk-Ole*.

"She came, that first time, over the crest of a tiny upland that lay in some great forest,—Brocheliaunde, I think. I knew it must be autumn, for the grass was brown and every leaf upon the trees was brown. And she too was all in brown, and her big hat, too, was of brown felt, and about it curled a long ostrich feather dyed brown; and my first thought, as I now remember, was how in the dickens could any mediaeval lady have come by such a garb, for I knew, somehow, that this was a woman of the Middle Ages.

"Only her features were those of Stella, and the eyes of this woman were filled with an unutterable happiness and fear, as she came toward me,—just as the haunting eyes of Stella were upon the night she married Peter Blagden, and I babbled nonsense to the moon.

"'Oh, I have wanted you,—I have wanted you!' she said; and afterward, unarithmetically dimpling, just as she used to do, you may remember: '*Depardieux*, messire! have you then forgotten that upon this forenoon we hunt the great boar?'"

"'Stella!' I said, 'O dear, dear Stella! what does it mean?'

"'You silly! it means, of course, that Ole-Luk-Oie is kind, and has put us both into the glaze of the mustard-jar—only I wonder which one we have gotten into?' Stella said. 'Don't you remember them, dear—the blue mustard-jar and the red one your Mammy had that summer at the Green Chalybeate, with men on them hunting a boar?'

"'They stood, one on each corner of the mantelpiece,' I said; 'and in the blue one she kept matches, and in the other—'

"'She kept buttons in the red one,' said Stella,—'big, shiny white buttons, with four holes in them, that had come off your underclothes, and were to be sewed on again. One day you swallowed one of 'em, I remember, because you *would* keep it in your mouth while you swung in the hammock. And you thought it would surely kill you, so you knelt down in the dry leaves and prayed God He wouldn't let it kill you.'

"'But you weren't there,' I protested; 'nobody was there. So nobody ever knew anything about it, though may be you—' For I had just remembered that Stella was dead, only I knew it was against some rule to mention it.

"'Well, at any rate I'm *here*,' said Stella, 'and Ole-Luk-Oie is kind; and we had better go and hunt the great boar at once, I suppose, since that is what the people on the mustard-jars always do.'

"'But how did you come hither, O, my dear—?'

"'Why, through your wanting me so much,' she said. 'How else?'

"And I understood. . .

"So we went and slew the great boar. I slew it personally, with a long spear, and with Stella clasping her hands in the background. Only there was a nicked place in the mustard-jar, where I had dropped it on the hearth some fifteen years ago, and my horse kept stumbling over this crevice, so that I knew it was the red jar and the buttons we were riding around. And afterward I made a song in honour of my Stella,—a song so perfect that I presently awoke, weeping with joy that I had made a song so beautiful, and with the knowledge I could not now recollect a single word of it; and I knew that neither I nor any other man could ever make again a song one-half so beautiful. . .

"Since then Ole-Luk-Oie—or someone—has been very kind at times. He always lets me into pictures, though, never into mouse-holes and hen-houses and silly places like that, as he did little Hjalmar. I don't know why. . .

"Once it was into the illustrations to the *Popular Tales of Poictesme*, and we met my great grandfather Jurgen there. And once it was into the picture on the cover of that unveracious pamphlet the manager of the Green Chalybeate sends in the spring to everybody who has once been there. That time was very odd.

"It is a picture of the Royal Hotel, you may remember, as it used to be a good ten years ago. Both fountains were playing in the sunlight,—they were torn down when I was at college, and I had almost forgotten their existence; and elegant and languid ladies were riding by, in victorias, and under tiny parasols trimmed with fringe, and all these ladies wore those preposterously big sleeves they used to wear then; and men in little visored skull caps were passing on tall old-fashioned bicycles, just as they do in the picture. Even the silk-hatted gentleman in the corner, pointing out the beauties of the building with his cane, was there.

"And Stella and I walked past the margin of the picture, and so on down the boardwalk to the other hotel, to look for our parents. And we agreed not to tell anyone that we had ever grown up, but just to let it be a secret between us two; and we were to stay in the picture forever, and grow up all over again, only we would arrange everything differently. And Stella was never to go driving on the twenty-seventh of April, so that we would be quite safe, and would live together for a long, long while.

"She wouldn't promise, though, that when Peter Blagden asked to be introduced, she would refuse to meet him. She just giggled and shook her sunny head. She hadn't any hat on. She was wearing the blue-and-white sailor-suit, of course." . . .

4

BUT A SERVANT WAS LIGHTING up the front-hall, and the glare of it came through the open door, and now the room was just like any other room.

"And you are Robert Townsend!" the marquise observed. "The one my mother doesn't approve of as a visitor!"

Madame d'Arlanges said, with a certain lack of sequence: "And yet you are planning to do precisely what Peter Blagden did. He liked Stella, she amused him, and he thought her money would come in very handy; and so he, somehow, contrived to marry her in the end, because she was just a child, and you were a child, and he wasn't. And he always lied to her about—about those business-trips—even from the very first. I knew, because I'm not a sentimental person. But, Bob, how can you stoop to mimic Peter Blagden! For you are doing precisely what he did; and for Rosalind, just as it was for Stella, it is almost irresistible, to have the chance of reforming a man who has notoriously been 'talked about.' Still, I see that for Stella's sake you won't lie as steadfastly to Rosalind as Peter did to Stella. It is none of my business of course; oh, I don't meddle. I merely prophesy that you won't."

But those lights had made an astonishing difference. And so, "But why not?" said I. "It is the immemorial method of dealing with savages; and surely women can never expect to become quite civilised so long as chivalry demands that a man say to a woman only what he believes she wants to hear? Ah, no, my dear Lizzie; when a man tries to get into a woman's favour, custom demands that he palliate the invasion with flatteries and veiled truths—or, more explicitly, with lies,—just as any sensible explorer must come prepared to leave a trail of looking-glasses and valueless bright beads among the original owners of any unknown country. For he doesn't know what obstacles he may encounter, and he has been taught, from infancy, to regard any woman as a baleful and unfathomable mystery—"

"She is never so—heaven help her!—if the man be sufficiently worthless."

"I rejoice that we are so thoroughly at one. For upon my word, I believe this widespread belief in feminine inscrutability is the result of a conspiracy on the part of the weaker sex; and that every mother is somehow pledged to inculcate this belief into the immature masculine mind. Apparently the practice originated in the Middle Ages, for it never seemed to occur to anybody before then that a woman was particularly complex. Though, to be sure, Catullus now—" "This is not a time for pedantry. I don't in the least care what Catullus or anyone else observed concerning anything—" "But I had not aspired, my dear Lizzie, to be even remotely pedantic. I was simply about to remark that Catullus, or Ariosto, or Coventry Patmore, or King Juba, or Posidonius, or Sir John Vanbrugh, or perhaps, Agathocles of Chios, or else Simonides the Younger, has conceded somewhere, that women are, in certain respects, dissimilar, as it were, to men." "I am merely urging you not to marry this silly little Rosalind, for the excellent reason that you *did* love my darling Stella even more than I, and that Rosalind is in love with you." "Do you really think so?" said I. "Why, then, actuated by the very finest considerations of decency and prudence and generosity, I shall, of course, espouse her the very next November that ever is."

The marquise retorted: "No,—because you are at bottom too fond of Rosalind Jemmett; and, besides, it isn't really a question of your feeling toward *her*. In any event, I begin to like you too well, Bob, to let you kiss me any more."

I declared that I detested paradox. Then I went home to supper.

5

BUT, FOR ALL THIS, I meditated for a long while upon what Lizzie had said. It was true that I was really fond of "proper" little Rosalind Jemmett; concerning myself I had no especial illusions; and, to my credit, I faced what I considered the real issue, squarely.

We were in Aunt Marcia's parlour. Rosalind was an orphan, and lived in turn with her three aunts. She said the other two were less unendurable than Aunt Marcia, and I believed her. I consider, to begin with, that a person is not civilised who thumps upon the floor upstairs with a poker, simply because it happens to be eleven o'clock; and moreover, Aunt Marcia's parlour—oh, it really was a "parlour,"—was entirely too like the first night of a charity bazaar, when nothing has been sold.

The room was not a particularly large one; but it contained exactly three hundred and seven articles of bijouterie, not estimating the china pug-dog upon the hearth. I know, for I counted them.

Besides, there were twenty-eight pictures upon the walls—one in oils of the late Mr. Dumby (for Aunt Marcia was really Mrs. Clement Dumby), painted, to all appearances, immediately after the misguided gentleman who married Aunt Marcia had been drowned, and before he had been wiped dry,—and for the rest, everywhere the eye was affronted by engravings framed in gilt and red-plush of "Sanctuary," "Le Hamac," "Martyre Chrétienne," "The Burial of Latané," and other Victorian outrages.

Then on an easel there was a painting of a peacock, perched upon an urn, against a gilded background; this painting irrelevantly deceived your expectations, for it was framed in blue plush. Also there were "gift-books" on the centre table, and a huge volume, again in red plush, with its titular "Album" cut out of thin metal and nailed to the cover. This album contained calumnious portraits of Aunt Marcia's family, the most of them separately enthroned upon the same imitation rock, in all the pride of a remote, full-legged and starchy youth, each picture being painfully "coloured by hand."

6

"Do you know why I want to marry you?" I demanded of Rosalind, in such surroundings, apropos of a Mrs. Vokins who had taken a house in Lichfield for the winter, and had been at school somewhere in the backwoods with Aunt Marcia, and was "dying to meet me."

She answered, in some surprise: "Why, because you have the good taste to be heels over head in love with me, of course."

I took possession of her hands. "If there is anything certain in this world of uncertainties, it is that I am not the least bit in love with you. Yet, only yesterday—do you remember, dear?"

She answered, "I remember."

"But I cannot, for the life of me, define what happened yesterday. I merely recall that we were joking, as we always do when together, and that on a wager I loosened your hair. Then as it tumbled in great honey-coloured waves about you, you were silent, and there came into your eyes a look I had never seen before. And even now I cannot define what happened, Rosalind! I only know I caught your face between my hands, and for a moment held it so, with fingers that have not yet forgotten the feel of your soft, thick hair,—and that for a breathing space your eyes looked straight into mine. Something changed in me then, my lady. Something changed in you, too, I think."

Then Rosalind said, "Don't, Jaques—!" She was horribly embarrassed.

"For I knew you willed me to possess you, and that possession would seem as trivial as a fiddle in a temple. . . Yet, too, there was a lustful beast, somewhere inside of me, which nudged me to—kiss you, say! But nothing happened. I did not even kiss you, my beautiful and wealthy Rosalind."

"Don't keep on talking about the money," she wailed. "Why, you can't believe I think you mercenary!"

"I would estimate your intellect far more cheaply, my charming Rosalind, if you thought anything else; for of course I am. I wanted to settle myself, you conceive, and as an accomplice you were very eligible. I now comprehend it is beyond the range of rationality, dear stranger, that we should ever marry each other; and so we must not. We must not, you comprehend, since though we lived together through ten patriarchal lifetimes we would die strangers to each other. For you, dear clean-souled girl that you are, were born that you might be the wife of a strong man and the mother of his sturdy children. The world was made for you and for your offspring; and in time your children will occupy this world and make the laws for us irrelevant folk that scribble and paint and design all useless and beautiful things, and thus muddle away our precious lives. No, you may not wisely mate with us, for you are a shade too terribly at ease in the universe, you sensible people."

"But I love Art," said Rosalind, bewildered.

"Yes,—but by the tiniest syllable a thought too volubly, my dear. You are the sort that quotes the Rubaiyat. Whereas I—was it yesterday or the day before you told me, with a wise pucker of your beautiful low, white brow, that I had absolutely no sense of the responsibilities of life? Well, I really haven't, dear stranger, as you appraise them; and, indeed, I fear we must postpone our agreement upon any possible subject, until the coming of the Coquecigrues. We see the world so differently, you and I,—and for that same reason I cannot but adore you, Rosalind. For with you I can always speak my true thought and know that you will never for a moment suspect it to be anything but irony. Ah, yes, we can laugh and joke together, and be thorough friends; but if there is anything certain in this world of uncertainties, it is that I am not, and cannot be, in love with you. And yet—I wonder now?" said I, and I rose and paced Aunt Marcia's parlour.

"You wonder? Don't you understand even now?" the girl said shyly. "I am not as clever as you, of course; I have known that for a long while,

Jaques; and tonight in particular I don't quite follow you, my dear, but I love you, and—why, there is *nothing* I could deny you!"

"Then give me back my freedom," said I. "For, look you, Rosalind, marriage is proverbially a slippery business. Always there are a variety of excellent reasons for perpetrating matrimony; but the rub of it is that not any one of them insures you against tomorrow. Love, for example, we have all heard of; but I have known fine fellows to fling away their chances in life, after the most approved romantic fashion, on account of a pretty stenographer, and to beat her within the twelvemonth. And upon my word, you know, nobody has a right to blame the swindled lover for doing this—"

I paused to inspect the china pug-dog which squatted on the pink-tiled hearth and which glared inanely at the huge brass coal-box just opposite. Then I turned from these two abominations and faced Rosalind with a bantering flirt of my head.

"—For put it that I marry some entrancing slip of girlhood, what am I to say when, later, I discover myself irrevocably chained to a fat and dowdy matron? I married no such person, I have indeed sworn eternal fidelity to an entirely different person; and this unsolicited usurper of my hearth is nothing whatever to me, unless perhaps the object of my entire abhorrence. Yet am I none the less compelled to justify the ensuing action before an irrational audience, which faces common logic in very much the attitude of Augustine's famed adder! Decidedly I think that, on the whole, I would prefer my Freedom."

It was as though I had struck her. She sat as if frozen. "Jaques, is there another woman in this?"

"Why, in a fashion, yes. Yet it is mainly because I am really fond of you, Rosalind."

She handed me that exceedingly expensive ring the jeweler had charged to me. I thought her action damnably theatrical, but still, it was not as though I could afford to waste money on rings, so I took the trinket absent-mindedly.

"You are unflatteringly prompt in closing out the account," I said, with a grieved smile. . .

"Good-bye!" said Rosalind, and her voice broke. "Oh, and I had thought—! Well, as it is, I pay for the luxury of thinking, just as you forewarned me, don't I, Jaques? And you won't forget the hall-light? Aunt Marcia, you know—but how glad *she* will be! I feel rather near to Aunt Marcia tonight," said Rosalind.

SHE LEFT LICHFIELD THE NEXT day but one, and spent the following winter with the aunt that lived in Brooklyn. She was Rosalind Gelwix the next time I saw her. . .

And Aunt Marcia, whose taste is upon a par with her physical attractions, inserted a paragraph in the "Social Items" of the Lichfield *Courier-Herald* to announce the breaking-off of the engagement. Aunt Marcia also took the trouble to explain, quite confidentially, to some seven hundred and ninety-three people, just why the engagement had been broken off: and these explanations were more creditable to Mrs. Dumby's imagination than to me.

And I remembered, then, that the last request my mother made of me was to keep out of the newspapers—"except, of course, the social items" . . .

Chapter 20

He Dines Out, Impeded by Superstitions

Within the week I had repented of what I termed my idiotic quixotism, and for precisely nine days after that I cursed my folly. And then, at the Provises, I comprehended that in breaking off my engagement to Rosalind Jemmett I had acted with profound wisdom, and I unfolded my napkin, and said:

"Do you know I didn't catch your name—not even this time?"

She took a liberal supply of lemon juice. "How delightful!" she murmured, "for I heard yours quite distinctly, and these oysters are delicious."

I noted with approval that her gown was pink and fluffy; it had also the advantage of displaying shoulders that were incredibly white, and a throat which was little short of marvellous. "I am glad," I whispered, confidentially, "that you are still wearing that faint vein about your left temple. I thought it admirable for early morning wear upon the house tops of Liege, but it seems equally effective for dinner parties."

She raised her eyebrows slightly and selected a biscuit.

"You see," said I, "I was horribly late. And when Kittie Provis said, 'Allow me,' and I saw—well, I didn't care," I concluded, lucidly, "because to have every one of your dreams come true, all of a sudden, leaves you past caring."

"It really is funny," she confided to a spoonful of *consomme a la Julienne*.

"After almost two years!" sighed I, ever so happily. But I continued, with reproach, "To go without a word—that very day—"

"Mamma—" she began.

I recalled the canary-bird, and the purple shawl. "I sought wildly," said I; "you were evanished. The *proprietaire* was tearing his hair—no insurance—he knew nothing. So I too tore my hair; and I said things. There was a row. For he also said things: 'Figure to yourselves, messieurs! I lose the Continental—two ladies come and go, I know not who—I am ruined, desolated, is it not?—and this pig of an American blusters— ah, my new carpets, just down, what horror!' And then, you know, he launched into a quite feeling peroration concerning our notorious custom of tomahawking one another—

"Yes," I coldly concluded into Mrs. Clement Dumby's ear, "we all behaved disgracefully. As you very justly observe, liquor has been the curse of the South." It was of a piece with Kittie Provis to put me next to Aunt Marcia, I reflected.

And mentally I decided that even though a portion of my assertions had not actually gone through the formality of occurring, it all might very easily have happened, had I remained a while longer in Liege; and then ensued a silent interval and an entree.

"And so—?"

"And so I knocked about the world, in various places, hoping against hope that at last—"

"Your voice carries frightfully—"

I glanced toward Mrs. Clement Dumby, who, as a dining dowager of many years' experience, was, to all appearances, engrossed by the contents of her plate. "My elderly neighbour is as hard of hearing as a telephone-girl," I announced. She was the exact contrary, which was why I said it quite audibly. "And your neighbour—why, *his* neighbour is Nannie Allsotts. We might as well be on a desert island, Elena—" And the given name slipped out so carelessly as to appear almost accidental.

"Sir!" said she, with proper indignation; "after so short an acquaintance—"

"Centuries," I suggested, meekly. "You remember I explained about that."

She frowned,—an untrustworthy frown that was tinged with laughter. "One meets so many people! Yes, it really is frightfully warm, Colonel Grimshaw; they ought to open some of the windows."

"Er—haw—hum! Didn't see you at the Anchesters."

"No; I am usually lucky enough to be in bed with a sick headache when Mrs. Anchester entertains. Of two evils one should choose the lesser, you know."

In the manner of divers veterans Colonel Grimshaw evinced his mirth upon a scale more proper to an elephant; and relapsed, with a reassuring air of having done his duty once and for all.

"I never," she suggested, tentatively, "heard any more of your poem, about—?"

"Oh, I finished it; every magazine in the country knows it. It is poor stuff, of course, but then how could I write of Helen when Helen had disappeared?"

The lashes exhibited themselves at full length. "I looked her up," confessed their owner, guiltily, "in the encyclopaedia. It was very instructive—about sun-myths and bronzes and the growth of the epic, you know, and tree-worship and moon-goddesses. Of course"— here ensued a flush and a certain hiatus in logic,—"of course it is nonsense."

"Nonsense?" My voice sank tenderly. "Is it nonsense, Elena, that for two years I have remembered the woman whose soft body I held, for one unforgettable moment, in my arms? and nonsense that I have fought all this time against—against the temptations every man has,—that I might ask her at last—some day when she at last returned, as always I knew she would—to share a fairly decent life? and nonsense that I have dreamed, waking and sleeping, of a wondrous face I knew in Ilium first, and in old Rome, and later on in France, I think, when the Valois were kings? Well!" I sighed, after vainly racking my brain for a tenderer fragment of those two-year-old verses, "I suppose it is nonsense!"

"The salt, please," quoth she. She flashed that unforgotten broadside at me. "I believe you need it."

"Why, dear me! of course not!" said I, to Mrs. Dumby; "immorality lost the true *cachet* about the same time that ping-pong did. Nowadays divorces are going out, you know, and divorcees are not allowed to. Quite modish women are seen in public with their husbands nowadays."

"H'mph!" said Mrs. Dumby; "I've no doubt that you must find it a most inconvenient fad!"

I ate my portion of duck abstractedly. "Thus to dive into the refuse-heap of last year's slang does not quite cover the requirements of the case. For I wish—only I hardly dare to ask—"

"If I were half of what you make out," meditatively said she, "I would be a regular fairy, and couldn't refuse you the usual three wishes."

"Two," I declared, "would be sufficient."

"First?"

"That you tell me your name."

"I adore orange ices, don't you? And the second?" was her comment.

"Well, then, you' re a pig," was mine. "You are simply a nomenclatural Berkshire. But the second is that you let me measure your finger—oh, any finger will do. Say, the third on the left hand."

"You really talk to me as if—" But this non-existent state of affairs proved indescribable, and the unreal condition lapsed into a pout.

"Oh, very possibly!" I conceded; "since the way in which a man talks to a woman—to *the* woman—depends by ordinary upon the depth—"

"The depth of his devotion?" she queried, helpfully. "Of course!"

I faced the broadside, without flinching. "No," said I, critically; "the depth of her dimples."

"Nonsense!" Nevertheless, the dimples were, and by a deal, the more conspicuous. We were getting on pretty well.

I bent forward; there was a little catch in my voice. Aunt Marcia was listening. I wanted her to listen.

"You must know that I love you," I said, simply, "I have always loved you, I think, since the moment my eyes first fell upon you in that—other pink thing. Of course, I realize the absurdity of my talking in this way to a woman whose name I don't know; but I realise more strongly that I love you. Why, there is not a pulse in my body which isn't throbbing and tingling and leaping riotously from pure joy of being with you again, Elena! And in time, you will love me a little, simply because I want you to,—isn't that always a woman's main reason for caring for a man?"

She considered this, dubious and flushed.

"I will not insist," said I, with a hurried and contented laugh, "that you were formerly an Argive queen. I mean I will not be obstinate about it, because that, I confess, was a paraphrase of my verses. But Helen has always been to me the symbol of perfect loveliness, and so it was not unnatural that I should confuse you with her."

"Thank you, sir," said she, demurely.

"I half believe it is true, even now; and if not—well, Helen was acceptable enough in her day, Elena, but I am willing to Italianise, for I have seen you and loved you, and Helen is forgot. It is not exactly the orthodox pace for falling in love," I added, with a boyish candour, "but it is very real to me."

"You—you couldn't have fallen in love—really—"

"It was not in the least difficult," I protested.

"And you don't even know my *name*—"

"I know, however, what it is going to be," said I; "and Mrs. 'Enry 'Awkins, as we'll put it, has found favour in the judgment of connoisseurs. So after dinner—in an hour—?"

"Oh, very well! since you're an author and insist, I will be ready, in an hour, to decline you, with thanks."

"Rejection not implying any lack of merit," I suggested. "This is damnable iteration; but I am accustomed to it."

But by this, Mrs. Provis was gathering eyes around the table, and her guests arose, with the usual outburst of conversation, and swishing of dresses, and the not always unpremeditated dropping of handkerchiefs and fans. Mrs. Clement Dumby bore down upon us now, a determined and generously proportioned figure in her notorious black silk.

"Really," said she, aggressively, "I never saw two people more engrossed. My dear Mrs. Barry-Smith, you have been so taken up with Mr. Townsend, all during dinner, that I haven't had a chance to welcome you to Lichfield. Your mother and I were at school together, you know. And your husband was quite a beau of mine. So I don't feel, now, at all as if we were strangers—"

And thus she bore Elena off, and I knew that within ten minutes Elena would have been warned against me, as "not quite a desirable acquaintance, you know, my dear, and it is only my duty to tell you that as a young and attractive married woman—"

2

"And so," I said in my soul, as the men redistributed themselves, "she is married,—married while you were pottering with books and the turn of phrases and immortality and such trifles—oh, you ass! And to a man named Barry-Smith—damn him, I wonder whether he is the hungry scut that hasn't had his hair cut this fall, or the blancmange-bellied one with the mashed-strawberry nose? Yes, I know everybody else. And Jimmy Travis is telling a funny story, so *laugh*! People will think you are grieving over Rosalind. . . But why in heaven's name isn't Jimmy at home this very moment,—with a wife and carpet-slippers and a large-size bottle of paregoric on his mantelpiece,—instead of here, grinning like a fool over some blatant indecency? He ought to marry; every young man ought to marry. Oh, you futile, abject, burbling twin-brother of the first patron that procured a reputation for Bedlam! why aren't *you* married—married years ago,—with a home of your own, and a victoria for Mrs. Townsend and bills from the kindergarten every quarter? Oh, you bartender of verbal cocktails! I believe your worst enemy flung your mind at you in a moment of unbridled hatred."

So I snapped the stem of my glass carefully, and scowled with morose disapproval at the unconscious Mr. Travis, and his now-applauded and very Fescennine jest. . .

I FOUND HER INSPECTING A bulky folio with remarkable interest. There was a lamp, with a red shade, that cast a glow over her, such as one sometimes sees reflected from a great fire. The people about us were chattering idiotically, and something inside my throat prevented my breathing properly, and I was miserable.

"Mrs. Barry-Smith,"—thus I began,—"if you've the tiniest scrap of pity in your heart for a very presumptuous, blundering and unhappy person, I pray you to forgive and to forget, as people say, all that I have blatted out to you. I spoke, as I thought, to a free woman, who had the right to listen to my boyish talk, even though she might elect to laugh at it. And now I hardly dare to ask forgiveness."

Mrs. Barry-Smith inspected a view of the Matterhorn, with careful deliberation. "Forgiveness?" said she.

"Indeed," said I, "I *don't* deserve it." And I smiled most resolutely. "I had always known that somewhere, somehow, you would come into my life again. It has been my dream all these two years; but I dream carelessly. My visions had not included this—obstacle."

She made wide eyes at me. "What?" said she.

"Your husband," I suggested, delicately.

The eyes flashed. And a view of Monaco, to all appearances, awoke some pleasing recollection. "I confess," said Mrs. Barry-Smith, "that—for the time—I had quite forgotten him. I—I reckon you must think me very horrid?"

But she was at pains to accompany this query with a broadside that rendered such a supposition most unthinkable. And so—

"I think you—" My speech was hushed and breathless, and ended in a click of the teeth. "Oh, don't let's go into the minor details," I pleaded.

Then Mrs. Barry-Smith descended to a truism. "It is usually better not to," said she, with the air of an authority. And latterly, addressing the facade of Notre Dame, "You see, Mr. Barry-Smith being so much older than I—"

"I would prefer that. Of course, though, it is none of my business."

"You see, you came and went so suddenly that—of course I never thought to see you again—not that I ever thought about it, I reckon—" Her candour would have been cruel had it not been reassuringly over-emphasized. "And Mr. Barry-Smith was very pressing—"

"He would be," I assented, after consideration. "It is, indeed, the single point in his outrageous conduct I am willing to condone."

"—and he was a great friend of my father's, and I *liked* him—"

"So you married him and lived together ever afterward, without ever throwing the tureen at each other. That is the most modern version; but there is usually a footnote concerning the bread-and-butter plates."

She smiled, inscrutably, a sphinx in Dresden china. "And yet," she murmured, plaintively, "I *would* like to know what you think of me."

"Why, prefacing with the announcement that I pray God I may never see you after tonight, I think you the most adorable creature He ever made. What does it matter now? I have lost you. I think—ah, desire o' the world, what can I think of you? The notion of you dazzles me like flame,—and I dare not think of you, for I love you."

"Yes?" she queried, sweetly; "then I reckon Mrs. Dumby was right after all. She said you were a most depraved person and that, as a young and—well, *she* said it, you know—attractive widow—"

"H'm!" said I; and I sat down. "Elena Barry-Smith," I added, "you are an unmitigated and unconscionable and unpardonable rascal. There is just one punishment which would be adequate to meet your case; and I warn you that I mean to inflict it. Why, how dare you be a widow! The court decides it is unable to put up with any such nonsense, and that you've got to stop it at once."

"Really," said she, tossing her head and moving swiftly, "one would think we *were* on a desert island!"

"Or a strange roof"—and I laughed, contentedly. "Meanwhile, about that ring—it should be, I think, a heavy, Byzantine ring, with the stones sunk deep in the dull gold. Yes, we'll have six stones in it; say, R, a ruby; O, an opal; B, a beryl; E, an emerald; R, a ruby again, I suppose; and T, a topaz. Elena, that's the very ring I mean to buy as soon as I've had breakfast, tomorrow, as a token of my mortgage on the desire of the world, and as the badge of your impendent slavery." And I reflected that Rosalind had, after all, behaved commendably in humiliating me by so promptly returning this ring.

Very calmly Elena Barry-Smith regarded the Bay of Naples; very calmly she turned to the Taj Mahal. "An obese young Lochinvar," she reflected aloud, "who has seen me twice, unblushingly assumes he is about to marry me! Of course," she sighed, quite tolerantly, "I know he is clean out of his head, for otherwise—" "Yes,—otherwise?" I prompted.

"—he would never ask me to wear an opal. Why," she cried in horror, "I couldn't think of it!" "You mean—?" said I.

She closed the album, with firmness. "Why, you are just a child," said Mrs. Barry-Smith. "We are utter strangers to each other. Please remember that, for all you know, I may have an unbridled temper, or an imported complexion, or a liking for old man Ibsen. What you ask— only you don't, you simply assume it,—is preposterous. And besides, opals *are* unlucky."

"Desire o' the world," I said, in dolorous wise, "I have just remembered the black-lace mitts and reticule you left upon the dinner-table. Oh, truly, I had meant to bring 'em to you—Only *do* you think it quite good form to put on those cloth-sided shoes when you've been invited to a real party?"

For a moment Mrs. Barry-Smith regarded me critically. Then she shook her head, and tried to frown, and reopened the album, and inspected the crater of Vesuvius, and quite frankly laughed. And a tender, pink-tipped hand rested upon my arm for an instant,—a brief instant, yet pulsing with a sense of many lights and of music playing somewhere, and of a man's heart keeping time to it.

"If you were to make it an onyx—" said Mrs. Barry-Smith.

Chapter 21

He is Urged to Desert His Galley

She had been a widow even when I first encountered her in Liege. I may have passed her dozens of times, only she was in mourning then, for Barry-Smith, and so I never really saw her.

It seems, though, that "in the second year" it is permissible to wear pink garments in the privacy of your own apartments, and that if people see you in them, accidentally, it is simply their own fault.

And very often they are punished for it; as most certainly was I, for Elena led me a devil's dance of jealousy, and rapture, and abject misery, and suspicion, and supreme content, that next four months. She and her mother had rented a house on Regis Avenue for the winter; and I frequented it with zeal. Mrs. Vokins said I "came reg'lar as the milkman."

2

Now of Mrs. Vokins I desire to speak with the greatest respect, if only for the reason that she was Elena Barry-Smith's mother. Mrs. Vokins had, no doubt, the kindest heart in the world; but she had spent the first thirty years of her life in a mountain-girdled village, and after her husband's wonderful luck—if you will permit me her vernacular,—in being "let in on the groundfloor" when the Amalgamated Tobacco Company was organised, I believe that Mrs. Vokins was never again quite at ease.

I am abysmally sure she never grew accustomed to being waited on by any servant other than a girl who "came in by the day"; though, oddly enough, she was incessantly harassed by the suspicion that one or another "good-for-nothing nigger was getting ready to quit." Her time was about equally devoted to tending her canary, Bill Bryan, and to furthering an apparently diurnal desire to have supper served a quarter of an hour earlier tonight, "so that the servants can get off."

Finally Mrs. Vokins considered that "a good woman's place was right in her own home, with a nice clean kitchen," and was used to declare that the fummadiddles of Mrs. Carrie Nation—who was in New York that winter, you may remember, advocating Prohibition,—would never have been stood for where Mrs. Vokins was riz. Them Yankee huzzies, she estimated, did beat her time.

3

It was, and is, the oddest thing I ever knew of that Elena could have been her daughter. Though, mind you, even today, I cannot commit myself to any statement whatever as concerns Elena Barry-Smith, beyond asserting that she was beautiful. I am willing to concede that since the world's creation there may have lived, say, six or seven women who were equally good to look upon; but at the bottom of my heart I know the concession is simply verbal. For she was not pretty; she was not handsome; she was beautiful. Indeed, I sometimes thought her beauty overshadowed any serious consideration of the woman who wore it, just as in admiration of a picture you rarely think to wonder what sort of canvas it is painted on.

Yes, I am quite sure, upon reflection, that to Elena Barry-Smith her beauty was a sort of tyrant. She devoted her life, I think, to the retention of her charms; and what with the fixed seven hours for sleep—no more and not a moment less,—the rigid limits of her diet, the walking of exactly five miles a day, and her mathematical adherence to a predetermined programme of massage and hair-treatment and manicuring and face-creams and so on, Elena had hardly two hours in a day at her own disposal.

She would as soon have thought of sacrificing her afternoon walk to the Musgrave Monument and back, as of having a front-tooth unnecessarily removed; and would as willingly have partaken of prussic acid as of candy or potatoes. She was, in fine, an artist of the truest type, in that she immolated her body, and her own preferences, in the cause of beauty.

Nor was she vain, or stupid either, though what I have written vaguely sounds as though she were both. She was just Elena Barry-Smith, of whom your memory was always how beautiful she had been at this or that particular moment, rather than what she said or did. And I believe that every man in Lichfield was in love with her.

But, in recollection of any person with whom you have had intimate and tender intercourse, the pre-eminent feature is the big host of questions which you cannot answer, or not, at least, with certainty. . .

FOR INSTANCE: THE NIGHT OF the Allardyce dance, after seeing Elena home, I stepped in for a moment to get warm and have her mix me a highball. We sat for a considerable while on the long sofa in the dimly-lighted dining room, talking in whispers so as not to disturb the rest of the house: and Elena was unusually beautiful that night, and I was more than usually in love, more thanks to three of the five drinks she mixed. . .

"You ought to be ashamed of yourself," she stated, sighing.

I did not say anything.

"Oh, well, then—! If you will just promise me," she stipulated, "that you will never in any way refer to it afterwards—"

So I promised. . . And the next day she met me, cool as the proverbial cucumber, and never once did she "refer to it afterwards," nor did I think it wise to do so either. But the incident, however delightful, puzzled me. It puzzles me even now. . .

5

IN ANY EVENT, SHE WAS not only beautiful but exceedingly well-to-do likewise, since her dead father and her husband also had provided for her amply; and Lichfield sniggered in consequence, and as a matter of course assumed my devotion to be of astute and mercenary origin. But I had, in this period, a variety of reasons to know that Lichfield was for once entirely in the wrong; and that what Lichfield mistook to be the begetter of, was in reality—so we will phrase it—the almost unnecessary augmenter of my infatuation. Of course I did not exactly object to her having money. . .

Meantime Elena was profoundly various. I told her once that being married to her would be the very next thing to owning a harem. And in consequence of this same mutability, it was as late as March before Elena Barry-Smith made up her mind to marry me; and I was so deliciously perturbed that the same night I wrote to tell Bettie Hamlyn all about it. I had accepted Rosalind more calmly somehow. Now I was dithyrambic; and you would never have suspected I had lived within fifty miles of Bettie for an entire two years without attempting to communicate with her, for very certainly my letter did not touch upon the fact. I was, in fine, supremely happy, and I wanted Bettie, first of all, to know of this circumstance, because my happiness had always made her happy too.

The act was natural enough; only Elena telephoned, at nine the following morning, that she had altered her intention.

"My regret is beyond expression," said I, politely, "I shall come for my tea at five, however."

She entered upon a blurred protest. "You have already broken my heart," I said, with some severity, "and now it would appear you contemplate swindling the remainder of my anatomy out of its deserts. You are a curmudgeon." And I hung up the receiver.

And my first thought was, "Oh, how gladly I would give the gold of Ormus and of Alaska just to have my letter back!" But I had mailed it, shuffling to the corner in my slippers, and without any collar on, in the hushed middle of the night, because my letter had seemed so important then.

6

"WILL YOU NOT HAVE ME, lady?" I began that afternoon.

"No, my lord," she demurely responded, "for I've decided it would be too much like living in my Sunday-clothes."

And "I give it up. So what's the answer?" was my annotation.

"Oh, I'm not making jokes today. Why are you so—Oh, as we used to say at school," she re-began, *"Que diable allais-tu faire dans cette galere?"*

"I was born in a vale of tears, Elena, and must take the consequences of being found in such a situation."

She came to me, and her finger-tips touched my hand ever so lightly. "That is another quotation, I suppose. And it is one other reason why I mean not to marry you. Frankly, you bore me to death with your erudition; you are three-quarters in love with me, but you pay heaps less attention to what I say about anything than to what Aristotle or some other old fellow said about it. Oh, that I should have lived to be jealous of Aristotle! Indeed I am, for I have the misfortune to be hideously in love with you. You are so exactly the sort of infant I would like to adopt."

"Love," I suggested, "while no longer an excuse for marriage, is at least a palliation."

"Listen, dear. From the first I have liked you, but that was not very strange, because I like almost everybody; but it was strange I should have remembered you and have liked the idea of you ever since you went away that first time."

"Oh, well, this once I will excuse you—"

"But it happened in this way: I had found everybody—very nice, you know—particularly the men,—and the things which cannot be laughed at I had always put aside as not worth thinking about. You like to laugh, too, but I have always known—and sometimes it gets me real mad to think about it, I can tell you—that you could be in earnest if you chose, and I can't. And that makes me a little sorry and tremendously glad, because, quite frankly, I *am* head over heels in love with you. That is why I don't intend to marry you."

And I was not a little at sea. "Oh, very well!" I pleasantly announced, "I shall become a prominent citizen at once, if that's all that is necessary. I will join every one of the patriotic societies, and sit perpetually on platforms with a perspiring water-pitcher, and unveil things every week, with felicitous allusions to the glorious past of our grand old State; and have columns of applause in brackets on the front page of the *Courier-Herald*. I will even go into civic politics, if you insist upon it, and leave round-cornered cards at all the drugstores, so that everybody who buys a cigar will know I am subject to the Democratic primary. I wonder, by the way, if people ever survive that malady? It sounds to me a deal more dangerous that epilepsy, say, yet lots of persons seem to have it—"

But Elena was not listening. "You know," she re-began, "I could get out of it all very gracefully by telling you you drink too much. You couldn't argue it, you know—particularly after your behavior last Tuesday."

"Oh, now and then one must be sociable. You aren't a prude, Elena—"

"However, I am not really afraid of that, somehow. I even confess I don't actually *mind* your being rather good for nothing. No woman ever really does, though she has her preference, and pretends, of course, to mind a great deal. What I mean, then, is this: You don't marry just me. I—I have very few relations, just two brothers and my mother; yet, in a sense, you know, you marry them as well. But I don't believe you would like being married to them. They are so different from you, dear. Your whole view-point of life is different—"

I had begun to speak when she broke in: "No, don't say anything, please, until I'm quite, quite through. My brothers are the most admirable men I ever knew. I love them more than I can say. I trust them more than I do you. But they are just *good*. They don't fail in the really important things of life, but they are remiss in little ways, they—they don't *care* for the little elegantnesses, if that's a word. Even Arthur chews tobacco when he feels inclined. And he thinks no *man* would smoke a cigarette. Oh, I can't explain just what I mean—"

"I think I understand, Elena. Suppose we let it pass as said."

"And Mamma is not—we'll say, particularly highly educated. Oh, you've been very nice to her. She adores you. You won *her* over completely when you took so much trouble to get her the out-of-print paper novels—about the village maidens and the wicked dukes—in that idiotic Carnation Series she is always reading. The whole affair was just like both of you, I think."

"But, oh, my dear—!" I laughed.

"No, not one man in a thousand would have remembered it after she had said she did think the titles 'were real tasty'; and I don't believe any other man in the world would have spent a week in rummaging the second-hand bookstores, until he found them. Only I don't know, even yet, whether it was really kindness, or just cleverness that put you up to it—on account of me. And I do know that you are nice to her in pretty much the same way you were nice to the negro cook yesterday. And I have had more advantages than she's had. But at bottom I'm really just like her. You'd find it out some day. And—and that is what I mean, I think."

I spoke at some length. It was atrocious nonsense which I spoke; in any event, it looked like atrocious nonsense when I wrote it down just now, and so I tore it up. But I was quite sincere throughout that moment; it is the Townsend handicap, I suspect, always to be perfectly sincere for the moment.

"Oh, well!" she said; "I'll think about it."

7

THAT NIGHT ELENA AND I played bridge against Nannie Allsotts and Warwick Risby. I was very much in love with Elena, but I hold it against her, even now, that she insisted on discarding from strength. However, there was to be a little supper afterward, and you may depend upon it that Mrs. Vokins was seeing to its preparation.

She came into the room about eleven o'clock, beaming with kindliness and flushed—I am sure,—by some slight previous commerce with the kitchen-fire.

"Well, well!" said Mrs. Vokins, comfortably; "and who's a-beating?"

I looked up. I must protest, until my final day, I could not help it. "Why, we is," I said.

And Nannie Allsotts giggled, ever so slightly, and Warwick Risby had half risen, with a quite infuriate face, and I knew that by tomorrow the affair would be public property, and promptly lost the game and rubber. Afterward we had our supper.

When the others had gone—for my footing in the house was such that I, by ordinary, stayed a moment or two after the others had gone,— Elena Barry-Smith came to me and soundly boxed my jaws.

"That," she said, "is one way to deal with you."

A minute ago I had been ashamed of myself. I had not room to be that now; I was too full of anger. "I did make rather a mess of it," I equably remarked, "but, you see, Nannie had shown strength in diamonds, and I simply couldn't resist the finesse. So they made every one of their clubs. And I hadn't any business to take the chance of course at that stage, with the ace right in my hand—"

"Arthur would have said, before he'd thought of it, 'You damn fool—!' And then he would have apologised for forgetting himself in the presence of a lady," she said, in a sorry little voice. "Yes, you—you *have* hurt me," she presently continued,—"just as you meant to do, if that's a comfort to you. I feel as though I'd smacked a marble statue. You are the sort that used to take snuff just before they had their heads cut off, and when *they* were in the wrong. And I'm not. That's always been the trouble."

"Elena!" I began,—"wait, just a moment! I'm in anger now—!" It was not much to stammer out, but for me, who have the Townsend temper, it was very hard to say.

"You talk about loving me! and I believe you do love me, in at any rate a sort of way. But you'll never forget, you never *have* forgotten, those ancestors of yours who were in the House of Burgesses when I hadn't any ancestors at all. It isn't fair, because we haven't got the chance to pick our parents, and it's absurd, and—it's true. The woman is my mother, and I'll be like her some day, very probably. Yes, she *is* ignorant and tacky, and at times she is ridiculous. She hadn't even the smartness to notice it when you made a fool of her; and if anybody were to explain it to her she would just laugh and say, 'Law, I don't mind, because young people always have to have their fun, I reckon.' And she would forgive you! Why, she adores you! she's been telling me for months that you're 'a heap the nicest young man that visits with me.'"

Afterward Elena paused for an instant. "I think that is all," she said. "It's a difference that isn't curable. Yes, I simply wanted to tell you that much, and then ask you to go, I believe—"

"So you don't wish me, Elena, in the venerable phrase, to make an honest woman of you?"

She had half turned, standing, in pink and silver fripperies, with one bared arm resting on the chair back, in one of her loveliest attitudes. "What do you mean?"

"I was referring to what happened the other night, after the Allardyce dance."

And Elena smiled rather strangely. "You baby! how much would it shock you if I told you no woman really minds about that either? Any way, you have broken your solemn promise," she said, with indignation.

"Ah, but perfidy seemed, somehow, in tone with an establishment wherein one concludes the evening's entertainment by physical assault upon the guests. Frankly, my dear"—I observed, with my most patronizing languor,—"your breeding is not quite that to which I have been accustomed, and I have had a rather startling glimpse of Lena Vokins, with all the laboriously acquired veneering peeling off. Still, in view of everything, I suppose I do owe it to you to marry you, if you insist—"

"Insist! I wouldn't wipe my feet on you!"

"That especial demonstration of affection was not, as I recall, requested of you. So it is all off? along with the veneering, eh? Well, perhaps I did attach too much importance to that diverting epilogue to the Allardyce dance. And as you say, Elena—and I take your word for it, gladly,—once one has become used to granting these little favors indiscriminately—"

"Get out of my house!" Elena said, quite splendid in her fury, "or I will have you horsewhipped. I was fond of you. You would not let me be in peace. And I didn't know you until tonight for the sneering, stuck-up dirty beast you are at heart—" She came nearer, and her glittering eyes narrowed. "And you have no hold on me, no letters to blackmail me with, and nobody anywhere would take your word for anything against mine. You would only be whipped by some real man, and probably shot. So do you remember to keep a watch upon that lying, sneering mouth of yours! And do you get out of my house!"

"It is only rented," I submitted: "yet, after all, to boast vaingloriously of their possessions is pardonable in those who have risen in the world, and aren't quite accustomed to it. . ." There were a pair of us when it came to tempers.

8

AND I WENT HOMEWARD ALMOST physically sick with rage. I knew, even then, that, while Elena would forgive me in the outcome, if I set about the matter properly, I could never bring myself to ask forgiveness. If only she had been in the wrong, I could have eagerly gone back and have submitted to the extremest and the most outrageous tyranny she could devise.

But—although I would never have blackmailed her, I think,—she had been mainly in the right. She had humiliated me, with a certain lack of decorum, to be sure, but with some justice: and to pardon plain retaliation is beyond the compass of humanity. At least, it ranks among achievements which have always baffled me.

Chapter 22

He Cleans the Slate

I t was within a month of this other disaster that Jasper Hardress came
to America, accompanied by his wife. They planned a tour of the
States, which they had not visited in seven years, and more particularly,
as his forerunning letter said, they meant to investigate certain mining
properties which Hardress had acquired in Montana. So, not unstirred
by trepidations, I met them at the pier.

For I was already in New York, in part to see a volume of my short
stories through the press—which you may or may not have read, in its
elaborate "gift-book" form, under the title of *The Aspirants*,—and in
part about less edifying employments. I was trying to forget Elena, and
in Lichfield it was not possible to induce such forgetfulness without
affording unmerited pleasure for gabbling busybodies. . . It was not in
me to apologise, except in a letter, where the wording and interminable
tinkering with phraseology would enable me to forget it was I who
was apologising, until a bit of nearly perfect prose was safely mailed;
and I knew she would not read any letter from me, because Elena
comprehended that I always persuaded her to do what I prompted, if
only she listened to me.

As it was, I talked that morning for an hour or more with fat Jasper
Hardress. . . Even now I find the two errands which brought him to
America of not unlaughable incongruity.

2

For, first, he came as an agent of the Philomatheans, who were
endeavouring to secure official recognition by the churches of America
and England of a revised translation of, in any event, the New Testament.

He told me of a variety of buttressing reasons,—which I suppose
are well-founded, though I must confess I never investigated the matter.
He told me how the Authorised Version was a paraphrase, abounding
in confusions and in mistranslations from the Greek of Erasmus's
New Testament, which, as the author confessed, "was rather tumbled
headlong into the world than edited." And he told me how the edition

of Erasmus itself was hastily prepared from careless copies of inaccurate transcriptions of yet further copies of divers manuscripts of which the oldest dates no further back than the fourth century, and is in turn, most probably, just a liberal paraphrase, as all the others are, of still another manuscript.

So that the English version, as I gathered, may be very fine English, but has scarcely a leg left, when you consider it as a safe foundation for superiority, or pillorying, or as a guide in conduct.

I suspect, however, that Jasper Hardress somewhat overstated the case, since on this subject he was a fanatic. To me it seemed rather quaint that Hardress or anybody else should be bothering about such things.

And as he feelingly declaimed concerning the great Uncials, and explained why in this particular verse the Ephraem manuscript was in the right, whereas to probe the meaning of the following verse we clearly must regard the Syriac version as of supreme authority, I could well understand how at one period or another his young wife must inevitably have considered him in the light of a rather tedious person.

And I told him that it hardly mattered, because the true test of a church-member was the ability to believe that when the Bible said anything inconvenient it really meant something else.

But actually I was not feeling over-cheerful, because Jasper's second object in coming to America was to leave his wife in Sioux City, so that she could secure a divorce from him, on quite un-Scriptural grounds. Hardress told me of this at least without any excitement. He did not blame her. He was too old for her, too stolid, too dissimilar in every respect, he said. Their marriage had been a mistake, that was all,—a mismating, as many marriages were. She wanted to marry someone else, he rather thought.

And "Oh, Lord! yes!" I inwardly groaned. "She probably does."

Aloud I said: "But the Bible—Yes, I *am* provincial at bottom. It's because I always think in nigger-English and translate it when I talk. It was my Mammy, you see, who taught me how to think,—and in our nigger-English, what the Bible says is true. Why, Jasper, even this Revised Version of yours says flatly that a man—"

"Child, child!" said Jasper Hardress, and he patted my hair, and I really think it crinkled under his touch, "when you grow up—if indeed you ever do,—you will find that a man's feeling for his wife and the mother of his children, is not altogether limited by what he has read in a book. He wants—well, just her happiness."

I looked up without thinking; and the aspect of that gross and unattractive man humiliated me. He had reached a height denied to such as I; and inwardly I cursed and envied this fat Jasper Hardress. . . I would have told him everything, had not the waiter come just then.

3

AND THE SAME AFTERNOON I was alone with Gillian Hardress, for the first time in somewhat more than two years. We had never written each other; I had been too cautious for that; and now when the lean, handsome woman came toward me, murmuring "Jack—" very tenderly,—for she had always called me Jack, you may remember,—I raised a hand in protest.

"No,—that is done with, Jill. That is dead and buried now, my dear."

She remained motionless; only her eyes, which were like chrysoberyls, seemed to grow larger and yet more large. There was no anger in them, only an augmenting wonder.

"Ah, yes," she said at last, and seemed again to breathe; "so that is dead and buried—in two years." Gillian Hardress spoke with laborious precision, like a person struggling with a foreign language, and articulating each word to its least sound before laying tongue to its successor.

"Yes! we have done with each other, once for all," said I, half angrily. "I wash my hands of the affair, I clean the slate today. I am not polite about it, and—I am sorry, dear. But I talked with your husband this morning, and I will deceive Jasper Hardress no longer. The man loves you as I never dreamed of loving any woman, as I am incapable of loving any woman. He dwarfs us. Oh, go and tell him, so that he may kill us both! I wish to God he would!"

Mrs. Hardress said: "You have planned to marry. It is time the prodigal marry and settle down, is it not? So long as we were in England it did not matter, except to that Faroy girl you seduced and flung out into the streets—"

"I naturally let her go when I found out—"

"As if I cared about the creature! She's done with. But now we are in America, and Mr. Townsend desires no entanglements just now that might prevent an advantageous marriage. So he is smitten—very conveniently—with remorse." Gillian began to laugh. "And he discovers that Jasper Hardress is a better man than he. Have I not always known that, Jack?"

Now came a silence. "I cannot argue with you as to my motives. Let us have no scene, my dear——"

"God keep us respectable!" the woman said; and then: "No; I can afford to make no scene. I can only long to be omnipotent for just one instant that I might deal with you, Robert Townsend, as I desire—and even then, heaven help me, I would not do it!" Mrs. Hardress sat down upon the divan and laughed, but this time naturally. "So! it is done with? I have had my dismissal, and, in common justice, you ought to admit that I have received it not all ungracefully."

"From the first," I said, "you have been the most wonderful woman I have ever known." And I knew that I was sincerely fond of Gillian Hardress.

"But please go now," she said, "and have a telegram this evening that will call you home, or to Kamchatka, or to Ecuador, or anywhere, on unavoidable business. No, it is not because I loathe the sight of you or for any melodramatic reason of that sort. It is because, I think, I had fancied you to be not completely self-centred, after all, and I cannot bear to face my own idiocy. Why, don't you realize it was only yesterday you borrowed money from Jasper Hardress—some more money!"

"Well, but he insisted on it: and I owed it to you to do nothing to arouse his suspicions——"

"And I don't hate you even now! I wish God would explain to me why He made women so."

"You accuse me of selfishness," I cried. "Ah, let us distinguish, for there is at times a deal of virtue in this vice. A man who devotes himself to any particular art or pursuit, for instance, becomes more and more enamoured of it as time wears on, because he comes to identify it with himself; and a husband is fonder of his wife than of any other woman,—at least, he ought to be,—not because he considers her the most beautiful and attractive person of his acquaintance, but because she is the one in whom he is most interested and concerned. He has a proprietary interest in her welfare, and she is in a manner part of himself. Thus the arts flourish and the home-circle is maintained, and all through selfishness."

I snapped my fingers airily; I was trying, of course, to disgust her by my callousness. And it appeared I had almost succeeded.

"Please go!" she said.

"But surely not while we are as yet involved in a question of plain logic? You think selfishness a vice. None the less you must concede that the world has invariably progressed because, upon the whole, we find civilisation to be more comfortable than barbarism; and that a wholesome apprehension of the penitentiary enables many of us to rise to deaconships. Why, deuce take it, Jill! I may endow a hospital because I want to see my name over the main entrance, I may give a beggar a penny because his gratitude puts me in a glow of benevolence that is cheap at the price. So let us not rashly declare that selfishness is a vice, and—let us part friends, my dear."

And I assumed possession of the thin hands that seemed to push me from her in a species of terror, and I gallantly lifted them to my lips.

The ensuing event was singular. Gillian Hardress turned to the door of her bedroom and brutally, as with two bludgeons, struck again and again upon its panels with clenched hand. She extended her hands to me, and everywhere their knuckles oozed blood. "You kissed them," she said, "and even today they liked it, and so they are not clean. They will never again be clean, my dear. But they were clean before you came."

Then Gillian Hardress left me, and where she had touched it, the brass door knob of her bedroom door was smeared with blood. . .

4

When I had come again to Lichfield I found that in the brief interim of my absence Elena Barry-Smith, without announcement, had taken the train for Washington, and had in that city married Warwick Risby. This was, I knew, because she comprehended that, if I so elected, it was always in my power to stop her halfway up the aisle and to dissuade her from advancing one step farther. . . "I don't know *how* it is!—" she would have said, in that dear quasi-petulance I knew so well. . .

But as it was, I met the two one evening at the Provises', and with exuberant congratulation. Then straddling as a young Colossus on the hearth-rug, and with an admonitory forefinger, I proclaimed to the universe at large that Mrs. Risby had blighted my existence and beseeched for Warwick some immediate and fatal and particularly excruciating malady. In fine, I was abjectly miserable the while that I disarmed all comment by being quite delightfully boyish for a whole two hours.

I must record it, though, that Mrs. Vokins patted my hand when nobody else was looking, and said: "Oh, my dear Mr. Bob, I wish it had been you! You was always the one I liked the best." For that, in view of every circumstance, was humorous, and hurt as only humour can.

So in requital, on the following morning, I mailed to Mrs. Risby some verses. This sounds a trifle like burlesque; but Elena had always a sort of superstitious reverence for the fact that I "wrote things." It would not matter at all that the verses were abominable; indeed, Elena would never discover this; she would simply set about devising an excellent reason for not showing them to anybody, and would consider Warwick Risby, if only for a moment, in the light of a person who, whatever his undeniable merits, had neither the desire nor the ability to write "poetry." And, though it was hideously petty, this was precisely what I desired her to do.

So I dispatched to her a sonnet-sequence which I had originally plagiarized from the French of Theodore Passerat in honour of Stella. I loathed sending Stella's verses to anyone else, somehow; but, after all, my one deterrent was merely a romantic notion; and there was not time to compose a new set. Moreover, "your eyes are blue, your speech is gracious, but you are not she; and I am older,—and changed how utterly!—I am no longer I, you are not you," and so on, was absolutely appropriate. And Elena most undoubtedly knew nothing of Theodore Passerat. And Stella, being dead, could never know what I had done.

So I sent the verses, with a few necessitated alterations, to the address of Mrs. Warwick Risby.

5

I HAD WITHIN THE WEEK, an unsigned communication which, for a long while afterward, I did not comprehend. It was the photograph of an infant, with the photographer's address scratched from the cardboard and without of course any decipherable postmark; and upon the back of the thing was written: "His has been the summer air, and the sunshine, and the flowers; and gentle ears have listened to him, and gentle eyes have been upon him. Let others eat his honey that please, so that he has had his morsel and his song."

I thought it was a joke of some sort.

Then it occurred to me that this might be—somehow—Elena's answer. It was an interpretation which probably appealed to the Supernal Aristophanes.

Chapter 23

He Reviles Destiny and Climbs a Wall

B ut now the spring was come again, and, as always at this season, I was pricked with vague longings to have done with roofs and paven places. I wanted to be in the open. I think I wanted to fall in love with somebody, and thereby somewhat to prolong the daily half-minute, immediately after awakening in the morning, during which I did not think about Elena Risby.

I was bored in Lichfield. For nothing of much consequence seemed, as I yawned over the morning paper, to be happening anywhere. The Illinois Legislature had broken up in a free fight, a British square had been broken in Somaliland, and at the Aqueduct track Alado had broken his jockey's neck. A mob had chased a negro up Broadway: Russia had demanded that China cede the sovereignty of Manchuria; and Dr. Lyman Abbott was explaining why the notion of equal suffrage had been abandoned finally by thinking people.

Such negligible matters contributed not at all to the comfort or the discomfort of Robert Etheridge Townsend; and I was pricked with vague sweet longings to have done with roofs and paven places. If only I possessed a country estate, a really handsome Manor or a Grange, I was reflecting as I looked over the "Social Items," and saw that Miss Hugonin and Colonel Hugonin had re-opened Selwoode for the summer months. . .

So I decided I would go to Gridlington, whither Peter Blagden had forgotten to invite me. He was extremely glad to see me, though, to do him justice. For Peter—by this time the inheritor of his unlamented uncle's estate,—had, very properly, developed gout, which is, I take it, the time-honoured appendage of affluence and, so to speak, its trade-mark; and was, for all his wealth, unable to get up and down the stairs of his fine house without, as we will delicately word it, the display and, at times, the overtaxing of a copious vocabulary.

2

I was at Gridlington entirely comfortable. It was spring, to begin with, and out of doors in spring you always know, at twenty-five, that something extremely pleasant is about to happen, and that She is quite probably around the very next turn of the lane.

Moreover, there was at Gridlington a tiny private garden which had once been the recreation of Peter Blagden's aunt (dead now twelve years ago), and which had remained untended since her cosseting; and I in nature took charge of it.

There was in the place a wilding peach-tree, which I artistically sawed into shape and pruned and grafted, and painted all those profitable wounds with tar; and I grew to love it, just as most people do their children, because it was mine. And Peter, who is a person of no sensibility, wanted to ring for a servant one night, when there was a hint of frost and I had started out to put a bucket of water under my tree to protect it. I informed him that he was irrevocably dead to all the nobler sentiments, and went to the laundry and got a wash-tub.

Peter was not infrequently obtuse. He would contend, for instance, that it was absurd for any person to get so gloriously hot and dirty while setting out plants, when that person objected to having a flower in the same room. For Peter could not understand that a cut flower is a dead or, at best, a dying thing, and therefore to considerate people is just so much abhorrent carrion; and denied it would be really quite as rational to decorate your person or your dinner table with the severed heads of chickens as with those of daffodils.

"But that is only because you are not particularly bright," I told him. "Oh, I suppose you can't help it. But why make *all* the actions of your life so foolish? What good do you get out of having the gout, for instance?"

Whereupon Mr. Blagden desired to be informed if I considered those with-various-adjectives-accompanied twinges in that qualified foot to be a source of personal pleasure to the owner of the very-extensively-hiatused foot. In which case, Mr. Blagden felt at liberty to express his opinion of my intellectual attainments, which was of an uncomplimentary nature.

"Because, you know," I pursued, equably, "you wouldn't have the gout if you did not habitually overeat yourself and drink more than is good for you. In consequence, here you are at thirty-two with a foot the same general size and shape as a hayrick, only rather less symmetrical, and quite unable to attend to the really serious business of life, which is to present me to the heiress. It is a case of vicarious punishment which strikes me as extremely unfair. You have made of your stomach a god, Peter, and I am the one to suffer for it. You have made of your stomach,"

I continued, venturing aspiringly into metaphor, "a brazen Moloch, before which you are now calmly preparing to immolate my prospects in life. You ought to be ashamed of yourself, Peter!"

Mr. Blagden's next observation was describable as impolite.

"Fate, too," I lamented, in a tragic voice, "appears to have entered into this nefarious conspiracy. Here, not two miles away, is one of the greatest heiresses in America,—clever, I am told, beautiful, I am sure, for I have yet to discover a woman who sees anything in the least attractive about her,—and, above all, with the Woods millions at her disposal. Why, Peter, Margaret Hugonin is the woman I have been looking for these last three years. She is, to a hair, the sort of woman I have always intended to make unhappy. And I can't even get a sight of her! Here are you, laid up with the gout, and unable to help me; and yonder is the heiress, making a foolish pretence at mourning for the old curmudgeon who left her all that money, and declining to meet people. Oh, but she is a shiftless woman, Peter! At this very moment she might be getting better acquainted with me; at this very moment, Peter, I might be explaining to her in what points she is utterly and entirely different from all the other women I have ever known. And she prefers to immure herself in Selwoode, with no better company than her father, that ungodly old retired colonel, and a she-cousin, somewhere on the undiscussable side of forty—when she might be engaging me in amorous dalliance! That Miss Hugonin is a shiftless woman, I tell you! And Fate—oh, but Fate, too, is a vixenish jade!" I cried, and shook my fist under the nose of an imaginary Lachesis.

"You appear," said Peter, drily, "to be unusually well-informed as to what is going on at Selwoode."

"You flatter me," I answered, as with proper modesty. "You must remember that there are maids at Selwoode. You must remember that my man Byam, is—and will be until that inevitable day when he will attempt to blackmail me, and I shall kill him in the most lingering fashion I can think of,—that Byam is, I say, something of a diplomatist."

Mr. Blagden regarded me with disapproval.

"So you've been sending your nigger cousin over to Selwoode to spy for you! You're a damn cad, you know, Bob," he pensively observed. "Now most people think that when you carry on like a lunatic you're simply acting on impulse. I don't. I believe you plan it out a week ahead. I sometimes think you are the most adroit and unblushing looker-out for number one I ever knew; and I can't for the life of me understand why I don't turn you out of doors."

"I don't know where you picked up your manners," said I, reflectively, "but it must have been in devilish low company. I would cut your acquaintance, Peter, if I could afford it." Then I fell to pacing up and down the floor. "I incline, as you have somewhat grossly suggested, to a certain favouritism among the digits. And why the deuce shouldn't I? A fortune is the only thing I need. I have good looks, you know, of a sort; ah, I'm not vain, but both my glass and a number of women have been kind enough to reassure me on this particular point. And that I have a fair amount of wits my creditors will attest, who have lived promise-crammed for the last year or two, feeding upon air like chameleons. Then I have birth,—not that good birth ensures anything but bad habits though, for you will observe that, by some curious freak of nature, an old family-tree very seldom produces anything but wild oats. And, finally, I have position. I can introduce my wife into the best society; ah, yes, you may depend upon it, Peter, she will have the privilege of meeting the very worst and stupidest and silliest people in the country on perfectly equal terms. You will perceive, then, that the one desirable thing I lack is wealth. And this I shall naturally expect my wife to furnish. So, the point is settled, and you may give me a cigarette."

Peter handed me the case, with a snort. "You are a hopelessly conceited ass," Mr. Blagden was pleased to observe, "for otherwise you would have learned, by this, that you'll, most likely, never have the luck of Charteris, and land a woman who will take it as a favour that you let her pay your bills. God knows you've angled for enough of 'em!"

"You are painfully coarse, Peter," I pointed out, with a sigh. "Indeed, your general lack of refinement might easily lead one to think you owed your millions to your own thrifty industry, or some equally unpleasant attribute, rather than to your uncle's very commendable and lucrative innovation in the line of—well, I remember it was something extremely indigestible, but, for the moment, I forget whether it was steam-reapers or a new sort of pickle. Yes, in a great many respects, you are hopelessly parvenuish. This cigarette-case, for instance—studded with diamonds and engraved with a monogram big enough for a coach-door! Why, Peter, it simply reeks with the ostentation of honestly acquired wealth,—and with very good tobacco, too, by the way. I shall take it, for I am going for a walk, and I haven't any of my own. And some day I shall pawn this jewelled abortion, Peter,—pawn it for much fine gold; and upon the proceeds I shall make merriment for myself and for my friends." And I pocketed the case.

"That's all very well," Peter growled, "but you needn't try to change the subject. You know you *have* angled after any number of rich women who have had sense enough, thank God, to refuse you. You didn't use to be—but now you're quite notoriously good-for-nothing."

"It is the one blemish," said I, sweetly, "upon an otherwise perfect character. And it is true," I continued, after an interval of meditation, "that I have, in my time, encountered some very foolish women. There was, for instance, Elena Barry-Smith, who threw me over for Warwick Risby; and Celia Reindan, who had the bad taste to prefer Teddy Anstruther; and Rosalind Jemmett, who is, very inconsiderately, going to marry Tom Gelwix, instead of me. These were staggeringly foolish women, Peter, but while their taste is bad, their dinners are good, so I have remained upon the best of terms with them. They have trodden me under their feet, but I am the long worm that has no turning. Moreover, you are doubtless aware of the axiomatic equality between the fish in the sea and those out of it. I hope before long to better my position in life. I hope—Ah, well, that would scarcely interest you. Good morning, Peter. And I trust, when I return," I added, with chastening dignity, "that you will evince a somewhat more Christian spirit toward the world in general, and that your language will be rather less reminiscent of the blood-stained buccaneer of historical fiction."

"You're a grinning buffoon," said Peter. "You're a fat Jack-pudding. You're an ass. Where are you going, anyway?"

"I am going," said I, "to the extreme end of Gridlington. Afterward I am going to climb the wall that stands between Gridlington and Selwoode."

"And after that?" said Peter.

I gave a gesture. "Why, after that," said I, "fortune will favour the brave. And I, Peter, am very, very brave."

Then I departed, whistling. In view of all my memories it had been strangely droll to worry Peter Blagden into an abuse of marrying for money. For this was on the twenty-eighth of April, the anniversary of the day that Stella had died, you may remember. . .

3

AND A HALF-HOUR SUBSEQUENTLY, TRUE to my word, I was scaling a ten-foot stone wall, thickly overgrown with ivy. At the top of it I paused, and sat down to take breath and to meditate, my legs meanwhile bedangling over an as flourishing Italian garden as you would wish to see.

"Now, I wonder," I queried, of my soul, "what will be next? There is a very cheerful uncertainty about what will be next. It may be a spring-gun, and it may be a bull-dog, and it may be a susceptible heiress. But it is apt to be—No, it isn't," I amended, promptly; "it is going to be an angel. Or perhaps it is going to be a dream. She can't be real, you know—I am probably just dreaming her. I would be quite certain I was just dreaming her, if this wall were not so humpy and uncomfortable. For it stands to reason, I would not be fool enough to dream of such unsympathetic iron spikes as I am sitting on."

"Perhaps you are not aware," hazarded a soprano voice, "that this is private property?"

"Why, no," said I, very placidly; "on the contrary I was just thinking it must be heaven. And I am tolerably certain," I commented further, in my soul, "that you are one of the more influential seraphim."

The girl had lifted her brows. She sat upon a semi-circular stone bench, some twenty feet from the wall, and had apparently been reading, for a book lay open in her lap. She now inspected me, with a sort of languid wonder in her eyes, and I returned the scrutiny with unqualified approval in mine.

And in this I had reason. The heiress of Selwoode was eminently good to look upon.

Chapter 24

He Reconciles Sentiment and Reason

So I regarded her for a rather lengthy interval, considering meanwhile, with an immeasurable content how utterly and entirely impossible it would always be to describe her.

Clearly, it would be out of the question to trust to words, however choicely picked, for, upon inspection, there was a delightful ambiguity about every one of this girl's features that defied such idiotic makeshifts. Her eyes, for example, I noted with a faint thrill of surprise, just escaped being brown by virtue of an amber glow they had; what colour, then, was I conscientiously to call them?

And her hair I found a bewildering, though pleasing, mesh of shadow and sunlight, all made up of multitudinous graduations of some anonymous colour that seemed to vary with the light you chanced to see it in, through the whole gamut of bronze and chestnut and gold; and where, pray, in the bulkiest lexicon, in the very weightiest thesaurus, was I to find the adjective which could, if but in desperation, be applied to hair like that without trenching on sacrilege? . . . For it was spring, you must remember, and I was twenty-five.

So that in my appraisal, you may depend upon it, her lips were quickly passed over as a dangerous topic, and were dismissed with the mental statement that they were red and not altogether unattractive. Whereas her cheeks baffled me for a time,—but always with a haunting sense of familiarity—till I had, at last, discovered they reminded me of those little tatters of cloud that sometimes float about the setting sun,—those irresolute wisps which cannot quite decide whether to be pink or white, and waver through their tiny lives between the two colours.

2

To this effect, then, I discoursed with my soul, what time I sat upon the wall-top and smiled and kicked my heels to and fro among the ivy. By and by, though, the girl sighed.

"You are placing me in an extremely unpleasant position," she complained, as if wearily. "Would you mind returning to your sanatorium and allowing me to go on reading? For I am interested in my book, and I can't possibly go on in any comfort so long as you elect to perch up there like Humpty-Dumpty, and grin like seven dozen Cheshire cats."

"Now, that," I spoke, in absent wise, "is but another instance of the widely prevalent desire to have me serve as scapegoat for the sins of all humanity. I am being blamed now for sitting on top of this wall. One would think I wanted to sit here. One would actually think," I cried, and raised my eyes to heaven, "that sitting on the very humpiest kind of iron spikes was my favorite form of recreation! No,—in the interests of justice," I continued, and fell into a milder tone, "I must ask you to place the blame where it more rightfully belongs. The injuries which are within the moment being inflicted on my sensitive nature, and, incidentally, upon my not overstocked wardrobe, I am willing to pass over. But the claims of justice are everywhere paramount. Miss Hugonin, and Miss Hugonin alone, is responsible for my present emulation of Mohammed's coffin, and upon that responsibility I am compelled to insist."

"May one suggest," she queried gently, "that you are probably—mistaken?"

I sketched a bow. "Recognising your present point of view," said I, gallantly, "I thank you for the kindly euphemism. But may one allowably demonstrate the fallacy of this same point of view? I thank you: for silence, I am told, is proverbially equal to assent. I am, then, one Robert Townsend, by birth a gentleman, by courtesy an author, by inclination an idler, and by lucky chance a guest of Mr. Peter Blagden, whose flourishing estate extends indefinitely yonder to the rear of my coat-tails. My hobby chances to be gardening. I am a connoisseur, an admirer, a devotee of gardens. It is, indeed, hereditary among the Townsends; a love for gardens runs in our family just as a love for gin runs in less favoured races. It is with us an irresistible passion. The very founder of our family—one Adam, whom you may have heard of,—was a gardener. Owing to the unfortunate loss of his position, the family since then has sunken somewhat in the world; but time and poverty alike have proven powerless against our horticultural tastes and botanical inclinations. And then," cried I, with a flourish, "and then, what follows logically?"

"Why, if you are not more careful," she languidly made answer, "I am afraid that, owing to the laws of gravitation, a broken neck is what follows logically."

"You are a rogue," I commented, in my soul, "and I like you all the better for it."

Aloud, I stated: "What follows is that we can no more keep away from a creditable sort of garden than a moth can from a lighted candle. Consider, then, my position. Here am I on one side of the wall, and with my peach-tree, to be sure—but on the other side is one of the most famous masterpieces of formal gardening in the whole country. Am I to blame if I succumb to the temptation? Surely not," I argued; "for surely to any fair-minded person it will be at once apparent that I am brought to my present very uncomfortable position upon the points of these very humpy iron spikes by a simple combination of atavism and injustice,—atavism because hereditary inclination draws me irresistibly to the top of the wall, and injustice because Miss Hugonin's perfectly unreasonable refusal to admit visitors prevents my coming any farther. Surely, that is at once apparent?"

But now the girl yielded to my grave face, and broke into a clear, rippling carol of mirth. She laughed from the chest, this woman. And perched in insecure discomfort on my wall, I found time to rejoice that I had finally discovered that rarity of rarities, a woman who neither giggles nor cackles, but has found the happy mean between these two abominations, and knows how to laugh.

"I have heard of you, Mr. Townsend," she said at last. "Oh, yes, I have heard a deal of you. And I remember now that I never heard you were suspected of sanity."

"Common-sense," I informed her, from my pedestal, "is confined to that decorous class of people who never lose either their tempers or their umbrellas. Now, I haven't any temper to speak of—or not at least in the presence of ladies,—and, so far, I have managed to avoid laying aside anything whatever for a rainy day; so that it stands to reason I must possess uncommon sense."

"If that is the case," said the girl "you will kindly come down from that wall and attempt to behave like a rational being."

I was down—as the phrase runs,—in the twinkling of a bed-post. On which side of the wall, I leave you to imagine.

"—For I am sure," the girl continued, "that I—that Margaret, I should say,—would not object in the least to your seeing the gardens, since they interest you so tremendously. I'm Avis Beechinor, you know,—Miss Hugonin's cousin. So, if you like, we will consider that a proper introduction, Mr. Townsend, and I will show you the gardens, if—if you really care to see them."

My face, I must confess, had fallen slightly. Up to this moment, I had not a suspicion but that it was Miss Hugonin I was talking to: and

I now reconsidered, with celerity, the information Byam had brought me from Selwoode.

"For, when I come to think of it," I reflected, "he simply said she was older than Miss Hugonin. I embroidered the tale so glibly for Peter's benefit that I was deceived by my own ornamentations. I had looked for corkscrew ringlets and false teeth a-gleam like a new bath-tub in Miss Hugonin's cousin,—not an absolutely, supremely, inexpressibly unthinkable beauty like this!" I cried, in my soul. "Older! Why, good Lord, Miss Hugonin must be an infant in arms!"

But my audible discourse was prefaced with an eloquent gesture. "If I'd care!" I said. "Haven't I already told you I was a connoisseur in gardens? Why, simply look, Miss Beechinor!" I exhorted her, and threw out my hands in a large pose of admiration. "Simply regard those yew-hedges, and parterres, and grassy amphitheatres, and palisades, and statues, and cascades, and everything—*everything* that goes to make a formal garden the most delectable sight in the world! Simply feast your eyes upon those orderly clipped trees and the fantastic patterns those flowers are laid out in! Why, upon my word, it looks as if all four books of Euclid had suddenly burst into blossom! And you ask me if I would *care*! Ah, it is evident *you* are not a connoisseur in gardens, Miss Beechinor!"

And I had started on my way into this one, when the girl stopped me.

"This must be yours," she said. "You must have spilled it coming over the wall, Mr. Townsend."

It was Peter's cigarette-case.

"Why, dear me, yes!" I assented, affably. "Do you know, now, I would have been tremendously sorry to lose that? It is a sort of present—an unbirthday present from a quite old friend."

She turned it over in her hand.

"It's very handsome," she marvelled. "Such a pretty monogram! Does it stand for Poor Idiot Boy?"

"Eh?" said I. "P.I.B., you mean? No, that stands for Perfectly Immaculate Behaviour. My friend gave it to me because, he said, I was so good. And—oh, well, he added a few things to that,—partial sort of a friend, you know,—and, really—Why, really, Miss Beechinor, it would embarrass me to tell you what he added," I protested, and modestly waved the subject aside.

"Now that," my meditations ran, "is the absolute truth. Peter did tell me I was good. And it really would embarrass me to tell her he added 'for-nothing.' So, this far, I have been a model of veracity."

Then I took the case,—gaining thereby the bliss of momentary contact with a velvet-soft trifle that seemed, somehow, to set my own grosser hand a-tingle—and I cried: "Now, Miss Beechinor, you must show me the pergola. I am excessively partial to pergolas."

And in my soul, I wondered what a pergola looked like, and why on earth I had been fool enough to waste the last three days in bedeviling Peter, and how under the broad canopy of heaven I could ever have suffered from the delusion that I had seen a really adorable woman before today.

3

But, "She is entirely too adorable," I reasoned with myself, some three-quarters of an hour later. "In fact, I regard it as positively inconsiderate in any impecunious young person to venture to upset me in the way she has done. Why, my heart is pounding away inside me like a trip-hammer, and I am absolutely light-headed with good-will and charity and benevolent intentions toward the entire universe! Oh, Avis, Avis, you know you hadn't any right to put me in this insane state of mind!"

I was, at this moment, retracing my steps toward the spot where I had climbed the wall between Gridlington and Selwoode, but I paused now to outline a reproachful gesture in the direction from which I came.

"What do you mean by having such a name?" I queried, sadly. "Avis! Why, it is the very soul of music, clear, and sweet and as insistent as a bird-call, an unforgettable lyric in four letters! It is just the sort of name a fellow cannot possibly forget. Why couldn't you have been named Polly or Lena or Margaret, or something commonplace like that, Avis—dear?"

And the juxtaposition of these words appealing to my sense of euphony, I repeated it, again and again, each time with a more relishing gusto. "Avis dear! dear Avis! dear, *dear* Avis!" I experimented. "Why, each one is more hopelessly unforgettable than the other! Oh, Avis dear, why are you so absolutely and entirely unforgettable all around? Why do you ripple all your words together in that quaint fashion till it sounds like a brook discoursing? Why did you crinkle up your eyes when I told you that as yet unbotanised flower was a *Calycanthus arithmelicus*? And why did you pout at me, Avis dear? A fellow finds it entirely too hard to forget things like that. And, oh, dear Avis, if you only knew what nearly happened when you pouted!"

I had come to the wall by this, but again I paused to lament.

"It is very inconsiderate of her, very thoughtless indeed. She might at least have asked my permission, before upsetting my plans in life. I had firmly intended to marry a rich woman, and now I am forming all sorts of preposterous notions—"

Then, on the bench where I had first seen her, I perceived a book. It was the iron-gray book she had been reading when I interrupted her, and I now picked it up with a sort of reverence. I regarded it as an extremely lucky book.

Subsequently, "Good Lord!" said I, aloud, "what luck!"

For between the pages of Justus Miles Forman's *Journey's End*— serving as a book-mark, according to a not infrequent shiftless feminine fashion,—lay a handkerchief. It was a flimsy, inadequate trifle, fringed with a tiny scallopy black border; and in one corner the letters M. E. A. H., all askew, contorted themselves into any number of flourishes and irrelevant tendrils.

"Now M. E. A. H. does not stand by any stretch of the imagination for Avis Beechinor. Whereas it fits Margaret Elizabeth Anstruther Hugonin uncommonly well. I wonder now—?"

I wondered for a rather lengthy interval.

"So Byam was right, after all. And Peter was right, too. Oh, Robert Etheridge Townsend, your reputation must truly be malodorous, when at your approach timid heiresses seek shelter under an alias! 'I have heard a deal of you, Mr. Townsend'—ah, yes, she had heard. She thought I would make love to her out of hand, I suppose, because she was wealthy—"

I presently flung back my head and laughed.

"Eh, well! I will let no sordid considerations stand in the way of my true interests. I will marry this Margaret Hugonin even though she is rich. You have begun the comedy, my lady, and I will play it to the end. Yes, I fell honestly in love with you when I thought you were nobody in particular. So I am going to marry this Margaret Hugonin if she will have me; and if she won't, I am going to commit suicide on her door-step, with a pathetic little note in my vest-pocket forgiving her in the most noble and wholesale manner for irrevocably blighting a future so rich in promise. Yes, that is exactly what I am going to do if she does not appreciate her wonderful good fortune. And if she'll have me—why, I wouldn't change places with the Pope of Rome or the Czar of all the Russias! Ah, no, not I! for I prefer, upon the whole, to be immeasurably, and insanely, and unreasonably, and unadulteratedly happy. Why, but just to think of an adorable girl like that having so much money!"

All in all, my meditations were incoherent but very pleasurable.

Chapter 25

He Advances in the Attack on Selwoode

"Well?" said Peter.

"Well?" said I.

"What's the latest quotation on heiresses?" Mr. Blagden demanded. "Was she cruel, my boy, or was she kind? Did she set the dog on you or have you thrashed by her father? I fancy both, for your present hilarity is suggestive of a gentleman in the act of attendance on his own funeral." And Peter laughed, unctuously, for his gout slumbered.

"His attempts at wit," I reflectively confided to my wine-glass, "while doubtless amiably intended, are, to his well-wishers, painful. I daresay, though, he doesn't know it. We must, then, smile indulgently upon the elephantine gambols of what he is pleased to describe as his intellect."

"Now, that," Peter pointed out, "is not what I would term a courteous method of discussing a man at his own table. You are damn disagreeable this morning, Bob. So I know, of course, that you have come another cropper in your fortune-hunting."

"Peter," said I, in admiration, "your sagacity at times is almost human! I have spent a most enjoyable day, though," I continued, idly. "I have been communing with Nature, Peter. She is about her spring-cleaning in the woods yonder, and everywhere I have seen traces of her getting things fixed for the summer. I have seen the sky, which was washed overnight, and the sun, which has evidently been freshly enamelled. I have seen the new leaves as they swayed and whispered over your extensive domains, with the fret of spring alert in every sap cell. I have seen the little birds as they hopped among said leaves and commented upon the scarcity of worms. I have seen the buxom flowers as they curtsied and danced above your flower-beds like a miniature comic-opera chorus. And besides that—"

"Yes?" said Peter, with a grin, "and besides that?"

"And besides that," said I, firmly, "I have seen nothing."

And internally I appraised this bloated Peter Blagden, and reflected that this was the man whom Stella had loved; and I appraised myself, and remembered that this had been the boy who once loved Stella. For, as I have said, it was the twenty-eighth of April, the day that Stella had died, two years ago.

THE NEXT MORNING I DISCOURSED with my soul, what time I sat upon the wall-top and smiled and kicked my heels to and fro among the ivy.

"For, in spite of appearances," I debated with myself, "it is barely possible that the handkerchief was not hers. She may have borrowed it or have got it by mistake, somehow. In which case, it is only reasonable to suppose that she will miss it, and ask me if I saw it; on the contrary, if the handkerchief is hers, she will naturally understand, when I return the book without it, that I have feloniously detained this airy gewgaw as a souvenir, as, so to speak, a *gage d'amour*. And, in that event, she ought to be very much pleased and a bit embarrassed; and she will preserve upon the topic of handkerchiefs a maidenly silence. Do you know, Robert Etheridge Townsend, there is about you the making of a very fine logician?"

Then I consulted my watch, and subsequently grimaced. "It is also barely possible," said I, "that Margaret may not come at all. In which case— Margaret! Now, isn't that a sweet name? Isn't it the very sweetest name in the world? Now, really, you know, it is queer her being named Margaret— extraordinarily queer,—because Margaret has always been my favourite woman's name. I daresay, unbeknownst to myself, I am a bit of a prophet."

3

BUT SHE DID COME. SHE was very much surprised to see me.

"You!" she said, with a gesture which was practically tantamount to disbelief. "Why, how extraordinary!"

"You rogue!" I commented, internally: "you know it is the most natural thing in the world." Aloud I stated: "Why, yes, I happened to notice you forgot your book yesterday, so I dropped in—or, to be more accurate, climbed up,—to return it."

She reached for it. Our hands touched, with the usual result to my pulses. Also, there were the customary manual tinglings.

"You are very kind," was her observation, "for I am wondering which one of the two he will marry."

"Forman tells me he has no notion, himself."

"Oh, then you know Justus Miles Forman! How nice! I think his stories are just splendid, especially the way his heroes talk to photographs and handkerchiefs and dead flowers—"

Afterward she opened the book, and turned over its pages expectantly, and flushed a proper shade of pink, and said nothing.

And then, and not till then, my heart consented to resume its normal functions. And then, also, "These iron spikes—" said its owner.

"Yes?" she queried, innocently.

"—so humpy," I complained.

"Are they?" said she. "Why, then, how silly of you to continue to sit on them!"

The result of this comment was that we were both late for luncheon.

4

BY A PECULIAR COINCIDENCE, AT twelve o'clock the following day, I happened to be sitting on the same wall at the same spot. Peter said at luncheon it was a queer thing that some people never could manage to be on time for their meals.

I fancy we can all form a tolerably accurate idea of what took place during the next day or so.

It is scarcely necessary to retail our conversations. We gossiped of simple things. We talked very little; and, when we did talk, the most ambitiously preambled sentences were apt to result in nothing more prodigious than a wave of the hand, and a pause, and, not infrequently, a heightened complexion. Altogether, then, it was not oppressively wise or witty talk, but it was eminently satisfactory to its makers.

As when, on the third morning, I wished to sit by Margaret on the bench, and she declined to invite me to descend from the wall.

"On the whole," said she, "I prefer you where you are; like all picturesque ruins, you are most admirable at a little distance."

"Ruins!"—and, indeed, I was not yet twenty-six,—"I am a comparatively young man."

As a concession, "In consideration of your past, you are tolerably well preserved."

"—and I am not a new brand of marmalade, either."

"No, for that comes in glass jars; whereas, Mr. Townsend, I have heard, is more apt to figure in family ones."

"A pun, Miss Beechinor, is the base coinage of conversation tendered only by the mentally dishonest."

"—Besides, one can never have enough of marmalade."

"I trust they give you a sufficiency of it in the nursery?"

"Dear me, you have no idea how admirably that paternal tone sits upon you! You would make an excellent father, Mr. Townsend. You really ought to adopt someone. I wish you would adopt *me*, Mr. Townsend."

I said I had other plans for her. Discreetly, she forbore to ask what they were.

5

"Avis—"

"You must not call me that."

"Why not? It's your name, isn't it"

"Yes,—to my friends."

"Aren't we friends—Avis?"

"We! We have not known each other long enough, Mr. Townsend."

"Oh, what's the difference? We are going to be friends, aren't we—Avis?"

"Why—why, I am sure I don't know."

"Gracious gravy, what an admirable colour you have, Avis! Well,—I know. And I can inform you, quite confidentially, Avis, that we are not going to be—friends. We are going to be—"

"We are going to be late for luncheon," said she, in haste. "Good-morning, Mr. Townsend."

6

Yet, the very next day, paradoxically enough, she told me:

"I shall always think of you as a very, very dear friend. But it is quite impossible we should ever be anything else."

"And why, Avis?"

"Because—"

"That"—after an interval—"strikes me as rather a poor reason. So, suppose we say this June?"

Another interval.

"Well, Avis?"

"Dear me, aren't those roses pretty? I wish you would get me one, Mr. Townsend."

"Avis, we are not discussing roses."

"Well, they *are* pretty."

"Avis!"—reproachfully.

Still another interval.

"I—I hardly know."

"Avis!"—with disappointment.

"I—I believe—"

"Avis!"—very tenderly.

"I—I almost think so,—and the horrid man looks as if he thought so, too!"

There was a fourth interval, during which the girl made a complete and careful survey of her shoes.

Then, all in a breath, "It could not possibly be June, of course, and you must give me until tomorrow to think about November," and a sudden flutter of skirts.

I returned to Gridlington treading on air.

7

FOR I WAS, BY THIS time, as thoroughly in love as Amadis of Gaul or Aucassin of Beaucaire or any other hero of romance you may elect to mention.

Some two weeks earlier I would have scoffed at the notion of such a thing coming to pass; and I could have demonstrated, logically enough, that it was impossible for Robert Etheridge Townsend, with his keen knowledge of the world and of the innumerable vanities and whims of womankind, ever again to go the way of all flesh. But the problem, like the puzzle of the Eleatic philosophers, had solved itself. "Achilles cannot catch the tortoise," but he does. It was impossible for me to fall uncomfortably deep in love—but I had done so.

And it pricked my conscience, too, that Margaret should not know I was aware of her identity. But she had chosen to play the comedy to the end, and in common with the greater part of trousered humanity, I had, after all, no insuperable objection to a rich wife; though, to do me justice, I rarely thought of her, now, as Margaret Hugonin the heiress, but considered her, in a more comprehensive fashion, as the one woman in the universe whose perfections triumphantly overpeered the skyiest heights of preciosity.

Chapter 26

He Assists in the Diversion of Birds

We met, then, in the clear May morning, with what occult trepidations I cannot say. You may depend upon it, though, we had our emotions.

And about us, spring was marshaling her pageant, and from divers nooks, the weather-stained nymphs and fauns regarded us in candid, if preoccupied, appraisement; and above us, the clipped ilex trees were about a knowing conference. As for the birds, they were discussing us without any reticence whatever, for, more favoured of chance than imperial Solomon, they have been the confidants in any number of such affairs, and regard the way of a man with a maid as one of the most matter-of-fact occurrences in the world.

"Here is he! here is she!" they shrilled. "See how they meet, see how they greet! Ah, sweet, sweet, sweet, to meet in the spring!" And that we two would immediately set to nest-building, they considered a foregone conclusion.

2

I HAD TAKEN BOTH HER firm, warm hands in salutation, and held them, for a breathing-space, between my own. And my own hands seemed to me two very gross, and hulking, and raw, and red monstrosities, in contrast with their dimpled captives, and my hands appeared, also, to shake unnecessarily.

"Now, in a moment," said I, "I am going to ask you something very important. But, first, I have a confession to make."

And her glad, shamed eyes bemocked me. "My lord of Burleigh!" she softly breathed. "My liege Cophetua! *My* king Cophetua! And did you think, then, I was blind?"

"Eh?" said I.

"As if I hadn't known from the first!" the girl pouted; "as if I hadn't known from the very first day when you dropped your cigarette case! Ah, I had heard of you before, Peter!—of Peter, the misogynist, who was ashamed to go a-wooing in his proper guise! Was it because you were afraid I'd marry you for your money, Peter?—poor, timid Peter! But, oh, Peter, Peter, what possessed you to take the name of that notorious Robert Townsend?" she demanded, with uplifted forefinger. "Couldn't you think of a better one, Peter?—of a more respectable one, Peter? It really is a great relief to call you Peter at last. I've had to try so hard to keep from doing it before, Peter."

And in answer, I made an inarticulate sound.

"But you were so grave about it," the girl went on, happily, "that I almost thought you were telling the truth, Peter. Then my maid told me—I mean, she happened to mention casually that Mr. Townsend's valet had described his master to her as an extraordinarily handsome man. So, then, of course, I knew you were Peter Blagden."

"I perceive," said I, reflectively, "that Byam has been somewhat too zealous. I begin to suspect, also, that kitchen-gossip is a mischancy petard, and rather more than apt to hoist the engineer who employs it. So, you thought I was Peter Blagden,—the rich Peter Blagden? Ah, yes!"

Now the birds were caroling on a wager. "Ah, sweet! what is sweeter?" they sang. "Ah, sweet, sweet, sweet, to meet in the spring."

But the girl gave a wordless cry at sight of the change in my face. "Oh, how dear of you to care so much! I didn't mean that you were *ugly*, Peter. I just meant you are so big and—and so like the baby that they probably have on the talcum-powder boxes in Brobdingnag—"

"Because I happen to be really Robert Townsend—the notorious Robert Etheridge Townsend," I continued, with a smile. "I am sorry you were deceived by the cigarette-case. I remember now; I borrowed it from Peter. What I meant to confess was that I have known all along you were Margaret Hugonin."

"But I'm not," the girl said, in bewilderment. "Why—Why I *told* you I was Avis Beechinor."

"This handkerchief?" I queried, and took it from my pocket. I had been absurd enough to carry it next to my heart.

"Oh—!" And now the tension broke, and her voice leapt to high, shrill, half-hysterical speaking.

"I am Avis Beechinor. I am a poor relation, a penniless cousin, a dependent, a hanger-on, do you understand? And you—Ah, how—how funny! Why, Margaret *always* gives me her cast-off finery, the scraps, the remnants, the clothes she is tired of, the misfit things,—so that she won't be ashamed of me, so that I may be fairly presentable. She gave me eight of those handkerchiefs. I meant to pick the monograms out with a needle, you understand, because I haven't any money to buy such handkerchiefs for myself. I remember now,—she gave them to me on that day—that first day, and I missed one of them a little later on. Ah, how—how funny!" she cried, again; "ah, how very, very funny! No, Mr. Townsend, I am not an heiress,—I'm a pauper, a poor relation. No, you have failed again, just as you did with Mrs. Barry-Smith and with Miss Jemmett, Mr. Townsend. I—I wish you better luck the next time."

I must have raised one hand as though in warding off a physical blow. "Don't!" I said.

And all the woman in her leapt to defend me. "Ah no, ah no!" she pleaded, and her hands fell caressingly upon my shoulder; and she raised a penitent, tear-stained face toward mine; "ah no, forgive me! I didn't mean that altogether. It is different with a man. Of course, you must marry sensibly,—of course you must, Mr. Townsend. It is I who am to blame—why, of *course* it's only I who am to blame. I have encouraged you, I know—"

"You haven't! you haven't" I barked.

"But, yes,—for I came back that second day because I thought you were the rich Mr. Blagden. I was so tired of being poor, so tired of being dependent, that it simply seemed to me I could not stand it for a moment longer. Ah, I tell you, I was tired, tired, tired! I was tired and sick and worn out with it all!"

I did not interrupt her. I was nobly moved; but even then at the back of my mind some being that was not I was taking notes as to this girl, so young and desirable, and now so like a plaintive child who has been punished and does not understand exactly why.

"Mr. Townsend, you don't know what it means to a girl to be poor!—you can't ever know, because you are only a man. My mother—ah, you don't know the life I have led! You don't know how I have been hawked about, and set up for inspection by the men who could afford to pay my price, and made to show off my little accomplishments for them, and put through my paces before them like any horse in the market! For we are poor, Mr. Townsend,—we are bleakly, hopelessly poor. We are only hangers-on, you see. And ever since I can remember, she has been telling me I must make a rich marriage—*must* make a rich marriage—"

And the girl's voice trailed off into silence, and her eyes closed for a moment, and she swayed a little on her feet, so that I caught her by both arms.

But, presently, she opened her eyes, with a wearied sigh, and presently the two fortune-hunters stared each other in the face.

"Ah, sweet! what is sweeter?" sang the birds. "Can you see, can you see, can you see? It is sweet, sweet, sweet!" They were extremely gay over it, were the birds.

After a little, though, I opened my lips, and moistened them two or three times before I spoke. "Yes," said I, "I think I understand. We have both been hangers-on. But that seems, somehow, a long while ago. Yes, it was a knave who scaled that wall the first time,—one who needed and had earned a kicking from here to Aldebaran. But I think that I loved you from the very moment I saw you. Will you marry me, Avis?"

And in her face there was a wonderful and tender change. "You care for me—just me?" she breathed.

"Just you," I answered, gravely.

And I saw the start, and the merest ghost of a shiver which shook her body, as she leaned toward me a little, almost in surrender; but, quickly, she laughed.

"That was very gentlemanly in you," she said; "but, of course, I understand. Let us part friends, then,—Robert. Even if—if you really cared, we couldn't marry. We are too poor."

"Too poor!" I scoffed,—and my voice was joyous, for I knew now that it was I she loved and not just Peter Blagden's money; "too *poor*, Avis! I am to the contrary, an inordinately rich man, I tell you, for I have your love. Oh you needn't try to deny it. You are heels over head in love with me. And we have made, no doubt, an unsavoury mess of the past; but the future remains to us. We are the earthen pots, you and I, who wanted to swim with the brazen ones. Well! they haven't quite smashed us, these big, stupid, brazen pots, but they have shown us that they have the power to do it. And so we are going back where we belong—to the poor man's country, Avis,—or, in any event, to the country of those God-fearing, sober and honest folk who earn their bread and, just occasionally, a pat of butter to season it."

The world was very beautiful. I knew that I was excellent throughout and unconquerable. So I moved more near to her.

"For you will come with me, won't you, dear? Oh, you won't have quite so many gowns in this new country, Avis, and, may be, not even a horse and surrey of your own; but you will have love, and you will have happiness, and, best of all, Avis, you will give a certain very undeserving man his chance—his one sole chance—to lead a real man's life. Are you going to deny him that chance, Avis?"

Her gaze read me through and through; and I bore myself a bit proudly under it; and it seemed to me that my heart was filled with love of her, and that some sort of new-born manhood in Robert Etheridge Townsend was enabling me to meet her big brown eyes unflinchingly.

"It wouldn't be sensible," she wavered.

I laughed at that. "Sensible! If there is one thing more absurd than another in this very absurd world, it is common-sense. Be sensible and you will be miserable, Avis, not to mention being disliked. Sensible! Why, of course, it is not sensible. It is stark, rank, staring idiocy for us two not to make a profitable investment of, we will say, our natural endowments, when we come to marry. For what will Mrs. Grundy say if we don't? Ah, what will she say, indeed? Avis, just between you and me, I do not care a double-blank domino what Mrs. Grundy says. You will obligingly remember that the car for the Hesperides is in the rear, and that this is the third and last call. And in consequence—will you marry me, Avis?"

She gave me her hand frankly, as a man might have done. "Yes, Robert," said Miss Beechinor, "and God helping us, we will make something better of the future than we have of the past."

In the silence that fell, one might hear the birds. "Sweet, sweet, sweet!" they twittered. "Can you see, can you see, can you see? Their lips meet. It is sweet, sweet, sweet!"

3

BUT, BY AND BY, SHE questioned me. "Are you sure—quite sure," she queried, wistfully, "that you wouldn't rather have me Margaret Hugonin, the heiress?"

I raised a deprecatory hand. "Avis!" I reproached her; "Avis, Avis, how little you know me! That was the solitary fly in the amber,—that I thought I was to marry a woman named Margaret. For I am something of a connoisseur in nomenclature, and Margaret has always—*always*— been my pet detestation in the way of names."

"Oh, what a child you are!" she said.

Chapter 27

He Calls, and Counsels,
and Considers

I am now" said I, in my soul, "quite immeasurably, and insanely, and unreasonably, and unadulteratedly happy. Why, of course I am."

This statement was advanced just two weeks later than the events previously recorded. And the origin of it was the fact that I was now engaged to Avis Beechinor though it was not as yet to be "announced"; just this concession alone had Mrs. Beechinor wrested from an indignant and, latterly, a tearful interview. . . For I had called at Selwoode, in due form; and after leaving Mrs. Beechinor had been pounced upon by an excited and comely little person in black.

"Don't you mind a word she said," this lady had exhorted, "because she is *the* Gadarene swine, and Avis has told me everything! Of course you are to be married at once, and I only wish *I* could find the only man in the world who can keep me interested for four hours on a stretch and send my pulse up to a hundred and make me feel those thrilly thrills I've always longed for."

"But surely—" said I.

"No, I'm beginning to be afraid not, beautiful, though of course I used to be crazy about Billy Woods; and then once I was engaged to another man for a long time, and I was perfectly devoted to him, but he *never* made me feel a single thrilly thrill. And would you believe it, Mr. Townsend?—after a while he came back, precisely as though he had been a bad penny or a cat. He had been in the Boer War and came home just a night before I left, wounded and promoted several times and completely covered with glory and brass buttons. He came seven miles to see me, and I thoroughly enjoyed seeing him, for I had on my best dress and was feeling rather talkative. Well! at ten I was quite struck on him. At eleven perfectly willing to part friends, and at twelve *crazy* for him to go. He stayed till half-past, and I didn't want to think of him for days. And, by the way, I am Miss Hugonin, and I hope you and Avis will be very happy. *Good-bye!*"

"Good-bye!" said I.

AND THAT, ODDLY ENOUGH, WAS the one private talk I ever had with the Margaret Hugonin whom, for some two weeks, I had believed myself to be upon the verge of marrying; for the next time I conversed with her alone she was Mrs. William Woods.

"Oh, go away, Billy!" she then said, impatiently "How often will I have to tell you it isn't decent to be always hanging around your wife? Oh, you dear little crooked-necktied darling!"—and she remedied the fault on tiptoe,—"*please* run away and make love to somebody else, and be sure to get her name right, so that I shan't assassinate the wrong person,—because I want to tell this very attractive child all about Avis, and not be bothered." And subsequently she did.

But I must not forestall her confidences, lest I get my cart even further in advance of my nominal Pegasus than the loosely-made conveyance is at present lumbering.

3

AND MEANWHILE PETER BLAGDEN AND I had called at Selwoode once or twice in unison and due estate. And Peter considered "Miss Beechinor a damn fine girl, and Miss Hugonin too, only—"

"Only," I prompted, between puffs, "Miss Hugonin keeps everybody, as my old Mammy used to say, 'in a perpetual swivet.' I never understood what the phrase meant, precisely, but I somehow always knew that it was eloquent."

"Just so," said Peter. "You prefer—ah—a certain amount of tranquillity. I haven't been abroad for a long while," said Mr. Blagden; and then, after another meditative pause: "Now Stella—well, Stella was a damn sight too good for me, of course—"

"She was," I affably assented.

"—and I'd be the very last man in the world to deny it. But still you *do* prefer—" Then Peter broke off short and said: "My God, Bob! what's the matter?"

So I think I must have had the ill-taste to have laughed a little over Mr. Blagden's magnanimity in regard to Stella's foibles. But I only said: "Oh, nothing, Peter! I was just going to tell you that travelling *does* broaden the mind, and that you will find an overcoat indispensable in Switzerland, and that during the voyage you ought to keep in the open air as much as possible, and that you should give the steward who waits on you at table at least ten shillings,—I was just going to tell you, in fine, that you would be a fool to squander any money on a guide-book, when I am here to give you all the necessary pointers."

"But I didn't mean to go to Europe exactly," said Mr. Blagden; "—I just meant to go abroad in a general sense. Any place would be abroad, you know, where people weren't always remembering how rich you were, and weren't scrambling to marry you out of hand, but really cared, you know, like she does. Oh, may be it *is* bad form to mention it, but I couldn't help seeing how she looked at you, Bob. And it waked something—Oh, I don't know what I mean," said Peter—"it's just damn foolishness, I suppose."

"It's very far from that," I said; and I was honestly moved, just as I always am when pathos, preferably grotesque, has caught me unprepared. This millionaire was lonely, because of his millions, and Stella was dead; and somehow I understood, and laid one hand upon his shoulder.

"Oh, *you* can't help it, I suppose, if all women love by ordinary because he is so like another person, where as men love because she is so different. My poor caliph, I would sincerely advise you to play the fool just as you plan to do,—oh, anywhere,—and without even a Mesrour. In fine go Bunburying at once. For very frankly, First Cousin of the Moon, it is the one thing worth while in life."

"I half believe I will," said Peter. . . So he was packing in the interim during which I pretended to be writing, and was in reality fretting to think that, whilst Avis was in England by this, I could not decently leave America until those last five chapters were finished. So, in part as an excuse for not scrawling the dullest of nonsense and subsequently tearing it up, I fell to considering the unquestionable fact that I was in love with Avis, and upon the verge of marrying her, and was in consequence, as a matter of plain logic, deliriously happy.

"For when you are in love with a woman you, of course, want to marry her more than you want anything else. In nature, it is a serious and— well, an almost irretrievable business. And I shall have to cultivate the domestic virtues and smoke cheaper cigarettes and all that, but I shall be glad to do every one of these things, for her sake—after a while. I shall probably enjoy doing them."

And I read Bettie Hamlyn's letter for the seventeenth time. . .

FOR BETTIE HAD ANSWERED THE wild rhapsody which I wrote to tell her how much in love I was with Elena Barry-Smith. And in the nature of things I had not written Bettie again to tell her I was, and by a deal the more, in love with Avis Beechinor. The task was delicate, the reasons for my not unnatural change were such as you must transmit in a personal interview during which you are particularly boyish and talk very fast.

Besides, I do not like writing letters; and moreover, there was no real need to write. I was going to Gridlington; what more natural than to ride over to Fairhaven some clear morning and tell Bettie everything? I pictured her surprise and her delight at seeing me, and reflected it would be unfair to her to render an inaccurate account of matters, such as any letter must necessarily give.

Only, first, there was the garden of Peter's aunt,—which sounds like an introductory French exercise,—and then Avis came. And, somehow, I had not, in consequence, traversed the scant nine miles that lay as yet between me and Bettie Hamlyn. I kept on meaning to do it the next day.

And the next day after this I really did.

"For I ought to tell Bettie about everything," I reflected. "No matter if the engagement is a secret, I ought to tell Bettie about it."

5

WHEN I HAD DONE SO, Bettie shook her head. "Oh, Robin, Robin!" she said, "how did I ever come to raise a child that doesn't know his own mind for as much as two minutes? And how dared that Barry-Smith person to slap you, I would like to know."

"Now you're jealous, Bettie. You are thinking she infringed upon an entirely personal privilege, and you resent it."

"Well,—but I've the right to, you see, and she hadn't. I consider her to be a bold-faced jig. And I don't approve of this Avis person either, you understand; but we poor mothers are always being annoyed by slushy, mushy Avises. I suppose there's a reason for it. She'll throw you over, you know, as soon as *her* mother has had an inning or two. That's why she took her to Europe," Bettie explained, with a fine confusion of personalities. "Only she just wanted any quiet place where she could take aromatic spirits of ammonia and point out between doses that she has given up her entire life to her child and has never made any demands on her and hasn't the strength to argue with her, because her heart is simply broken. We mothers always say that; and the funny part is that if you say it often enough it invariably works far better than any possible argument."

I told her she was talking nonsense, and she said, irrelevantly enough: "Setebos, and Setebos, and Setebos! I don't think very highly of Setebos sometimes, because He muddles things so. Oh, well, I shan't cry Willow. Besides there *aren't* any sycamore-trees in the garden. So let's go into the garden, dear. That sounds as if I ate in the back pantry, doesn't it? Of course you aren't of any account any more, and you never will be, but at least you don't look at people as though they were a new sort of bug whenever they have just thought a sentence or two and then gone on, without bothering to say it."

So we went into Bettie's garden. It had not changed. . .

6

NOTHING HAD CHANGED. IT WAS as though I had somehow managed, after all, to push back the hands of the clock. Fairhaven accepted me incuriously. I was only "an old student." In addition, I was vaguely rumoured to write "pieces" for the magazines. Probably I did; "old students" were often prone to vagaries after leaving King's College; for instance, they told me, Ralph Means was a professional gambler, and Ox Selwyn had lately gone to Shanghai and had settled there,—and Shanghai, in common with most other places, Fairhaven accorded the negative tribute of just not absolutely disbelieving in its existence.

Nothing had changed. The Finals were over; and with the noisy exodus of the college-boys, Fairhaven had sunk contentedly into an even deeper stupor, as Fairhaven always does in summer. And, for the rest, the unpaved sidewalks were just as dusty, the same deep ruts and the puddles which never dry, not even in mid-August, adorned Fairhaven's single street; the comfortable moss upon Fairhaven's roofs had not varied by a shade; and George Washington or Benjamin Franklin might have stepped out of any one of those brass-knockered doorways without incongruity and without finding any noticeable innovation to marvel at.

Nothing had changed. In the precise middle of the campus Lord Penniston, our Governor in Colonial days, still posed, in dingy marble;

and the fracture of the finger I had inadvertently broken off, the night that Billy Woods and I painted the statue all over, in six colours, was white and new-looking. Kathleen Eppes had married her Spaniard and had left Fairhaven; otherwise the same girls were already planning their toilets for the Y.M.C.A. reception in October, which formally presents the "new students" to society at large; and presently these girls would be going to the germans or the Opera House with the younger brother of the boy who used to take them thither. . .

Nothing had changed; not even I was changed. For I had soon discovered that Bettie Hamlyn did not care a pin for me in myself. She was simply very fond of me because, at times, I reminded her of a boy who had gone to King's College; and her reception of me, for the first two days, was unmistakably provisional.

"Very well!" I said.

And I did it. For I knew how difficult it was to deceive Bettie, and in consequence all my faculties rose to the challenge. I did not merely mimic my former self, I was compelled, almost, to believe I was indeed that former self, because not otherwise could I get Bettie Hamlyn's toleration. Had I paused even momentarily to reflect upon the excellence of my acting, she would have known. So I resolutely believed I was being perfectly candid; and with constant use those older tricks of speech and gesture and almost of thought, at first laborious mimicry, became well-nigh involuntary.

In fine, we could not wipe away five years, but with practice we found that you would very often forget them, and for quite a while. . .

I had explained to Bettie's father I was going to board with them that summer. Had I not been so haphazard in the progress of this narrative, I would have earlier announced that Bettie's father was the Latin professor at King's College. He was very old and vague, and his general attitude toward the universe was that of remote recollection of having noticed something of the sort before. Professor Hamlyn, therefore, told me he was glad to hear of my intended stay beneath his roof; hazarded the speculation that I had written a book which he meant to read upon the very first opportunity; blinked once or twice; and forthwith lapsed into consideration of some Pliocene occurrence which, if you were to judge by the expression of his mild old countenance, he did not find entirely satisfactory. . .

So I spent three months in Fairhaven; and Bettie and I read all the old books over again, and were perfectly happy.

AND WHAT I WROTE IN those last five chapters of my book was so good that in common decency I was compelled to alter the preceding twenty-nine and bring them a bit nearer to Bettie's standard. For I was utilising Bettie's ideas. She did not have the knack of putting them on paper; that was my trivial part, as I now recognised with a sort of scared reverence.

"Of course, though, you had to meddle," I would scold at her. "I had meant the infernal thing to be a salable book. Today it is just a stenographic report of how these people elected to behave. I haven't anything to do with it. I wash my hands of it. I consider you, in fine, a cormorant, a conscienceless marauder, a meddlesome Mattie, *and* a born dramatist."

"But, it's *much* better than anything you've ever done, Robin—"

"That is what I'm grumbling about. I consider it very unfeeling of you to write better novels than I do," I retorted. "But, oh, how good that scene is!" I said, a little later.

"Let's see—'For you, dear clean-souled girl, were born to be the wife of a strong man, and the mother of his dirty children'—no, it's 'sturdy', but then you hardly ever cross your T's. And where he goes on to tell her he can't marry her, because he is artistic, and she is too practical for them to be real mates, and all that other feeble-mindedness? Dear me, did I forget to tell you we were going to cut that out?"

"But I particularly like that part—"

"Do you?" said Bettie, as her pen scrunched vicious lines through it. Then she said: "I only hope she had the civility and self-control not to laugh until you had gone away. And 'We irrelevant folk that design all useless and beautiful things,' indeed! No, I couldn't have blamed her if she laughed right out. I wonder if you will never understand that what you take to be your love for beautiful things is really just a dislike of ugly ones? Oh, I've no patience with you! And wanting to print it in a book, too, instead of being content to make yourself ridiculous in tete-a-tetes with minxes that don't especially matter!"

"Well—! Anyhow, I agree with you that, thanks to your editing and carping and general scurrility, this book is going to be," I meekly stated, "a little better than *The Apostates* and not just 'pretty much like any other book'."

"Do you know that's just what I was thinking," said Bettie, dolefully. She clasped both hands behind her crinkly small black head, and in that queer habitual pose appraised me, from between her elbows, in that way which always made me feel I had better be careful. "Damn you!" was her verdict.

"Whence this unmaidenliness?" I queried, with due horror.

"You are trying to prove to me that it has been worth while. This nasty book is coming alive, here in our own eight-cornered room, with a horrid crawly life of its own that it would never have had if you hadn't been learning things my boy knew nothing about. That's what you are crowing in my face, when you keep quiet and smirk. Oh, but I know you!"

"You do think, then, that, between you and me, it is really coming alive?"

"Yes,—if that greatly matters to the fat literary gent that I don't care for greatly. Yes, the infernal thing will be a Book, with quite a sizable B. I am feeding its maw with more important things than a few ideas, though. The thing is a monster that isn't worth its keep. For my boy was worth more than a Book," she said, forlornly,—"oh, oceans more!"

8

ALL IN ALL, WE WERE a deal more than happy during these three very hot months. It was a sort of Lotus Eaters' existence, shared by just us two, with Josiah Clarriker intruding occasionally, and with echoes from the outer world, when heard at all, resounding very dimly and unimportantly. I began almost to assume, as Fairhaven tacitly assumed, that there was really no outer world, or none at least to be considered seriously. . .

For instance: Marian Winwood had come to Lichfield, and wrote me from there, "hoping that we would renew an acquaintance which she remembered so pleasurably." It did not seem worth while, of course, to answer the minx; I decided, at a pinch, to say that the Fairhaven mail-service was abominable, and that her letter had never reached me. But the young fellow who two years ago had wandered about the Green Chalybeate with her had become, now, as unreal as she. I glimpsed the couple, with immeasurable aloofness, as phantoms flickering about the mirage of a brook, throwing ghostly bread crumbs to Lethean minnows.

And then, too, when the police caught Ned Lethbury that summer, it hardly seemed worth while to wonder about his wife. For she was, inexplicably, with him, all through the trial at Chiswick, you may remember, though you were probably more interested at the time by the Humbert trial in Paris. In any event, no rumor came to me in Fairhaven to connect Amelia Lethbury with Nadine Neroni, but, instead, a deal of journalistic pity and sympathy for her, the faithful, much-enduring wife. Still quite a handsome woman, they said, for all her suffering and poverty. . . And when he went to the penitentiary, Amelia Lethbury disappeared, nobody knew whither, except that I suspected Anton von Anspach knew. I could not explain the mystery. I did not greatly care to, for to me it did not seem important, now. . .

9

MEANTIME, I MEDITATED.

"I am in love with Avis—oh, granted! I am not the least bit in love with—we will euphemistically say 'anyone else.' But confound it! I am coming to the conclusion that marrying a woman because you happen to be in love with her is about as logical a proceeding as throwing the cat out of the window because the rhododendrons are in bloom. Why, if I marry Avis I shall probably have to live with her the rest of my life!

"What if that obsolete notion of Schopenhauer's were true after all,— that love is a blind instinct which looks no whit toward the welfare of the man and woman it dominates, but only to the equipment a child born of them would inherit? What if, after all, love tends, without variation, to yoke the most incompatible in order that the average type of humanity may be preserved? Then the one passion we esteem as sacred would be simply the deranged condition of any other beast in rutting-time. Then we, with the pigs and sparrows, would be just so many pieces on the chess-board, and our evolutions would be just a friendly trial of skill between what we call life and death.

"I love Avis Beechinor. But I have loved, in all sincerity, many other women, and I rejoice today, unfeignedly, that I never married any of them. For marriage means a life-long companionship, a long, long journey wherein must be adjusted, one by one, each tiniest discrepancy between the fellow-wayfarers; and always a pebble if near enough to the eye will obscure a mountain.

"Why, Avis cannot attempt a word of four syllables without coming at least once to grief! It is a trifle of course, but in a life-long companionship there are exactly fourteen thousand trifles to one event of importance. And deuce take it! the world is populated by men and women, not demi-gods; the poets are specious and abandoned rhetoricians; for it never was, and never will be, possible to love anybody 'to the level of every-day's Most quiet need by sun or candlelight.'

"Or not to me at least.

"In a sentence, when it comes to a life-long companionship, I prefer not the woman who would make me absolutely happy for a twelvemonth, but rather the woman with whom I could chat contentedly for twenty years, and who would keep me to the mark. I am rather tired of being futile; and not for any moral reason, but because it is not worthy of *me*. In fine, I do not want to die entirely. I want to leave behind some not inadequate expression of Robert Etheridge Townsend, and I do not care at all what people say of it, so that it is here when I am gone. Oh, Stella understood! 'I want my life to count, I want to leave something in the world that wasn't there before I came.'

"Now Bettie—"

I arose resolutely. "I had much better go for a long, and tedious, and jolting, and universally damnable walk. Bettie would make something vital of me—if I could afford her the material—"

And I grinned a little. "'Go, therefore, now, and work; for there shall no straw be given you, yet shall ye deliver the tale of bricks.' Yes, you would certainly have need of a miracle, dear Bettie—"

10

I STARTED FOR THAT WALK I was to take. But Dr. Jeal and Colonel Snawley were seated in armchairs in front of Clarriker's Emporium, just as they had been used to sit there in my college days, enjoying, as the Colonel mentioned, "the cool of the evening," although to the casual observer the real provider of their pleasure would have appeared to be an unlimited supply of chewing-tobacco.

So I lingered here, and garnered, to an accompaniment of leisurely expectorations, much knowledge as to the fall crops and the carryings-on of the wife of a celebrated general, upon whose staff the Colonel had served during the War,—and there has never been in the world's history but one war, so far as Fairhaven is concerned,—and how the Colonel walked right in on them, and how it was hushed up.

Then we discussed the illness of Pope Leo and what everybody knew about those derned cardinals, and the riots in Evansville, and the Panama Canal business, and the squally look of things at Port Arthur, and attributed all these imbroglios, I think, to the Republican administration. Even at our bitterest, though, we conceded that "Teddy's" mother was a Bulloch, and that his uncle fired the last shot before the Alabama went down. And that inclined us to forgive him everything, except of course, the Booker Washington luncheon.

Then half a block farther on, Mrs. Rabbet wanted to know if I had ever seen such weather, and to tell me exactly what Adrian, Junior— no longer little Adey, no indeed, sir, but ready to start right in at the College session after next, and as she often said to Mr. Rabbet you could hardly believe it,—had observed the other day, and quick as a flash too, because it would make such a funny story. Only she could never quite decide whether it happened on a Tuesday or a Wednesday, so that, after precisely seven digressions on this delicate point, the denouement of the tale, I must confess, fell rather flat.

And then Mab Spessifer demanded that I come up on the porch and draw some pictures for her. The child was waiting with three sheets of paper and a chewed pencil all ready, just on the chance that I might pass; and you cannot very well refuse a cripple who adores you and is not able to play with the other brats. You get instead into a kind of habit of calling every day and trying to make her laugh, because she is such a helpless little nuisance.

And tousled mothers weep over you in passageways and tell you how good you are, and altogether the entire affair is tedious; but having started it, you keep it up, somehow.

11

IN FINE, IT IS A symbol that I never took the walk which was to dust the cobwebs from my brain and make me just like all the other persons, thick about me, who grow up, and mate, and beget, and die, in the incurious fashion of oxen, without ever wondering if there is any plausible reason for doing it; and my brief progress was upon the surface very like that of the bedeviled fellow in *Les Facheux*. Yet I enjoyed it somehow. Never to be hurried, and always to stop and talk with every person whom you meet, upon topics in which no conceivable human being could possibly be interested, may not sound attractive, but in Fairhaven it is the rule; and, oddly enough, it breeds, in practice, a sort of family feeling,—if only by entitling everybody to the condoned and matter-of-course stupidity of aunts and uncles,—which is not really all unpleasant.

So I went home at half-past seven, to supper and to Bettie, in a quite contented frame of mind. It did not seem conceivable that any world so beautiful and stupid and well-meaning could have either the heart or the wit to thwart my getting anything I really wanted; and the thought elated me.

Only I did not know, precisely, what I wanted.

Chapter 28

HE PARTICIPATES IN SUNDRY CONFIDENCES

I was in the act of writing to Avis when the letter came; and I put it aside unopened, until after supper, for I had never found the letters of Avis particularly interesting reading.

"It will be what they call a newsy letter, of course. I do wish that Avis would not write to me as if she were under oath to tell the entire truth. She communicates so many things which actually happened that it reads like a 'special correspondent' in some country town writing for a Sunday morning's paper,—and with, to a moral certainty, the word 'separate' lurking somewhere spelt with three E's, and an 'always' with two L's, and at least one 'alright.' No, my dear, I am at present too busy expressing my adoration for you to be exposed to such inharmonious jars."

Then I wrote my dithyrambs and sealed them. Subsequently I poised the unopened letter between my fingers.

"But remember that if she were here to *say* all this to you, your pulses would be pounding like the pistons of an excited locomotive! Nature, you are a jade! I console myself with the reflection that it is frequently the gift of facile writing which makes the co-respondent,—but I *do* wish you were not such a hazardous matchmaker. Oh, well! there was no pleasant way of getting out of it, and that particular Rubicon is miles behind."

I slit the envelope.

I read the letter through again, with redoubling interest, and presently began to laugh. "So she begins to fear we have been somewhat hasty, asks a little time for reconsideration of her precise sentiment toward me, and feels meanwhile in honour bound to release me from our engagement! Yet if upon mature deliberation—eh, oh, yes! twaddle! *and* commonplace! and dashed, of course, with a jigger of Scriptural quotation!"

I paused to whistle. "There is strange milk in this cocoanut, could I but discern its nature."

I did, some four weeks later, when with a deal of mail I received the last letter I was ever to receive from Avis Beechinor.

Wrote Avis:

DEAR ROBERT

Thank you very much for returning my letters and for
the beautiful letter you wrote me. No I believe it better
you should not come on to see me now and talk the matter
over as you suggest because it would probably only make
you unhappy. And then too I am sure some day you will be
friends with me and a very good and true one. I return the
last letter you sent me in a seperate envelope, and I hope it
will reach you alright, but as I destroy all my mail as soon as
I have read it I cannot send you the others. I have promised
to marry Mr. Blagden and we are going to be married on the
fifteenth of this month very quietly with no outsiders. So
good bye Robert. I wish you every success and happiness that
you may desire and with all my heart I pray you to be true to
your better self. God bless you allways. Your sincere friend,

AVIS M. BEECHINOR

I indulged in a low and melodious whistle. "The little slut!"

Then I said: "Peter Blagden again! I *do* wish that life would try
to be a trifle more plausible. Why, but, of course! Peter meant to go
chasing after her the minute my back was turned, and that was why
he salved his conscience by presenting me with that thousand 'to get
married on,' Even at the time it seemed peculiarly un-Petrine. Well,
anyhow, in simple decency, he cannot combine the part of Shylock
with that of Judas, and expect to have back his sordid lucre, so I am
that much to the good, apart from everything else. Yes, I can see how
it all happened,—and I can foresee what is going to happen, too, thank
heaven!"

For, as drowning men are said to recollect the unrecallable, I had
vividly seen in that instant the two months' action just overpast, and its
three participants,—the thin-lipped mother, the besotted millionaire,
and the girl shakily hesitant between ideals and the habits of a lifetime.

"But I might have known the mother would win," I reflected: "Why,
didn't Bettie say she would?"

I refolded the letter I had just read, to keep it as a salutary relic; and
then:

"Dear Avis!" said I; "now heaven bless your common-sense! and I don't especially mind if heaven blesses your horrific painted hag of a mother, also, if they've a divine favor or two to spare."

And I saw there was a letter from Peter Blagden, too. It said, in part:

I am everything that you think me, Bob. My one defence is that I could not help it. I loved her from the moment I saw her. . . You did not appreciate her, you know. You take, if you will forgive my saying it, too light a view of life to value the love of a good woman properly, and Avis noticed it of course. Now I do understand what the unselfish love of woman means, because my first wife was an angel, as you know. . . It is a comfort to think that my dear saint in heaven knows I am not quite so lonely now, and is gladdened by that knowledge. I know she would have wished it—

I read no further. "Oh, Stella! they have all forgotten. They all insist today that you were an angel, and they have come almost to believe that you habitually flew about the world in a night-gown, with an Easter lily in your hand—But I remember, dear. I know you'd scratch her eyes out. I know you'd do it now, if only you were able, because you loved this Peter Blagden."

Thereafter I must have wasted a full quarter of an hour in recalling all sorts of bygone unimportant happenings, and I was not bothering one way or the other about Avis. . .

3

IN THE MOONLIGHTED GARDEN I found Bettie. But with her was Josiah Clarriker, Fairhaven's leading business-man. He shook hands, and whatever delight he may have felt at seeing me was admirably controlled.

"Now don't let me interfere with your eloquence," I urged, "but go right on with the declamation."

"I make no pretension to eloquence, Mr. Townsend. I was merely recalling to Miss Hamlyn's attention the beautiful lines of our immortal poet, Owen Meredith, which run, as I remember them:

> "*I thought of the dress she wore that time*
> *That we stood under the cypress-tree together,*
> *In that land, in that clime,*
> *And I turned and looked, and she was sitting there*

> In the box next to the stage, and dressed
> In that muslin dress, with that full soft hair
> And that jessamine blossom at her breast.'"

"But I am not permitted to wear flowers when Mr. Townsend is about," said Bettie. "Did you know, Jo, that he is crazy about that too?"

"Well—! Anyhow, Meredith is full of very beautiful sentiments," said Mr. Clarriker, "and I have always been particularly fond of that piece. It is called *'Ox Italians.'*"

"Yes, I have been previously affected by it," said I, "and very deeply moved."

"And so—as I was about to observe, Miss Hamlyn,—you will notice that the poet Meredith gowned one of the most beautiful characters he ever created in white, and laid great stress upon the fact that her beauty was immeasurably enhanced by the dainty simplicity of her muslin dress. This fabric, indeed, suits all types of faces and figures, and is Economical too, especially the present popular mercerised waistings and vestings that are fast invading the realm of silks. We show at our Emporium an immense quantity of these beautiful goods, in more than a hundred styles, elaborate enough for the most formal occasions, at fifty and seventy-five cents a yard; and—as I was about to observe, Miss Hamlyn,—I would indeed esteem it a favour should you permit me to send up a few samples tomorrow, from which to make a selection at, I need not add, my personal expense.

"You see, Mr. Townsend," he continued, more inclusively, "we have no florists in Fairhaven, and I have heard that candy—" He talked on, hygienically now. . .

4

"And that," said I, when Mr. Clarriker had gone, "is what you are actually considering! I have always believed Dickens invented that man to go into one of the latter chapters of *Edwin Drood*. It is the solitary way of explaining certain people,—that they were invented by some fagged novelist who unfortunately died before he finished the book they were to be locked up in. As it was, they got loose, to annoy you by their incredibility. No actual human being, you know, would suggest a white shirtwaist as a substitute for a box of candy."

"Oh, I have seen worse," said Bettie, as in meditation. "It's just Jo's way of expressing the fact that I am stupendously beautiful in white.

Poor dear, my loveliness went to his head, I suppose, and got tangled with next week's advertisement for the *Gazette*. Anyhow, he is a deal more considerate than you. For instance, I was crazy to go to the show on Tuesday night, and Josiah Clarriker was the only person who thought to ask me, even though he is one of those little fireside companions who always get so syrupy whenever they take you anywhere that you simply can't stand it. The combination both prevented my acceptance and accentuated his devotion; and quite frankly, Robin, I am thinking of him, for at bottom Jo is a dear."

I laid one hand on each of Bettie's shoulders; and it was in my mind at the time that this was the gesture of a comrade, and had not any sexual tinge at all. I wished that Bettie had better teeth, of course, but that could not be helped.

"You are to marry me as soon as may be possible," said I, "and preferably tomorrow afternoon. Avis has thrown me over, God bless her, and I am free,—until of course you take charge of me. There was a clever woman once who told me I was not fit to be the captain of my soul, though I would make an admirable lieutenant. She was right. It is understood you are to henpeck me to your heart's content and to my ultimate salvation."

"I shall assuredly not marry you," observed Miss Hamlyn, "until you have at least asked me to do so. And besides, how dared she throw you over—!"

"But I don't intend to ask you, for I have not a single bribe to offer. I merely intend to marry you. I am a ne'er-do-well, a debauchee, a tippler, a compendium of all the vices you care to mention. I am not a bit in love with you, and as any woman will forewarn you, I am sure to make you a vile husband. Your solitary chance is to bully me into temperance and propriety and common-sense, with precisely seven million probabilities against you, because I am a seasoned and accomplished liar. Can you do that bullying, Bettie,—and keep it up, I mean?"

And she was silent for a while. "Robin," she said, at last, "you'll never understand why women like you. You will always think it is because they admire you for some quality or another. It is really because they pity you. You are such a baby, riding for a fall—No, I don't mean the boyishness you trade upon. I have known for a long while all that was just put on. And, oh, how hard you've tried to be a boy of late!"

"And I thought I had fooled you, Bettie! Well, I never could. I am sorry, though, if I have been annoyingly clumsy—"

"But you were doing it for me," she said. "You were doing it because you thought I'd like it. Oh, can't you understand that I *know* you are worthless, and that you have never loved any human being in all your life except that flibbertigibbet Stella Blagden, and that I know, too, you have so rarely failed me! If you were an admirable person, or a person with commendable instincts, or an unselfish person, or if you were even in love with me, it wouldn't count of course. It is because you are none of these things that it counts for so much to see you honest with me— sometimes,—and even to see you scheming and play-acting—and so transparently!—just to bring about a little pleasure for me. Oh, Robin, I am afraid that nowadays I love you *because* of your vices!"

"And I you because of your virtues," said I; "so that there is no possible apprehension of either affection ever going into bankruptcy. Therefore the affair is settled; and we will be married in November."

"Well," Bettie said, "I suppose that somebody has to break you of this habit of getting married next November—"

Then, and only then, my hands were lifted from her shoulders. And we began to talk composedly of more impersonal matters.

5

IT WAS TWO DAYS LATER that John Charteris came to Fairhaven; and I met him the same afternoon upon Cambridge street. The little man stopped short and in full view of the public achieved what, had he been a child, were most properly describable as making a face at me.

"That," he explained, "expresses the involuntary confusion of Belial on re-encountering the anchorite who escaped his diabolical machinations. But, oh, dear me! haven't you been translated yet? Why, I thought the carriage would have called long ago, just as it did for Elijah."

"Now, don't be an ass, John. I *was* rather idiotic, I suppose—"

"Of course you were," he said, as we shook hands. "It is your unfailing charm. You silly boy, I came from the pleasantest sort of house-party at Matocton because I heard you were here, and I have been foolish enough to miss you. Anne and the others don't arrive until October. Oh, you adorable child, I have read the last book, and every one of the short stories as well, and I want to tell you that in their own peculiar line the two volumes are masterpieces. Anne wept and chuckled over them, and so did I, with an equal lack of restraint; only it was over the noble and self-sacrificing portions that Anne wept, and she laughed at the places where you were droll intentionally. Whereas I—!! Well, we will let the aposiopesis stand."

"Of course," I sulkily observed, "if you have simply come to Fairhaven to make fun of me, I can only pity your limitations."

He spoke in quite another voice. "You silly boy, it was not at all for that. I think you must know I have read what you have published thus far with something more than interest; but I wanted to tell you this in so many words. *Afield* is not perhaps an impeccable masterwork, if one may be thus brutally frank; but the woman—modeled after discretion will not inquire whom,—is distinctly good. And what, with you only twenty-five, does *A field* not promise! Child, you have found your metier. Now I shall look forward to the accomplishment of what I have always felt sure that you could do. I am very, very glad. More so than I can say. And I had thought you must know this without my saying it."

The man was sincere. And I was very much pleased, and remembered what invaluable help he could give me on my unfinished book, and what fun it would be to go over the manuscript with him. And, in fine, we became again, upon the spot as it were, the very best of friends.

6

IT WAS EXCELLENT TO HAVE Charteris to talk against. The little man had many tales to tell me of those dissolute gay people we had known and frolicked with; indeed, I think that he was trying to allure me back to the old circles, for he preoccupied his life by scheming to bring about by underhand methods some perfectly unimportant consummation, which very often a plain word would have secured at once. But now he swore he was not "making tea."

That had always been a byword between us, by the way, since I applied to him the phrase first used of Alexander Pope—"that he could not make tea without a conspiracy." And it may be that in this case Charteris spoke the truth, and had come to Fairhaven just for the pleasure of seeing me, for certainly he must have had some reason for leaving the Musgraves' house-party so abruptly.

"You are very well rid of the Hardresses," he adjudged. "Did I tell you of the male one's exhibition of jealousy last year! I can assure you that the fellow now entertains for me precisely the same affection I have always borne toward cold lamb. It is the real tragedy of my life that Anne is ethically incapable of letting a week pass without partaking of a leg of mutton. She is not particularly fond of it, and indeed I never encountered anybody who was; she has simply been reared with the notion that 'people' always have mutton once a week. What, have you never noticed that with 'people,' to eat mutton once a week is a sort of guarantee of respectability? I do not refer to chops of course, which are not wholly inconsistent with depravity. But the ability to eat mutton in its roasted form, by some odd law of nature, connotes the habit of paying your pew-rent regularly and of changing your flannels on the proper date. However, I was telling you about Jasper Hardress—" And Charteris repeated the story of their imbroglio in such a fashion that it sounded farcical.

"But, after all, John, you *did* make love to her."

"I have forgotten what was exactly the last observation of the lamented Julius Caesar," Mr. Charteris leisurely observed,—"though I remember that at the time it impressed me as being uncommonly appropriate—But to get back: do you not see that this clause ought to come here, at the end of the sentence? And, child, on all my ancient bended knees, I implore you to remember that 'genuine' does not mean the same thing as 'real' . . ."

7

MEANWHILE HE AND BETTIE GOT on together a deal better than I had ever anticipated.

Charteris, though, received my confidence far too lightly. "You are going to marry her! Why, naturally! Ever since I encountered you, you have been 'going to marry' somebody or other. It is odd I should have written about the Foolish Prince so long before I knew you. But then, *I* helped to mould you—a little—"

And resolutely Bettie said the most complimentary things about him. But I trapped her once.

"Still," I observed, when he had gone, and she had finished telling me how delightful Mr. Charteris was, "still he shan't ever come to *our* house, shall he?"

"Why, of course not!" said Bettie, who was meditating upon some cosmic question which required immediate attention. And then she grew very angry and said, "Oh, you *dog!*" and threw a sofa-cushion at me.

"I hate that wizened man," she presently volunteered, "more bitterly than I do any person on earth. For it was he who taught you to adopt infancy as a profession. He robbed me. And Setebos permitted it. And now you are just a man I am going to marry—Oh, well!" said Bettie, more sprightlily, "I was getting on, and you are rather a dear even in that capacity. Only I wonder what *becomes* of all the first choices?"

"They must keep them for us somewhere, Bettie dear. And that is probably the explanation of everything."

And a hand had snuggled into mine. "You do understand without having to have it all spelt out for you. And that's a comfort, too. But, oh," said Bettie, "what a wasteful Setebos it is!"

Chapter 29

He Allows the Merits of Imperfection

I was quite contented now and assured as to the future. I foreknew the future would be tranquil and lacking in any particular excitement, and I had already ceded, in anticipation, the last tittle of mastery over my own actions; but Bettie would keep me to the mark, would wring—not painlessly perhaps—from Robert Townsend the very best there was in him; and it would be this best which, unalloyed, would endure, in what I wrote. I had never imagined that, for the ore, smelting was an agreeable process; so I shrugged, and faced my future contentedly.

One day I said, "Tomorrow I must have holiday. There are certain things that need burying, Bettie dear, and—it is just the funeral of my youth I want to go to."

"So it is tomorrow that we go for an admiring walk around our emotions!" Bettie said. She knew well enough of what event tomorrow was the anniversary, and it is to her credit she added: "Well, for this once—!" For of all the women whom I had loved, there was but one that Bettie Hamlyn had ever bothered about. And tomorrow was Stella's birthday, as I had very unconcernedly mentioned a few moments earlier, when I was looking for the Austin Dobson book, and had my back turned to Bettie.

2

Next day, in Cedarwood, a woman in mourning—in mourning fluffed and jetted and furbelowed in such pleasing fashion that it seemed flamboyantly to demand immediate consolation of all marriageable males,—viewed me with a roving eye as I heaped daffodils on Stella's grave. They had cost me a pretty penny, too, for this was in September. But then I must have daffodils, much as I loathe the wet, limp feel o. them, because she would have chosen daffodils. . . Well! I fancied this woman thought me sanctioned by both church and law in what I did,—and viewed me in my supposedly recent bereavement and gauged my potentialities,—viewed me, in short, with the glance of adventurous widowhood.

My faith (I meditated) if she knew!—if I could but speak my thought to her!

"Madam,"—let us imagine me, my hat raised, my voice grave,—
"the woman who lies here was a stranger to me. I did not know her.
I knew that her eyes were blue, that her hair was sunlight, that her
voice had pleasing modulations; but I did not know the woman. And
she cared nothing for me. That is why my voice shakes as I tell you of
it. And I have brought her daffodils, because of all flowers she loved
them chiefly, and because there is no one else who remembers this. It
is the flower of spring, and Stella—for that was her name, madam,—
died in the spring of the year, in the spring of her life; and Stella
would have been just twenty-six today. Oh, and daffodils, madam,
are all white and gold, even as that handful of dust beneath us was
all white and gold when we buried it with a flourish of crepe and
lamentation, some two years and five months ago. Yet the dust there
was tender flesh at one time, and it clad a brave heart; but we thought
of it—and I among the rest,—as a plaything with which some lucky
man might while away his leisure hours. I believe now that it was
something more. I believe—ah, well, my *credo* is of little consequence.
But whatever this woman may have been, I did not know her. And she
cared nothing for me."

I reflected I would like to do it. I could imagine the stare, the squawk,
the rustling furbelows, as madam fled from this grave madman. She
would probably have me arrested.

You see I had come to think differently of Stella. At times I
remembered her childish vanity, her childish, morbid views, her childish
gusts of petulance and anger and mirth; and I smiled,—oh, very tenderly,
yet I smiled.

Then would awake the memory of Stella and myself in that ancient
moonlight and of our first talk of death—two infants peering into
infinity, somewhat afraid, and puzzled; of Stella making tea in the
firelight, and prattling of her heart's secrets, half-seriously, half in fun;
and of Stella striving to lift a very worthless man to a higher level and
succeeding—yes, for the time, succeeding; and of Stella dying with a
light heart, elate with dreams of Peter Blagden's future and of "a life
that counted"; and of what she told me at the very last. And, irrationally
perhaps, there would seem to be a sequence in it all, and I could not
smile over it, not even tenderly.

And I would depicture her, a foiled and wistful little wraith, very
lonely in eternity, and a bit regretful of the world she loved and of
its blundering men, and unhappy,—for she could never be entirely

happy without Peter,—and I feared, indignant. For Stella desired very heartily to be remembered—she was vain, you know,—and they have all forgotten. Yes, I am sure that even as a wraith, Stella would be indignant, for she had a fine sense of her own merits.

"But I am just a little butterfly-woman," she would say, sadly; then, with a quick smile, "Aren't I?" And her eyes would be like stars—like big, blue stars,—and afterward her teeth would glint of a sudden, and innumerable dimples would come into being, and I would know she was never meant to be taken seriously. . .

But we must avoid all sickly sentiment.

You see the world had advanced since Stella died,—twice around the sun, from solstice to solstice, from spring to winter and back again, travelling through I forget how many millions of miles; and there had been wars and scandals and a host of debutantes and any number of dinners; and, after all, the world is for the living.

So we of Lichfield agreed unanimously that it was very sad, and spoke of her for a while, punctiliously, as "poor dear Stella"; and the next week Emily Van Orden ran away with Tom Whately; and a few days later Alicia Wade's husband died, and we debated whether Teddy Anstrother would do the proper thing or sensibly marry Celia Reindan: and so, a little by a little, we forgot our poor, dear Stella in precisely the decorous graduations of regret with which our poor dear Stella would have forgotten any one of us.

Yes, even those who loved her most deeply have forgotten Stella. They remember only an imaginary being who was entirely perfect, and of whom they were not worthy. It is this fictitious woman who has usurped the real Stella's place in the heart of the real Stella's own mother, and whom even Lizzie d'Arlanges believes to have been once her sister, and over whom Peter Blagden is always ready to grow maudlin; and it is this immaculate woman—who never existed,—that will be until the end of Avis' matrimonial existence the standard by which Avis is measured and found wanting. And thus again the whirligig of time, by an odd turn, brings in his revenges.

And I? Well, I was very fond of Stella. And the woman they speak of today, in that hushed, hateful, sanctimonious voice, I must confess I never knew. And of all persons I chiefly rage against that faultless angel, that "poor dear Stella," who has pilfered even the paltry tribute of being remembered from the Stella that today is mine alone. For it is to this fictitious person that the people whom my Stella loved, as she did not love me, now bring their flowers; and it was to this person they erected their pompous monument,—nay, more, it was for this atrocious woman they ordered the very coffin in which my Stella lay when I last saw her. And it is not fair.

And I? Well, I was very fond of Stella. It would be good to have her back,—to have her back to jeer at me, to make me feel red and uncomfortable and ridiculous, to say rude things about my waist, and indeed to fluster me just by being there. Yes, it would be good. But, upon the whole, I am not sorry that Stella is gone.

For there is Peter Blagden to be considered. We can all agree today that Peter is a good fellow, that he is making the most of his Uncle Larry's money, and that he is nobody's enemy but his own; and we have smugly forgotten the time when we expected him to become a great lawyer. We do not expect that of Peter now; instead, we are content enough—particularly since Peter has so admirably dressed his part by taking to longish hair and gruffness and a cane,—to point him out to strangers in Lichfield as "one of our wealthiest men," and to elect him to all civic committees, and to discuss his semi-annual sprees and his monetary relations with various women whom one does not "know." And the present Mrs. Blagden, too, appears content enough.

And as Stella loved him—

Well, as it was, Peter was then off on his honeymoon, and there was only I to bring the daffodils to Stella. She was always vain, was Stella; it would have grieved her had no one remembered.

3

THEN I CAUGHT THE AFTERNOON train for Fairhaven, and went back to my capable fiancee.

But I walked over to Willoughby Hall that night and found Charteris alone in his queer library, among the serried queer books and the portraits of his "literary creditors." When I came into the apartment he was mending a broken tea-cup, for he peculiarly delighted in such infinitesimal task-work; but the vexed countenance at once took on the fond young look my coming would invariably provoke, and he shoved aside the fragments. . .

We talked of trifles; apropos of nothing, Charteris said, "Yes,—but, then, I devoted the morning to drawing up my will." And I laughed over such forethought.

The man rose and with clenched fist struck upon the littered table. "It is in the air. I swear to you that, somehow, *I* have been warned. But always I have been favoured—Why, man, I protest that never in my life have I encountered any person in associating with whom I did not condescend, with reason to back me! Yet today Death stands within arm's reach, and I have accomplished—some three or four little books! And yet—why, *Ashtaroth's Lackey*, now—Yes, by God! it is perfected speech such as few other men have ever written. I know it, and I do not care at all even though you piteous dullards should always lack the wit to recognise and revere perfected speech when it confronts you. But presently I die! and there is nothing left of me save the inefficient testimony of those three or four little books!"

I patted his shoulder and protested he had over-worked himself.

"Eh, well," he said, and with that easy laugh I knew of old; "in any event, I have been thinking for a whole two hours of my wife, and of how from the very beginning I have utilised her, and of how good and credulous she is, and of how happy I have made her—! For I have made her happy. That is the preposterous part of it—"

"Why, yes; Anne loves you very dearly. Oh, I think that everybody is irrationally fond of you, John. No, that is not a compliment, it is rather the reverse. It is simply an instance of what I have been brooding over all this afternoon,—that we like people on account of their good qualities and love them on account of their defects. I honestly believe that the cornerstone of affection is the agreeable perception of our superiority in some one point, at least, to the beloved. And that is why so many people are fond of you, I think."

He laughed a little. "And *de te fabula*—Yet I would distinguish. You think me a futile person and not, as we will put it, a disastrously truthful person, and so on through the entire list of all those so-called vices which are really just a habit of not doing this or that particular thing. Well! it is no longer *a la mode* to talk about God,—yet I must confess to an old-fashioned faith in our Author's existence and even in His amiability. I believe He placed me in this colourful world, and that He is not displeased because I have spent therein some forty-odd years pleasurably. Then too I have not wasted that pleasure, I have philanthropically passed it on. I have bequeathed posterity the chance to spend an enjoyable half-hour or so over one or two little books. That is not much to claim, but it is something."

John Charteris was talking to himself now.

"Had I instead the daily prayers of seven orphans, or the proud consciousness of having always been afraid to do what I wanted to,—which I take to be the universally accredited insurance of a blissful eternity,—or even a whole half-column with portrait in the New York papers to indicate what a loss my premature demise had been to America,—or actually all three together, say, to exhibit as the increment of this period, I honestly cannot imagine any of the more intelligent archangels lining up to cheer my entry into Paradise. I believe, however, that to be contented, to partake of the world's amenities with moderation as a sauce, and to aggrieve no fellow-being, except in self-protection, and to make other people happy as often as you find it possible, is a recipe for living that will pass muster even in heaven. There you have my creed; and it may not be impeccable, but I believe in it."

"You have forgotten something," I said, with a grin. "'One must not think too despondently nor too often of the grim Sheriff who arrives anon to dispossess you, no less than all the others, nor of any subsequent and unpredictable legal adjustments.' See, here it is, your own words printed in the book."

"Dear me, did I say that? How nicely phrased it is! Well! you and I have defiantly preserved the gallant attitude in an era not very favorable thereto. And we seem to prosper—as yet—"

"But certainly! We are the highly exceptional round pegs that flourish like green bay-trees in a square hole," I summed it up. "Presently of course our place knoweth us not. But in the mean while—well, as it happens, I was recalling today how adroitly I scaled the summit of human wisdom when I was only fourteen. For I said then, 'You can have a right good time first, any way, if you keep away from ugly things and fussy people.' And at twenty-five I stick to it."

"I wonder now if it is not at a price?" said Charteris, rather mirthlessly. "Either way, you have as yet the courage of the unconvicted. And you have managed, out of it all, to get together the makings of an honest book. I do not generally believe in heaping flattery upon young authors, but if I had written that last book of yours it would not grieve me. Even so, I wonder—? But it is dreary here, in this old house, with all my wife's high-minded ancestors chilling the air. Come, let us concoct some curious sort of drink."

I looked at him compassionately. "And have Bettie staying up to let me in and smelling it on me! You must be out of your head."

And then Charteris laughed and derided me, and afterward we chatted for a good two hours,—quite at random, and disposing of the most important subjects, as was our usage when in argument, in a half-sentence.

It was excellent to have Charteris to talk against, and I enjoyed it. Taking him by and large, I loved the little fellow as I have loved no other man.

Chapter 30

HE GILDS THE WEATHER-VANE

B ut I would not go along with Charteris the next morning when he
came by the Hamlyns' on his way to King's College. I could not,
because I was labouring over a batch of proof-sheets; and as I laboured
my admiration for the very clever young man who had concocted this
new book augmented comfortably; so that I told Charteris he was a
public nuisance, and please to go to Tillietudlem.

He had procured the key to the Library,—for the College had not
opened as yet,—and meant to borrow an odd volume or so of Lucian.
Charteris had evolved the fantastic notion of treating Lucian's Zeus as a
tragic figure. He sketched a sympathetic picture of the fallen despot, and of
the smokeless altars, girdled by a jeering rabble of so-called philosophers,
and of how irritating it must be to anybody to have your actual existence
denied. Did I not see the pathos of poor Zeus's situation with the god
business practically "cornered," and the Jews getting all the trade?

I informed him that the only pathos in life just at present was my
inability to disprove, in default of abolishing, the existence of people
who bothered me when I was busy. So Charteris went away, just as
Byam brought the mail from the post-office.

2

THERE WERE TWO CHEQUES FROM magazines. Life was very
pleasant, in a quiet uneventful world. The *Fairhaven Gazette* for the
week had come, too, to indicate that, as usual, nothing of grave import
was happening in an agreeably monotonous world. True, the Bulgarians
were issuing an appeal to civilization on the ground that they objected
to being massacred, and cyclones were wrecking towns and killing
quite a number of persons in Florida, and the strikes in Colorado were
leading to divers homicides; but in Fairhaven these things did not seem
to matter. And so the front page of the *Gazette* was, rightfully, reserved
for Plans of the College for the Session of 1903–4. . .

I looked again. The President was explaining that he had intended
no discourtesy to Sir Thomas Lipton by declining to attend the

Seawanhaka-Corinthian Yacht Club dinner; Major Delmar had failed to beat Lou Dillon's time, on the same track; the National Dressmakers' Association had declared that the kangaroo walk and Gibson shoulders would shortly be eschewed by all really fashionable women; and these matters were more interesting, of course, but certainly no cause for excitement. Well, I reflected, no news was good news proverbially; and I was content to let the axiom pass.

In fine, there was nothing to worry over anywhere. And the book was going to be good, quite astonishingly good. . .

And yonder Bettie waited for me, and I could hear the piano that proclaimed she was not idle. I was ineffably content; and at ease within a rather kindly universe, taking it by and large. . .

"Quite a nice Setebos, after all! a big, fine generous-hearted fellow, who doesn't bother to keep accounts to the last penny. I heartily approve of Setebos, and Bettie ought not to rag Him so. She would think it tremendously nice and boyish of me if I were to go impulsively and tell her something like that—"

So I decided I had worked quite long enough.

3

But as I reached out toward the portieres, a man came into the room, entering from the hall-way. And I gave a little whistling sound of astonishment and hastened to him with extended hand.

"My dear fellow," I began; "why, have you dropped from the moon?"

"They—they told me you were here," said Jasper Hardress, and paused to moisten his lips. "My wife died, yonder in Montana, ten days ago last Thursday,—yes, it was on a Tuesday she died, I think."

And I was silent for a breathing-space. "Yes?" I said, at last; for I had seen the shining thing in Jasper Hardress's hand, and I was wondering now why he had pocketed the toy, and for how long.

"It was of a fever she died. She was delirious,—oh, quite three days. And she talked in her delirium."

I began to smile; it was like witnessing a play. "Yonder is Bettie and my one chance of manhood; and blind chance, just the machination of a tiny microbe, entraps me as I tread toward all this. I was wrong about Setebos. Heine was right; there is an Aristophanes in heaven."

I said, aloud: "Well, Hardress, you wouldn't have me dispute the veracity of a lady?"

But the man did not appear to hear me. "Oh, it was very horrible," he said. "Oh, I would like you, first of all, to comprehend how horrible it was. She was always calling—no, not calling exactly, but just moaning one name, and over and over again. He had been so cruel, she said. He didn't really care for anything, she said, except to write his hateful books. And I had loved her, you understand. And for three whole days I must sit there and hear her tell of what another man had meant to her! I have not been wholly sane, I think, since then, for I had loved her for a long time. And her throat was so little that I often thought how easy it would be to stop the moaning and talking, but somehow I did not like to do it. And it isn't my honour that I mean to avenge. It is Gillian that I must avenge,—Gillian who died because a coward had robbed her of the will to live. For it was that in chief. Why, even you must understand that," he said, as though he pleaded with me.

And yonder Bettie played,—with lithe fingers which caressed the keys rather than struck them, I remembered. And always at the back of my mind some being that was not I was taking notes as to how unruffled the man was; and I smiled a little, in recognition of the air, as Bettie began *The Funeral March of a Marionette*. . .

"Yes," I said; "I think I understand. There is something to be advanced upon the other side perhaps; but that scarcely matters. You act within your rights; and, besides, you have a pistol, and I haven't. I am getting afraid, though, Jasper. I can't stand this much longer. So for God's sake, make an end of this!"

Jasper Hardress said: "I mean to. But they told me he was here? Yes, I am sure that someone told me he was here."

I think I must have reeled a little. I know my brain was working automatically. Gillian Hardress had always called me Jack; and Jasper Hardress was past reason; and yonder was Bettie, who had made life too fine and dear a thing to be relinquished. . .

"Jasper," someone was saying, and that someone seemed to laugh, "we aren't living in the Middle Ages, remember. No, just as I said, I cannot stand this nonsense any longer, and you must make an end of this foolishness. Just on a bare suspicion—just on the ravings of a delirious woman—! Why, she used to call *me* Jack,—and I write books—Why, you might just as logically murder *me*!"

"I thought at first it was you. Oh, only for a moment, boy. I was not quite sane, I think, for at first I suspected you of such treachery as in my sober senses I know you never dreamed of. And I had forgotten you were just a child—But she was conscious at the end," said Jasper Hardress, "and when I—talked with her about what she had said in delirium, she told me it was Charteris whose son we christened Jasper Hardress some two years ago—"

I said: "I never knew there was a child." But I was thinking of a hitherto unaccounted-for photograph.

"He only lived three months. I had always wanted a son. You cannot fancy how proud I was of him." Hardress laughed here.

"And she told you it was Charteris! in the moment of death when—when you were threatening me, she told you it was Charteris!"

"It is different when you are dying. You see—Gillian knew that eternity depended on what she said to me then—" He spoke as with difficulty, and he kept licking at restless lips.

"Yes,—she did believe that. And she told you—!" I comprehended how Gillian Hardress had loved me, and my shame was such that now it was the mere brute will to live which held me. But it held me, none the less. Besides, I saw the least unpleasant solution.

"I suppose I can't blame you," I said,—"for if she told you, why, of course—" Then I barked out: "He was here a moment ago. You must have come around one corner, in fact, just as he turned the other. You will find him at Willoughby Hall, I suppose. He said he was going straight home."

For I knew that Charteris was at King's College, a mile away from Willoughby Hall; and, I assured myself, there would be ample time to warn him. Only how much must now depend upon the diverting qualities of Lucian! For should the Samosatan flag in interest, John would be leaving the College presently; and there is but one street in Fairhaven.

4

I HAD MY HAND UPON the garden-gate, and Hardress had just turned the corner below, going toward Cambridge Street, when Bettie came upon the porch.

"Well," she said, "and who's your fat friend, Mr. Sheridan?"

"I can't stop now, dear. I forgot to tell John about something which is rather important—"

"Gracious!" Bettie Hamlyn said; "that sounds like shooting. Why, it is shooting, isn't it?"

"Yes," said I.

"—Quite as though the Monnachins and the Massawomeks and all the other jaw-breakers were attacking Fairhaven as they used to do on alternate Thursdays, and affording both of us an excellent opportunity to get nicely scalped in time for dinner. So I don't mind confessing that it was against precisely such an emergency I declined to turn out an elaborate suite of hair; and now I expect the world at large to acknowledge that I acted very sensibly."

"It is much more likely to be some drunken country-man on his monthly spree—" I was reflecting while Bettie talked nonsense that there had been no less than four shots. I was wondering whom the last was for. It would be much pleasanter, all around, if Hardress had sent it into his own disordered brain. Yes, certainly, three bullets ought amply to account for an unprepared and unarmed and puny Charteris. . .

So I said: "Well, I suppose my business with John must wait for a while. Besides, Bettie, you are such a dear in that get-up. And if you will come down into the garden at once, I will explain a few of my reasons for advancing the assertion."

Standing upon the porch, she patted me ever so lightly upon the head. "What a child it is!" she said. "I don't think that, after all, I shall put twenty-six candles on your cake next week. The fat and lazy literary gent is not really old enough, not really more than ten."

"—And besides, apart from the proposed discussion of your physical charms, I have something else quite equally important to tell you about."

"Oh, drat the pertinacious infant, then I'll come for half an hour. Just wait until I get a hat. Still, what a worthless child it is! to be quitting work before noon."

And she would have gone, but I detained her. "Yes, what a worthless child it is,—or rather, what an unproverbial sort of busy bee it has been, Bettie dear. For his has been the summer air, and the sunshine, and the flowers; and gentle ears have listened to him, and gentle eyes have been upon him. Now it is autumn. And he has let others eat his honey-which I take to include all that he actually made, all that wasn't in the world before he came, as Stella used to say,—so that he might have his morsel and his song. And sometimes it has been Sardinian honey, very bitter in the mouth,—and even then he has let others eat it—"

"You are a most irrelevant infant," said Miss Hamlyn, "with these insectean divagations—Dear me, what lovely words! And of course if you really want to drag me into that baking-hot garden, and have the only fiancee you just at present possess laid up by a sunstroke—"

The Epilogue: Which Suggests that Second Thoughts—

So I waited there alone. Whatever the four shots implied, I must tell Bettie everything, because she was Bettie, and it was not fair I should have any secrets from her. "Oh, just be honest with me," she had said, in this same garden, "and I don't care what you do!" And I had never lied to Bettie: at worst, I simply had not told her anything concerning matters about which I was glad she had not happened to ask any questions. But this was different. . .

Dimly I knew that everything must pivot on my telling Bettie. John was done for, the Hardress woman was done for, and whether or no Jasper had done for himself, there was no danger, now, that anyone would ever know how that infernal Gillian had badgered me into, probably, three homicides. There might be some sort of supernal bookkeeping, somewhere, but very certainly it was not conformable to any human mathematics. . . And therefore I must tell Bettie.

I must tell Bettie, and abide what followed. She had pardoned much. It might be she would pardon even this, "because I had been honest with her when I didn't want to be." And in any event—even in her loathing,—Bettie would understand, and know I had at least kept faith with her. . .

I must tell Bettie, and abide what followed. For living seemed somehow to have raised barriers about me a little by a little, so that I must view and talk with all my fellows more and more remotely, and could not, as it were, quite touch anybody save Bettie. At all other persons I was but grimacing falsely across an impalpable barrier. And now just such a barrier was arising between Bettie and me, as I perceived in a sort of panic. Yes, it was rising resistlessly, like an augmenting mist not ever to be put aside, except by plunging forthwith into hours, or days, or even into months perhaps, of ugliness and discomfort. . .

It was the season of harvest. The leaves were not yet turned, and upon my face the heatless, sun-steeped air was like a caress. The whole world was at full-tide, ineffably sweet and just a little languorous: and bees were audible, as in a humorous pretence of vexation. . .

The world was very beautiful. I must tell Bettie presently, of course; only the world was such a comfortable place precisely as it was; and I began to wonder if I need tell Bettie after all?

For, after all, to tell the truth could resurrect nobody; and to know the truth would certainly make Bettie very unhappy; and never in my life have I been able to endure the contact of unhappiness.

A NOTE ABOUT THE AUTHOR

James Branch Cabell (1879–1958) was an American writer of escapist and fantasy fiction. Born into a wealthy family in the state of Virginia, Cabell attended the College of William and Mary, where he graduated in 1898 following a brief personal scandal. His first stories began to be published, launching a productive decade in which Cabell's worked appeared in both *Harper's Monthly Magazine* and *The Saturday Evening Post*. Over the next forty years, Cabell would go on to publish fifty-two books, many of them novels and short-story collections. A friend, colleague, and inspiration to such writers as Ellen Glasgow, H.L. Mencken, Sinclair Lewis, and Theodore Dreiser, James Branch Cabell is remembered as an iconoclastic pioneer of fantasy literature.

A NOTE FROM THE PUBLISHER

Spanning many genres, from non-fiction essays to literature classics to children's books and lyric poetry, Mint Edition books showcase the master works of our time in a modern new package. The text is freshly typeset, is clean and easy to read, and features a new note about the author in each volume. Many books also include exclusive new introductory material. Every book boasts a striking new cover, which makes it as appropriate for collecting as it is for gift giving. Mint Edition books are only printed when a reader orders them, so natural resources are not wasted. We're proud that our books are never manufactured in excess and exist only in the exact quantity they need to be read and enjoyed.

bookfinity™

Discover more of your favorite classics with Bookfinity™.

- Track your reading with custom book lists.
- Get great book recommendations for your personalized Reader Type.
- Add reviews for your favorite books.
- AND MUCH MORE!

Visit **bookfinity.com** and take the fun Reader Type quiz to get started.

Enjoy our classic and modern companion pairings!

Classic & Modern

9 781513 295800